Hard Case Book V

Blood and Fear

(The John Harding Series)

by

Bernard Lee DeLeo

✱✱✱✱✱

PUBLISHED BY:

Bernard Lee DeLeo and RJ Parker Publishing Inc.

ISBN-13: 978-1507742938
ISBN-10: 1507742932

www.RJPARKERPUBLISHING.com

DEDICATION

As it will be with every novel I write from now until my own End of Days, I dedicate this novel to my deceased angel, wife, and best friend: *Joyce Lynn Whitney DeLeo*.

Chapter 1

Sometimes a Great Notion

As coach of Al's softball team, the A's, I enjoyed every second working with the girls. Especially entertaining in our endeavor was my assistant coach, the over six months pregnant Lynn Montoya, also known as Cruella Deville, or Crue for short. In our age category, we garnered some very vocal Oakland parents, used to big mouths having their way on playing time, and game interference. Although Lynn and I made it very clear from the beginning there would be no pressure on the girls, we absorbed the usual loud mouthed crap about nearly everything. I had made sure Lynn understood this very weird paradigm, where like little league baseball, parents go absolutely nuts sometimes.

We're playing a team on Owen Jones Field, a real nice setting for any sport. Al was scheduled to pitch. When the other team's coach heard she was a lefthander, we had a problem. The opposing coach wanted to see her pitching style with the umpire, judging whether her delivery was within the rules. Lynn, of course, wanted to disembowel both the opposing coach, and the volunteer umpire. I reasoned with her, reminding Lynn we would have to face exactly this type of very strange maneuverings.

"But damn! This is the definition of chicken-shit. Thirty seconds alone with that nitwit coach, and she'd be begging me to let Al pitch any damn way she wanted. It's adolescent girls' softball, for God's sake!"

I spent a few seconds chortling over Lynn's spot on description. She began playing off my amusement as a sign I would embrace a no holds barred confrontation, pointing at the small faces of confusion on our bench. "Step up, Hard Case! These girls depend on you being a mentor, friend, protector, and-"

Lynn took a deep breath after eyeballing our softball league A's team members' faces. "This is a lot harder than I had envisioned, and we're not even playing the game yet."

I clasped her arm gently. At least she called me by my UFC handle, Hard Case. I think that was a sign of respect, possibly. "Let me handle the goofball intricacies of girls' softball, Crue. The damn girls love you. Your coaching patience needs to infiltrate your coaching persona. It won't be but a blink of the eye before you're doing cub-scouts, T-ball, and eventually soccer Mom responsibilities with Clint Jr. This is great practice. I need your stone cold, bad ass back up for me, without physical confrontations or verbal spewing we can be kicked out of the league for. C'mon, Crue, Al's depending on you."

The logic washed down over my assistant coach's persona in a reluctant acceptance of fact. "Let me handle this, HC. I hear you."

Lynn walked around the dugout cage, treading slowly toward the umpire and opposing coach, while I listened intently, and Al stood waiting for the A's representative. Lynn put a comforting arm around Al's shoulders. "I'm here, kid. Don't let these two get your mind out of the game. What is it exactly, Coach, that you don't like about Al's delivery? Let's go over your objections on a word by word illustration. The only thing I see differently Al does in pitching is to throw left-handed. That is not illegal."

The opposing coach stammered, her thought processes disturbed by a cold factual challenge. "She doesn't... ah... have the same delivery."

"Oh," Lynn dived in. "Let me get this straight. If a girl pitches left-handed in this softball league, it's some kind of voodoo?"

6

"No," the umpire stated. "I see nothing deceptive about her stance or delivery. If you have any further objection, Ms. Wintos, say so now. Otherwise, let's continue. We're already behind getting this game started."

Wintos began walking away, but the umpire stopped her. "I know you Ms. Wintos. Please say you have no further problems with this little girl's pitching style right now, or I will find a representative from your team to do so."

The shrew at the base of Marion Wintos's mind made her presence known. Fists clenched, and facial features twisted as if she were illustrating someone being possessed by an evil entity, she twirled around, hunched at the waist. The umpire took an involuntary step back, although he was familiar with the woman's demeanor on the softball field. Wintos pointed a finger at the umpire, the trembling with rage smile on her face a precursor of doom.

"Fine, Bobby! I know you're sleeping with half the softball league's 'young moms'. I'd bet you have a bun in the oven of this-"

Wintos never saw Lynn move, but in the next second she found herself kneeling on the ground with hand locked in an unbreakable grip, pain lancing through her entire body, capable only of a small breathless panting rasp without words. The umpire reached for Lynn, but his hand was engulfed in mine, as my rather huge shadow blocked his advance. I shook the umpire's hand gently. I needed to avert this disaster or it would end the game before the girls even had a chance to play.

"Let me handle this, Bobby," I urged the young volunteer umpire.

"Su...sure, John."

I hunched down slightly so I could meet Lynn's eyes. She tried looking away, but she was lost the moment her husband Clint joined me on the field. "We discussed this, Lynn. I heard what this young woman was about to say, but we're here to see Al pitch, remember?"

Lynn took a deep breath while releasing Marion Wintos's hand. "Sorry John."

She then grabbed Marion's chin in a grip best described as an angry bear-trap. "I know what you were about to say concerning me, girlfriend. It would be best if you understand that would not go well for you. If you had completed the phrase I saved you from spewing, you'd have a broken arm instead of a slightly sprained hand. Now what say we play ball? How about it, Marion?"

"Please let me go… please?"

Lynn released her. She pointed one finger toward the Wintos's dugout without looking. "I see your husband and brother hurrying to your idiot rescue. Save them some pain, and intercept them."

Marion immediately ran to engage the shocked advance of her husband and brother. Clint engulfed his wife in his arms. "Nice start, Hon. Five minutes on the field of a girls' softball game you're coaching, and you nearly cause a riot."

"Did not." Lynn allowed Clint to escort her to our team area.

My stepdaughter Alice, of course was enjoying it all. Although, she wants to pitch, Al loves the complete disintegration of adults around her. I have wondered if her intuition of what might happen between us nitwit adults was the reason she wanted to sign up for softball. She knew she wasn't to blame for any of it, but instinctively knew she could cause chaos anyway.

"C'mon, lefty. Let's get you with the rest of your team for the opening ceremony." I looked at the nineteen year old volunteer umpire with compassion. I had no idea if he was guilty of Wintos's charge, but I had a suspicion he might be guilty of it with her. "Call it straight to the best of your ability, Bobby. I'll back your play no matter what."

Bobby visibly relaxed. "I will, Mr. Harding. Honest. Thanks."

"Just John is fine. Thanks for volunteering to umpire the game, Bobby. If you need a water or anything, look my way. I'll get it for you without anyone seeing."

"Thanks. Uh… you don't think I'm really-"

"Don't know, don't care," I cut him off. "Have a good game, Blue."

Bobby nodded. "I'll do my best, Sir."

I led Al around the cage, and into our team area, where Lynn cautioned her batters to be patient. We were the away team today so we were up to bat first. Clint busily engaged Al's nervous teammates, urging them to relax and have a good time. He was going to be a natural when Lynn gave birth to Clint Jr. Clint came to every practice, shagging balls, pitching batting practice, giving fielding tips, and helping Lynn run the girls through drills. It had been fun preparing for this first game of the season.

Supposedly having the girls line at the cage shouting rhymes like 'pitcher has a rubber arm' or 'swing batter/batter' when the opposing team came to bat was the way we were to coach spirit. I preferred to let the girls cheer when they wanted to. Lynn and I led by example. We planned to encourage our girls, but hold off on the more unsavory styles of team spirit. We did coach our girls through hitting and fielding practice about reality in the game. We explained they may have to perform with a hundred voices yelling derogatory remarks at the top of their lungs. In any case, we were ready to have a good time, win or lose. Our parents… not so much.

Although Al was ten years old, I was hearing critics yelling no way should Al be pitching. See, there were other older girls who could pitch faster, but they couldn't get the ball over the plate. Al pitched a moderately fast underhand slung ball, but her advantage was she got it over the plate. Like Lynn told her, she only needed to get the other team to swing at the ball, and rely on her fielders to catch it. The opposing pitcher for the Owls walked the first four batters, giving away a run with the bases still loaded. When Al was about to bat, I patted her shoulder.

"I know Lynn told you to be patient. I also know you can hit a ball no matter where it's pitched, Al. This pitcher will want to throw a strike. It may not be a perfect one, but take a swing at it. The fielders are all asleep by now. If they make a play on anything hit, it will be a shock to me. Swing away, Al."

"Did you just countermand my orders, John?" Lynn had slid in next to me on the bench after I returned from coaching Al.

"Watch, Lynn. We didn't come out here to snooze through a bunch of walks."

The Owls' pitcher threw the first pitch high and outside. Al creamed it into the right field corner. It took the right fielder so long to track down the ball, Al could have walked around the bases. Just like that, Al had a grand slam, and we were ahead five to zip. There was a six run rule, so we scored the sixth run, and our girls hit the field. Al pitched down the heart of the plate. The Owls got a couple runs back due to fielding errors, but the girls were awake behind Al. They didn't take a chance on weaving around playing with the grass. They knew there was a chance the batter would hit the ball on every pitch.

Unfortunately, Al could only pitch three innings by rule. We were well ahead by then, but our second pitcher walked the bases loaded, putting the Owls into the game again, when she then walked in two runs, followed by a couple of hits, our lead was only four. Lynn and I encouraged our pitcher to simply play catch with the catcher. She did, allowing two more runs, but also getting two outs. We were hearing it from the parents on our side. One really nasty guy projected one of those annoying voices you can hear for a mile in any direction. The problem was he wanted me to yank the girl pitching. I had no intention of that. Silence came shortly after. When I glanced behind me, I spotted Lucas sitting next to loudmouth. I exchanged grins with Lynn. When Pappy sits down next to you, you automatically shut up. Yep, all my monsters were here to watch this first journey into the unknown. The next batter hit a foul popup on the first base side. Al caught it easily.

"Great job out there, girls," Lynn greeted them. "Remember, we're here to have a good time. Everyone misses the ball once in a while. Just watch the major leaguers. Make sure you hustle after the ball, and throw it in. They have a new pitcher. By the looks of her warm up tosses, you girls better be thinking swing. She throws a fastball, and it'll be over the plate before you can blink. You're up first, Al. Show us how it's done."

"Elbows in, Al." I patted her shoulder as she walked by. "Level swings, like when we took you all to the batting cages."

Al nodded, donning her batting helmet, and strapping it tight under her chin. Lucky thing too, because the first pitch beaned her. Lynn and I ran out to check on her. Al's no sissy. I helped her up, with Lynn looking into her eyes closely. Al shook us off.

"Wow, I got conked," Al stated. She immediately sighted in on Lora who was on her way to the field. Samira was trying to slow her down, but not having much luck. Al's wave stopped her. "I'm okay, Ma. Stay there."

I reinforced Al's declaration as did Lynn. "Do you want to run the bases, Al, or come out of the game?"

"I'm good to go, Dad." Al handed me her bat, and ran to first base escorted by a round of heartfelt applause.

"Is she okay, John?" Bobby watched her run to first base, but knew it was his responsibility to ask.

"We'll watch her, Bobby." Jafar was our first base coach, and I could see Al joking with him as he looked her over.

Lynn noticed the opposing pitcher grinning while we walked to our area. "Hey, John. Do they allow chin music at this level?"

I had noticed too. "Not on purpose, but the girls get a bit wild, although I thought her warmup tosses were all right over the plate. It'll probably have the desired effect."

"Al took it well," Lynn whispered. "If it had been any of the other girls, we would have had to call an ambulance."

I clasped our next batter's shoulder. "Hang in there, Carrie."

"That was scary, John." Carrie looked at me, her eyes big. "I thought Al was bad hurt."

I knelt down in front of her. I smiled reassuringly, I hope. Hell, the kid just watched her teammate take a fastball to the head. "If you feel like jumping away from the plate, do it. If you feel like swinging, swing away."

Carrie looked at Al, who was already dancing at the first base bag, clapping her hands and shouting encouragement. Carrie's lips tightened. "I'll do okay."

The first pitch to Carrie was another inside hard one. Carrie stepped back, but moved right into the box again. I had to contend with Lynn, who wanted to tear through the fence. She pointed at the opposing team's pitcher. "Did you see that? The little brat is still smiling."

"She's doing the same thing you would have done as a kid, Crue."

Lynn sputtered, searching for a retort. She smiled and grabbed the chain link fence. "Yeah… I would have."

The pitcher did her windup, and Jafar sent Al to second base before she realized Al had moved away from the base. Al stole third base the moment the pitcher began her windup. She drew a throw, but it was a panicked toss that bounced into foul territory behind third base. Al never paused, nearly running over Casey, my third base coach. She ran across home plate, only to turn and hug Carrie before pumping her fists in the air while skipping towards us. Lynn was the first to meet her, gathering my happy stepdaughter in her arms. I fist bumped Al with quiet pride.

"Damn, kid, that was some in your face base running."

"That was easy, Lynn," Al told her. She spun to the fence with her teammates around her. "C'mon Carrie!"

I could tell the pitcher was really pissed off. She had been stomping around the pitcher's mound instead of running home, which would have been what she should have done on the misthrow to third base. I called timeout to hoots and catcalls from our opposing team parents. I guided Carrie off to the side.

"Jump backwards on the next two pitches, no matter what she throws, Carrie. On the third pitch, swing level." I put my mitts on her shoulders. "It's a suggestion. Jump out every time if you want, but definitely do so the next couple of pitches, okay?"

Carrie nodded, looking out at the pitcher. "I understand."

I patted her shoulder. "No pressure, Carrie. It's a softball game, not a war."

Carrie giggled. "Thanks, John."

With me behind the chain link fence next to Lynn, we waited while Carrie moved into the batter's box. The first pitch was high inside, and Carrie jumped quickly. The second pitch was low and inside, but Carrie stood in, her bat in ready position. I grinned over at Lynn, who met my satisfied gaze with nodding acceptance.

"Carrie ain't scared," Lynn said.

With the count three balls and no strikes, the pitcher threw a fastball down the heart of the plate. Carrie smashed it up the middle, and directly into the opposing pitcher's side. The ensuing recovery allowed Carrie to make second base without a throw, with her teammates screaming joyfully on the sideline. The opposing pitcher had absorbed Carrie's smash, rolled in pain for only a moment, and then dived for the errant ball. She wisely chose not to make a throw without any chance of getting the runner at second. She smacked her glove with the ball as the coaches ran out to check on her. The pitcher then pointed at Carrie with the same grin she had after beaning Al.

"Damn, that is me," Lynn conceded. "Can we trade for her?"

I laughed at that remark. "Nope. She can take it and dish it out, but I wish she'd simply pitch. The girl might have struck out the side, depending on how Al did."

"I love this shit, HC," Lynn admitted. "I hope Al's into every sport year round. I'm addicted already. I am a soccer Mom! You, of course, will front me so I don't kill anyone."

That was a crackup. "Agreed. We need the monster squad to continue on this endeavor into sports or band or anything Al deems worthy. So far, she's our only entrant, but soon Clint Junior, along with Jafar's and Casey's kids, will join the ranks, eager for our coaching prowess."

Lynn shrugged. "If we live, HC. I'm not forgetting the front line war we face, where survival may be a problem in our goofy world."

Such is life in monster world. "Amen to that, Crue."

Our first excursion into the official sports world wound down to a win by a few runs. The girls all shook hands, the parents eyeballed each other as bitter enemies, and we coaches announced pizza on us at the local Red Boy Pizza, only a few minutes away. My crew, who were engaged in our other business at Oakland Investigations, Bond Retrieval, and Security, met us for a quick hello and pizza. They had weekend duty during this first taste of team sport schedules. Lora, who ran operations, confused dates on our first sporting excursion. We were supposed to be cutting way back on jobs until June, so we could all enjoy this unusual pastime - unusual for us anyway.

See, we're on a break from things. At the beginning of the year, we saved America, killed a bunch of terrorists at sea, and on land. Then I fought a UFC fighter nicknamed The Rattler on Valentine's Day at the Mandalay Bay after being tortured by my trainers for a couple months of hell. Sure, we didn't let our Oakland front business go down the tubes, but we planned to take it slow until the end of softball season. Because they get bored easily, my monsters helped me with the girls' softball practices. Yeah, even monsters need downtime, and we were enjoying the hell out of it.

My partner, Tommy Sands, was the first through the door. I waved him over. He came with Devon Constantine and Jesse Brown. Lynn and my wife Lora began chortling away watching my fight corner guys walking toward us together. They were all well over six feet tall, black, wearing black, and looked as if they needed a cattle truck to move them around. The place quieted. The girls were used to having my entire bunch around at different times, but the parents not so much. I waved them down at the end of our table near the rest of us monsters. They were all smiles, waving at the girls, and hugging Al, who hopped up to meet them.

"I got beaned today with a fastball," Al stated proudly. "Then I stole all the way around the bases and scored."

"Sit down here with your Uncles, girl," Jesse said, guiding her with him. "We need a complete accounting of the game. I'll need an entire pizza and a pitcher of beer though for snacks."

"Jess hasn't eaten all day," Dev explained. "We've been on the escort trail since early this morning. T anchored us at the office, watching weather and traffic, but we still got caught on the bridge. Luckily, we drove the new limo, so our guests were entertained. I see you were prepared for Jess, John."

While they were sitting down, Dev was pointing at the pitchers of beer and two giant pizzas waiting for them. "Of course. No way would I invite Jess into a pizza place celebration, and make him wait for food. He'd start gnawing on the table legs."

"You got that right, brother," Jess confirmed, piling a plate I handed him with slices, while Dev poured mugs of beer. "I'm ready, Al. Give us the recap, and don't leave anything out."

The late afternoon celebration proceeded on a high note until Tommy, who was facing the door, saw something not to his liking. When I turned to see what grabbed his attention in a bad way, I spotted Baatar Okoye. When I kicked the shit out of him the last time I saw the Big O, he weighed over three hundred pounds. At nearly six and a half feet tall, that is an impressive size. He had lost around forty pounds, and looked like he was made out of iron. Big O stood patiently at the entrance, waiting for someone, without the usual arrogant smile I'd knocked off his face during our last rumble behind The Warehouse Bar. Alexi Fiialkov walked in next to him. He gave me a small wave, but did not approach the table.

"Damn, John, after you nearly knocked Big O into a different dimension, I didn't figure to ever see him around again," Tommy said, with vocal agreement from the others.

"Don't start anything!" Lora felt the need to tell me something I didn't need Sherlock Holmes to figure out all by myself.

16

"Alexi's with him, Hon," I replied, standing. "No way he brings the Big O with him unless something really strange is going on. I'll go see what he wants. We'll talk outside, so no one gets nervous."

"You talked to him the last time outside, John," Lynn reminded me. "I have my cell-phone. Call me if you need the medical examiner and a meat wagon."

I admit the monsters enjoyed the reference, including me, when Big O's guys had to drag him away from our last meeting. I may have said a few unkind things like I might kill him the next time he crossed my path. "That won't be necessary, Crue, but thanks. Be right back."

Alexi Fiialkov is a Russian mobster, who has decided to turn his prior business into legitimate holdings, which he has. He has also helped us stop terrorist threats beyond imagining, including an anthrax attack we stopped only a short time ago. His family lives here, and I know from being his friend, he cares about my crew and this country. He is a friend in every sense of the word. I don't trust many people, but I trust Alexi. We shook hands with warm regard for each other.

"May we talk outside for a moment, John?"

"Certainly." I kept my mouth shut, and avoided eye contact with the Big O. I have a rather dim view of past enemies. Most are dead.

Outside in the rather fast cooling temperatures, I halfway wished I'd brought my jacket. Big O held out his hand solemnly. "I work for Mr. Fiialkov now. I do not fight. I am sorry for past problems, Mr. Harding."

Well this is a nice surprise. I don't like playing games with old enemies, but Alexi had been backing him on the fight circuit. If the Big O decided to quit fighting, I couldn't think of anything insurmountable in letting bygones be bygones. I shook his hand.

"You look well, Big. If you're working for Alexi, I trust anything he does. We have no problems from now on."

"Thank you. I am glad to be out of the fight game," Big O admitted. "I thought I was more than a street brawler. I am glad for this chance with Mr. Fiialkov."

"Very good," Alexi said, clapping the Big O on the shoulder. "Wait for me in the car. I will be there shortly."

"Yes, Sir." Big O turned after a slight nod in my direction, walking toward Alexi's vehicle.

"Did you have to order Big to apologize?"

"He had a choice, John. Baatar Okoye could have went back to Nigeria or pursued street fighting here. You showed him he could not hope to compete in the UFC. He wisely chose to take a position with me he is very good at. I wished to settle any past grievances before allowing him to continue. I had high hopes for him, as I did Van Rankin, whom you killed in the ring. I did not wish for my employee, Mr. Okoye, to continue until you were forced to kill him."

I grinned at Alexi. "Plus, you have The Rattler under contract. Congratulations, both to him and you. He was getting screwed."

"Yes, and he will not be fighting in any matches with you. I believe Eugene will rise in the UFC to the top if I keep him away from you."

Eugene and I settled our differences in a violent manner twice on the Mandalay Bay stage. I didn't know how he felt about it, but I'd had enough of Eugene. "You can tell him I don't want to fight him again either."

Alexi laughed. "I would be here propositioning you to do exactly that if not for the fact you have broken him. I looked into

18

his eyes. He doesn't believe he can beat you. It may be a temporary thing, but I would not put him in the cage against you again until he has something to lose, like the UFC Heavyweight Belt. I will work him into a position from the beginning to do just that. I noted the UFC still does not want to promote your rising star after beating The Rattler, John. Those two killings in the cage have the powers that be in the UFC worried. I believe a few of them thought you were going to kill Eugene."

"Was not." Maybe, but it's a rough sport to gauge how far you should go.

"Yes… I have no doubt you were going to do exactly that if need be. That has no bearing in my decision to not try and put Rattler against you. He doesn't believe he can beat you. You don't believe anyone can beat you."

"I do, but I don't care." I sensed we were dancing for some reason. I was glad Big O wouldn't be coming around at odd times, trying to ankle bite me into kicking his ass once again. I wasn't convinced I could beat Rattler, but I'd beat Big O every time we threw hands. "I suspect you stopped to see me on something other than the fight game. I think you've prepped me enough. What's on your mind?"

"Direct as always. Subtlety is not your strong suit, my friend. Another Russian mobster, named Yuri Kornev, immigrated from his holdings on the East Coast to the East Bay. He sent some men around to let me know he was in the area. I sent word to him I am no longer a player in such matters. We found my messenger's body tortured as in the old country. It was my mistake to send someone to reason with such a beast. Even in my old days I never did such a thing. This will not affect me. He knows I am no longer in the trade, but to do such a thing while knowing the truth is reprehensible. Such is the world nowadays, my friend. I only came to make amends with Baatar, and to warn you of his presence."

This was odd. "So, you didn't strike back at this Yuri guy?"

Alexi smiled. "I struck back just now, John. You know about him, and I will feed you any information or knowledge I learn concerning his movements. I have already sent a file to Denny with all the details of what I know at this time. I think when he sees what Yuri is capable of, you'll be getting a call from him. Have you ever considered another street fight for a rather large sum of money, John?"

This conversation is getting more interesting by the minute. "I haven't been asked, Alexi. You probably know we're not hurting for money. I doubt Tommy would like me risking the ranking I've achieved by beating Rattler in the UFC on a street fight."

"We both know you don't fight for the money. You never did. It was the main reason I could not perceive what you were up to, until I learned about your day-job. Is that not true?"

"Maybe." There wasn't any use in pretending with Alexi. I nearly killed him over pressure he brought to bear on me in back of The Warehouse Bar to throw a fight. "What's this all about?"

"Yuri is trying to insert himself into my backstreet fighting endeavors. He has a fighter who is unbeaten. He is a Bulgarian, nicknamed The Assassin. Yuri wants to challenge any fighter I have. The stakes will be high. This Marko Hristov was mentored by Yuri from the time his parents met with an unfortunate accident when he was twelve."

Uh oh. "Accident?"

"They were killed because the boy's Father worked for Yuri, by a rival syndicate," Alexi explained. "It was ruled a traffic accident, but I do not believe it was, nor did Yuri. The boy lived. His first kills at age fifteen were his parents' murderers. In the past decade Yuri has had him trained in special skills. Although he is being groomed for ultimate fighting, Marko has been killing for his mentor a long time."

"You're in a position to ignore him, my friend. Why risk anything. You own the nicest street fighting warehouse setting anywhere, and you already have an inside track with backers for anything you do in the UFC. What kind of strings is this Yuri pulling behind the curtain?"

Alexi tilted his hands in an 'it is what it is' fashion. "This challenge comes at an awkward time for me, John. I am trying to have all aspects of my holdings legal, with the small exception in betting at the fights I host. The politicos look the other way while betting and taking free cage-side seats, so that is not a problem. If Yuri gets ignored, I believe he plans to cause enough problems with the illegal betting so as to scare away our key crowd. Once I lose the look the other way politicos, I'm in deep trouble."

There goes my vacation, but not my coaching job. "I don't need to hear what Denny says. I'm in, but I have to coach Al's softball team. If that's a problem, then take a hike. Another point to consider is I might lose. There are no guarantees in this game, especially under street fighting rules."

"I would rather enter this venture with you, rather than any other fighter. You look good, and I know you train everyday no matter what happens in the future. You set your mind on something, make the endeavor work, and you lead a team of killers I have never seen the like of. If problems do occur, your crew either fix the problems, or they bury them. Lastly, you act on the side of what is right, although the sheer number of sociopaths who have joined your crew would be a case study that would make the X-Files believable in comparison."

Now even I'm wondering where we're going with this. "Denny runs the operation, Alexi."

That statement caused much mirth on the part of the old gangster. He even clapped his hands in appreciation. "I…I am sure Mr. Strobert masterminded much of what brought your crew together. Part of it I suspect is because he joined together the most

21

dangerous loners on earth with only one person they respected enough to lead them – you. We have all done much good, although the work sometimes took place outside the parameters of the law. In the case of Ms. Montoya/Dostiene, the work sometimes takes place outside the realm of horrific imaginings. In any case, you hold this crew together. I know if you agree to fight, nothing on earth Yuri could do to threaten you or your family would be more than pissing into the wind. He mentioned your people after I met with him in spite of his horrid handling of my first approach. His arrogance I admit makes me forget how arrogant I was in his position. I have learned humility since meeting you, a well taught, and much appreciated lesson, John."

"Okay… I'm in. I'll have to endure torture on your behalf from family corners because of it though. My crew will shake their heads and laugh, make fun of me, and create new nicknames of shame for me. Lora accepts anything, but forgets nothing. Tommy will want to prod me into my banana dry-suit, and feed me to the sharks as he did training me for the Rattler. Al will give me her tight lipped scowl, which will rip my heart out; but what do you care, you unfeeling wretch?"

I smiled, as I again drew big laughs at that statement. "Enough of the laugh track, when do we meet?"

Alexi waved me off for a few more seconds, unable to continue for a moment after being labeled an unfeeling wretch I'll wager. "You are most entertaining, my friend. May we meet again at six o'clock tomorrow evening at The Warehouse Bar? It will of course be my treat, and please bring anyone who would like to accompany you. I know Tommy will be at your side. He will be pleased at the amount of money to be had in a back alley brawl where he can again work his betting magic with guaranteed money."

"I'll tell him, but Tommy is a bit jaded after the Rattler win. He seems to think I owe it all to his torture sessions in the Bay. Those training sessions will not be happening under any circumstances. Pain used to be my friend. Tommy's made pain into an enemy."

"I admit when I heard of his training regimen putting you alongside the boat in a yellow dry-suit being poked with poles, and bumped by sharks, I thought even beating Eugene would not be worth it. I am result oriented though, and respect Tommy's outcome, but I understand you not resuming such training."

"Good… because I'm not, even if it means death by Assassin," I replied.

"Such will not be the case. I use Jack Korlos in all important matches. You know him. He has never had a death happen in any match he's refereed."

"Jack's the best. He'll sap the Assassin or me if we don't stop when he tells us to stop. I'll see you tomorrow at six."

"Until then, my friend." Alexi walked away with a wave, and I went in to face my crew.

Lora and Al were already watching the door, so I knew my extended meeting with Alexi had their imaginations working overtime. The rest of the gang only glanced from pizza devouring when I reached the table. Lora took a deep breath and reached for my hand as I sat down. I think her feminine sixth sense kicked in although I smiled at her with what I thought was reassuring good humor.

"What have you done, Mellow Yellow?"

Lora prodded me with one of the nicknames given to me during my Bay training inside a yellow dry-suit. It received appreciative laughter of course. "Nothing, Hon. Tommy and I have to meet Alexi at The Warehouse Bar tomorrow night to discuss a business proposal."

23

"Partial truth," Tommy said. "I see in his eyes though that's all we're getting for now, Lora. I'm coming over to the house after we leave here. I feel a storm brewing on the horizon."

Tommy's pronouncement elicited smiling but questioning looks from my monsters. I drank down half my mug of beer before expounding any further. "All of you are invited to the house after we leave here. There will be refreshments served. For now, let's enjoy the girls' celebration."

"You promised to be our coach, Dad," Al said.

I met her questioning look with my Dark Lord stare and voice. "When has the Dark Lord broken his word to you, daughter and minion of the Dark Lord?"

That provoked a giggle from Al, and her teammates within hearing. She immediately jumped to her feet, head bowed. "Yes, Dark Lord."

Her impromptu adlib drew general laughter. Discussion stayed on track, talking softball and what we still needed to work on. Tommy eyeballed me through our entire pizza celebration. I figured I'd be hearing about it at the house. Better there than here. The girls took in the whole process with their parents eyeballing me with I'm sure conflicting emotions. The entire crew of my monsters showing up probably made them a bit uneasy, but too bad. If anything bad happened around the girls in this particular public place, the only casualties would be bad. Those thoughts no sooner passed into my head than the opposing coach and his brother show up, ready for action, or what they thought would be action. I know it seemed confrontational to them as my monster crew and I groaned together. The husband pointed at Lynn, provoking amusement inappropriate, but unavoidable as we all knew if Lynn got busy, nothing but scraps of flesh would be left of these two innocent dolts. Clint stood up, waving us down, including Lynn who he had to force back into her seat.

24

"Hi, I'm Clint Dostiene. This is Lynn, my wife. We all know Marion was upset. She made a remark best not repeated in front of the kids, which my wife could not let stand." Clint took out a notepad and pen from his pack. He scribbled on it for a moment, tore off the page, and handed it to Marion's husband. "There's my address and phone number. My advice is to make your complaint to the board. Don't make this an issue here in front of the kids. It will end badly for you."

"You're cocky with all your friends around you!" The husband was approaching the river of no return.

Clint turned to us monsters with a grin. "No matter what happens, stay out of it. Are we clear?"

We all said 'clear' in chorus, except for Lynn, who continued to smilingly eyeball the husband. "That means you too, Crue."

"Fine! I relinquish this opportunity to the 'man from nowhere'."

That drew laughs from even Clint, to the tag Lucas had put on him during our last caper. "Thank you, my dear. Now, let's let bygones be bygones. This won't end well, guys. If we all stay within the softball rules, and don't make disparaging remarks about one another, we'll get along fine. Threaten my wife again, and that would not only be impolite, but an action with consequences."

The idiot husband moved into the airspace of a man so dangerous even his brothers in arms from our monster squad didn't invade his airspace. "You don't scare me. You'd best corral your wife if you want to keep on in this league."

Clint leaned in close so no one else could hear. The husband's eyes got real wide for a moment while he backed away. He corralled his brother-in-law with a quick shoulder grip, guiding him out the exit. "Finally, someone who understands English."

Clint sat down and resumed eating pizza and drinking beer. Lynn couldn't resist. "What did you say 'man from nowhere'.

Clint shrugged. "I told him he was being unreasonable. He agreed."

"I'll bet," Lynn replied. "Nice work... man from nowhere."

Chapter 2

New Player

Al went to bed at ten, under protest, while I enjoyed interrogation 101. I explained it in simple terms exactly what was said, including the invitation at The Warehouse Bar. Although there were clucking noises during my explanation, I believed everyone understood who Yuri Kornev was. They knew what he did if he didn't like the message, he killed the messenger. No one had seen The Assassin, Marko Hristov fight.

"Jess and I will see what we can find out about the fighter," Devon said. "At least you'll get to meet the guy first. When do we start training on the Lora?"

"That kind of talk will get you killed, Dev. Anyone else thinking about an at sea training regimen involving poles and Tasers better leave the room now."

"It helped you win the fight against Rattler," Tommy pointed out.

I put up my hands. "Stop with the result oriented regurgitation of fact. I beat Rattler: period. It's in the past. I am never donning the banana suit again or going anywhere but over the Bay waters on a boat. Like I said, anyone forcing that issue needs to say goodnight, and find their way home. Otherwise, let's keep our heads in the game. Alexi is an ex-mobster we trust through hard won past issues. Yuri is a mobster force moving into our territory. Denny's on his way over now with some added news about our new turf invader. Any ideas about handling this Kornev guy before Denny arrives?"

"I sense a direct approach spiking through your mind," Lynn said. "I think you're wondering what the fastest way is for returning to nothing other than coaching girls' softball, and drinking Bud and Beam at The Warehouse."

Much enjoyment and toasting went on for a few moments over that assessment. "I admit it. I'm into this small window of time without weapons of mass destruction threats, and playing bump the banana with the sharks. I've indulged in a couple of the Bud and Beam brothers, so this might be a good time to get into specifics, Crue."

Lynn stood to address my concern. "We have a tip about a new gang moving into our territory by an extremely reliable source. Why fuck around the edges. Let's hit this nail with a hammer and be done with it. Why play footsie with the locals who'll get drawn into it no matter what we do? When you meet with this Yuri tomorrow, we'll all be there too as Warehouse Bar customers. When he leaves, we'll take him out along with his assassin. It'll be a springtime feeding for the sharks in place of bumping the big banana."

"I like your thinking, Crue." Man, I'm overthinking this shit. I was considering local feedback, which would be minimal. Hell, we're all professional killers with a shadowy government cover. Lora had stayed silent, but I could tell she liked Lynn's plan. Then the doorbell rang. "I'll get it. I smell the Spawn of Satan at my doorstep."

"Hey... my BFF is married to him, and having his baby." Lynn shook her finger at me warningly. "Ease up, or we will put you in the Bay with poles and Taser training."

I smiled, glancing around the room. "First off, there ain't enough of you. Secondly, I will hear what Spawn has to say in the matter."

Lora touched my arm as I answered the door, her hand gliding lightly over it. I noticed. At the door, I saw it was indeed Denny and his wife Maria. She's a billionaire backer of our endeavors if we feel something occurs beyond the coffers our reticent government provides. Maria Brannigan is a singular case, rough handled by Lynn when we took down her brother, but now a no holds barred best friend of the most dangerous woman alive. I respect that, as do all my cohorts. Denny, on the other hand, is on a case by case basis. We'd do quite a bit for him on command, but we would delve deeper. He knows it, and tries to keep himself in check.

I opened the door. "Hi Maria. You look wonderful. Denny... not so much."

While Maria hugged me, giggling at my jab at Denny, he never lost his mission face. "Thank God Alexi called me right away. This Kornev move into the Bay Area means a hell of a lot more than a fight, and the usual gangster action. He's being forceful with Alexi because he has no shipping contacts on the West Coast. He's targeted Alexi's deep water port possessions for something more than smuggling trinkets. Yuri's in link with a Bulgarian arms dealer. He calls himself The Ghost. Lately, the bastard's been supplying not only rogue Isis factions, but also Boko Haram in Nigeria. He's the perfect money laundering outlet for both to clean their robbing and kidnapping money, while supplying them with everything he can get his hands on."

I admit I'd never seen Denny this on edge. Maybe Fatherhood is lighting his paternal instincts. "Lynn already instinctively came up with a kill plan in advance of ground gained in useless ploys with the locals. I meet with Yuri, and his fighter tomorrow night, and we nuke them all, including any names Lynn tortures out of them. Easy pickings."

Maria liked Lynn's idea. "Yes! Lynn has found a perfect solution to these people."

Denny hugged her to him with real emotion. "I wish it could be that easy. John's crew would go through whoever Yuri has like a hot knife through butter. The parameters have changed in that we can get a lead on the most notorious arms dealer on the planet. It will mean, with John's permission, that we allow Alexi and Kornev to vie against each other head to head. We know Alexi's holdings are legal now, but for the sporadic backstreet fights he's taken over from those two prior termites, Bonasera and Alexander. I hear they're working for him full time now."

"Yeah, Alexi's not greedy. He gives the people he displaces a helping hand. He owns that sweat-bag's soul, Ray Alexander. Ray's into Alexi for so much money, none of us may live to see the day he gets clear of that debt. Boo hoo… I'll light a candle for him… the asshole. Alexi keeps everything on the up and up since taking over the fights. Jim and Ray could be bought. It made people uneasy about the fights. You know yourself Tommy and I would play the marks. I would hold off dropping a guy to not piss off the losers.

Denny smiled, closing my door behind him. "Like you did to Jesse?"

"Don't go there, Den. It won't go well for you. Mr. Brown lost fair and square. If I did some playacting, it was to smooth over the loss with the crowd. Partnering with me and Tommy has made him a fortune. I take care of my people, unlike some other gasbags who like to shoot their mouths off about other people's failings. Hell… you ordered me killed. The only thing stopping you was the fact you had no one else but Lucas, Casey, and Clint that could get the job done. You only rescinded the order because Clint told you if anything happened to me, he'd be at your bedside one night."

Denny shrugged with an engaging smile. "Who's perfect? We all make mistakes. I've learned from mine. That's why you have final say over anything we do. I'm not some blind newbie. I know who your crew swears allegiance to, and it ain't me. I facilitate what needs to be done. Yuri Kornev needs to be yesterday's news, but so does the Bulgarian arm's dealer. I admit I haven't thought of a way you could get that done without possibly kicking the crap out of his fighter, 'The Assassin'. I figure if you can scramble Assassin's marbles, Yuri may want to buy you on a steady basis. He already knows you're a freelancer. What do you think of that angle, John?"

"I like it," I admitted. "It may be the only way to get in on the operation Yuri's trying to steal from Alexi. We'd have to make it up to Alexi some time down the way though."

"We saved his granddaughter's life," Denny lanced into the conversation. "He owes us until time stops, damn it!"

"No, he doesn't. You need to take a step back. Let me handle the details. You come on in, and I'll lay out our initial operation and why. That way, the gang can unload on me. You only input positive comments. We need you as our facilitator. I don't want any evil thoughts directed at you for the operational phase. Things have changed since you, Lucas, Casey, and I worked this end of the street. You backed Clint to get his honey, Lynn Montoya, out of a bad spot, and recruited the worst nightmare anyone ever dreamed of to our side. Trust me to run this the way you want."

Denny gripped my wrist. "I trust you with my life, Maria's life, and my unborn child's life, John. I give you direction, sometimes a gamble, to aim our resources at a threat to the USA. I have no intention of botching the groundwork we've laid into place... ever. Let's go face our friends. I'll give them the basics with the facts about taking down Yuri Kornev and why. I'll allow you to explain the course for altering his plans while gaining the name and whereabouts of 'The Ghost'."

"Understood. You've made me so dry talking to you, even the Bud and Beam brothers will have to be sipped to get through this caper."

"I think I'll have one with you, John." Denny took Maria's arm and followed me into our meeting.

It didn't take long after the usual greetings to explain the situation. I had replenished everyone's drinks, including mine. Tommy of course decided to harpoon me again.

"I understand everything now," Tommy said. "This is for the sake of the nation to get this 'Ghost' guy. Playing the angles with Yuri can be done easily if John beats this Assassin fighter Yuri's promoting through the ranks. All the more reason for you to order Mellow Yellow into the Bay, Denny. Issue the order now."

With everyone laughing, Denny shook his head. "I'm afraid not, T. I want to see my kid born and raised if I can. What would be my chances of survival if I order you into the Bay, John?"

"Uh... possibly ten seconds after it leaves your mouth. Pay no attention to T. His eyes lit up when I explained the meeting with Alexi. He pictured being on the side of The Lora with a pole in one hand, and a Taser in the other. What Tommy needs to understand is the only thing for him off the side of The Lora is another swimming lesson. Anyone have input as to this Kornev business?"

"We could still pluck the two of them from The Warehouse Bar, and take them for a cruise. I'd get the Bulgarian Ghost's name in thirty seconds," Lynn offered. "You wouldn't have to take a chance on getting your ass kicked at all."

Not bad. "Nice input, Lynn. How about it, Denny?"

Denny took a moment. He didn't want to word what he had to say wrongly. "In different circumstances I'd jump at that one, Lynn. It will take John at least another month to recover completely from his fight with 'Rattler'. In that time, I'm hoping Yuri will be in contact with the Bulgarian, and possibly host him here in the area to look over shipping arrangements he hopes to gain control of. We need to wipe this guy out of existence along with any Boko Haram connections we can find. It would be a much easier outcome to control if he popped into our area."

"That makes sense, Denny," Lynn replied. "It still hinges on John and Tommy making a fight deal with Kornev. I like the Las Vegas fights at the Mandalay Bay. Does John's street-fighting screw our chances of getting him into another UFC fight at the Mandalay, Tommy?"

"If he loses, it could permanently wreck his chances."

"That does it, John. It's into the Bay for you, oh great banana."

"I'll tell you what. Anyone thinking to put me in the Bay next to my beloved's named boat put your money where your mouth is. I'm giving 20 to 1 odds. Any takers?"

Lots of smiles, but only silence to accompany them. Good choice.

* * *

Tommy and I walked into The Warehouse Bar for the first time since before I introduced Rattler to the canvas on Valentine's Day. Being an Oakland police officer hangout separates our 'Warehouse' from anywhere else. It's the safest place in Oakland to have a drink or good food. I love the place. Plus, many of my Oakland PD friends hang out here, along with the best barkeep ever: Marla.

"Champ!" Marla rushed around the bar to hug me. "Where the hell have you been? Ditched your friends after the big win, huh?"

"Never. I'm coaching Al's girls' softball team, and time away has been short."

"Alexi called to let me know you have another fight meeting. I would have figured with the exchanges I saw, you'd be fighting again next year. You don't look so bad. I made a bundle on that fight, John. Best of all... you were never really in danger. I've seen some hard ass features on peoples' features before, but the look you were wearing that night had me feeling sorry for Rattler. So, a girls' softball coach, huh? Al's lovin' it with your crew pitching in, I'll bet."

"We won our first game today. Al pitched, and played great. My crew is really into it. Lynn's my assistant coach, if you can believe it."

"Cruella Deville coaching." Marla paused, shaking her head. "That girl-"

"Hey! Can I get some service around here?" A big blustery asshole at the bar wearing jeans and a gray muscle shirt called out loud enough for people down the block to hear. "Quit stroking Coach Pervert, and bring me another round, Marla!"

Before Tommy could reach out to corral me, I had Mr. Muscle up on his toes at the bar, my hand clamped around his chin in a tightening press leading to destruction. "What did you say about me, Pussy? I hope I heard you wrong, pal."

My close buddies from Oakland PD, Enrique Rodriguez and Earl Taylor rushed out of the gaming room. Earl wound around to grab my wrist. He'd been a Marine the same time I was. Now he's an Oakland police officer, but he and I were still Marines. "Don't kill him, John."

"He's a newbie, Hard Case," Marla added. "I'll kick his butt to the street."

I stared into the newbie's eyes, while blocking any action from his legs. His hands were busily trying to separate me from his neck. It wasn't working well for him. "You'd best make an apology right now before I force my Oakland PD friends to arrest me for your killing. No one jokes or calls me a child predator unless they're too stupid to live. Repeat what you said ass-wipe, and I crush your throat!"

"I...I'm done! I'm sorry," the turd said.

Seeing in my face we were not done, Marla jumped me, clinging to me in an effort to thwart my base tendencies. I didn't like this guy's tone. He thought there would never come a time in his wasted life where someone with violent tendencies would erase him. Lesson coming up. I'd had enough of these tulips, bullying and conning 'the young and the restless'. Then something appeared in behind those beady eyes – something strange. I let him go, patting Marla's hands wrapped around me.

I didn't take my eyes off of the bastard in front of me. "It's a setup. Thank you my friends for delaying me a moment so my brain would work. Yuri decided to test the waters with this punk. He'll be here in a few minutes expecting a bar fight, which I was nearly on the verge of causing."

"Who you callin' a punk, mother-"

I had him this time by the throat with only his toes dangling trying to meet the floor. "Be careful, chump. There are no take backs. Answer one question, and I let you live. Play bad boy with me, and I rip your Adam's Apple out. I'll hold it in front of your eyes while you figure out what happened. Wanna' play, bad boy?"

His negative head shake was all he could muster, but it was enough. "Did a guy pay you to pop off like this, trying to cause trouble?"

A minute, gasping head nod put him back on the floor, holding his neck with both hands, while the sparse crowd in the bar went about their business. This place was like 'Cheers' in the TV show. Everyone knew my name, and they didn't care what the hell I did with the blueberry muffin at the bar. I patted his cheek.

"Tell me what I suspect already, and walk out untouched."

"I...I got paid," he admitted while massaging his neck. "Didn't get any names. A nobody in a suit... you know... looking like he's somebody's enforcer, gets in my face and asks if I want to make some money. I told him hell yeah! This ain't the way it was supposed to go."

As if illustrating the point, in walked Alexi, the guy I assumed was Yuri Kornev, but also 'The Assassin' himself, Marko Hristov. I shoved my bar buddy against the bar. "Stay here. Finish your drink, and then walk out."

He nodded, and I pushed against the bar before leaning with my arms folded. I knew the guy who paid him wouldn't be in this fight deal group. I exchanged glances with Earl and 'Rique while the new arrivals approached us. They smiled. Game on.

"Marla… I'm mighty dry, and I'm buying my friends in the bar anything they're drinking." My answer to this goofball no win situation was to win. I could tell Tommy approved of my first maneuvers. The trouble maker downed his drink, and slid around the group, moving quickly toward the door.

She slapped the side of my head with real compassion, and a little angst. "I'll have them at hand for you in seconds, Champ."

Marko Hristov shaved his head, wore an earring of a skull on his right ear, and kept a closely shaved stubble beard. My height and maybe ten or fifteen pounds heavier, Marko moved with a fighter's light stride with little side to side movement. His slate gray suit looked form fitted to his body, nearly a second skin. Muscles bulged through the material everywhere. He looked up to the mark to me.

Yuri could have been a walking illustration of a Hollywood gangster. His shoulders hunched slightly, and at a couple inches over six feet, he carried about thirty extra pounds. His graying black hair, cut and styled to perfection barely touched the collar of his black suit coat. He had one of those crooked grins that form after time when the guy usually has a cigar sticking in one end most of the time.

"Did something happen, John," Alexi asked.

"Someone bought some bait, used it to prime the trap, but the wolf smelled a rat, and sprung the trap without damage. No need to discuss your guests' ploy right now, Alexi."

"Are you accusing me of something, pug?" Yuri wasn't happy with my inferences.

"It almost worked," Tommy said. "John's been around. He doesn't get caught easily. Let's get a table and talk over this fight deal. John needs something to rest his drinks on."

"I don't think I like you two," Yuri said. "Are these really the best you can do, Alexi? Harding won't last fifteen seconds against The Assassin. Show me what you got, Harding. Why the hell do I have to make all these intricate arrangements for a pug like you?"

"He just beat 'The Rattler' in a huge match at the Mandalay Bay," 'Rique said. "What the hell did your pug do?"

The Assassin reached for 'Rique. I snatched his wrist, while blocking him into the bar. I saw Oakland's finest coming quick to back 'Rique, and they weren't reaching for party favors inside their jackets. Earl and 'Rique stepped away, with at least four of their fellow officers surrounding them. Marko tried to move, but quickly found I had leverage he couldn't break free of. Surprise showed in his eyes. "Don't do it. These men around you are Oakland police officers. Touch one of them, and there not only won't be a fight, but you'll spend some time in jail. Let's quit insulting each other and sit down."

Yuri clasped Marko's shoulder. "Let us sit as he suggests, Marko. We will settle with the pug soon. This was a bad venue for the meeting, Alexi."

Alexi smiled while I released Marko. "I think it a perfect setting, Yuri. Marla, I wish to take care of all open tabs here. I apologize for the disturbance, my friends. Please return to your meals and drinks. We will proceed in a much more reserved manner."

Alexi's instant generosity ended the tense standoff with many happy faces around us. I exchanged silent understanding with my friends. 'Rique patted my shoulder. "I hope Earl and I get security duty if the fight gets arranged, John."

"If it does, count on it," I replied. 'Rique and Earl had been watching my back for a long time in the street fighting game. We also had an arrangement due to them knowing my background for a while with government agencies. They let me know if anything has a terrorist angle from what they hear or see.

Marla led us to a table that was cordoned off in a room corner after Alexi made his reservations earlier. Tommy and I kept a polite distance from our companions, not willing to make any fake forgiving gestures, or put ourselves within reach of these bozos. Marla expertly took drink orders, and supplied menus. When we were settled into our seats, I drank down my Beam brother, and half my Bud brother. From now on, I planned to make this meeting entertaining and enjoyable – for me at least.

"You drink like a Cossack," Yuri commented with thoughtful speculation, as Marla slipped in a refill on my Jim Beam. "It is a wonder you have survived the street fighting, and UFC matches. You have quickness and strength, but no will power I think."

Tommy chuckled. "Well that was an eye opening first dip in the pool. I think it best if you simply tell us the deal. We'll make a decision from that without personal comment. How's that?"

"Yuri is offering fifty thousand dollars for John to fight Marko," Alexi said. "It will not be a UFC fight nor will it be under the same rules. The fight will be refereed by Jack Korlos. John and Marko will be given a list of what each fighter can do without getting sapped. The winner is whoever Jack states has won the fight. Both of you are familiar with his work, because both John and Marko have fought street fights with Jack refereeing. I take ten percent of all side bets, and an even split on any money from video rights or sales. I do not take care of collections other than guarding the process. For an extra five percent, my people will act as intermediaries. Are there any questions?"

I nodded at Tommy. It was a nice piece of change. No, we didn't need any money, but in this case we definitely had a dog in the hunt. Terrorists and their enablers are our business. It would be in bad taste for me to get preachy about laundering money. With the vast amounts we have taken from recently deceased bad guys who died violently at our hands, I don't get moralistic about money. After going through a past period of not having any, a fifty thousand dollar guaranteed cash payout makes us smile even now.

"We'll take it," Tommy said.

"Since Yuri has already made the offer, and knows the parameters, the deal's done. He and I have a separate wager which will remain between us. The only other matter is when. How much time will you require for training and rehab from your 'Rattler' fight, John?"

"Six weeks would be great."

"Good," Alexi said. "Yuri already agreed to a time parameter up to two months. Let us agree on middle April for the fight then. I will spell out all the details in contract letters to both parties. Is there anything else?"

"Yes," Marko spoke for the first time, his voice like small rocks ground together in a mixer. "What will happen to me if I kill this man?"

"Nothing," Alexi said. "We don't allow killings, and Jack Korlos has not lost a single fighter, but accidents happen. It's a rough sport."

"It will not be an accident," Marko said.

"Jack will tell you to stop if he sees John's in danger, or has tapped out, or been knocked out. If you try to continue, he will sap you in the back of the head. It's bad business to allow killings to happen with many political figures in attendance."

Marko smiled as Alexi finished. "I will be careful then."

"If we are finished, Marko and I will take our leave. I do not care for these two gentlemen. I will leave them to overindulge in peace."

Without another word, Yuri walked away with Marko following. I then explained the ploy Kornev had tried on me. Alexi listened intently until I finished. I could nearly feel the inner rage building inside him.

"I cannot believe what a fool I am. Nothing in our violent universe happens by accident. The last fighter Marko beat here three weeks ago was one of my top heavyweight prospects: Eric Minor. Marko nearly killed him. An odd thing occurred at a restaurant bar I was not present at to the young fighter. A guy at the bar kept a steady flow of invective aimed at Eric going until the bartender called the police. The instigator threw a punch, and Eric decked him. Even with witnesses, the police arrested Eric. It took me a few days to get him released on bail, because of the so called victim's injuries. The fight took place a day after he was released. I don't know if Eric could have beaten Marko, but the jail time robbed him of a step. I should have known that bastard Kornev was behind it."

"Kornev didn't really care about putting me in jail. I think it was a test. Care to share your wager with Kornev, Alexi?"

"If you think it involves shipping, you are correct. Ownership will not be in play, but access to my port facilities without interference will be. I calculated if you lose the fight, I will simply tip off Denny as to when any shipment leaves my port facilities or arrives bearing Kornev's ownership."

Tommy and I enjoyed that tidbit of duplicity. I sipped while Marla brought over appetizers, accompanied by refills. This Yuri and Marko show today pissed me off. I'm no wallflower cowered by name calling or threats, even from terrorist enablers. Business is business. The stakes were high, separate from the cash. I don't laugh off threats. I trusted Jack Korlos implicitly. If Marko put me down, he would make sure I didn't die. Jack would also sap the shit out of me if I continued on after being ordered to stop. I felt the great banana rising in me. Maybe it was too soon to retire my Mellow Yellow dry-suit. Back alley/street fight brawls were an inexact science. The gloves were thinner, and it was a go until someone drops match. We'd have that excellent cage Alexi inherited after I whooped the Syrian Slayer, so at least Tommy and I wouldn't have to watch out for crowd interference as in the old days. Yep, memories of my prior training in the Bay would have to be erased from my mind. I never thought anything would get me back in the damn banana suit, but I had a sixth sense for bad situations. My spidey-sense was tingling loudly like the 'Bells of St. Mary's'.

"I see that look in your eyes," Tommy said, drawing Alexi's attention. We had been eating and drinking quietly without the deal making couple present. "Do you know something we don't?"

"No, but I know I'm not taking this Marko lightly. Those two bother me. When I look at them, I see dead people and a bad moon rising. I'm going back in the Bay, T. I won't be whining about it either. We need to get Yuri out in the open with the people he's fronting for."

"Jesus… you're not kidding?" Tommy couldn't believe it. I didn't blame him, but I had to stay alive to keep my Al and her softball friends alive.

41

"We still have to keep working, and I can't miss my softball coach duties. We'll take The Lora out on the Bay as much as we did for Rattler. I want to be as sharp as I was at the Mandalay Bay this last time – no kidding, no playing, and no complaints."

Tommy shook his head and drained his drink. "You're scarin' me, brother."

"Gonna' get serious again, T."

Alexi had watched the exchange with first amusement and then complete concentration. "What is it you sense, John. I agree with your plan to be ready, but this sounds like much more."

I sipped the Beam brother, and nodded in agreement. "I'm still alive and well because I don't ignore my hunches. Yuri and Marko make me nervous. When I get nervous, I get violent. Nothing makes me more violent than training in the Bay."

"I have never said sure thing out loud," Alexi said. "The shape you were in, and the speed during the match with Rattler were amazing. You would have won the UFC heavyweight title. If they saw your fight in Las Vegas, the side hand strike should have been enough to make Yuri reconsider any match between you and Marko. You pinned him like a child against the bar only moments ago. You are right, John. Something is wrong with this picture."

"Exactly. I don't plan to find out the night of the match what it is I missed either."

"Crue's going to love your new determination."

I drank my newly arrived Beam brother with Lynn Montoya in mind, standing with pole ready to poke the Banana swimming alongside The Lora with vicious intensity, while giggling uncontrollably. "Yeah, T, I know."

Recognizing my mood, Marla arrived with a refresher. I held it up in toasting form. "Training in the Bay is hell on earth. Here's to hell on earth."

We toasted and drank in solemn agreement.

* * *

I pitched batting practice with the same concentration I ran a terrorist operation. I fast pitched with only one goal in mind – don't hit my players. Being a dedicated coach, I did not make that kind of error. I had struck out the first three batters with three pitches each. I watched them roll their eyes at me. See, although I only pitch at a speed similar to other teams' best pitcher, I still get the eye-roll because I'm an adult. I stopped the practice.

"Hey... you ladies may not like me pitching to you with respect, but if you think 'The Jaguars' plan to let you beat them down out of first place by lobbing 'hit me' softballs at you, I believe your judgment is impaired."

Lynn and I exchanged smiling acknowledgement this bunch of girls on our team were more of the 'show me' type player. Al was up next. She walked to the plate all business. She hit everything I threw to the deep part of the park in which we were playing, making my crew of Tommy, Jafar, and Clint get some exercise. I didn't make the girls shag every ball over their heads, except if they thought they could make a play on an overeager teammate. We had a rule – three strikes or fifteen minutes. Al always went the distance. She led by example. Every girl after her had blood in her eye. The batting practice went well after that. I made a personal note – lead off batting practice with Al. Then came the unexpected.

Lynn coached first base, because we doubled batting practice with run the bases correctly drills. She whistled. Lynn was jerking a thumb at the parking lot on our left. "Look who came to see you work, Coach. I've seen his picture. It looks like 'The Assassin' himself, Marko… uh… something or other."

"The name is Hristov, lady." Apparently, it was a sin not to know Marko's name.

Lynn cut him off. "Hey Hysterectomy… Vasectomy… Molotov… whatever. This is a girls' softball practice, Homey. Get your ass off my field before I call the cops… or worse."

With the girls giggling, and me trying not to, we all watched the veins in Marko's head pop out. His fists clenched tightly at his sides, before he shook one of them at me. "I wish to speak with the Pug."

Lynn smiled, waving her hands in a helpful manner. "See, you should have just said that. We don't have a Pug on the field. Maybe you have the wrong park, Jethro."

"I am not this Jethro! That man, there," Marko's gravel tongue rises in anger as he shakes a fist at me.

"Oh… you mean John. Sorry, big fella, no can do." Go have a seat on the bench. When John finishes practice, I'm sure he'll give you a listen."

Marko's ADD kicked in, and his attention span went into die mode. He reached to yank Lynn out of his way, only to have her duck inside, grip his jacket with her left hand, while the magically appearing butterfly knife shot forward under his groin. She whispered in his ear. Marko nodded, hands dropping to his sides. He then backed away from the knife, twisted toward me, as he walked away from the field.

"I wait for you, big man. Yuri sent me." He stormed to a nearby park tree, leaned against it, and folded his arms.

No one will be sending you anywhere soon, chump, I promised myself. "Thanks, Crue. Shall we hit a few balls, girls? Let's give the shag brigade out there some exercise."

We practiced for another half hour, and then I called it a day. The girls had a great time, but I was concerned the parents would be hearing another exciting tale of the dastardly Cruella Deville. I worked on a cover story while joining Lynn at the dugout.

"What did you tell my visitor?"

"I told him to go ahead, lay a hand on me, and I'd carve my initials in his dick. Then I told him to wait on the sideline. I bet you thought I was out of control, didn't you?"

"I didn't care. Hell... we would have carted him to a car saying we needed to rush him to the hospital. Unfortunately, he would have disappeared on the way there, never to be heard from again."

"How many girls do you think saw my knife?"

"Too many, but I'll claim you simply told an observer to stand by a tree to wait for practice to end, and he did so without further argument."

"Damn, Mellow, you almost sound like you could run for office," Lynn replied.

I guess I'll be back to the banana nicknames. "Tommy told you, huh?"

"Yep. You better go talk to that idiot before he goes ballistic, and I have to put him down like a rabid dog. I'll go tell our boys about the altercation. That will give you some time to talk with your playmate."

"This should be good. I have no clue what Yuri would want to talk with me about."

"If Yuri's here, are you going to talk with him in that limo I see out in the parking lot?"

"Sure, Crue. Why?"

"The boys and I will be watching. If you drive away with him, at least wave that you're okay. We have a date on a cruise today. Casey, Jess and Dev are already loading their fishing tackle."

"Thanks for the reminder. I'll keep that in mind. If they drive away to kill me elsewhere maybe I'll still wave." I continued on to Marko while Lynn laughingly met our guys coming in from the deep outfield.

"Hey, Marko, what's with the visit business during my coaching stint? Yuri could have called Alexi if he needed to meet again," I said.

"Yuri wants a meet with just you," Marko snarled, poking a finger in my chest. "You should not have kept him waiting."

"I see you like to talk with your hands. I like to break things. Poke me again, and we'll have to postpone the fight while your broken hand mends."

Marko grinned. "We see soon who gets broken. Come with me."

He led the way to Yuri's limo while I began looking forward to my training session. This guy was way too confident. Marko and Yuri weren't dummies. They'd seen the films of my Rattler fight. Jafar had searched everywhere for some clips of Marko's fights. He had them on a movie clip with Tommy, Jess, and Dev commenting on them in voice over for me. I would be training with those in mind, but it appeared I would need a bit more imagination to figure out what Marko might have up his sleeve. I

46

hated guess work, but sometimes it's all we have. At the limo, Marko opened the rear door, and I slid in opposite Yuri. He was by himself. Marko sat next to his boss.

"For a guy who doesn't like my company, you seem to be seeing a lot of me by choice." Yuri wore his smug grin mask. In addition to training, I'd better hone my detective skills. I smelled a rat, and these two made me uneasy.

"I wanted to speak with you about the coming match without Alexi or your partner in attendance," Yuri explained. "I like sure things. This match means a lot to Marko's rise into the UFC, and my getting a piece of the action around here. I'm sure Alexi informed you that access to his port facilities would also be part of a win for us. I have an offer for you. If you will make a believable fight of it, but lose, I will add five hundred thousand to the fifty you were offered. It would also mean Marko won't kill you in the cage."

I kept my face in neutral while he talked. Maybe this was what they were so confident about. "I'm surprised Alexi didn't mention he tried to pay me to take a dive. I don't do that."

"He did tell me, but we are offering much more money than you ever dreamed of making on a fight," Yuri replied. "No one need know about any of this. I certainly would not tell anyone. Depending on the side-bets which will be huge, I could cut you in for another hundred grand in addition to the offer. You also have a business which could profit greatly from a collaboration like I'm offering."

Time to put my suave politically aware personality into gear. Otherwise, I see murder and mayhem before I exit the limo. "While I appreciate your very generous offer, as I stated before, I don't do that, not for any price."

I'm afraid Yuri hadn't thought his ploy through before putting it into effect. I could tell by the stunned look on his face, he had figured I would jump at the chance to screw over everyone in my life who trusted me. Now, he was left with a refusal, and no way of knowing whether I would tell Alexi or not. That would mean in his kingpin mind he would have to kill me rather than allow me to leave the limo. I decided to put his mind at ease. We needed more info on his cohorts.

"I don't speak about deals made to me. If you're thinking I'll run out and tell Alexi, I don't do that either. This offer will remain between you and me. If we're done with the meeting, I have training to do."

"You'll regret this Harding," Yuri said as I opened the limo door, watching for any movements I didn't like.

"It's possible, but my answer is the final one. Good day, gentlemen." Man I'm slick. Maybe Lynn's right. I should start running for office.

"I kill you in the cage," Marko promised me. "It will matter not how much training you do."

That's what you think, Jethro. "Let me know how that works out for you, Marko. I don't like your chances; but then again, anything's possible. Bye for now."

The limo sped off once I closed the door. Al and my crew were waiting for me. Al looked relieved. She senses things no one else does. So does my crew, but they were simply smiling. They didn't care what happened in the limo. Once I exited it, everything was cake with frosting. Clint put away his .45 caliber Colt from under the towel he was holding. I have no doubt the limo would have never made it out of the parking lot. He knew where I was sitting in the limo. Clint would have put a clip into the idiots on the other side of me, while running to get a better shot at the driver.

"Did you have a nice meeting, brother?"

"Yeah, Clint, it was very enlightening."

"They wanted you to take a dive," Tommy said with conviction.

Tommy knows how this business works, inside and out. He knew Yuri and Marko would have stayed the hell away from me unless they were worried. Then they would bypass Alexi, and do a meeting like this. I don't have to break my word. I knew Tommy would figure it out the moment those two arrived at the park.

"You're right, partner, and they offered some big money – over half a mil. I guess they must have finally decided to watch the Rattler fight." That was my guess. Being the arrogant assholes they are, Yuri and Marko may not have even done their homework until the match was agreed to.

Tommy smiled. "Arrogance, overconfidence, and easy wins does it to these idiots every time. It looks like you were right, John. For them to offer that kind of money on a two bit, backstreet warehouse fight, they have a lot at risk."

"I know you don't take a dive for anyone, Dad. Can I go swing while you talk?" Al gets bored with business.

"Sure. We won't be long."

"I know," Al replied with a giggle. "You get to be the Great Banana this afternoon since it's a school holiday."

I put on my Dark Lord mask of evil retribution. Laughs were about all it drew. That's fine, because I planned to embrace the training rather than bitching about it. "Go on. Don't think I'll forget how much you're enjoying my torture though." I switched to my fist up Dark Lord voice. "The Dark Lord will have his revenge, young acolyte!"

On cue, Al spun, dipped her head, and said, "Yes, Dark Lord."

She ran off immediately to play on the playground. As I watched where she was heading, I noted movement with my peripheral vision. A guy left his vehicle to plod along nonchalantly toward the playground, along the outskirts. He halted as he came parallel with the swing set Al chose. My people were the best in the world. They missed nothing.

"Son-of-a-bitch! Kornev put a guy onto my girl, Al! Excuse me boys. I have some business to attend to." Lynn turned to flank the guy. "Call Denny. Clean up on aisle seven."

"Wait, Crue," I said. "Let's put away the equipment in my soccer mom van while we keep an eye on him. I have his license plate number now. If he's shadowing Al, he'll follow us, or make a report. Either way, we can collect him later. Run the plate, J. Make sure an actual person owns it or we may have to collect him now."

"On it." Jafar ran over to his car, and in minutes jogged over to us. "His name's Jordan Azi. I sent him on to Denny. Laredo's with him at home base. They are working over the names associated with Yuri's operation from Boko Haram, Soldiers of Allah, and a Pakistani based group, Jamaat al-Fuqra. Denny wanted to make sure we had pictures of all the players known to be associates. They're running the Azi name now."

"Good. Let's load our gear, and wait for Denny. If Azi looks promising, you and Clint could tail him, Crue."

"Oh, hell no, Dark Lord. I have a boat cruise scheduled this afternoon. I'll ride with you and Al. Let 'the man from nowhere' tail Azi if we don't snatch him right now."

"Is that okay with you, Clint? I don't want Crue to miss a neat torture session on my training cruise."

Clint had been enjoying the whole thing. He nodded agreeably. "Consider it done. Do I observe only?"

"For now," I replied, carting the team bags over to my newly acquired soccer mom van. "We've found out one piece of info here. Yuri's having my family tailed. We all know where that will get him. Both Tommy and I will have to start taking extra precautions until we end this Yuri business."

"The moment I heard about Kornev, and then met him, I've been taking a lot of extra precautions," Tommy stated. "I hope the big bad you're after comes in range by fight time. That Boko Haram bunch kidnaps and robs for a living. Ain't that special our government thinks we should have some of our own Boko's for diversity's sake?"

We all laughed, but everything Tommy said was true. We keep letting in people from nations who slip in, build terrorist cell links to their home country, and wait for the day they can unleash hell on earth here. Then Azi did a real stupid thing. I saw him look toward the ball field - not seeing anyone, he didn't look toward the parking lot, he approached Al. So much for planning.

"Take him at his car when I herd him this way."

I ran towards Al at a dead run. When I run, people look up. Al looked up, saw me running, and stopped swinging. She noticed the guy coming toward her then, and dismounted from the swing. The playground wasn't crowded, but it sure wasn't empty. I wondered what Azi had in mind. It wouldn't matter now. He didn't know it yet, but Azi was going to disappear without a trace. I slowed to a jog. Azi had noticed where Al's eyes focused. He saw me. His eyes widened, and he went left at a brisk pace. Yeah, that'll help him.

"We're going now, Al."

She walked to me and took my hand. "Was that a bad guy, Dad?"

"Yep. Unfortunately for him, we know he's a bad guy."

51

We both watched as Azi circled toward his car. When he reached it, there was a short meet up with Clint and Lynn. His unconscious body was bound and thrown into the backseat within seconds. Clint gave Lynn a kiss, and then drove off with Azi in his car. Tommy and Jafar were the lookouts. They all joined us at the soccer mom van.

"Wow Lynn, that was fast!" Al was impressed by the abduction of the abductor.

"It was, wasn't it? Maybe I need to get into calf roping or something at the rodeo, Al. What do you think?"

"Maybe after the baby," Al suggested.

We monsters enjoyed that line. Al went home with Jafar in our soccer mom van. He had ridden to practice with us while Samira helped Lora at the office. I went with Lynn for our boat cruise where it seemed Azi would be an added chore for Cruella Deville aboard the good ship 'Lora'. She was humming and whistling as she slid behind the steering wheel of her Toyota, waiting with a happy expression for me to get belted in.

"We goin' ta' have some fun now, partner," Lynn announced complete with goofy cowboy drawl.

Chapter 3

Journey Into Terror

Tommy drifted over to where Lynn sweated even in the ocean breeze as she worked the pole Tommy had invented for poking John as he swam alongside The Lora. The tip although well padded, was a painful jolt when it landed squarely. Lynn grinned and poked. John twirled in the water, snapped the pole with a vicious side-hand strike that nearly tore the pole out of Lynn's hands. Clint, who had shark duty with his MP5, laughed appreciatively. Tommy shook his head.

"Damn. John's quick as he was before the Rattler fight."

Lynn pulled the mangled pole out of the water, and flung it on the deck. "I'm done. That's enough exercise for me. Let's get John on deck. He's killing me. I would have thought he'd need a few days to get into this again, but either I'm slowing down, or he is indeed fast as hell still. He and I have Azi to play with."

"I hear you," Tommy said. "Shut her down Lucas!"

* * *

The Lora slowed to a stop. I looked up in surprise, but Tommy was there waving me on board. Damn. I had my mad on today. Between that meeting with Yuri, and the Boko Haram guy doing an approach on Al, I lost all track of reality. I didn't argue. I'm not stupid. I got the hell on board. I could tell from Lynn and Tommy's faces I must have done real well.

"That was your best ever in the Bay session yet," Tommy admitted. "You have a hard-on for this Yuri and Marko show, and you demonstrated it today. They were right to try and get you to take a dive. The only killin' 'The Assassin' will be doing is with his mouth, and not for long. I never get cocky, but damn, brother, you impressed me today."

"Thanks, T. Yeah, I am in all the way on this one. I'll get a shower, and then we'll do the long awaited discussion with Azi. Did Denny call yet?"

"Nope." Lynn patted my 'Great Banana' shoulder. "That last smash nearly ripped my arms out of socket. Denny must have found out a lot on this Azi character. Otherwise, he would have called by now. Get this straight in your head. Denny will be pleading for this dude to get turned over to him. I think we need to make him disappear."

"I agree. These people are in our backyard now, for whatever moronic reason the government pushes in the media. What the hell would be the use of holding onto a Boko Haram baby killer? If Denny calls while I'm in the shower, and pulls any of that whiney crap saying we have to hug this particular terrorist, he'd better get in a helicopter and find us before Azi goes bye/bye. I don't like his chances."

"Take your shower," Lynn said, staring at Azi restrained in the corner. "I'll warm him up while you're gone. All you Snow White's fishing off the boat either better get a grip, or head to the bridge with Lucas."

Devon and Jesse reeled in, and fled to the bridge without a word of argument. Casey chuckled and kept fishing. Lynn walked over in front of Azi, and crouched down to his level. "Hi there, Fuzzy. Here's how this goes. I'm going to show you a taste of what hell on earth will be for you if I don't get the answers to the questions I have." Lynn paused, as humming innocence pleas bounded out from behind the duct tape over Azi's mouth. Lynn projected her absolutely terrifying face of uncaring bloodlust. "I see you don't understand. Let me help you."

54

The screams began almost immediately as I went below decks for a shower. The worst part of these screams was the fact Lynn would not stop until she heard the prisoner's final benediction. I admit I grinned going down to take a shower. Lynn loved Al like her own kid. That colors our horizons in monster land. When I returned, Azi blubbered stuff from nearly his birth as I watched a professional work. Lynn patted his cheek, making shushing noises.

"Denny called," Clint said. "This Azi guy is a true Boko Haram bad guy. His picture flashed in reference to five kidnapping and extortion jobs overseas, including a village extermination. He works for 'The Ghost'.

I accepted the double Beam brother he offered with beaming appreciation. "I hate to say this, but how do we know it."

Clint enjoyed my rhetorical question for a moment. "Lynn's in fine form today. She knows this fuck had every intention of snatching Al off the playground. I believe my better half is in gathering form for anything you or Denny need ask, brother."

I acknowledged his input with a downing of my Beam brother, which Clint replenished immediately. "Thanks. I will join Crue's party, and see what dastardly deeds lie in the future."

Lynn wasn't touching Azi, or trying to make friends. I could tell she had made contact way down deep inside of our guest. Azi now knew there were truly moments worse than hell. By the looks of him, Lynn had exercised her nearly surgeon like skills with a scalpel, followed with a salt water dousing of the wounds, Clint did with a spray bottle. Very effective. That particular method could be reinforced with the spray bottle each time Azi hesitated. After a few treatments, Azi would then become nearly clairvoyant in his answers. I networked with Denny to do a long question and answer session, with both Jafar and Laredo checking every word, while data mining across the globe. Laredo Sawyer, our West Coast

Avengers pilot, and mentor to Jafar's IT skills, confirmed the answer parameters, which was all we could do for now.

"Take care of Azi, and I'll meet you at the base to go over the intel," Denny said. "I know he tried to take Al. There are no take backs for that. Will you be sober enough to visit Azi's place before the other rat he's rooming with scurries away?"

Denny knew all too well my sojourns into the Bay demanded some pain killer when I again boarded the boat. "I'll take Casey and Lucas with me. Crue and Clint will drive Azi's vehicle over for her minions to dismantle. If he's home, we'll bring the roomie with us for Crue to question and confirm Azi's answers."

"Good deal, John. I'll call in the minions." Denny disconnected.

I turned then to Lynn. "Want us to warm this roomie, Sam Edoja, before we arrive at the base?"

"Maybe. Leave him alone for now, except whatever you need for Sammy to accept the invitation. Want to hot shot Azi here, or feed him to our cleaners alive?"

I took a syringe out of my bag. "We don't have time to make sure our fined friends find him. We're far enough out to leave Azi off here."

I gave Azi his hot shot to hell, and then stripped him. Lynn sliced him with her scalpel from chest to groin before Clint and I tossed Azi into the water. "I'll clean the deck. You two relax on the bridge, and tell Lucas what we have in mind. Ask Dev and Jess if they can drive and be lookouts for our Edoja grab.

"Will do. I've been on the wagon for a week now. I think I'll indulge in a glass of Berringer's if you have a bottle," Lynn said.

56

"There's three in the refrigerator," I replied, while taking the cleaning elements from our above deck storage locker. After Clint and Lynn adjourned to the bridge, Lucas steered The Lora toward port while I cleaned the deck. Casey helped me, having reeled his line in when the boat moved. "Any luck today, Case?"

"Jess caught a couple sturgeon, but that was it. Dev and I got nada. I'm glad Lucas already had the van. We won't have to swing by the base to get it. Do you want to wait for dark, or are we doing the snatch and grab in daylight?"

The base, also known as The House of Pain, housed our moving vehicles, control center, and holding cells. Lynn's minions now took care of it 24/7. Gus Denova, Quays Tannous and Silvio Ruelas, who Denny refers to as Lynn's minions, did anything and everything we needed prepped or disappeared. Lynn rehabilitated them, and by rehabilitation I mean they were once used by the Muslim Brotherhood. A couple sessions with Lynn, and they were so helpful, we decided to recruit them rather than kill them. Since coming over from the dark side, Denova, Tannous, and Ruelas did excellent work, so much so, I obtained residences for the three men. They still looked at their shoes every time Cruella Deville walked into the room they were in.

"We'll take them the moment we get over there, Case. We may be able to gather a lot more intel from what's in their place. After we get Edoja, I'll find out where his car is, pop him in the trunk, and deliver him to Crue. You and Lucas can head for home then."

"I watched your training exercise today. I never thought you'd get back in the Bay. I heard you have a bad feelin' about this 'Assassin' match. This Azi guy sure proved you had reason. I don't know how many of these Boko Haram freaks are around, but I'm sure you've heard what they've done. That Nigerian sect will do anything. If there are any more of them in with Kornev, I hope Crue gets all the names out of Edoja. Azi didn't mention any, and I know he would have, but maybe he's low on the totem pole."

"I'll make that a priority when we're questioning them. I'll grab our memory card for the Azi session to show Edoja. Crue won't like it, but we may need to move faster than we like."

"Those damn recorded torture sessions have really saved us some time," Casey agreed. "Maybe she won't be pissed off today. She worked up a real sweat putting you through your paces. I think she only does them now to see if she can get someone watching to puke."

Very true. "I won't mention it to her until we see how snatching Edoja goes. If he gives us any shit, I'll hold off on showing him the recording of his buddy being brought to justice."

"That'll work." Casey led the way to the bridge which is spacious on The Lora. Everyone seemed in fine spirits, but Lynn was conversing with someone on the satellite phone with serious intent. Lynn smiled after a time, agreed, and told the other party she'd run it by me.

Putting aside the phone, Lynn sipped her wine Clint had been holding for her. "Samira wants to help do the snatch on Edoja. She's meeting us at the dock, so she can go along with you guys. Before you come unglued, Jafar's coming with her. Samira must have done one of her more persuasive hammerings on her young husband. What do you think?"

"I think she can do it, but I'm wondering if Jafar is counting on me not allowing her," I replied. "She could walk to the door, ring the bell, get checked out by Edoja, and step aside the moment he opens the door. Is that what she had in mind?"

"Almost verbatim," Lynn said, "only she wants to zap the guy in the doorway herself."

"That damn girl is going to drive Jafar nuts," Lucas said, glancing away from his steering. "She did real well on the 'Knockout Game' action, but that had more surprise going for it than this will have. Even with all of us at her side, for all we know

Edoja could answer the door with a gun. That's why John takes the first hit."

Lucas referred to our ending a gang doing sucker punches on innocent people at the mall, sometimes known as 'Polar Bear' attacks. Samira and Jafar partnered on a takedown of one participant. It had been her first time helping us on a job. She was trying to pattern herself on Lynn, but without the interrogation side. The other point he made was on a snatch like this, we normally pick the lock, and I bust in with Kevlar on. I take the first hit if the guy draws fast enough. Usually I take them down before they clear the holster. I also have backup in the form of men who can shoot the beak off a hummingbird at fifty yards. Jafar won't like this when I put the decision in his court again.

"I'll get off the boat and say it's okay with me if it's okay with Jafar. How's that?"

"Typical 'Denny Light' shirk the duty ploy," Lynn retorted to much appreciation.

* * *

Everyone comically skirted around Jafar and Samira with a quick wave, even Cruella Deville. Jafar stared expectantly at me, as did his pregnant wife, Samira. I smiled at them, after tying down The Lora securely to the dock. I could tell with one glance I'd guessed right that Jafar hoped to dump his no go decision in my lap. I don't think so, kid. We fight our own family battles here in monster land.

"Hi kids. I heard from Lynn what you'd like to do, Samira. You do understand I usually take the first hit through the door with Kevlar on, right?"

"Yes, John," Samira said with respectful acknowledgement. I had been one of her family's CIA guards attached from Marine Recon in Afghanistan when she was only a kid. I knew the lingo, so I'd been an obvious choice. "Did Lynn explain my simple

59

operational approach? I can do it without bullets firing or having to wound the suspect or worse."

"She did explain your plan, but although very tempting, I'm concerned about the danger. Since I believe you're capable of doing it, I will let Jafar have the last word. If it's okay with him, it's okay with me."

That statement evoked a squeal of delight from Samira, and a 'someone shot my dog' look from Jafar, confirming what I had suspected. The kid loved Samira more than life itself. He had high hopes for a future with Samira and children, but the cost of being in our group weighed heavily on him. I recruited him out of a jail cell. I gave him a dangerous new start. He loved it until a mission drew Samira into our group. Now, having won the hand and heart of the lovely Samira, who became our mission because she speaks out for change in Islam, Jafar wants to avoid being a barrier to her goals. Unfortunately for him, Samira wants more than speaking engagements. Lynn has made it plain to her she's not a Cruella Deville, nor could she hope to be - but she loves the interaction between Lynn and Clint, sharing everything in their lives. I doubt very much if she understands the danger as thoroughly as she claims, or the misery her demands to be more active in our group cause her mate. I'm not her Mommy though, so I passed the buck where it belongs.

Jafar stepped up. "I will not forbid this action. Such a decree would only alienate you from me. I am with John forever in this hellish endeavor to do what is right. I know you wish to help, but I doubt you see what it would mean to me if I lost you. I suspect because my friends laugh and joke about the unimaginable, you think the danger is a joke too. It is not. My friends' continued survival hinges on the fact they are so dangerous and skilled in these endeavors they are without peer. You are not Lynn, nor am I Clint Dostiene. They are something I sometimes think beyond your imagining. What they are together is not beyond my imagining. John's Lora does not wish to be Lynn or Lynn Light. That is all I will say. I will back your play, my love."

The kid made an impression on her, but I could tell she had already set her mind on completing at least this task with him or without him. She hugged him tightly. "I know you worry, but I must do this. I want to be more a part of this deadly business with you. I believe in this path, my love. I wish to walk it with you."

I grinned. She ate the kid's lunch. Done deal. Now, we needed to keep her alive so we didn't have to deal with those nasty unintended consequences. I put my arm around Jafar. "You have my permission to be first at the door on either side. Would you like that?"

Jafar vehemently shook his head. "I want you, Casey, and Lucas first in line."

"Lucas and Casey will have one side. You and I will have the other side, little brother. We will see the brave parakeet through this most dangerous endeavor, despite her questionable decisions."

That prompted a gasp from Samira, followed by a long cursing diatribe in Pashtu. I enjoyed it, but Jafar liked it even more as tears of laughter streamed down his cheeks, bent over at the waist. She was of course cursing me out. I understood Pashtu though, and reminded her of a duty one who loves has to a mate in Pashtu.

"Only the fortunate sometimes journey through their lives with one beloved beyond all things. To discard such a gift without thought is a mortal sin, punishable beyond imagining."

That sobered my little parakeet to reality, with Jafar gripping her hand with both of his. "It is just so, my love. This is not a game, and everything will not always come out right."

Samira patted his hands. "Step up, Homey. We're goin' ta' war, baby."

She nailed us good with that one, but she saved a final hug for Jafar, clinging tightly to him, tears running down her cheeks. "I know what loss is, my beloved. I will not lightly weigh my loss on you, but I must do this."

Jafar simply hugged her. "I know."

"Sorry to break this up, but we have a bad guy possibly holding onto much invaluable information. Let's go introduce him to Lynn Light."

While we laughingly strode off the pier Samira glanced back at me as I followed. "Your proverb will not be forgotten. There will be blood."

I nodded meekly in agreement. Such is life in monster world. We sometimes deal with situations where killing and torture have no part. It's an inexact science as a group leader. It was true what Jafar told his mate about our oddball group. We have the skills to react to any threat, but shit happens. When the BBC woman from my past and her asshole terrorist partner entered my home and took Lora and Al prisoner, only combat skill freed them. Lynn made their deaths legendary. Denny covered the act with a fatal car crash with the bodies burned beyond recognition. Luck played a part, but we do reduce the luck factor as much as humanly possible. I watched Jafar and Samira wrapped together as they walked along with some uneasiness. As Samira said when speaking of retaliation to my Pashtu reminder that there would be blood. When you care about someone, no matter what kind of skilled monster you are, there will also be fear.

* * *

We drove by the house Edoja and Azi shared. Not wanting a blood bath either in the house or on the street located in the Oakland hills, Laredo coordinated real time satellite imaging to Jafar in our ready van. I watched him closely as we passed the old house built on the steep slope of Lawlor Street. Jafar did not look happy with what he was seeing. At a glance, the only promising factors were the house had a ramshackle redwood fence shielding the front from the street, and the large gate did not have a lock on it.

"You have your game face on, little brother. What's the problem?"

"I'm getting four heat signatures. Edoji is not alone."

Casey, networked in with Jafar, pointed out a few possibilities. "It still looks good, John. There are three in the back part of the house, on the lower floor. I see on the plans, a long staircase separates the two house floors. Lucas and I can take the lower part. We'll approach alongside the house by that steep driveway. You and Jafar take the upper front where the porch is. The moment Samira gets a guy to the door, zap him, and throw a couple of flash-bangs down the staircase. Lucas and I will take it from there."

"I like it, Case, but we won't have as much backup at the door. What about it, J?"

Jafar took one look at Samira's stern face, and went for the alteration with tight mouthed acknowledgement. "Casey's plan is a good one. Let us get this done."

Jafar checked Samira's Kevlar under her clothing, tightening the Velcro straps slightly. With Dev driving, Jess had lookout duty. It would be their job to make sure we had a reasonable chance of slipping inside the fencing. Then they would circle the block and park where Dev could move into pickup position in seconds. Our ready van is an EMT vehicle with all the bells and whistles. We were all dressed as emergency medical techs. The ploy had worked so well in the past, we had adopted it as an operational choice. The moment after whoever on the upper floor opened the door, Jafar would shift the Taser into Samira's hands. I would be ready to maim or kill. I handed Lucas and Casey a couple of gas masks. Our flash-bangs could maim and kill too. They also affected breathing.

63

"We're ready, Dev. Take us in front."

"On our way." He rounded the block into position, while Jess watched for people moving on the sidewalks, or doing lawn chores outside.

"Clear," Jess said.

Dev stopped at the front gate, and our hit team piled out and quickly through the fence. Lucas and Casey scrambled down the steep driveway while Jafar and I split around Samira as she approached the door located on a small porch under an awning.

"There's too many windows down here at the back, John," Casey said in my ear. "It will only take seconds to get in after the bangs."

"Ringing the bell now, Case. Be ready in case they start bailing out the back rather than waiting for me to blow their eardrums out."

"You just keep Jafar's parakeet safe, boot camp," Lucas said. "This ain't our first swim in the pond, you disrespectful cracker."

The parakeet growled for Lucas's amusement while I, the boot camp cracker, prepared for violence. Jafar readied the Taser. Samira rang the bell. We all saw an indication someone looked through the peephole in the door. A deadbolt was slid into the open position. As the door began to open, Jafar slapped the Taser into Samira's hands. The moment the door opened to a point where the guy answering it was in view, Samira fired the Taser into him. She ramped the juice, and then cut it off. I grabbed the dropping shock victim, slamming him face first onto the floor, where Jafar restrained him.

I found the stairwell, which was indeed a long one. Hearing voices, I ran down the steps and pitched the flash-bang into the open living area. It blew to the usual screams of agony. Then I

64

threw in the second one. All quiet on the western front. I heard the door slam open at the back, while pulling my mask into place. My part was to stay out of the line of fire until I received a clear sign from Lucas. It came a moment later. I went down through the small doorway with plastic ties ready. We had all live casualties, so that was a good thing, because we didn't know who the hell was who, nor did we know if Edoje was the one Samira took down at the door.

"We have Edoje with us," Jafar said.

"Good." I quickly took pictures of our soon to be new guests at the House of Pain. I sent them directly to Laredo.

It was then time to cart our suspects upstairs. None of us felt like carrying them, so Lucas began kicking the shit out of them like he was waking a bunch of boot camps on their first day at the Marine Recruit Depot at Parris Island. They pissed and moaned, but Lucas did not cease until they were staggering up the stairs. We collected them in a little grouping near the front door, along with anything and everything having to do with computers or communications. They stared at us with hate filled eyes, mucous covered faces, and a little blood at noses and ears. I took a wet towel and wiped them off.

"In a couple minutes we're going to herd you guys into our transport. Anyone making a noise or slowing our progress loses something immediately." I had my butterfly knife with razor sharp blade at Edoje's right ear, drawing blood. "Want a demonstration?"

"We will come quietly!" Edoje spoke real fast for the group.

"Okay then, but remember any noise, and every one of you four loses an ear. Understand?" I had their attention. They nodded in energetic agreement. I called Dev, and we hurried the whole bunch out through the gate into our spacious EMT rig. Besides, we stuffed them into a corner on the floor. We hadn't counted on four ride along new companions, but we'd make due. Denny called as we were getting underway. "Terrorists Are Us. Welcome to the new terrorist Mecca where the USA lets in anyone from terrorist nations, as long as they come here to reduce our population."

I drew laughter from my friends inside the van, but Denny merely chuckled while letting the background noise subside. "Edoje's companions are all Nigerian Boko Haram. Did they have vehicles?"

"Hold on, and I'll check a couple of things." I turned to the huddled masses yearning to be free in the van corner. "Anyone not demonstrating English understandably dies right now. Who would like to live?"

They demonstrated the English language until Lucas had to bop them in the head. "Shut the fuck up. He wanted a simple answer, not a damn speech."

"Next on our question list is how many vehicles do you jerks have, and where are the keys. I saw two vehicles at the driveway entrance, inside the gate. Do you have any others?"

"No, they are our only transportation," one of the others with Edoje admitted.

Edoje stared at the speaker in surprise. "These people will torture us if we lie, idiot! They are not cops. We will all die shortly. Speak the truth, and maybe it will be a quick kill rather than a torturous death. There is a van parked in front. All the vehicle keys are on hooks at the left side of the entrance."

"Did you get that, Den?"

"I'll send a team. Can I have these guys for trading purposes after Crue interrogates them? Before you ask, I don't have a clue who let them in, or how they weren't arrested way before now. It would be a good question for Crue to work on. It would be good to know if both the entire Senate and House are selling us out for money, or if this is just a vote getting ploy to legalize everyone

66

who crosses the border, even if they want to kill us all. At least we'd have some idea where we stand in all this crap."

"I think we know where we stand... right next to the other seventy percent of our citizens who keep demanding we lock down immigration and the borders, all to no avail. I'm venting. I'll find out a few facts, or Crue will."

"She certainly will. This is straight from her – warm them up."

I grinned. "On it. See you in a few minutes."

"Jafar. Load the Azi interrogation video for these gentlemen to see."

"Ten seconds," Jafar acknowledged, working his laptop with smiling concentration.

When he had it loaded, he turned the sound to max, and knelt so our Boko Haram party of four could see how we found out about them. After a few minutes of watching Crue at work, they began turning their heads away in fear and disgust. Lucas let off an arc from his stun-gun in their faces.

"Anyone looking away better get set for some bad time with the blue arc in places you don't ever want jolted electrically."

It was a cinch after that for quiet contemplation of the video. At the end, I crouched down to engage my guests. "We're driving to meet the lady who did the interrogation on Azi. If I were you guys, I'd be dreaming of ways to be helpful. How did you ass-wipes get into the country? I already know you're all Boko Haram."

"Aboard a container ship in the East," Edoje admitted. "There is a Jamaat al-Fuqra faction operating at the docks. They work for the Bulgarian, as do we."

"What's the Bulgarian's name?"

"I don't know. They call him 'The Ghost'. Nobody talks to or meets this man. We are under Yuri Kornev at this time. He would know the Bulgarian's name. I have heard Kornev speak of meeting with the Bulgarian soon."

"Nice start, Sam. You and your buddies keep thinking of ways to make our video lady pleased. Otherwise, she gets really mean, like when your buddy Azi decided he was not going to talk… but he did… eventually."

* * *

Clint opened the large pull down metal door for our ready van, and closed it behind us. Crue met us with her minions, Quays Tannous, Silvio Ruelas, and Gus Denova. Casey and I helped the Nigerians to their feet. They saw who was meeting them, and wanted to climb over me to get back in the van.

"We are being cooperative!" Edoje pleaded.

"Ahhhhh… they really are warmed up." Lynn smiled directly into each man's face. "Did you see that horrible video? I know it was very upsetting. My men will take you down to interrogation. Be ready to give us your life's history or I'm going to be upset. We don't want that, now do we?"

Four heads shook in the negative in sync. Denny joined us as Lynn and Clint escorted their unhappy group to interrogation with the minions' help.

"Hell of a day. You did very well, Samira. I'm not crazy about you doing it, but your approach was professionally smooth. Lynn watched it, and she said you timed the Taser hit right on the button. I know Jafar will caution you. Take nothing for granted if you really are going to take a more active role."

"I want to without any reservations," Samira replied. "I know John will not allow me to endanger his team's lives, but today was a good start."

We sat down together in our conference room. Jafar took the electronics and communications contraband to Laredo. They would hack into and data mine all the gear we had confiscated. I explained to Denny what Edoje had told me. "We nabbed them without anyone noticing. Their disappearances will screw with Yuri's head. He won't know for certain if the Bulgarian summoned them, or they took off on their own. You were right about Yuri and the Bulgarian meeting soon, so we may be able to keep all the participants under observation. If Crue extracts any names from the Pakistani group, Jammaat al-Fuqra, are we going to move on them immediately, or wait to see who arrives with the Bulgarian?"

"I'd like to wait, John. Thanks to the importance Yuri puts on this port deal, I want all the players we can entice. I'm working on a picture of the Bulgarian, but having no luck so far – he uses disguises everywhere. What I can't understand is even with his own private plane, he still has to go through customs, yet we have no pictures of him. I get the feeling someone is protecting him. I'll be careful allowing anyone in on this until we break it open."

"Damn," Lucas said, "another sellout. You better watch your back, Denny. Could this mole be high enough to take a meeting with any of our benefactors?"

"I don't know, but I'm not finding out by sharing info on this op. Luckily, I didn't read anyone in on this, because Yuri's ploy to pressure Alexi's operations with the street fight decoyed me. I wanted further ahead on the investigation after Crue questioned Azi and his friends."

"What about approaching it from the Jamaat angle," I suggested. "Once Lynn records some names and locations, we could do an information gathering visit to get pictures. If we find an important member, we could snatch only him, see what he knows about the Bulgarian, and you can have him to trade."

"I like it. I'll stay here with Jafar and Laredo. Clint and Lynn won't be long, so I'll have some names in the al-Faqra sect to consider for abduction. Samira can stay or go. Everyone else may as well go get some rest. You certainly had a busy day, John. Go over all your security measures. The rest of you need to check on all family precautions until we end this."

"John's in shape," Lucas stated. "I watched him today. It's possible Yuri is not only uneasy about Marko's match with John, he's getting scared. I don't know what those characters have planned, but they're getting sloppy. Daytime kidnappings, Nigerians, Bulgarians, Pakistanis, and even the good old Russians plotting together with the Lord knows how many other Middle East terror threads. I'm wondering what the hell more this Yuri has in mind."

I stood. "Lynn will find a next step for us to follow. I get the feeling things are moving along faster than we anticipated."

"All the more reason for extra precautions," Denny said. "That goes for you and Jess, Dev. Don't assume these idiots won't try something on the extended families. C'mon, little parakeet. Let's go see how your husband and Laredo are doing."

Samira spun on me, finger under my chin. "You have made me into a noisy bird, John! Now everyone is calling me this parakeet bird."

"Not everything is about you, little parakeet. Sometimes, it's just for entertainment." I waved her off as she prepared to launch again. "Say no more. Your warbling these past few minutes has convinced me you shall indeed be known as 'The Parakeet'."

"I'll tell Lora you're picking on me."

"Keep talking, and the next mission you'll go on will be from a wheelchair in a rest home for the aged."

Samira gasped. "That is blackmail!"

"No. It's called action and reaction. Not another chirp out of you for tonight, little parakeet. Don't forget to tell Lynn all about your exciting day as a bird of prey."

I enjoyed being fervently cursed out in Pashtu until Samira entered our control room behind Denny. "That young lady has a filthy mouth."

"You do seem to provoke those malevolent feelings in the females you've been around lately, Dark Lord," Dev stated. "You've certainly reached Samira's last nerve."

"Malevolent, huh? Damn, Jess, I think Rose has been smoothing Dev's rough edges off. She's improved his vocabulary."

"Oh, she's done wonders for him," Jess piled on. "He takes off his shoes before entering the house. Dev says 'please' and 'thank you' now, along with 'yes ma'am', and 'no ma'am'. I've heard a rumor he sits down to pee too."

Jess had the rest of us but good with that ace, including Dev.

"What can I say? I'm whipped," Dev admitted.

"Don't worry about it, kid," Lucas said. "It just means you accept life as it was meant to be, except for the shark whisperer here. Be careful what kind of advice he gives you. I'm done for the day. I know you scheduled practice early for the girls because of this goofy Thursday teacher's conference. What's it look like for out in the Bay tomorrow?"

Torture and routine until I get past 'The Assassin'. "I'll have to let you know depending on what target we get next. I was hoping if we don't have the usual business tomorrow, we could go out on the Bay early, say around ten. I'll get the training in, and then some rest for Al's softball practice. Our business meetings will have to be fitted in as time allows."

"When are you working the rest of the routine?" Dev counterstrikes me right in the kisser. "You have to make time for work on the bags and your ground game."

"There probably won't be any ground game, but I guess we'll see what we can see, brother. I have workout bags installed for easy workouts at my house. You and Jess know I have a full gym over at the office. I'll work everything into my schedule, including the ground game. Take stock of anything and everything else out of place or missing in your lives? And I do mean everything. We're officially on war footing until we get in front of them. We all know what this kind of drama entails. The bad guys think we'll be a step behind. I'll keep you all informed every moment until we strike."

"I've already broken the news to Rose," Dev said. "She knows the score now. I'll have to make sure her two kids don't take any unnecessary chances. We all move on our personal 911 calls anyway. Jafar and Laredo get a beep, and they spike the rest of us into instant action. I'm glad you're taking this Marko guy seriously, John. This could get out of hand real quick, if Yuri gets nervous over the gaps in his crew disappearing."

"All true, Dev. Bombs in the backyard ain't going to happen. Any unannounced family visits, and we go all in immediately. Yeah, gray area innocents will die, I'm afraid. I don't believe in reaction. Guilt by association means death by association if we go to Death Con."

"Amen to that," Jess said. "I don't want anything happening like when that BBC reporter from your past life took Lora and Al hostage. I'm sick of these stupid gangs. Dev and I played around the fringes back when we were growing up. We can't take chances.

Like you said, there may definitely be the old unintended consequences for some kids caught in the gang fear factor. I have someone now I don't want in on the danger, but I know there's no way to guarantee that."

"You can quit, Jess. The retirement package is extraordinary. There won't be any hand to mouth existence if you give this up." I don't want anyone staying in this game of ours without a clear danger quotient in mind. "I know the danger, and the threat of loss. Do not stay in our crew if you cannot deal with loss. We all know it's there. When it comes, it will be beyond imagining. I hope to avoid that accounting, but I sure as hell can't guarantee it won't come at our loved ones. Let's not ignore that part of this deadly game we play, because if it inevitably happens, there are no take backs."

Jess held out his hand and I shook it with solemn acknowledgement. "I'm in for the duration, John. We'll have to rely on our intel to keep us away from the unimaginable."

"Yeah... we will, brother."

No one laughed the rest of our way.

* * *

We all enjoyed the scene at my house though. I was the first drop off. Guess what? We had a contingent of the Nigerian Rastafarians on the sidewalk in front of my house. At least they were dressed like Rastafarians dress in the Hollywood shows I've seen them portrayed in. We'd been in lockdown for business or personal calls. With Lora at the office with Al, we could make light of this, but I could see everyone was looking at me for permission. We made all the Nigerians disappear that we knew about, so how did this bunch get my address along with directions to come here.

"I'll lead. I know damn well Cruella will ream my ass out for not waiting for her, but I'm tired. Want to go for the big scare?"

"Hell yeah!" Lucas was not pleased. "I'm not tired. Let me go pull some dreadlocks out by the roots. That'll get their attention."

"This means the news leaked. No way in hell that happens unless we have bigger fish in our pond. I need to front this, and see if I can get any names before I start the punishment phase."

"Thou shalt not cross the John Harding perimeter line without permission from John, or the word of God." Jess illustrated my position exactly the way it should be.

When the five of us left the ready van, we sucked all the energy right out of the Rastafarian congregation. The group of seven had been jiving on the sidewalk together, much to the dismay of my neighbors peeking at us from behind closed drapes. The lead guy, nearly my height, and maybe twenty or thirty pounds heavier counted participants while scratching at his trim beard. He decided wrongly he had enough guys to get the job done.

"You 'dat mon, Harding?" He asked me politely with a calypso lilt in his voice.

"Yes, I'm John Harding. What can I do for you?"

"One of my boys saw you take some of my crew with you somewhere, mon. Where are 'da?"

In seconds, everyone had a weapon except for our Rasti's. They noticed, as my guys herded them together toward the ready van. We didn't talk anymore. We herded... roughly... with a couple of small pistol whippings thrown in for good behavior. Once we were all in the now crowded van, I plastic tied their hands behind them, and sat them down. I photographed each one, and sent the pictures to Denny, while Casey put on Nitril gloves for a pat down. Casey discovered weapons galore, including two 9mm Glocks. I sent in the serial numbers. Jess drove the van on a return path to our base once again. The rest of us checked the ID's as I scanned and sent each one. When I finished, I turned to our guests.

74

"Okay. What was the meeting at my house about besides finding your posse?" I addressed the guy who had conversed with me first.

"We say nothing. I want a lawyer."

"Did you hear that, guys? They want their ACLU packet – ass kissing media reporters, live cameras recording how deprived their youth was, and lawyers."

"I have my tablet with Crue's earlier interrogation," Lucas said.

"What my friend is saying is although we don't have any of that bullshit you'd like to have, we do have this gem – and yes, the star of the video clip is one of the assholes from your posse."

Lucas held the tablet steady for them to see. To say they were impressed would be an understatement. "See boys, we didn't want you punks to think you've been snatched off the street by people who give a shit what the hell you want. You all congregated at the home of my Marine Recon brother, John Harding. That's not quite as bad as your buddy Azi tried to do, but he's paid for his sins. Who wants to be the first to tell us the tale of woe bringing your punk asses into a van traveling to the last place on earth you want to be."

Lucas presented our position very well. At least three of the seven were ready to start screaming out answers, but my original greeter on the street still thought this was a bluff. Some folks are just too stupid to live.

"You do not scare me, mon. The rest of you... shut up. Say nothing when we get to their station. Then say only four words 'I want a lawyer'."

"Oh Lord, please let Crue still be at the 'House of Pain'," Dev prayed for our amusement. "Yeah... you guys are going to the station for sure. It's the last stop to the Seventh Level of Hell.

75

When we open the door, and you're greeted by the one and only Cruella Deville, everything will be a bit clearer."

Denny texted me when we were only minutes away. I relayed the info. "They're all illegals. Every ID is a fraud. Denny has hits on four of them including big mouth, for kidnapping, murder, and of course blackmail."

"Do not speak!" Loudmouth wasn't getting the message. You have to know when to hold 'em, and know when to fold 'em.

"Shut the hell up, pussy," Lucas fired back in loudmouth's face. Then loudmouth spit in Lucas's face. My knife-hand strike to his throat made sure he would be lucky to ever spit again.

Lucas wiped away the remnants of loudmouth retribution with grinning appreciation as loudmouth's survival stayed in jeopardy straight on until we were parked inside the 'House of Pain. He threw open the door. Sure enough, there was Cruella Deville, arms folded with look of calm anticipation on her face. Lucas grabbed the fighting for his life loudmouth, and flung him onto our cement floor.

"This bastard spit on me, Crue. John adjusted him immediately with one of those damn knife-hand strikes to the throat. He's still breathing, so he can write whatever he has to say."

Lynn smirked as gasps and cringes of recognition greeted her. She looked inside at the other Nigerian guests with her monster face of utter cold, calculating terror. "Spit on you, did he, Pappy. Well, now... you know what that means. Brave boy has volunteered to be an example for the rest of his posse. John... you know I've warned you about altering my toys before I see them."

I bowed my head comically for my companions. "I'm so ashamed, Crue. It was pure instinct. This man touched a nerve when he spit into our beloved grandfather's face."

"Grandfather!? Why you disrespectful peckerwood!" Casey, while laughing his ass off, was trying to soothe the inner beast of Grandfather Blake to no avail. "Put the Cheeseburger on the grill too, Lynn! This age insult cannot go unpunished!"

I enjoyed my return to the 'Rattler' nickname I'd accrued in my first fight with him by getting my face pummeled almost into the maiming category. Yep. The monster squad continued our enjoyment of entertainment within the ranks, including Denny, who had joined us from the control room. Denny laughingly put an arm around Lucas's shoulders.

"It's okay, Pa. We have to enjoy the lighter moments where we can."

"Don't start with me, Spawn! It's not you being held up for ridicule."

I sensed a deeper ingredient to this continued outrage. "You have our attention, Pa. What is it that's really bothering you?"

Lucas didn't waste any time either. "I want another pirate mission before I get too old to go out on one."

Uh oh, I didn't like the sound of that. "We're not allowed to have a pirate mission, brother. The part where you took over ownership, and then stated, 'nothing can be damaged or out of place' on our pirate boat exempts us from missions even if anyone was thinking of conjuring one."

Amidst 'hell yeahs', and other significant agreement with my pirate comment, Lucas folded. "Yeah... I admit it. I never owned anything like the 'Sea Wolf'. With all the damn ocean going training maneuvers on 'The Lora', I've reconsidered my position on using the 'Sea Wolf' in enemy territory. I want another piece of those bastards!"

"Is this about you channeling the pirate attack in Nigeria with the subsequent kidnappings?" Denny was of course up to speed, and ready for any weakness in the Lucas 'Sea Wolf' confiscation.

Denny outfitted at great expense our aforementioned 'Sea Wolf'. It had everything a tight crew would want for blasting pirates into the hereafter or pinpointing their mother ships and bases. Lucas had unfortunately declared the vessel his during and after a very impressive demonstration of her value. The poor 'Sea Wolf' had been kept dormant since then.

"I screwed up, porting the 'Sea Wolf', and protecting her from what comes natural to a warship. I'm putting the 'Wolf' back in play, and I want a part sailing her into dangerous waters. Who the hell knows what the future holds? I want to go into harm's way with the 'Wolf' under my guiding hands. Anyone got a problem with that? Speak up!"

Crickets, moths caught around a porch light somewhere, fireflies enjoying an evening's rapture of flight – all made more noise than Lucas's audience of stone cold killers. Denny let the silence go on before capping it with a heartfelt, "by your command, Ahab. I believe we can get a pirate adjustment into the schedule after the softball season ends. Our benefactors have in fact been clamoring for a return of the Sea Wolf to the high seas. I'll put together an op where we'll have a fleet on maneuvers near where we operate. I see we have a volunteer if he lives, to help persuade any of our Boko Haram friends to cooperate, so I'll leave this in your capable hands, Crue."

When we turned our attention to the volunteer, he had expired. Lynn checked him over with a smile. "It's a good thing my minions are still here. Nice demo on why knife-hand strikes are only legal for body strikes, John. Let's keep this simple. Line up the Bokos. Any of them still not wanting to talk get a quick throat strike from the adjuster."

We lined them, but it was useless. They were ready to kill each other to tell us anything we wanted to know. Lynn had Quays

Tannous, and Gus Denova take charge of the prisoners, along with a list of questions Denny dictated to them. Silvio Ruelas was already with our other prisoners.

Lynn faced off with each one, patting their cheeks, and generally scaring the shit out of them. "If I get a bad report about you bunch being uncooperative, I'll come back here in the morning with my operating room tools. Don't let them get off subject, Quays."

"Shall I call you when we finish and report in," Quays asked.

"No, it can wait for morning. Put the dead spitter in a body bag in the freezer. We'll get rid of him at sea when John works out tomorrow off The Lora."

Quays grinned at Gus. Both men looked then at me.

"What?"

"Nothing, John," Gus answered. "Quays, Silvio, and I were going to have a pool with dates when Tommy would coerce you into the Bay again."

I shrugged as everyone else enjoyed the thought of a Bay pool. "I have to be ready for this guy, Gus. Nothing incites murder and mayhem better than training in the Bay."

"We know this is important, John," Quays chimed in. "We will work our Nigerian guests into a frenzy of sharing. Gus thought showing them some past videos of our mentor, Cruella Deville, in action will keep them motivated."

"A wise plan," Lynn said, putting a mentor's arm around Quays. "Make me proud, boys. We have work ahead of us tomorrow."

Quays immediately came to a head bowed, at attention stance with his partner Gus Denova to say, "yes, mistress of the unimaginable. Your will be done."

"I like that, my treasured minions," the true mistress of the unimaginable stated as the rest of us appreciated the moment appropriately. She turned on the Nigerian guests. "Don't forget boys. You make my minions unhappy, you make me unhappy. The ways I get happy again will make your group beg for death as a long lost love."

I could tell on the Nigerians' faces they had no intention of incurring the wrath of the unimaginable. "Goodnight, Lynn. You're the best."

"Nice knife-hand strike, John. Damage my toys again before I get to see them, and there will be blood."

I did the at attention bow. "Yes, mistress of the unimaginable."

Chapter 4

Close to Home

"Hell of a day, John," Casey said as Dev drove us for drop off. "We sure got shortchanged on our off time between world ending threats."

"You get to fish, and see me dodging sharks in the Bay again, Case. That should count for something. Okay… let's get the pool going. I give Spawn a day to trade all the Nigerians for Pappy's pirate op with full permissions."

"A day?" Lucas rubbed his chin. "I'm in for a thousand on forty-eight hours."

"Damn, Lucas, cut a man out of the payoff in a heartbeat, and your partner too." Casey's whining had no effect. "Okay, I'm down for the in-between. Thirty-six hours."

"Shit!" Jess was unhappy. He called forward for Dev's commitment. "Brother! Let's go for the up-tight at midafternoon tomorrow."

"I don't gamble anymore, Jess," Dev called back. "I got Rose and the kids. The thrill is gone from the gamblin'."

"That settles it," Jess said, taking a deep breath. "Dev's definitely pissing while sitting down. I'm in on the down low then for one large. No way Denny takes it out past two days."

"The bets are down, but I have to text Lynn, Clint, Laredo, Jafar, and the minions," I told them. "If they don't get an opportunity to hone down our pool, they'll be whining for the next couple of months."

"Agreed," Lucas said. "It will make the pot bigger anyway. It's a thousand in though. If the minions want a dog in this hunt, they'll have to pool their money. How much are we paying them, John?"

"A lot. All three have houses, and a very ripe paycheck to be on call 24/7. They've done a terrific job keeping the House of Pain in top condition. They really earn their money when we have layovers like tonight. It's the price of being able to go home, confident we won't have murderers getting free, and causing an untold amount of damage."

"That was the bitch about our central command," Casey went on. "It was a great place for interrogations, holding cells, high tech command, and even as a safe house. It sucked taking care of it. Those guys are worth their weight in gold. Not to mention, they make Crue happy. She loves having minions she's tortured into the light. Crue treats Danessa like her own daughter. Clint's happy because Danessa loves Tonto, and cleans their house. They bought her a damn car, and are paying her way through college. You don't suppose Crue feels guilty about the way she turned Danessa around, do you?"

Casey got the laughs he was shooting for with all of us trying to imagine Lynn feeling guilty about anything. "She does have a soft spot though. Getting at it sometimes is a mystery."

"Clint seems to find it regularly," I replied. "We better hope Lynn has the baby before Denny schedules any pirate operations."

"Sure, but you know what she'll do then," Lucas added.

"You guys will have to go to war with a baby on board unless you find her something to focus on other than motherhood," Jess said. "I don't like your chances. Maybe John can invent some secret mission to keep Crue and Clint at home with the baby."

"Hey, that's not bad, Jess." I didn't believe in wishing for bad things to happen, but having something for Clint and Lynn to do where they could have the new baby with them would be for the best. Having Lynn on board The Sea Wolf, either with the baby, or worrying because someone else was looking after the baby, could end in the rest of us losing our minds or our lives. "I will keep that suggestion in mind."

"John," Dev called out. "You have company in front of your house again."

I moved forward as Dev slowed. I could make out who it was with streetlamp light. "That's my neighbor, Della Sparks, Lora, and the new neighbor from across the street. He doesn't look happy."

"Want us to stop for a while, John?"

"No. If Lora came out of the house, I don't think this will take an intervention, Lucas. I'll see you all tomorrow. It's going to be a busy day."

Outside as our ready van drove away, I waved to my wife. "Is this a neighborhood watch meeting?"

Della and Lora were amused. Not so much my new neighbor, Doug Ferguson. He's one of those neighbors who never minds his own business. If a lawn isn't mowed, the weeding around the house has been neglected, or a car is parked too far from the curb, Doug feels it's his duty to leave a full critique letting the guilty party know about their transgressions. I'd already been served my summons to yard duty twice, and Doug had only been in the neighborhood for two months. Although I do it, I'm not much of a gardener, and I don't obsess over my lawn much.

Doug was over six feet of pent up rage, but he's no dummy. He didn't race out of his house to confront the Nigerian Posse when they were here, but you can bet he seethed at the window sill with his hands clenched so tightly he drew blood. In his middle forties with two teenage daughters in high school, he had his hands full, and it showed. Doug's ruddy complexion, coupled with a construction worker's body build, made the guy an imposing figure. I liked him. He cared about where he lived. He always waved, even though he didn't care much for my yard upkeep attitude. His wife Pam was his alter ego. She calmed him down. A thin brunette with soft voice, and always calm exterior, Pam could quiet Doug with only a touch, as if her hand on his arm signaled he had plunged off the cliff of insanity. She joined him now in the chilling March early evening temperature.

"Hi, John," Doug shook hands with me. "I noticed you had some trouble. I didn't care much for how those men were loaded into the van. Where did you take them?"

"They're being held in custody, pending deportation," I explained, which was close to the whole truth. "It turned out they were all here illegally, and four of them are wanted by the Nigerian government for crimes committed there. We had to detain some of their groups' other members earlier. They came to my house unhappy their friends had been arrested."

"Oh... sorry... I thought you owned a private security firm that does investigations on the side along with bond skips."

I showed him and Pam my FBI and Homeland Security ID's. "I'm also a consultant with various other groups, including our local police."

"He does cage fightin' too," Della added. "Not to mention he keeps the gangbangers away from our kids, and off our block."

"Cage fighting? You mean like UFC? We don't watch it, but I know it's a really brutal sport."

Della chuckled as did Lora, and I knew what was coming. "Yeah, John got into a match at the Mandalay Bay with this guy named the Rattler. Rattler remade John's face into hamburger, so he had a nickname for a while of Cheeseburger... Cheese for short."

"Did you ever fight again, John?" Pam was hanging onto Doug tightly with some obvious underlying reason for this discussion.

It was Lora's turn to speak before I could get a word out. "John broke Rattler's jaw a split second after the first fight ended, but lost on the technicality. The rematch was last month on St. Valentine's Day. Rattler and his handlers promoted it as the St. Valentine's Day Massacre. It was... for the Rattler."

"When they were carting Rattler to the emergency room, did you really say 'Happy Valentine's Day' like your partner Tommy told me," Della asked. "That doesn't sound like you, John."

"I told them I said that when they asked so they'd have to throttle back the laughs on nationwide TV. It seems Tommy didn't care much for my small prank. I told Eugene the usual 'nice fight' stuff. You and Pam seem very animated tonight. Is something else wrong besides my having to coral those Nigerian bad boys?"

Doug began to say something, sputtered a bit, and then hugged Pam. "You tell him, Hon. I'll lose it, and start ranting."

Pam reached to frame his face for a moment with her hand before turning to me. "My oldest daughter has a stalker. We suspect it's her ex-boyfriend, but she hasn't been able to snap a picture of him. Whoever it is even came into our home yesterday while Doug was at work, the kids were in school, and I was grocery shopping. He left pictures of Callie on her bed, in school, at the mall, and... and an incident where she was smoking grass at a party. We don't know what to do. Doug would end up in prison, and possibly harm the wrong man. Could we hire you to find out who is behind this?"

I'm already getting eyeballed by Lora and Della. They expect me to ride in on my white steed, and solve this neighborhood dilemma. I did have an idea though. "I have wide angle HD cameras pointing out at the neighborhood for security. I will go over my recordings. Maybe I can find the stalker without a lot of expense."

"That's incredible!" Doug liked my plan. Good, because shadowing teeny girls looking for lovesick puppy boyfriends sets off my barf reflex. That he came into their house put a monster spin on it I needed to check out. "Thanks, John."

"I have to ask this for all the usual reasons. I'll bet you didn't know Callie was smokin' weed, and there might be a hidden element in this stalker scenario too. The Internet is rife with goons looking for easy marks to either terrorize or fixate on. My advice is to rip all electronic devices away from her, demand pass codes, find out if there's more to this than a 'can't let go' ex-boyfriend."

"Done deal. The moment I get in the house I will find out everything you've outlined. I can't have this – strangers invading my house. Like Pam said, I'll be dead or in prison without solving anything."

"How old is Callie by the way?"

Doug took a deep breath. "She's a senior, and just turned eighteen as she reminds us in every second sentence. Callie will protest everything I do, but Pam and I will make sure she understands the danger we're in. It's not her fault, but I can't risk someone burning our damn house down, or kidnapping Callie when they get frustrated."

Amen to that. "I will pursue this until I have your answers, Doug. If it's a simple overzealous ex, we'll let the police handle it from there. They'll warn him off while you and I keep a lookout for him here. If it's more complicated, I'll bring my team in on it. I'll call you tomorrow with how well I do."

Doug nodded complacently. Pam waved and led her husband away toward their house without another word.

"Damn, John… apparently all those blows to your thick skull haven't short circuited your reasoning ability," Della prodded me.

"I have a job to do, Mrs. Sparks," I replied, complete with dusting off my shoulders comically. "I'd suggest you stay inside, and mind your own business. I'll be walking your twins and Al into school tomorrow as always. They will be safe or I will be dead."

Della gripped my arm. "I know that, John. I could tell on your features that guy going into Doug and Pam's house put you on the scent big time. Has Darin been walking with you too? I'm worried about that boy."

"He does sometimes, but he's in his last year at this level. Although he gets a kick out of walking with us, he doesn't do so on a regular basis. He's been great since Terry Nelson disappeared."

Della reached up to pat my face. "Yeah… Terry Nelson disappeared alright. They haven't found him in any landfills, so I expect you had to place him somewhere he wouldn't be found."

Damn it! See, this cloak and dagger stuff only works to a certain extent before something gets noticed. "I have no idea what you're talking about, Della. Terry's probably on a beach somewhere drinking Mai Tai's, and getting wasted."

Della snorted while turning to her house. "Yeah, I'll bet that's where Terry is. Goodnight you two. I'll have the twins ready in the morning."

Lora leaned into me as we negotiated the walk to our door. "I hope the stalker thing is something simple. You have allowed your downtime to die again."

"We can't have guys running around in our houses when we're not there. If I get a good ID of him on our security cam recording, I'll turn him over to the police. I want to see for myself whether this is an overzealous boyfriend, or perhaps Callie played around in the wrong sandbox on the Internet."

"Doug is a little intense."

"I'll get something to eat while I go over my cam feeds, and find out if maybe Doug needs to be worried." Al met us at the door. "Hey Al, how do you like the two high school girls across the street?"

"The younger one, Nadine, is nice. The older sister is a stoner. She usually has the redeye express going whenever I see her. Is she in trouble?" Al followed me toward the kitchen. Lora motioned me down, showing me the plate she had ready for heating.

I angled my satellite laptop where I wanted it, and tapped into my security feed. I let Al cycle through the hours I suspected on screen while I forked food into my mouth. The break in happened during the nearly two hours Pam was at the grocery store from noon to two.

"There he is." Al pointed at the left screen. "He's staying real close to the houses. He moves like you and your guys do… real quick like… and then stops in between, sensing movement."

He sure does. "Good eye. Back it up a moment to where he comes into view. Then let's get a frame by frame from there. He wore a hoodie, but his face isn't covered. Watch for any turn toward our cams."

Although tedious, I knew he would not be able to resist glancing at our house. It's human nature. Sure enough, Al caught him in a full face look into our HD low light cams. We messed with it to get the best quality snap for running it with my state of the art, Company backed facial recognition software. Surprisingly, I had Lora on my lap, and Al huddled next to us as we watched the faces streak across the screen. Twenty minutes later we had our guy. I nearly pitched Lora onto the floor.

"What's wrong, John?" Lora scrunched her eyes to read the fine print. "Uh oh. What the hell could Callie be doing to draw a guy like this into doing a stalker stunt?"

"Murder and rape?" Al read along with us. "Why is this Gavin Comstock on the street instead of prison?"

"The last sighting I read about was in Oregon. This would fit his profile. No one ever linked his four known victims to him in any way. He hits random victims. The last rape/murder tied to him happened nearly two years ago. The only reason they found a lead to follow was because of a convenience store video of Comstock stalking a teenage girl into the store. She was found dead near the convenience store. The police in Scranton, PA found DNA fibers on her too. They then knew who, but they had no idea where. Comstock leaves the area he strikes in."

"You know a lot about this guy, Dad."

"Tommy and I were called in by a bonding company in Reno. They had a sighting of Comstock, but wanted nothing to do with him. The family of the teenager in Scranton collected twenty-five grand reward money to catch her killer. If Tommy likes the gig, we give the referral twenty percent. We went to Reno, found Comstock, and waited for him to return to his motel room after an all-night binge. Never happened – it turned out he was stalking another victim. I watched the guy closely. By the time Tommy and I gathered him into custody, we had enough photo evidence to prove he planned to strike again in Reno. We Tased him into an electric trance. The locals loved sharing the big catch. Everyone was happy, until one of the guys working the desk released Comstock by mistake. There was nothing we could do."

Lora shifted to face me on my lap. "This isn't really about Callie. Is it?"

"I don't believe in coincidences, Baby. You and Al know that. My pal Gavin knew who captured him in Reno. Things just got a lot more complicated. Let's use my other adjoining cam feeds. Maybe he parked on the street."

I split screened each side of Doug's house, so we could see if he parked or left a vehicle we could get a license plate number from. My wide angle HD cams scoped both sides of the house three houses down on each side. I went backwards for a time, checking for traffic on the street driving past or parking. A black van slowed from one feed into the other, stopping within view of my left side cam. I had an unobstructed view to hone in on the van's license plate number. Comstock waited five full minutes before exiting the van for his approach on Doug's house. He was cat quick and smooth. It took only seconds for him to pick the lock.

"I believe Gavin is trying to hit Callie, but he's playing to get a crack at me. He is one arrogant prick. I wonder if he knows whether Doug and Pam talked with us. I'll bet he doesn't. My ladies. I have to move on this tonight. Tomorrow, this asshole could be taking potshots at our softball practice. He found me, and now I have to find him."

"We know," Lora agreed, leaving my lap reluctantly. "Gee, we nearly had an entire month after the Rattler fight to wind down into normal land. What I'd like to know is why it all explodes at the same time."

"It's feast or famine. I know one thing – I'd like to cross Gavin off our list. He's the one they let get away that bothered me and Tommy from day one. Yes!" I had the license number searched. It was a rental. Comstock had wrongly figured we would never be onto this so fast. Gavin thought he could do Callie, and somehow trap me into being killed too. I'd ask him about it once I had him in hand. I called Tommy.

Knowing I never call unless the sky is falling, Tommy hit all the high points. "No, I'm not drinking tonight. Yes, I had dinner. Where and when?"

"My place as quick as you can. I have Gavin Comstock stalking my across the street neighbor's teenage daughter while eyeballing my house. He didn't know I'd be read in as quickly as it happened. I have him in a hotel room over at the Hilton by the Oakland Airport not with his name of course, but with the same one he rented his murder van in."

"Son-of-a-bitch! Get ready to cross that bastard off the list. I'll be there in fifteen minutes. You're right about this, John. He ain't hittin' that girl across the street without eyes on taking you out at the same time somehow. See you in a few."

I called Samira and Jafar next. I explained in detail how I could use Samira to get Gavin answering the door without any problems. Samira was ecstatic. Jafar... not so much. "It's important, little brother."

"I know that, John. Two missions bunched up in a day is screwing with my head. I'll bring my gear. Couldn't you bang on the door, and shout 'open up... it's the FBI'."

"I could if I didn't care about gun battles in the middle of the Hilton Hotel. I just need the door to open. I'll take down Comstock the moment he unlocks the door while you grab your lovely wife away from the door."

"Be there, soon. We'll take our SUV. It will hold us all if we make you run alongside."

"You're getting to be quite the comedian, Jafar. How about if I squeeze your head like a jelly bean. Would you like to see how much fun that is?"

"Uh... no John, I'm good." Jafar disconnected.

"Jafar is funny," Al called over her shoulder, where she helped Lora put away the dishes.

"That's what he thinks too. Don't encourage him."

Lora stopped me from leaving the kitchen to get my bag. "Do you have any idea why Comstock would suddenly arrive in the area out of nowhere? Is there some kind of bad guy convergence going on I don't know about?"

"I'll ask him. For now, I'm thinking something big being planned on the horizon. The players are jamming their pieces into place. So far, we've moved fast enough. We stopped the one who had his eye on Al after I turned down Kornev, but that was a breach of personal security. The Nigerians parking their asses on my front lawn was another breach of security. Then a supposed coincidence with Comstock on the hunt for our neighbor girl across the street completes our odd trifecta. Everyone is interested in our ports. We have to protect Alexi's interests with the docks. We know he will warn us if something odd happens there as he has with the arrival of Yuri Kornev. I think Alexi suspects a lot worse from Kornev than sneaking in contraband. After the Anthrax scare so recently, the old man is keeping the port under strict observation. I hear Tommy's car."

I gave Lora a kiss and a hug along with her mini-me. Tommy waited by his car, arms folded. I brought out the huge traveling trunk with cargo type wheels along with my equipment bag. I told Tommy we needed to wait for Jafar and Samira. I also explained my door entry plan. "Jafar's bringing his SUV so he's driving."

"I like your idea for getting him to open the door. I bet Jafar wasn't too thrilled with it though. What's with you using Samara all of a sudden?"

"She asked. Right now, I only have Lynn to work any op requiring a woman. Danessa liked helping Clint and Lynn, but I'm not sure she's interested. Samira would be a real asset if used sparingly, and safely. With all the pregnancies, we're going to be a boy's only club if we can't get another woman."

"Danessa's street smart. She can spot a phony or con, and she knows what pain is," Tommy replied. "The downside is she has a large family, and her Mom is falling for Laredo. If something happened to her, the exposure would suck."

"All good points. Here they are." Jafar drove along my curb, slowing. Tommy and I put our gear bags in the back along with the trunk. When buckled into our seats, Jafar drove toward the Hilton. "You made good time, kid. Thanks."

"I called ahead to base. Gus Denova is still there working out some travel options Lynn gave him to investigate."

"Nice. What travel options?" I didn't know if I liked the sound of that. Lynn had been so excited with her creating ops for the team to entrap the terrorists we'd been hunting, coupled with directing the 'Hollywood Bounty Hunters' season ending hit, I was afraid she'd decided on another gig without telling me.

"I think it has to do with bringing the Hollywood crew to the Bay for a special season opening episode. She wants another extra special capture that will look great on film with them handing over a high value target to FBI Agents Clint and Cheese. I've heard her and the minions talking. I think she recruited the three of them as her entourage along with personal assistant Danessa."

"Very interesting development, my minion, and when exactly were you going to share this new information with your mentor? You know. The Denny Light that runs this team."

Jafar waved me off without turning. "Lynn swore me to secrecy… no… that's not true… she threatened me into secrecy. I figured at the rate we are going with crooks and terrorists popping into the open, you would need to know something about what Lynn has in mind. Besides, Lynn's scarier than you."

"I'm with you on that," Tommy said. Samira was enjoying the 'Fear Factor' Lynn generated in my friends. "Best you remember he who laughs last, laughs best, Samira. Your day will come on one of Cruella Deville's less enthusiastic days."

Samira shrugged in the front seat. "I spent a long time in an Afghan cave with only the Cheese between me and torturous death. I was a little kid, and I saw monsters in every shadow. My Father calmed me with only one caution. He told me when I awoke frightened, look for John. If he is alive, we are safe. He is still alive."

That admission brought on a few minutes of silence. "Thanks, Samira."

"It is okay, John. I still wish to poke you with poles in the water."

I grinned. "Of course you do."

* * *

Samira knocked on the door, holding a fresh batch of white towels I'd taken from the pool area. "Housekeeping. Clean towels for you."

The door cracked open with the chain still in place on the door. "I didn't order fresh towels. My room was done hours ago, but the towels weren't replaced!"

"I'm sorry, Sir. Did you leave them on the bathroom floor? We know to replace them then. Let me have your used ones, and you may have these fresh towels."

"Fine! Just a second." Comstock policed his room for wet towels before coming to the door. The moment he removed the chain, I smashed the door into him, followed by a bodily charge which ended when Comstock lay sprawled on the floor with his hands trying to fend off attackers.

I waved at him as Samira, Jafar, and Tommy entered with our gear. "Hi there, Gavin. I got your message while hearing about your stalking of my across the street neighbor's daughter, Callie. That ain't ever happening again. We're going to take you somewhere isolated, and find out what the hell brought your serial killing asshole self to the Bay Area. How we arrive at those findings will be completely up to you. I'm hoping you choose the hard way, so I can work a little magic on you while we drive to our 'House of Pain'. There, you will find someone arriving who will do things to you only curbed by her imagination, which is extensive. What's it going to be, you no good little prick!?"

I grabbed his Adam's Apple for a moment while he came to grips with what would happen if he began screaming. "I see in your face I'm getting my message across. That's good, because the alternative would be painful beyond your pathetic belief. I don't believe in coincidences, so I'll make a deal with your psychopathic ass. Tell me what brought you to the Bay at this time. After I investigate the truthfulness of your admission, I'll end you peacefully. Start bullshitting me, and we go see Cruella Deville. Believe me, you don't want that."

Gavin began spluttering for mercy, innocence, and lawyers. Not happening, my idiot scammer. "Shut the fuck up! Okay, I can deal with you wanting the hard way. I'll show you a little film. If it changes your mind, maybe I'll let you in again on the easy way out. If not, you will be disappointed in how little we care about your right to justice, Amigo."

I showed him the interrogation of Azi to his very obvious horror. I had to smack his face back on target with eyes open a couple of times. "I see you recognize my video subject. That's where you're going next if I don't get some really entertaining reasons you're here at all. The first thing I want out of you is a complete list of your victims. I know you'll want to let everyone know about your handy work."

Gavin was a psychopath, but he understood reality very well. He knew watching the film his two choices would be vengeance on a scale he couldn't contemplate, or full cooperation with a quick ending. Comstock wrote out the victim list first with smiling satisfaction. With some hesitation dispelled by the looks he got, Gavin outlined everything, including the fact he had been targeting not only Callie but my family as well. He'd found out about us through an anonymous source who knew all about his serial killing ass. They'd given him twenty-five thousand dollars to do what he does best – terrorize the innocent, and in my case, not so innocent people.

He had my attention. "Why on earth would you believe someone decided to launch a scum sucking prick like you for twenty-five big ones?"

Comstock grinned. "Why would I lie with something to face like you showed me on that vid? I'm dead. I can see that much in your eyes. I don't want to go out screaming. I've been asking around ever since I hit town. There's something big brewin'. There are other plans in place to keep the media busy too, but I was the star I figure. If you'd let me do Callie, and then come back for your wife and kid in a couple weeks, there wouldn't have been anything else on the news except for the Oakland Strangler."

One of these days I'll learn not to make promises I can't keep. By the time the red haze lifted, I had Tommy, Jafar, and Samira strung out across me, all to no avail. Poor old Gavin suffered something terrible when I busted his rib cage to bits before I broke his neck. Oh well. Win a few, lose a few, I always say. Gonna' bust me some poles in the water today. I held my hands up in acknowledgement.

"I'm okay... I'm okay."

"Yeah," Tommy panted, "but your buddy there is looking around at an impossible angle for him to actually still be alive."

"He was going on a boat trip tomorrow anyway." I stood and wheeled my large trunk over. "Nice work, Samira. I'll wheel dead Gavin down to the SUV. Gather everything with your gloves on. We'll take his bags next. I need you to investigate anything of interest on his phones and laptop tonight, little brother. I want to hit any accounts he has for hints where the twenty-five grand came from."

I stuffed Gavin into the trunk. It was easier since his head proved very maneuverable. "I'll be right back to help with his bags."

"Stay with my van, John." Jafar tossed me his keys. "It would be better if we check Comstock out of his room on-line, and then bring the rest of his gear down ourselves. We'll each walk out separately."

"Good input. I'll see you down there.

* * *

Tommy stretched a little, while looking over Jafar and Samira. "Are you two okay? I don't think John realizes what happened. Trying to stop him in mid-kill is dangerous even for innocent bystanders."

"I'm okay," Samira answered. "I will not try that again."

Jafar nodded his head. "Comstock experienced forty-five seconds of hell. I think I have had enough of field ops for the night. It will be a relief to scan over computer data. Perhaps I will then be able to sleep."

"I'll pack the belongings," Tommy said. "You two work on finding anything and everything of a communications or computer nature. Comstock had our names. I remember an old Louis Armstrong song called 'I'll Be Glad When You're Dead, You Rascal You'. That fits perfectly my sentiments about Comstock.

Will you actually be able to confirm the info he gave us before he boarded the train to Neverland?"

"Most of it," Jafar answered. "I will check his whereabouts, credit slips, reservations, and victims named, with their time of death and circumstances. Since Gavin will be going on his final ocean voyage, we may have to wait on giving closure to the victims, even though John surely did exactly that on a permanent basis."

"Amen," Tommy agreed.

* * *

Gus Denova opened our large rollup door. Jafar drove in. We unloaded the rolling Gavin. "I'll help Gus put Gav on ice, and be right back."

"Okay, John," Jafar responded.

On the way to our industrial type freezer room, Gus turned as if to say something to me a couple times, but without sound. "Spit it out, Gus. Did the Nigerians give you guys something making you uneasy?"

"It is as you say... an uneasiness. The Nigerians gave us plenty of facts, but they seemed genuinely surprised they weren't already freed and on the street. One of Kornev's powerful front groups, based in New Mexico, paid to have this bunch brought in over the Southern border. God knows how many payoffs took place to get them into and through Mexico. They arrived in Mexico by container ship, one our Nigerian buddies said had been hijacked, but now bore the documentation of Kornev's front group. Jafar texted me you think this guy Comstock was paid to draw headlines. I think the Nigerians were bought and paid for to do exactly that too. Kids snatched, and rape/murders would be a smorgasbord for the media. They would shelve a world war to delve into kidnappings and serial killers."

"I like your thinking, Gus. You've progressed far in your media understanding since Crue starred you in the 'Hollywood Bounty Hunters' episode."

He snorted comically at that remembrance. "I remember thinking every second not to screw up and end tied and gagged in a room with a disappointed Lynn Montoya. Yeah, John, I've come a long way in understanding what you and your crew are doing. It's damn rough justice, but I remember well how to play off the cops and feds in this country."

Gus gestured around him before looking at me. "Here in The House of Pain we make things better for real people, not psychopathic shitheads who think their fuckin' Mommy or Daddy abused them. I serve the Cruella Deville by choice. No one arrives here without cause. Quays, Silvio, and I all know we do here what is right. You have created personal lives for us we never dared pray to have. Many will die, my friend, before I allow that to be taken away. We will get to the bottom of this puzzle about using the media to sweep aside the horrendous. We will filter through these puzzle pieces until we know the truth."

Now that's what I'm talkin' about. I shoulder hugged another cold blooded killer with real emotion. "Yes! You have it exactly right, Gus. We have this game in play where we don't have to worry about being ready. We are ready. It may be now though we'll have to wait for our targets to deal with having chess pieces they were counting on removed from the board. That's all good though. We need to see the whole picture."

"It is good you trust us to do this work, John. If ever you need something done out of the public eye or your crew, let us know. We will get whatever it is you need done an accomplished task. No... we don't care what it is you want done."

Damn, that's plain enough. "I will keep that in mind, Gus. Between us, I don't think of you bunch as minions. I never did."

"We are proud to be the minions to the mistress of the unimaginable," Gus argued. "She broke us, and remade us in her image."

Very true. "Tomorrow I'd like you, Silvio, and Quays to hit the streets. Spread money, favors, or whatever you need to as quietly as possible. We need a hint of what's going on behind the scenes that would require such an elaborate ruse to capture the media's attention."

"We will work all our sources. Do you think they have any others like this Comstock guy running around looking for headlines?"

"Good question, Gus. Keep that in mind when you're on the prowl tomorrow. The fact dead Gavin had a personal connection from the past with me and Tommy makes Kornev and his operations the prime suspect. As you say, we need to find more puzzle pieces. I heard you minions are also putting together something with the 'Hollywood Bounty Hunters' for Crue."

Gus looked a little surprised. "I don't think she wanted anyone to know about that yet. I guess we left too many trails for our IT guys, huh?"

"Nothing gets past Laredo and Jafar, especially with Clint doing intermittent checks on security and content. What's with the secrecy? Lynn knows she can do anything she wants. Jafar told me they want to film another episode with a turnover of a bad guy to the cardboard FBI cutouts, me and Clint."

"It was supposed to be a surprise," Gus replied as we finished depositing Gavin for the night in the freezer with his cozy trunk holder. "We will be helping as 'grips' on set, managing, arranging, and getting our director anything she wants. We'll find the site she wants, and do all scene setup operations."

Lynn relieved our team of any active part on set. Very nice, especially if it brought her more directing gigs. Maybe when our pirate operation comes about, she'll be whisking around a movie set with Clint Jr. strapped to her, and won't make a lot of racket about not going. "You'll keep me informed of all this, right Gus?"

Gus smiled at me. "Only if you are cleared by the mistress of the unimaginable."

Great… I've been degraded in the chain of command below the minions.

* * *

Light rain hit overnight, but after retrieving our overnight freezer occupants, the sky cleared into a hazy sixty degree day. The Nigerians, bundled off for trade by Denny at dawn, left behind a wealth of information, but little of it useful in our present mission. Laredo and Jafar both arrived early to decipher the data, and confirm as many facts as possible. They would be concentrating on the money threads from all activity we uncovered. Comstock's twenty-five grand came from a front company in the Cayman Islands, Jafar busily went on the hunt to investigate. Denny was still in place, hungry for intel, and overseeing our IT forensics boys.

"The Nigerian government wanted the Boko Haram goons desperately," Denny told me. "They're willing to offer support and permission for anything we wish to do in the Gulf of Guinea. It seems they're having another increase in Boko terrorism against business interests in the country, along with hijackings in the Gulf. They confirmed what our overnight Boko boys claimed about container ships hijacked, and refitted for movement of drugs, weapons, contraband, and people. They realize it's only a matter of time before something very bad happens, and it is traced to their shores. They don't want to become another Somalia."

I shut our smaller company van door, while listening. I still didn't hear any theories about what all this intricate bullshit with bringing in Bokos, and hiring media grabbing serial killers had to do with anything. When Denny paused, I hit him with my concerns. It didn't faze him a bit. He even grinned in anticipation of my running out of words, so I cut it short. "I see in your face you're not confused at all. What's in the Spawn of Satan crystal ball you haven't told me?"

"You've already forgotten my wife's brother's empire built on chaos. Terrorism and crime bloom like wild weeds in chaos. Sure, we have to see this through while staying ahead of the game, but this shouldn't be a mystery to you, John. I'm even looking ahead to when the fight takes place you've agreed to. If you win, things will get real exciting on this new port and container ship front."

"I've been thinking about that too. I'm betting the next move on Yuri's part is moving the fight date to as soon as he possibly can without my backing out. Tommy or Alexi will hear about it from him the moment he starts trying to contact assets that no longer exist, or are on their way to Nigeria. Jafar and Laredo have all their burner phones, so they'll be able to tie in Yuri with his Nigerian buddies in a nice tight package."

"Although you worked over Rattler in the second fight without a lot of damage, are you willing to allow them to schedule the fight sooner, John?"

"Yesterday proved to me I'm still in the best shape I've ever been in. I could be talked into an earlier meeting with Marko. I'll have Tommy make such a change very expensive for Yuri. I am liking an earlier fight date before these weasels import a whole army of thugs looking to make your chaos theory viable."

"That would be my take on this too. Are you taking Al to school this morning?"

"Yep. I'll drop my dead weight off at 'The Lora' first. I'll still have plenty of time to take Al and the Sparks' twins to school. I might be able to let my across the street neighbors know everything is okay with their daughter Callie. They already know she's been going off the good girl reservation, so I'm figuring they mean to clamp down on her anyway.

Denny stayed silent for a moment. "Those are some impressive goals for the day. I won't insult your intelligence by saying I like all of them."

Denny grabbed me for the first time ever. "Listen to me, John! You're right about all of this. Something's wrong we can't hope to know in time. I wish I could decipher this shit, but I get more confused every second I look at it. That tells me we're somehow ahead of the game. I'm warning you this business with Yuri is a time bomb. I'd like to dismantle it before we lose the East Bay. We may have to go to war on American soil right now, brother."

I detached myself from his grip with slow assuredness. "This isn't like you. I told you I had a hunch at the beginning. We're playing it out. It's the only thing we can do. I have everyone, including the minions, hitting the streets today. If we miss something it won't be from lack of trying. I'll take the crew and snatch Yuri and Marko if you want. We'll take them straight out on a boat ride. Crue will know everything they know before 'The Lora' ports again without them."

"If the Bulgarian arms dealer was with them, I'd volunteer to drive. There's chatter about a weapon to be smuggled here in pieces. They mean to overcome the way we struck the Anthrax threat months ago."

"It would mean the chances are slim to none it's a bio weapon," I replied. "I've been so wrapped up with the Yuri and Marko show, I'd forgotten about the damn 'Ghost'. So the fight is still our key ingredient to drawing him out, unless we find what they're planning to strike with. Do any of your contacts have a clue as to what the hell type of weapon we're supposed to guard against?"

"Not yet, which may be why we need to get the 'Ghost' into Crue's hands," Denny admitted. "Get going. If I find out anything, I will meet you at the dock. Text me when you return to port."

"Will do. Calm down, Denny. I know we have a lot riding on this. Nothing else would get me back in the Bay playing shark tag while getting hammered with poles."

"I have a feeling it will be worth the dedication on this one, John. Could I ask one more favor? When you see Clint, please ask him not to make threats to civilian girls' softball parents."

Yeah, I chuckled over that one. "Sure, I'll ask. I don't know if it will do any good though. I guess Maria found out from her BFF what he said to the opposing coach's husband, huh?"

"Say another word, and you'll wake up with me next to your bed, and I won't be there to tuck you in."

Yep. That's the one Crue told us. "I'm glad the guy had the good sense to let his survival instinct kick in. Like I said, I'll make the request. Clint said it quietly, so no one else heard. I'll keep an eye on the husband, so he doesn't do something tragically stupid. This softball coaching mission is proving to be fraught with danger."

"Yeah," Denny replied, "to the other teams' coaches."

I nodded and waved. "Text you later."

* * *

After an active forty-five minutes of torturous Bay training, Lynn forgot to vary her striking times. When she poked me twice at fifteen second intervals, the third time the pole never reached me. I rotated after counting to thirteen, and hit the pole end with a knife-hand strike so potent, it ripped the pole out of her hands. She was not happy, as the rest of my crew chortled in appreciation of her cussing me out for a minute solid while rubbing her stinging hands together. I flipped over on my back, waved, and smiled. Then I stopped smiling. Only Clint's quick action saved me from getting Tased with my less than compassionate crew egging her on.

"Let me go! I'm cookin' the Cheeseburger!" Lynn struggled mightily, but was unable to break free.

I'm no dummy. My mind said dive... dive... dive. Down I went, reversing my direction, and grabbing onto the fantail while keeping my head down. After a few moments of hunching under cover in my banana suit, Jess walked over and waved me aboard, a big grin splitting his face. Tommy clapped me on the shoulders as I climbed aboard gingerly, scanning for Lynn's location. Not seeing her, I heaved a sigh of relief. Clint must have taken her below deck to warm up.

"That was hell-a-good!" Tommy helped me strip out of my banana yellow dry-suit. "How many in the pattern?"

"Only twice, T. Lynn was probably getting tired. I should have flipped and tapped it away. I didn't mean to piss her off." I put on my sweats over the long underwear I wore under the suit. I usually took a shower immediately following the workout, but I figured below decks was a dangerous place for me at the moment.

"I'll spell her sooner tomorrow," Tommy promised. "Crue was enjoying herself because she was getting more pokes past you than the first time we went out. Clint's trying to cool her off while reminding her we still have softball practice in a few hours. You did damn good, John. If that Bulgarian bastard can beat you in a match, I'll eat the damn mat."

Dev handed me a cup of coffee. "Want anything in it, brother?"

I shook my head, letting the coffee mug warm my hands. "Nope. I can't do all this and coach softball while enjoying my usual painkillers. Are you and Jess shagging balls today, or working?"

105

"We have an escort gig in SF. The traffic will be murder. Lora talked the couple into letting us escort them on the Alameda Ferry. She told them the view of the bridges is spectacular, and that we would bring them back after dark, so they can watch all the lights from the boat."

"Outstanding. Did you hire one of our cohorts on the other side of the Bay for driving duty?" We trade favors with three limo services on the San Francisco side for this reason. We don't trade much in rides though, since SF is much more popular than the East Bay. We trade muscle for them occasionally doing a limo ride for our clients. See, if they have questionable clients, or places to go, as when some adventurous idiots want to see the Tenderloin District, they call us. Either Tommy and I go with them, or Dev and Jess do it.

"Marty's driving for us," Jess answered. "He's still hyped over you and Tommy helping him escort those high maintenance dildos pretending to be made men from some crime family back East."

I laughed, remembering the two wise-guys. One of them tried to intimidate Tommy when we first met them, claiming they wouldn't pay extra for half ass protection, walking into Tommy's airspace. He let out a sudden burst of air with Tommy smiling at him. 'know what I have shoved down the front of your pants, Tony Soprano'."

The guy did indeed. When his buddy reached into his jacket, I snatched his wrist. Sometimes people think they've had their wrist snatched. If I snatch a wrist, there is a symphony of protesting bones, and the feeling if I squeezed any harder I could simply rip it off. After the demonstration, our two East Coast goombas decided to enjoy their tour of SF rather than try and prove what bad-asses they were. My Dad told me my Mom was Italian, so when I began excelling at languages in the Marines, I learned Italian too. I practiced on the wise-guys. It was a fun night, and

Marty got a huge tip. Anyway… that's how it's done if you don't want to constantly fight the damn traffic into Bagdad by the Bay.

"Tell Marty we enjoyed the tour with Tony Soprano and his acolyte. No blood, no foul. If you guys need anything, I'll be at home tonight with Lora and Al."

"The most excitement Dev and I expect is when we get to play at the 7D Experience on Fisherman's Wharf with the couple's two boys. Man, I love that zombie killin' game."

"Yeah, that is one of the most impressive gaming experiences down there. I need to take Al and Lora again. Al had a blast killing zombies on screen in that 3D theater mode. Lora… not so much."

"I'll rack up a big zombie body count for your approval."

"You do that, Jess. Thinking about you and Dev going head to head on the zombie killing experience is almost entertaining enough."

"I'll ruin him for the game. He sits down to pee now. Brother Dev won't have a chance. Even if he had a chance, he doesn't gamble, so I'd be wasting my time competing against Metro Man."

Jess, Tommy, and I were laughing so hard from that ace, with Lucas's bass yelping roar from the bridge, Dev couldn't get a word in edgewise. He shrugged it off as we wound down our enjoyment of his small roasting. Then, Cruella Deville and her better half climbed the stairs to our main deck.

"Give me a laugh, boys," Crue said. "I need it."

She and Clint definitely enjoyed the limo story, followed by our take on the zombie game. Lynn walked over and hugged me.

"That was one impressive strike, John. I'm sorry about losing it like that on you. I'm working on my taking as well as giving, but the damn hormones are raging. You wouldn't happen to have someone in mind I could work out my issues on, would you?"

"Not immediately, but as over the edge as Denny's been on this, it may happen real soon. He thinks this shit in the works is so bad, if the Bulgarian 'Ghost' guy showed up, he'd launch us like an Independence Day fireworks show, no holds barred."

"Well damn... that sounds worth waiting for. I take it, even after all we've found out, the next step is this goofy matchup, huh?"

"That sums it up," I admitted. "Oh yeah, Denny wants you to tone down your conversations with girls' softball parents, Clint. Shame on you."

Clint enjoyed his sendup at my hands. "Okay, fine, I'll allow Cruella Deville to interact with the pissed off parents. You do know of course the first one who raises a hand to her gets a third eye along with all of their posse... and no, she can't stop me. My lovely wife has acknowledged the danger involved with handling girls' softball parents as we do terrorists. We have decided to allow the vaunted Cheeseburger to handle all future interactions until they descend into violence, in which case innocents will die."

I waved in acknowledgement. "The Cheese will accept full intervention duties from now on, to ensure the continued wellbeing of fellow softball parent gamesters. Since we've already disposed of our unwanted soulless assholes, let's adjourn to the bridge with Lucas for the trip back. I have been informed we may have to let loose the full scope of bad endings we're geared up to do. If worse comes to worse, we hit everything suspect without mercy or any proof. This is one of those worst case scenarios where we don't have the facts, or any clues to lead us in a formidable direction. We all know things change. I have Crue's minions on the street, and Denny is working our IT boys with whip in hand. He will be meeting us at the dock if Jafar or Laredo discover something we can act on."

"You can bet old man Alexi is working this Kornev debacle with everything he has in reserve too," Casey added, taking a break from his fishing endeavor on the bow. "Did Denny have any theories about how this could have come about? I mean... hell... one minute we're pitting John in a match for some illusionary dock rights, and suddenly, we're fighting for our lives, and the survival of the country. Did I miss something?"

"I was supposed to text him when we were heading into port, which I did. He told me he'd see us at the dock. That means he has some clue what's going on. I wish that 'Ghost' bastard would come to town. I'm set on a 'game show' special, or in other terms, how many skin squares will it take to make a chessboard."

"I must admit," Lynn said as the rest of us hooted at my info gathering mention of Cruella Deville's more monstrous interrogation technique, "that is one of the most satisfying fact extraction methods I've developed."

"We also have a suspicion Kornev will try and move the fight to an earlier date. With the pressure building to get this 'Ghost' guy in town, I'm ready tomorrow if it works to get him here."

"I hate being optimistic about the damn fights, but you're as ready as you've ever been," Tommy stated. "If I'm contacted, I'll arrange a meeting right away. Do you want it at The Warehouse again?"

"It would be best for monitoring all accompanying traffic either inside or outside the bar. It would be a bonanza if the 'Ghost' snuck in, thinking to get a glimpse at who Marko will be fighting. I'm betting one of us could pick him out of a crowd."

"Are you talking about snatching him right on the spot, John?" Suddenly, Clint didn't look enthused. "We'd be tipping off everything. Remember, this guy may be a step higher in the food chain, but we don't want to lose any players scurrying for the tall grass when they find out 'Ghost' has been taken."

"Good point," I admitted. "We'll wait for Denny to meet us with what he has. Besides, it's wishful thinking the 'Ghost' would walk into the bar to observe anyway. He will already be on edge with the number of acolytes we've relieved him of in the last couple days. It will probably come down to picking him out at the fight by the way Yuri reacts to him, or a Marko loss as we've already discussed, could flush him out into the open."

"Lots of ifs and maybes in this," Casey remarked.

"There won't be if I get my hands on 'Ghost'," Lynn replied. She pointed. "There's Denny, and he has a real anxious look about him. Let's Taser his ass, just to chill him a little."

Chapter 5

Political Expediency

"**H**ey… what's so funny," Denny asked, as we hadn't quite finished enjoying Lynn's chill pill idea. "Never mind. I'm sure it had something vicious to do with me. We have a good idea what they're hoping to put together. It seems the Russians are allowing some very dangerous weapons to arrive on the open market using shell corporations. The latest one brokered by the 'Ghost' for sale to Boko Haram pirates in the Gulf of Guinea was an EMP bomb, smuggled aboard a container ship that was ported in the Nigerian International Port called Tin Can Island. The State Department believes it's the same EMP tech the Russians sold to North Korea. They can be put in a warhead, or detonated in place. It doesn't take much for one to completely disable a container ship, leaving it dead in the water. The low tech pirates can scramble on board without resistance in the dark. The container ship can't call for help or move."

"Wait a second." We all halted our disembarking tasks to hear what Casey had to say. "I thought we were the only ones who had anything potent enough to disable a vessel from a hand held weapon. If the Russians have something like that, why in hell would they sell it to those Boko nitwits or North Korea for that matter? Doesn't the potent stuff have to have a nuclear charge?"

"Right on all counts, Case," Denny said. "The Russians have a warhead very similar to what we've been working on to fire from launchers like an M136. The military grade black-market warheads and hand weapons have been smuggled out of Russia before. Once a guy with means like our Bulgarian arms dealer gets his hands on something as lethal as an EMP warhead, he has it deconstructed for mass assembly. It would be no trick to add a detonator or develop it to be fired from an RPG7. Naturally, the

111

non-nuke EMP warheads would be localized, but think of the infrastructure disaster if they're used on our electrical grid."

"You think these training camps already in place, Kornev has plans for, could be put into operation assembling these EMP warheads?"

"I do, Lucas," Denny answered. "In a concerted attack, they may not be able to cripple us completely, because we do have shielding, but not enough of it. Power stations, water utilities, trains, and financial district centers are susceptible to low yield EMP weapons. Smuggling the ingredients for mass production of these EMP weapons should be a top priority of every agency in the Federal Government. Guess what? We're it."

"It's not very smart using us like this," Lynn replied. "Perhaps now would be a good time to shut off all shipping from suspicious places, and close the damn borders with troops."

Denny shrugged. "Instead, they launch us. At least we won't have to put together a last minute attack on the high seas with something like anthrax involved. They caught North Korean cargo ships trying to get nuclear missiles through the Panama Canal as late as 2013, and they still allow the bastards to use the Canal. We don't have answers. All we have is a deadly solution."

"A temporary one at best," I added. "Let's get the hell out of here. We have softball practice later after I pick up Al from school. We'll all stay on this, and keep our eyes open until I can force Kornev's hand. Isn't there some EMP or microwave bursts that could be used in concert from container ships at a distance from port?"

"Hell yeah, they could," Clint agreed. "If the container ships are supplied off the shore before anyone knows what's happening, they could mount the more potent canons to get the job done. They have the deck space, and means to shield them from view. Now you're making sense with this shit. I confess to nodding off while you were discussing this small time EMP attack threat. Knowing how easily Kornev could build something unimaginable in a port he controls, I'm with Denny and John. This is the big time. If we want to fight an all-out war on American soil, I can't think of anything more potent to bring that about than bastards who think they can't be touched off shore firing EMP cannons in concert, or planting EMP bombs. These people are serious. We already have a population of smartphone zombies, who can't release the damn things from their hands for five minutes. Consider what knocking out all communications devices would do to the zombies. They'd probably start eating brains for real."

Denny waited for the zombie line appreciation to subside before going on. "Clint's exactly right, which is why we're going to end this threat. Until we know the scope of it, we'll have to play this dangerous game out to its conclusion. Let me know if Tommy or Alexi get word Kornev wants to meet. It would be a welcome sign we're at least worrying these assholes."

I didn't let on how really sick I was of this terrorist crap. I could tell from the grim faces around me I wasn't alone. When you lead a band of killers, it is very difficult to factor outside political stupidity into decisions made to confront threats. Sometimes the urge to first adjust the elected officials selling out our nation on a daily basis overwhelms me – not a good thing. "Tommy or I will let you know if we hear anything. I have to get Al from school. We'll continue our world saving duties after practice. I know the training gig today was tough, Lynn. You can take today off from practice if you want."

"No way," Lynn said. "The girls need their female role model to counteract the influence of the violent Cheeseburger."

I stared at the sky, shaking my head for the killer elite enjoying Lynn's reasoning for not taking a day off from practice. "Oh yeah... that's what they need."

    * * *

Lynn glanced over at her husband with a bemused smirk as he turned out of the marina parking lot. "You got on a roll back there with the boys. Is there something deeper going on I'm not aware of? Usually, Denny or John simply point you to the kill zone, and away you go… with me of course."

She reached over to fondle Clint from knee to chest as he drove when he remained silent. "If you don't answer me, I'm not letting you have your way with me before practice."

Clint curbed their Toyota. He enveloped Lynn in a torrid embrace from which she had no retreat or defense. When finally he pulled away as their friends drove by honking horns, and shouting derogatory remarks, Lynn panted while leaning over the center console into him. She managed to flip off their detractors to much amusement as the vehicles sped on. "Well okay… you have a passionate problem with our work somehow. Sharing means caring, Cowboy."

Clint put his finger in his mouth, making gagging noises for his amused wife. "Oh God… don't ever say that phrase again. The problem is I saw this video on the Internet about either a country's population maintain at least a 1.9 birth rate, or they cease to exist. All of Europe, America, and Canada are under that rate. The deadliest scourge of humanity now is at an over 8 percentile."

"Oh my goodness, you Islamophobic infidel! That's what sent you over the edge? You believe we're being bred into extinction? I have news for you, infidel. I plan on having at least six kids. I'm Latino by heritage, but red, white, and blue through and through. I'll raise an American Flag loving brood to counteract this world wide plague you speak of." Lynn held up her fist. "We will not be defeated!"

Clint enfolded her in his arms, reacting to her humor with amusement and hope. "Do you really mean that? I've always wanted a big family. Hell… I never had one, and I know if you did, you don't know who they are anyway. I love you more than anything on earth. I would love to father the brood you're espousing. I'm worried about keeping you alive until then."

"Screw that. It is what it is, Cowboy. We're rich. Money and self-indulgent bullshit is why Western Civilization is dwindling. We're monsters. We do what we do with the West Coast Avengers because we're the last entity on earth to call when a big bad surfaces, and we love what we do. Have you ever seen me mope around in abject angst while slicing pieces off of bad people? We're freaks, Clint. We don't belong around soccer moms, girls' softball leagues, or even just normal people – but here we are. I'm not giving it up, and I'm having babies with you until I can't have babies because we're rich, and I'm planning on being Psycho Mom. As a 'Man from nowhere' you don't understand how pumped I am at the thought of Psycho Mom at everything from birthday parties to marriages."

Clint gripped her hand with both of his. He kissed her hand with royal adoration showing on his features and through his eyes. "I have more imagination than you think, Dear. We only have one downside. If anything happens to either one of us, many innocents may die."

Lynn shrugged. "Most of them will be bad. Let's go home. I'm horny as hell after John disrespected me. Oh yeah, and how dare you stop me from Tasing that prick."

Clint leaned again into his seat while still gripping her hand in his right. "I didn't mean to be disloyal. I only meant to protect the best friend I've ever had. John put together the team that came and got me out of that hellhole I was in after I escaped, at Laredo's request. If not for him, I and Laredo would be dead as I plan on making everyone in charge of this latest bullshit threat."

Lynn leaned in to kiss him on the lips with tender feeling. "I know, love. Even thinking about Tasing John after his great strike to the pole was wrong. You do know I'd do it again in a heartbeat though, right?"

Clint nodded, gripping the wheel again. "I'd expect nothing less. I doubt John does either, but he'll be more observant about checking weapons the next time. He got complacent. It almost cost him a toasting."

Lynn giggled as Clint drove home. "Yeah, it did."

"He's my best friend, babe. John initiates things beyond imagining. He's kept you and I in action with backup. I don't want you Tasing him."

"What's in it for me?"

Clint laughed. He knew his wife would be immune to any plea from him about anyone. "Nothing. Would you at least keep it in mind when you thing about sparking him into oblivion?"

"I will under one condition."

"Name it," Clint replied immediately.

"When Clint Jr. arrives, you do the nighttime feedings, cuddling, and anything else he requires. I hate... hate... hate springing up at night unless it's to kill or torture something. You don't want that mentality with your son, and our future kids."

"Absolutely." Clint reached out his right hand without looking away from the road. "I agree to your terms. I have a feeling you'll take them away from me after you give birth to Clint Jr. but who knows. I agree without angst. I'd love to spring up with our newborn son. Shall we shake on it, or is my word enough."

"Damn it!" Lynn crossed her arms while leaning back in her seat. "You were going to jump up every time no matter what. I need to restate the terms."

"Fine, but I'm siding with Jess every time he accuses you of being a 'give but not take lightweight', I will have to agree with clear conscience you may be flawed, my love."

Lynn giggled appreciatively. "And then some, Cowboy, same as you. Damn, Clint, I never thought in a hundred years anyone could put America at risk in reality."

Clint snorted back an outright belly laugh, which earned him a glare from Cruella Deville, who shifted into an arms folded demeanor. "Sorry, babe. Were you being serious? The baby boom after World War II vets returned was the last significant time of cultural population upheaval in a good direction. Once abortion became a legitimate choice of birth control, along with sex, drugs, rock and roll a creed of lifestyle, family began to descend into darkness."

"You mean divorce, right?"

"Kids are kids," Clint replied. "They take the easy way out when not guided by principal from a two parent home. If you can be convinced an unborn baby is an unviable tissue mass, then Western Civilization is doomed no matter how many assholes we kill. You may be the most dangerous and immoral woman on the face of the earth, but you never mentioned aborting our child, Lynn. That fact goes way beyond a bunch of words. I love you so much, even the thought of losing you initiates my kill button. I won't bore you with what I'd do to any cult causing your death on a mission. We need to prevent anything like that happening. By the time the authorities caught or executed me, the death toll would be staggering – not to mention the West Coast Avengers, specifically John Harding would be at my side without hesitation."

Lynn leaned into Clint again as he drove. "That's straight up, Hon. I promise to be circumspect when shooting my mouth off or Tasering a friend like John. You have to allow me some space though. I'm not a robot. I'm a psychopathic whore who can't keep her hands off of you. Is that a bad thing?"

Clint clutched the steering wheel in both hands, squeezing the life out of it as if it were ambient. "Nope. Tonto and I flourish because of you. We both have purpose, family, and an outlet for duty. How we survive will be up to God, not us."

Lynn gripped Clint's arm. "You believe in God!"

"Hell yeah, I believe in God," Clint stated with some disbelief in his tone. "Damn... I'm sorry, honey. I thought you knew. I've seen so many things in combat surpassing normal human perception I have no doubt there is a God... a force beyond imagining... a force that cannot be conquered or swayed."

"I believe." Lynn relaxed in her seat. "I'm not waiting on heaven or hell, but I damn well believe in a presence beyond. Any universal force of creation would barf at the callings to prayer by a cult butchering human beings around the world. Surely the millions in the cult should have dealt with their failings long ago as Christianity did centuries past. Unfortunately for us, the death cult worshippers still butcher without protest from their clan, constantly executing ways to subjugate the world into their twisted perception. I'm glad you said something about this. I'm at a crossroads in believing we do what is justice in the world. I really don't give a shit. I guess that means a belief in God, or a universal force is really creepy coming from me."

Clint gripped her hand. "Nothing about you is creepy to me. We're running into all this shit because we're the best, and last call the jackasses in charge make. They know we operate without orders or authority. If we get the job call, the ones who pointed us at the target realize they have no control until the job's done. This op is beginning to look like one nasty possible kill zone."

"I've been thinking about what you said. If power to everything goes black there will be blood on a scale we have yet to see," Lynn replied. "If these Isis, Soldiers of Allah, Hamas, and the other ding-dongs all have hidden cells throughout the nation as they claim, we're in for some killin' if the power grid goes black."

"It's a damn shame the government is so down on militias. They're treated like terrorists, but in the event of an EMP attack, they would be low tech enough to fight the cells until we could get boots on the ground in numbers. I... hey... what the hell is going on now?" Clint had turned onto their street. Their fenced and gated property gave them plenty of time in the event of a frontal attack. It did not protect them outside the property. Danessa stood outside the gate with Tonto at her side. It was obvious their caretaker had been jogging with Tonto. A crowd of seven men in suits gestured and pressed closer, only to be warded off by the ever observant Tonto.

"Damn, Clint, I'm going to start the killin' early, honey," Lynn said as she exited the Toyota. "They're fuckin' with my protégé and the best damn dog since Lassie. Buckle up, Cowboy, it's goin' to be a bumpy ride."

"On it, babe." Clint followed his wife, gauging distances and hiding points for unseen snipers, his hand on the butt of his .45 caliber Colt. He had no fear. Clint could hit a target within a hundred yard range with deadly accuracy. He had no peer in close order combat, even amongst his killer elite brethren under John Harding. "Launch Tonto if it goes south."

"Will do," Lynn called out while diving directly in between the opposing forces. "Well hello boys. I'm not a strict Mom, but my ward Danessa is not allowed to play with strangers. I, on the other hand would love to mix it up with a bunch of third world troglodytes. What's your beef, and why the fuck should I care."

"We are here to collect Amara Nejem, woman," a foaming at the mouth Middle Eastern man shouted at Lynn, his moderate black beard catching most of the projectile spittle. "Show us to her immediately."

Lynn grinned, drinking in the tension, danger, and threat to loved ones with an all-encompassing pleasure built into her being.

She did not look away for an instant. "Dannie? Speak to me, kid. What the hell is this goon referring to?"

Danessa rushed to her mentor's side. Having experienced Lynn's monster side, both physically and mentally, she did not hesitate for a second – not because she was afraid for herself, but because she knew there could be seven dead bodies in an instant. "Amara from the Sacramento Masjid, we retrieved the little boy from last year, asked me for shelter. She wishes to quit Islam. It carries a death sentence. I'm not sure how they could have known Amara was here.. I jogged with Tonto after she arrived, same as usual. I shouldn't have!"

After a moment's emotional break, Danessa went on with her explanation. Tonto pranced over to sit next to her. "I should have texted you, Lynn. I never thought for a moment they would come to your house. She must have a tracker on her somewhere, or they have been monitoring her phone calls. I…I didn't know what else to do."

Lynn put an arm around Danessa, while holding concentration on the men. "It's okay, baby. It's a misunderstanding. Now, who wants to go home without being hurt, maimed or killed? You idiots have been very lucky so far. Danessa didn't say the magic word to our blood thirsty dog, Tonto. If she had, the only things left when we arrived would have been your bloody corpses. Seriously, are you stupid? Where the hell do you think you are, Tehran?"

The men had been staring in disbelief at the pregnant woman belittling them to their faces, shocked into inaction because of Lynn's dismissive attitude towards them as a threat. Clint quietly moved in behind the men, making eye contact with Tonto. He used his open hand held palm downward to signal Tonto silently into a crouch.

"We are through talking woman!" The bearded man who addressed Lynn originally, lost all semblance of sanity. "We are here on behalf of Amara's father! Bring her out to us now!"

"Well aren't you just the most precious thing," Lynn replied. "If you think I'm handing Amara over to you turds so her daddy can run her ass over in some parking lot, you need to change whatever you're smokin' in the hookah. Do yourself a favor. Gather your demented flock, and get the hell away from here while you're still in one piece. If I have to ask Tonto to escort you, some parts might make it to your vehicle, and others might not. Tonto tends to yank the wrong body parts sometimes."

One of the men at the rear eased a hand inside his jacket. Clint pistol whipped him. "No guns. Next one who reaches will need a body bag."

Stunned, the men lurched away from Clint, but the leader reached to grab Lynn. Tonto ripped the man to the sidewalk by the arm, pouncing across his chest, jaws enveloping his neck.

Lynn made a quick flipping action with her hand, returning the butterfly knife to the closed position with a sigh as Clint chuckled. "Damn it, Tonto! Did I ask for an intervention? Oh hell. Come over here dog and give me a hug."

Tonto leaped from the sobbing man to Lynn. She hugged the big dog. "Don't kiss me with that tongue you've had on that flake's neck. There's no tellin' where it's been or when the last time he washed it."

Lynn straightened. She kicked Tonto's victim in the side. "We're done here. Stand up before I get Tonto to help you. My girl Danessa is going to scan each one of your licenses, or whatever kind of ID you have, and take your pictures. I don't want to miss anything."

Clint showed his FBI credentials to the group of men once the leader staggered to his feet. "I'm Special Agent Clint Dostiene, and this is my wife, Special Agent Lynn Dostiene. Please get your licenses out now. Then, one at a time, hand them to Danessa. Don't hesitate, or Special Agent Tonto will assist you."

Tonto settled in front of the men, snarling face, and dripping fangs making it clear he could take down any runner within a split second. Tonto added a low pitched growl for good measure. Each man carefully retrieved their licenses, handing them to Danessa one at a time while she used the scanner app on her phone. When finished, she then took photos of each man.

"We will report this travesty to your superiors!"

"I don't think so," Lynn said. "Now that you've dried your eyes from Tonto's attitude adjustment, you worthless prick, listen up. Our security cameras have everything you've done since arriving here on HD video, including threatening our ward, Danessa. If you have a brain in your head, you'll go tell daddy dearest he'll have to do an 'Honor Killing' on some other poor sap in his family. Amara will be under our protection. We have your faces, names, and addresses. Guess who we come for if anything happens to Amara."

The leader began to spout another diatribe, but his companions dragged him away, the ease in which they'd been handled convincing the saner members of the group any further confrontation would end badly. Lynn hugged Danessa.

"Now that's what I'm talkin' about. I get just a little bored, and you give me an entertaining gift like that. You're a treasure, kid."

"With all those guys shouting at me at once, I almost yelled the magic word for Tonto," Danessa said, hugging Lynn back with all her might. "He is so good. Tonto never moved from my side. He sat still as can be, without interfering. You are an incredible trainer, Clint."

"I'm happy you didn't have to say the magic word, Dannie," Clint replied. "Tonto only intimidates for about two minutes after the word. Then he rips out throats. I guess now would be a good time to tell you if you use the magic word, when things are under control, follow it with 'Hold'."

"Good to know." Dannie sighed.

"Oops." Lynn laughed appreciatively at Clint's omission. "It would have been fine, Dannie. We would have simply called my minions for a cleanup on aisle seven. Then during John's ocean training workout, Clint and I would have fed the fish. Now what's this all about? Is Amara really inside?"

Danessa became very agitated. "Yes! Her Dad beat the crap out of her. Her nose is broken, and she's been switched with something. There are welts all over her body. Can we really protect her?"

"That's a rhetorical question, right Dannie," Clint asked with a smile. "We have so many damn bedrooms and bathrooms in our house John got for us, we could start our own abused women's shelter. I'm sorry your friend had to flee here, but I'm very glad she has you for a friend. Lynn and I have already been plotting other confrontations with the supposed followers of the religion of peace... actually submission. As Lynn said, you brought this to us at a good time. Did you show Amara the way to use our safe-room?"

"Yes," Danessa answered. "I never thought anyone could find her so quickly."

Clint shrugged. "All she needs is to keep her smartphone on, and they can track her, especially if daddy has been paying the bills. We'll have to smash a couple of her prized possessions, but such is life without beatings or death for the moment. Let's go inside. We'll need to formulate a plan for the next more violent approach."

Danessa gasped. "You…you think they'll come back?"

"Hell yeah, Dannie," Lynn answered. "We would have had to kill all of them right now on the sidewalk to avoid any after-hours' retribution. They can't get into our place anyway… lucky for them. C'mon. Let's talk Amara into attending Al's softball practice. It will get her mind off this mess. We'll bring Tonto along today too. This will be a great time to introduce John to the new trick Tonto does."

"Uh oh." Danessa backed away from her mentors with palms out, as both Lynn and Clint enjoyed the thought of Tonto's new trick being demonstrated. "I don't think I like the sound of that."

"It'll be fun," Lynn insisted. "It will definitely make Amara smile. Let's go recruit her for our practice session. We'll talk out the situation later with John after practice."

* * *

I noted our beat up girl in slightly too large sweats in the outfield shagging balls. Judging by the raccoon eyes, taped over nose, and split lip, she didn't need me to interrogate her. The fact she giggled and laughed next to Clint and Lynn's ward Danessa made me hopeful this was some kind of therapy session. As we gave the girls a five minute break while changing batters, Lynn filled me in with a very entertaining version I'm sure was deadly accurate – including my canine buddy, Tonto's part. Our main mission dog was following me around the field as if he hadn't seen me in weeks.

"She can stay, but she's too old to play."

Lynn appreciated that short rejoinder. "I wanted your opinion on whether bringing her here would endanger the other girls."

124

"You're joking. You must be. You, Clint, Casey, and Lucas are here helping the girls. How in hell would I be thinking you're endangering the girls? Even if someone showed with automatic weapons, they wouldn't get two steps out of their vehicles before Clint gave them new holes in their heads."

Lynn sighed. "I guess even being around us could be considered an endangerment. I know you feel the same way as Clint and I do, John. In this instance, we may need backup if they arrive as we think they will at some point to try and collect Amara. I didn't want to blindside you. These clowns don't quit. Ask Samira. If a young girl quits Islam as Amara's doing, she's marked for death."

"Noted." I didn't want a discussion of capability. Hell, I wouldn't throw a Seal Team at Lynn and Clint in their domain. The outcome would be questionable. Civilians don't recognize the categories. There are inadvertent killers, professional killers as the Seals are, and then there are Clint and Lynn... and much of my team: professional killers without conscience. Have we ever killed innocents? I expect so. Did we obsess over it for more than a few moments? Ah... no. "You know we're with you, Lynn. No explanation necessary, and I know you and Clint have already discussed plans if we have to add this new pack of hyenas onto our boating list. What's wrong with Tonto anyway? He's shadowing me as if I had bacon pinned to my jeans."

"Oh... that... Tonto is waiting for the right time to show you the new trick he's learned," Lynn said. "He didn't want to disrupt practice. Ask him."

The hairs were standing on the back of my neck, especially when I saw our outfield ball shaggers and coaches inching in closer. I stared at Tonto. The big mutt grinned at me in his usual calm, drooling way. I knew we needed to get on with practice so I threw caution to the wind, much to my regret.

"Okay, Tonto," I addressed him while leaning down with hands on knees, "show me your new trick, pal."

Tonto gave out a short bark, walked over next to me, lifted his leg, and peed on my tennis shoe. I didn't bother dancing out of the way. I was a day late and a dollar short perceiving this new smack-down for the Cheeseburger. I hung my head in deference to this ace. To say great hilarity ensued on the part of my ball field companions would be an incredible understatement. Lucas, for one, was rolling around on the ground, hooting helplessly. The girls, initially stunned, quickly joined into the merriment. Clint of course ran over with an award winning horrified look.

"Tonto? What have you done? Oh, for shame. Tell John you're sorry this instant."

Tonto dropped on his back, legs straight up, and head cocked off to the side, playing dead. This brought on more pandemonium. Finally, I shook my shoe out, and pointed at Clint. "Of course you know, this means war. Batter up!"

I walked over with soggy shoe to the pitching mound. Tonto popped out of his death act to follow me. Such is life in Cheeseburger land.

* * *

"That was so much fun, Mr. Harding," Amara said. "May I help with practice while I'm visiting every day?"

"Sure. We have another game on Saturday morning too. You can sit with us in the dugout," I answered. We had adjourned to a picnic table with all of us in attendance, including Jafar and Samira, who sat next to Amara. Only Casey, Tommy, Jess, Dev, Denny, Laredo, and Lora weren't on hand to enjoy Tonto's trick, but Clint had filmed it for them, sending off the video clip after practice resumed. "Although, you've gone through a lot, I guess Samira explained how difficult your future may be."

126

"Yes, she did." Amara gripped Samira's hand. "I will be shunned from now on by everyone in my family if I live. When my Father told me about the marriage he had arranged with a much older friend of his, who does financial dealings with him, I was shocked. He is in his forties. I have never been permitted to date, and now I am told I will be married to a man over twice my age. When I refused, and appealed to my Mother, she turned away. I am almost twenty. They... they changed. Everything changed. Even Imam Ahmad at the SALAM Center was forced to side with my Father. The Imam tried to reason with my parents, but there is much pressure on him to enforce any parental edict."

"I understand not wanting to be bludgeoned into an arranged marriage," I replied carefully. "Are you certain though that leaving Islam is what you want?"

Amara's bruised face contorted slightly in distaste. "It has been building for some time. When I helped Dannie unknowingly to find the kidnapped little boy in our Masjid, and the way those men went after her, it was a turning point. I later found out Imam Ahmad did indeed know there was something more to the boy's situation. I kept in touch with Dannie, and she gave me many links to Samira's speeches. It is all true! We women are nothing but slaves in Islam. My Father made this all clear to me when he tried to drag me to a meeting with his friend and I refused. He beat me until I thought he meant to kill me. I e-mailed Dannie. She drove to Sacramento right away, and I snuck out of the house when my Mother thought me too beaten to leave on my own. Dannie believes in God. Is there not but one God? Samira has admitted to me she cannot safely visit a Masjid except if disguised, because she tries to work within Islam to change the way women are treated. I will never go back. I will pray to Allah on my own. I know there is much danger for all of you. Is it possible to escape this without getting my friend Dannie killed?"

I saw my monsters grinning at me. Yeah, it probably wouldn't be Dannie that got killed. "We'll help you all the way through this. Clint and Lynn already stated they want you to stay with them until we can clear this mess up. I have to warn you though, and I'm sure Dannie has explained this to you, we're not the police. To end this threat so you can leave Islam, and live on your own, there will probably be casualties, even amongst your family members. We want to help you get free with as few people getting hurt as possible. We have a fund for this kind of thing."

"We do?" Lynn smirked at me.

"We do now," I corrected my error in thinking I could get anything past my companions, even to ease Amara's mind. "It's my fund."

"Like hell," Lucas piped in. "We share everything. Amara gets a new start somewhere, preferably far away from her family. Jafar can handle the new identity papers with Denny's signature. Amara and Dannie can put their heads together to pick a place she would like to start over in. I want this on the record for everyone though. It would be very bad if I come face to face with Daddy Dearest... clear?"

"Ditto," Lynn said, echoed by the entire team. "That's the drawback, Amara. There are, as John tries to point out to us constantly, inadvertent consequences. Our team doesn't take casualties. We give casualties. Hopefully, we'll have you in a new place before your Daddy knows what's happening. Clint and I will teach you the ways to stay in contact with us and Dannie if you need help. You have to be all in though, because if your Father or any family attack us before we get you to safety with a new identity, they won't survive."

Tears streamed down Amara's cheeks. She gestured at her face. "Could any of you do such a thing to your own daughter?"

There was no need to answer. We also had no doubt he would kill her, given the chance. My iPhone went off with an indication of a Denny message. I read the text with growing concern. "Well shit... Denny has the facts on the seven clowns sent after Amara. They're all Isis and Soldiers of Allah connected. Anyone else seeing a web of crap descending over us?"

Amara swiped at her eyes. "What does this mean? Are... are you saying my Father is a terrorist? He is a brutal and unforgiving man... but I do not think he has ever exploded bombs or plotted anything in my hearing. I would have mentioned such-"

"Relax, sister," Samira said soothingly. "John means there are connections between the men who tried to take you and terrorists."

"That your Father could reach out into a possible nationwide web for help in kidnapping you from our house makes us wonder if the net of these terrorist tools has finally closed," Lynn added. "I'm sure our boss Denny has already reached that conclusion. It means this may be a full strike through intimidation not only as a terrorist network, but also an attempt to bolster Sharia law."

"Lynn's right. If all these terrorist imports, we've been stupidly allowing to slip through our borders, close ranks in communication and purpose, they can strike at will while covering their tracks. If a family decides to crack down on a recalcitrant daughter, or an opportunity arises to further the takeover of the United States through Sharia law, these jokers have the puzzle pieces in place to do exactly that. It is unfortunate for you, but very fortunate for us we had this interaction, Amara."

"Then... you will still help me, Mr. Harding?"

"We'll be helping you no matter what. This other info has only to do with us. It paints a clearer picture of what we're up against on a more official level. We certainly won't hand you over to your family because things get tricky settling you into a new place. We have some new leads to follow on our regular cases now. Don't let any of this bother you. Lynn and Clint will take great care of you, and the rest of us are only a phone call away. I think we've covered everything we can at this time. C'mon Al, we'll have to ride with the damn windows open, because Tonto didn't only get my shoe."

"It's okay, Dad," Al said from where she was sitting on the ground petting the main culprit in making me disgustingly aromatic. "Tonto's sorry. He says he was forced into evil by his housemates."

"Be careful pulling the 'Dog Whisperer' card on us, Al," Lynn warned. "It won't go well for you. C'mon crew. Between boat cruises, confrontations, and softball practice, I'm running low on fuel. I think a quiet night at home is in order. Tomorrow's Saturday, so I'm thinking Sunday will be the first night we'll have to worry about late night visitors."

Then as we were walking to the parking lot Tommy arrived. He had texted me, wondering if we were still at the park. We met him with the usual fanfare of greetings, accusing him of being a slacker for not helping at practice. He had been taking my place at work, so I kept my mouth shut. His nose crinkled as we traded one liners.

"What is that smell?"

"I know Clint sent you the video, T. Don't dig a hole for yourself. I know you didn't only arrive here to perform a discovery phase of my Tonto decorated shoe."

"Alexi called. He wants us to meet with Yuri and Marko about an earlier match date just as all of you suspected. Grab Lora, change your piss-pants, and we'll have dinner with Al at The Warehouse. It's on for six."

At least we were ahead of one game in town. "That's perfect. Tommy, this is Amara Nejem. She'll be staying with Clint and Lynn until we can move her out of the area. Amara, this is my partner, Tommy Sands. You can trust him with anything."

130

Amara held out her hand to Tommy. "I am very glad to meet you, Sir."

Tommy shook her hand gently, peering with compassion at her face. "Nice meeting you too, Amara. Just call me Tommy. Does this have something to do with the religion of peace?"

"Yeah, it does, T. We're going to help her leave the religion of peace. Her Dad thinks of it more in the true meaning's form – her 'submission'. He rearranged her face, teaching Amara his take on the meaning."

Tommy shook his head. "Sorry to hear that, Amara, but you picked the best people in the world to help you survive it. Clint, I got your text about coaching third base tomorrow. Is that still the plan?"

"Yeah, T, I'm coaching first base. We have Jafar on this new wrinkle we're following. Casey and Lucas are bringing their wives to watch the game before we have pizza and beer. What did you think of Tonto's new trick?"

"Incredibly good," Tommy acknowledged. "In front of the entire softball team was an added bonus I didn't expect. You do know the damn thing already went viral on YouTube, right?"

"Of course it did," Clint replied. "I added it to the John Harding list there, titled Tonto schools John Harding."

"Gee thanks, Clint. As much fun as this disrespectful banter is, I'm going home. See you at six, T, if you can drag yourself away from the YouTube channel."

"Do you guys need backup in the bar?"

"We'll be fine, Lucas. Anyone wanting a free dinner is of course welcome to come, but I know we have the after game pizza fest tomorrow. Any updates I get from this meeting will be streamed to you. We all know what the new meeting is all about.

This could speed everything into high gear. I'm not cutting back, so anyone wanting to fish off the Lora tomorrow morning, we're leaving the pier at eight because the game's at 1 pm."

"Let's take The Sea Wolf tomorrow, John," Lucas said. "We need to do some shakedown cruises in case Denny ships her overseas for us when we get some action."

"Sounds good to me. Bring Dannie and Amara if they want to come, Lynn. Amara can see your sadistic side first hand."

"I would like that very much," Amara said.

"Yep. Gonna' get me some tomorrow morning after a good night's rest," Lynn remarked.

"No Tasers," I added.

"Heh…heh."

* * *

I escorted my lovely wife and daughter into The Warehouse by a quarter until six. I waved at some familiar faces, hearing 'Hey John' called out by some of my Oakland PD friends. Marla ran around from behind the bar to hug Lora and Al. This place was like 'Cheers' to me. I'd confronted bad guys, allies, potential friends, and even had my first date with Lora here. Tommy and I had made fight plans, met with potential opponents, and I'd nearly killed Alexi Fiialkov outside the bar during our initial meeting.

"Come right over here." Marla guided us to a large table, obviously reserved. "Alexi called ahead to have me prepare this dinner engagement. Lora and Al will be with you right here, Champ, at least until your fight opponents arrive. I have that meeting focused at the end of the bar, where I can keep you in company with the Bud and Beam brothers so nothing violent happens in the bar."

132

"Very astute, Marla," I replied, while seating my girls. "I know Al's starving, so would you bring over a complete appetizer plate, to curb any bad feelings caused by hunger?"

Marla laughed. "I didn't know you knew a word like astute. I'll bring on the food. Want the brothers now, Champ?"

"Oh... you betcha'," I replied without taking offense to Marla not knowing the full range of my expertise, including a vocabulary beyond one syllable words.

In moments, we had menus, drinks, appetizers, and a fun conversation about the softball game on Saturday. Lora even managed to do some fondling under the table to attract my attention while Al related details of her day at school... oh for shame. Tommy arrived next, only a heartbeat ahead of Alexi, Yuri, and Marko. When I stood to greet him, his brow furrowed, because he knew our meeting guests must be right behind him.

"Did you take a taxi over, or are you staying bright-eyed and busy tailed tonight?"

"I took a cab. I don't care what Yuri and the Assassin think. They're right behind me, aren't they?"

"Coming up on your left, Uncle Tommy. Holy crap, Dad, that guy's big."

"Quiet, Al. Polite speak only." Al was right. Marko looked huge in the black suit he was wearing. I shook hands with each one as they arrived at the table. "Marla has a spot near the bar for us reserved."

"Can we not meet your family?"

Not by choice, but polite speak only. "Sure, Marko. This is my wife Lora, and daughter Alice, Al for short. Ladies, this is Marko Hristov and Yuri Kornev."

Marko crouched near the table in front of Al. "Will you be seeing the fight, Al?"

"Nope. I saw the first Rattler fight without permission. I didn't like it."

Marko straightened with a laugh. "Yes, that was very brutal. This one will be too. I think it probably best if you do not see it. Would you like me to stop over after the fight to see if you and your Mom are okay?"

"Sure…" Al hesitated with perfect timing, "if you can still walk."

"You are a very outspoken little girl," Kornev observed. "Nice meeting you both. Come Marko, let us adjourn to our meeting place, and put our proposal on the table."

We had the corner end of the bar to ourselves. Marko and I took up a lot of room, but Marla had placed the stools so we had plenty of space. She also brought me refills, and Tommy what I was having.

"Can I get you anything, guys?"

"I would like some coffee, Marla, thank you," Alexi said. His companions echoed the order, and Marla had coffee for them within seconds.

"If you need anything, just wave at me." Marla walked away.

I took a long pull off my Bud brother refreshment, watching how annoyed Kornev became when I did it. "This is your show, Yuri. How can Tommy and I help you?"

"Are you coherent enough to talk business?"

"I'll manage. Tommy and I just arrived ourselves. What's the problem?"

"One of the problems is that I do not think you are simply a pug with a day-job. We first want to make sure you will not be a problem for us after Marko beats you. It is imperative when Marko wins that our holdings and business at the port will not be interfered with by you or anyone else employed by you. Secondly, we want the fight moved up. I have had men watch you train in the ocean – a very unusual training regimen. They report you are prepared now to fight. So is Marko."

"How soon do you want the fight to happen?" Tommy took over from there.

"We would like it to be next Friday night at 10 pm."

First, I was thinking thank God we trained near land, and we fed the fishes way out, well past where anything would drift in on the current before digested. Secondly, we used the radar installed on The Lora to warn of any approach within miles of our position. I nodded at Tommy, because next Friday seemed perfect to me. I would have liked for it to go down tomorrow, but I knew that couldn't happen.

"That would be acceptable," Tommy replied. "Anything else?"

Yuri glanced at Alexi, who took over the conversation with a grin. "They wish to have the knife-hand strike disallowed completely for the match."

Tommy and I erupted in laughter. It took a few moments to regain control. Alexi chortled along with us. Tommy wiped absently at his eyes. "I'll bet they would like the knife-hand strike banned. That ain't happenin'. Anything permitted in the UFC is permitted in our Oakland brawls. You two know that. What happened? Did you finally decide to watch the second Rattler fight? Damn, Marko, you were all set to kill John in the cage. Now you want to start banning legal strikes? What's next, we have to tie him up before the fight?"

Oh man, that was an ace. Marko's head looked ready to explode. Yuri gestured in calming fashion. "It was a suggestion after seeing the second Rattler fight, because even a rib shot can cause death."

"That should work out well for Marko then," Tommy said. "He wants to kill John, not the other way around, so maybe he should start working on his own knife-hand tools instead of whining about John using it."

I stepped in front of the body shot Marko threw at Tommy. It was a good one, but this ain't my first rodeo. I absorbed it, and did not blink. "No one throws a shot at Tommy, Marko. You have a beef, we'll go outside and do this in the parking lot dust out back. My Oakland PD friends won't care if I announce it first. If you start anything inside this bar, I get serious, because this is my chosen place. Tommy put it to you plainly. The knife-hand strike stays or the match is off. I won't break the rules in the cage unless you do. If you break the rules, I'll smash your larynx so you'll die before any help can save you."

"You throw another punch, asshole, and you're going to jail!" Marla had been obviously monitoring our physical interaction. "I have an entire bar of back up too!"

Indeed she did. Marla never raises her voice. When she did, she had six police officers ringing Marko, and they were armed. Yuri bear hugged Marko away from death, because his problem was I would have killed him on the spot if he threw another punch. Full contact martial arts is one thing, but kill strikes are another. I've administered them, and I know more than a few. Marko wisely allowed the 'hold me back' scenario from Yuri.

"Please," Alexi said, his hands in the air, speaking to some grim faced cops. "It is over gentlemen. Marla, I am taking care of all bills in the bar. Please tally them onto my tab with generous tip. We will cause no further problems, my friends."

Alexi knew how to hit the high note. A few of the officers patted my arm as they returned to their seats, but I kept my eyes on Marko. "Don't do anything else, Marko. If you do, the police will be the last thing you need to worry about. You and Yuri need to go. We'll be ready for the match at your chosen date. Hit the road."

Marko leaned toward me while supposedly being held back by Kornev. "You will see. I kill you in the cage, and visit your family to help them through it."

"I don't think that's going to work out the way you think, asshole!" Tommy moved to my side. "We were playing this straight up. You keep talkin' about a killin', and you're going to find out John takes your shit talk to heart. God knows you mentioning Lora and Al will get you to a place you never dreamed. My advice – shut the fuck up, and walk on out before you cement your death in stone."

Yuri and Marko chuckled at Tommy's warning, but they did the smart thing and left with Alexi waving to us as he left with them. Tommy knew me, which was why he sighed, picked up his Beam brother, drained it, picked up his Bud brother, drained it, and signaled Marla for another round. "Damn it, brother! You didn't need to take that shot for me."

I downed the brothers as Marla replaced them. "Yeah, I did, Tommy. We have other irons in this fire. We need to have this match take place. I'm not worried about anything happening to me. Hell, my monster squad would kill every single person even with knowledge of my death. It's our bond here on the West Coast. They would make sure nothing ever happened to either Lora or Al. I know damn well you would. I took a shot... big deal."

Tommy peered at me knowingly. "That strike told you something. You prick, you know something. Spit it out."

I put an arm around my brother by another mother with real feeling. "There may be someone who can clock me. The Assassin is not the one, brother."

Yeah, I took the blow meant for Tommy with more than one reason… big deal.

"So… that intervention was a learning experience, huh? I knew it! Okay… where do we go from here?"

"On to the match, T. You want the first stakeout at Clint and Lynn's place with me on Sunday? I'm doing the first watch."

Tommy held up a toast with his Beam, and I clicked glasses with him. "Damn right! I want to see if the sick bastard father shows. What'll be our reason for staking out Clint and Cruella's loft? The assholes would need a special forces strike team to take those two, and even then the outcome would be in doubt."

"You're right about that, but Denny would like some live ones, who might be connected to this other multiple Islamist group crap. I texted him my idea they may be developing Sharia Law strike groups where they can work at dual purposes on a nationwide basis."

Tommy leaned on the bar, sipping his Beam. "Remember the days when I thought we were just a couple of street-fighting, bond chasers. I never thought I'd look back on them like they were the good old days."

"If you want out, T, let me know. We're brothers. We'll get together on holidays, and kids' birthdays if this crap gets too much for you. I know the feeling. Denny says we've attracted a lot of attention from the higher echelon, who like our work. They'll throw us under the bus in a heartbeat, but Denny's plan is to relocate us if it gets too hot for us here. That's the main reason we clean our messes thoroughly. I love the East Bay, and I know you do too."

"Let's go eat. I'm through whinin' for tonight. Rachel would throw me under the bus if I move us out of the East Bay. You bunch have been a bit busier than I like lately, including that shithead trying to snatch Al. We sure didn't have much downtime after the Rattler fight. What there was of it was great, but short."

"Amen to that." We walked over to the table with fresh drinks as Marla arrived with our dinners. Apparently, Lora took the lead, and ordered for us. Nice. Al was none too happy.

"You should have Gronked him, Dark Lord."

Tommy and I sat down to enjoy that upbraiding for a few moments. Al had invented the word after I put the hurt on a guy named Gronk. Since then, she issues the order when she senses something off about someone, as my little Alice rightfully did in Las Vegas a while back at the airport. She spotted a killer hitting on Lora. I didn't think much about her concerns until the guy asked for a private conference, and threatened my family if I didn't throw the fight. I Gronked him.

Chapter 6

Let The Darkness Flow

I switched to the Dark Lord for the first time in a while. "The Dark Lord was doing research, and bar fight prevention."

"You did very well, DL," Lora said. "What did they want?"

"We're fighting next Friday night." I began digging into my hot turkey sandwich, not really wanting to set Lora off. Fail.

"You're going to what? I thought you needed at least a month to heal!"

"Calm down, Lora." Tommy came to my aid. "DL's in the best shape of his life. Come out on the boat tomorrow. He'll give you a demonstration. Lucas is going to let us sail in the Sea Wolf. He's angling for another pirate mission, I hear."

"Oh great. That sounds lovely. Where at this time, the Bermuda Triangle?"

Even Al got a kick out of that line. "No. The destination is still being decided. Want to come along, Hon? We don't have a nag in the crew."

Lora's face went through a few contorted changes of rage before settling on neutral accompanied with a shrug. "Sorry, John. I was around my sister too much over the holidays, followed by taking them to Las Vegas for the St. Valentine's Day Massacre. Are you really ready to fight again this quickly?"

"Come on board the Wolf tomorrow. I pissed off Lynn so badly with my pole strikes, she was going to Tase me. I'm ready. We have a few side deals riding on the outcome of the fight. Next Friday will be fine."

"C'mon, Mom. If the weather's nice, I'd love to go out on the Sea Wolf and watch Lynn poke Dad."

"Gee... thanks, Al."

"That does sound very tempting," Lora admitted. "Fine. If the Bay is relatively calm we'll go with you. We'll be back in plenty of time for the game, won't we?"

"Of course. The team can't play without the coaches and star player. Tommy will demonstrate my readiness. He and Lynn will put me through my bloody paces in the water."

"Forty-five minutes of hell on earth, Lora," Tommy added. "Any bad feelings you've ever had about the Cheeseburger will be rendered non-existent when you watch what Lynn and I do to him."

Lora grinned, while looking straight into my eyes with something other than retribution. She and I had found something in each other we had no intention of letting go. When after the first Rattler fight, she jumped into the locker room shower with me, no holds barred, I knew I had a partner. We may not agree at times, and the fights normal couples had couldn't be avoided; but in those gripping shower moments, Lora let everything loose. She didn't give a damn about what I was or what I did. Lora clutched my battered looking soul with screaming suppressed abandon, cementing the fact she was in for the long haul, no matter the outcome.

"The Dark Lord and I have a pact, Tommy. Sometimes, I forget to rein in my mouth before I speak." She reached over to grip my hand. "Contrary to the persona I sometimes allow to surface, I love this guy more than anything. I don't choose to observe his torture as a hobby. Since it is supposed to be a beautiful day, I can make an exception for John's forty-five minutes of discomfort. I'd be glad to come on board with Al."

Tommy smiled. "Understood, my friend. The Dark Lord does grow on us. He and I have been through the wringer together.

141

When you need someone standing at your side, the Cheese is the one to have."

Well okay, that filled up all my parameters for touchy/feely moments. I should be more feeling, but it's a process. As I gripped Lora's hand more firmly, I wondered if she knew how many I'd kill to keep her at my side. Looking into her eyes, I think she did. Life is a journey not to be taken lightly. At times… we are alone in all things. Sometimes, another human being crashes through our parameters of alone, and leaves us doubting everything. When Lora gripped me in the elementary school parking lot to say thanks for interceding with scary adults about Al, I damn well saw more in her eyes than gratitude. I'm here now, and I ain't letting go. She understands not everything can be peaches and cream. How much more understanding can a guy ask for – not much.

Al stood and placed a hand over ours. "Don't change, Dad. If Mom throws you under the bus, I'll Gronk her."

Yeah, that led to hilarity. Done deal.

* * *

Tommy busted me in on my right shoulder, but could not pull the pole away fast enough as I jettisoned out of the water, striking with every ounce of rage within me. I sheared the damn thing off, leaving Tommy standing at the railing with a pole missing a piece. I watched as he simply threw the pole into the water with disgust. I propelled on my back like a dolphin waiting for fish at the aquarium, pointing at him. He grinned appreciatively.

"C'mon out, Dark Lord. I wish to hell you were fighting for the damn Ultimate Fighting crown instead of with that pug, Assassin. If anyone can beat you in the UFC heavyweights, they should make an offer for a fight at the Mandalay Bay. I doubt very much after that second Rattler fight that any of them want a piece. Good workout. Right, Lynn?"

Lynn moved to the railing with a big smile as I treaded water with Lucas powering down. "Damn right, DL. You gave me and Clint Junior a hell of a workout. We don't want to fatten your head, but what the hell, you know the score. I know you well enough you won't be overconfident no matter what we say, so come on out of the water, Cheese."

As I moved to do exactly that with a big smile, one of my shark friends bumped against me, drawing a scream of anguish from Al, who had moved next to Lora. A split second later the burst from Clint's MP5 shot through the shark from head to tail. A repeat burst right through its disorganized head made it the new blood target. I streaked for the fantail. I had enough provocation to be on board in seconds afterward. I raised my banana suited arms out in happiness after I boarded the Sea Wolf.

"What... no hugs?" I meant it as a joke, but Al rushed forward hugging my gnarly yellow banana colored wetsuit with passion, in spite of the drenched in saltwater reality. I patted her back gingerly. "Hey... Al, don't insult my shark intervention guy Clint with shadows of doubt. He takes his job very seriously, kid."

Clint wrapped a comforting arm around Al. "Listen to the Dark Lord, Al. I would never allow a shark strike on DL. I admit that one fooled me. I figured him to be in a curious state. My bad. I'll be more careful in the future."

My monsters all laughed, except for Al. She was pissed. Al clutched Clint's shoulders as he knelt next to her. "Don't do that!"

Al wiped at the tears. "I'm sorry... but please don't do that."

Clint was caught unawares. He is so good, the rest of us simply accept his expertise in protection of the Cheeseburger without doubt. Al fronting him left a mark no humorous write-off would answer as she stared grimly into his eyes. Clint recovered in true monster form although I knew it rattled him. "All sharks die from this moment on, Al. You have my word."

Al hugged him without pretense, her head against his chest. "Thank you. I...I know how good you all are, but please don't let anything happen to my Dad in these training sessions."

Clint disengaged from Al, and held her at the shoulders. "You have my word, Al. Ask anyone here. It is my bond. I will waste sea life from now until kingdom come if they even appear while your Dad is in the water. I hope today's incursion into the training regimen doesn't discourage you and your Mom from sailing with us in the future."

Al sobbed at Clint's declaration. She gripped the sides of his head with tearful acknowledgement. "Thank you! I didn't mean to be such a baby."

Clint took her hands in both of his, kissing each of them. "We monsters sometimes go too far with our jokes, Al. Thank you for highlighting one that will never happen again. I was not on my game today. I took a few things for granted I normally don't. Thanks for pointing it out to me. Never hesitate for a moment to point out something you see that makes you uncomfortable. I heard about the way you nailed the killer at the Las Vegas airport, when an entire team of professionals thought nothing of him. This is your second right call. There's no way I should have let your Dad get bumped."

Al hugged Clint tightly. "I only thought the guy in the airport was going to have his way with my Mom, and DL was going to let him."

Oh yeah, the crew enjoyed that explanation. Then we had much bigger problems. Lucas speeded the Wolf to full speed without warning, adapting a zigzag pattern as we shot over the waves. "Incoming... two cruiser type vehicles... unknown origin... cannot get them on the radio."

144

Lucas kept it short and sweet. We were under attack. The monster squad didn't bother with surprised looks or worthless exclamations. Lynn grabbed Al up in her arms, and Lora by the hand, dragging them below decks. One look from Lynn, and Dannie followed her with Amara in hand without a word. The Wolf was a warship, which these attacking assholes didn't know. They would have had to have torpedoes to puncture the hull, and long range weapons to do any damage above decks at the distance Lucas put between us and them. Lucas networked Denny into our ears as we scrambled to battle stations. Casey manned the .50 caliber machine gun as Lucas activated our pop-out armament nests. I took the XM307 25mm grenade airburst gun which can fire 250 rounds per minute. Clint found a comfortable position with his MP5.

Also in the XM307 nest I had my M107 sniper rifle with swivel mounting. Picking off targets on a ship at sea is of course a difficult task at best, but as the old commercial stated back in the day: practice… practice… practice. The Spawn of Satan came on as we completed our readiness tasks. He at least began with asking about our safety first. Lucas had already signaled we could outrun them easily. That meant Denny could request prisoners, because Casey and I would disable their craft while Lucas maneuvered in and out of firing positions.

"Give it to me plain, John. I know you have Snow Whites on board. You call the shots. I've radioed the Coast Guard. I have-"

I had seen the overhead burst, thinking they had their own airburst weapon. Uh oh. We were deader than the proverbial doorknob instantly after the burst, including communications. I didn't waste time with analyzing the situation. Lucas jogged to my side, taking the M107. "EMP Case. Let's rip 'em. Fire at will, Clint."

The four of us fired everything we had, and let me tell you, we shocked our predators right to hell. Casey worked the below decks on both cruisers with armor piercing .50 caliber bursts. Lucas took out the bridge inhabitants with workman like accuracy. He knows how to shoot from the deck of a moving or floundering sea craft. Clint raked the bridges of both vessels with short bursts that finished off their equipment nearly as well as their EMP blast did ours. Then it was my turn when our pursuit lost forward motion. The 25mm grenade shots disintegrated everything above the waterline in airburst mayhem. By silent agreement, we did target practice after the boats were helpless. I didn't waste ammo, but I did add more devastating rounds to the carnage caused by my initial shots. My three brethren picked what they wanted to hit, and practiced. It would be hard to explain this to the Coast Guard in United States territorial waters, but such is life in monster land. We put away all our weapons, closing the pop-out nests. Clint went down to assure our passengers all was well, and to make sure they had enough emergency lighting to see. He came above decks with four beers.

"Damn exciting training day, John," Clint said, toasting us with his beer. "The girls are eating up the ice cream Lucas had in his freezer."

"We had the tools, we had the knowhow, it's Miller time," Casey added. "It's my turn on the XM307 next time, DL."

"They killed my baby," Lucas lamented, his hand patting the railing of the floundering Sea Wolf. "You know of course... this means war."

"You think you're pissed," Clint replied. "I have a steaming Cruella Deville below decks who not only didn't get to fire a weapon, she also won't find a survivor aboard either good ship lollipop to torture. God only knows the concessions I will have to make in smoothing over this debacle."

"Great shakedown cruise though," Casey said. "We may be dead in the water, but we're not in the Gulf of Guinea either. We'll have to have shielding when we go overseas with the Wolf. We'll have to have everything shielded with those Faraday Cages. We're lucky this happened. Man, I wish we could have chanced getting one alive, but I'm not fond of taking prisoners from sitting duck land. I wonder how much they'll be able to salvage on the wrecks. I know what the airbursts did to the decks, but I believe we can agree there won't be much left below decks either."

I pointed at what was left. They were doing a Titanic type sink below the waves. Casey had literally cut a groove below the waterline with the fifty in each boat so they looked like they were smiling as they sunk out of sight. "We'll let Denny send in people to pick apart the wreckage. Let's talk about these guys having EMP weapons. Anyone else thinking someone Denny's dealing with for the Gulf of Guinea operation leaked the info, and painted a target on us? It also means the boats had a prototype of some kind. They knocked us the hell out, and they had their systems shielded already, or they would have been taking a chance on damaging their own rides."

"No doubt this was a hit," Clint agreed. "They had no way of knowing the conventional weapons we have on the Wolf. Lucas was scary good with his sixth sense going out on the Wolf instead of The Lora. We had enough firepower on The Lora to give them a hell of a battle, but we don't know what kind of weapons they were bringing to the party. It's obvious they wanted to take the Wolf unharmed, and us prisoners… for a short time anyway."

"Shit! I almost forgot we have a satellite uplink in a shielded case below decks," Lucas said. "I'll go get it. Be right back."

Lucas handed it to Clint when he returned. Clint had us on with Denny in moments. We could tell he was on a helicopter.

"Damn, it's good to hear from you guys. I expected the worst," Denny said. "I commandeered a Coast Guard Pelican Transport. Laredo's driving. We'll get you all off the Sea Wolf. Anything left of the attack boats?"

147

"Not much, Denny," Clint answered. "You may be able to sift through the wreckage. They hit us with an EMP airburst weapon. We didn't wait for them to get close. No way they could have come after us without help."

"Understood. I'll pull some strings, and see if I can put this under top secret lockdown. I have two Coast Guard cruisers heading to your position. They'll be working salvage for bodies, and whatever they can find. I don't want you guys interacting with the Coast Guard. I have a man on each Coast Guard boat in case I don't get you away from there before they arrive. They will scour those attack boats for anything and everything. This puts a new face on our problems – namely as you guys have already figured, I have a leak on my end. Do you still have your banana suit on, John?"

"Unfortunately yes, Spawn."

"You don't have to do it, but the Coast Guard is forty-five minutes away from your position because I needed my guys on board. Would you swim over and see if you can find anything in the debris."

"You do understand there is blood in the water, right?"

"The sharks will never attack the Great Banana," Denny replied to much amusement from my compatriots. "Please... pretty please."

"Fine! I'm not doing a search operation for more than the emergency air breathing piece allows, I carry with me in training."

"Much appreciated, John. I'll be there very soon to start loading everyone. Spawn out."

"Go on, John. I'll do the best I can from our nest with the M107," Lucas said. "It's a damn good thing the nest pops out and in hydraulically without any electrical component."

"The rest of us will be on the railing, compadre," Clint added. "As I promised Al, we'll kill everything in the water near you if we can see it. We have the emergency inflatable if you'd like Case and I to paddle with you over there."

I arranged my hood and goggles, "Nope. I'll be okay. I want you guys to ensure our ladies make it aboard the helicopter with as few problems as possible. Lucas will watch my back... what he can see of it. Remember, I'm the yellow one, Lucas."

"Get in the fuckin' water, Recon! If you keep whinin' much longer, we'll have the damn Coast Guard on our backs."

After that reminder of duty I was in the water in short order, propelling full speed to the debris. Yep. There were bodies, body parts, and sharks. They were busy in the water. We probably waited too long for me to get in here. On the plus side, my yellow suit was not attractive to the sharks. Black looks much like their meals. I spent most of my time by the bodies, looking for ID's before the sharks intervened. When I surfaced after nearly twenty minutes, the bodies I'd encountered rendered nothing in the way of identification. While sifting through the debris after my initial ID hunt, I noticed movement a hundred yards away from our debris mess. Someone was stroking away from our danger zone. A live one! This was so good in relation to what I expected, I charged behind him so convincingly in noise and stroke, the idiot thought I was a great white moving in for the kill.

I stroked easily in next to him. His lips were already turning blue from hypothermia. It's cold in the Bay waters, low fifties and sometimes below. This guy was a good swimmer. I'll give him that. I removed my breathing apparatus, and stuck it in my wet suit pocket. "Hi there, cutie. Want to get out of the water in one piece?"

He recognized me as a human being and attacked, not to damage me, but to try and cling to me like a safety buoy in a tropical storm. This guy was seriously freaked out. I immediately dived, which caused him to release me instantly. I surfaced again

149

with a wave. Instead of the Dark Lord, I accessed the Terminator. "Come with me if you want to live!"

"Yes! Yes! Please… help me out of the water!"

"Follow me with strong strokes. It will help you keep warm. Make another move to grab me, and I take you for a dive."

He followed me on the swim back. Lucas had to plug a nice sized great white targeting my swimming partner dressed all in black. By the time we made it to the Sea Wolf, the guy was done. I had to haul him on board by the scruff of his neck. Laredo waved at me from the cockpit of his newly acquired Pelican Transport. Clint and Lucas waited for me, having already transferred our precious cargo with an ingenious transfer line from the Sea Wolf to the Pelican. It holds twenty-eight passengers and a crew of three, so we'd be fine.

"Nice catch, John," Clint said as he secured the prisoner, and threw a blanket around him. He and Lucas put him in the bucket next for transfer with Casey and Denny ready to receive.

"We go next, Recon," Lucas directed. "You then detach our bucket transfer and swim over. Don't bother with the banana suit. Strip down to your skivvies and dive over."

"The banana suit stays, Ahab. Now get your old ass over onto the helicopter before I heave you through the hatch."

Lucas was still chuckling as we sent him over. Clint was next. Then I undid the Pelican Transport apparatus for transfer. It only took me a couple moments to stroke over, and get hauled aboard. All I could think of was it would be nice to get out of the banana suit, and that it was a good thing the weather stayed calm, or we would have had a hellacious time transferring our people in rough seas. I stripped out of my dry-suit, and sat down in my long johns by Lora and Al. Dannie and Amara sat together on the other side of Al. Amara's eyes were as wide as saucers. I don't think she ever intended to have this much adventure. Al simply looked

150

excited. Lora put her arm around my neck, leaning into me despite the smell. Laredo exercised the smoothest takeoff possible once we drifted clear of the Sea Wolf, and we were on our way home.

"I should have brought along some Fabreeze pine scent with me," I joked.

"I'm glad to have you next to me. So much for a little jaunt around the Bay, huh?"

"We'll be back in time for the game. I see Denny and Lynn over comforting my swim partner in the back."

"Yeah, and he's not real pleased about it either," Lora replied.

"The other guys were laughing at him, Dad. He kept insisting he wouldn't say anything until he spoke to his lawyer."

"I don't think that will end well for him, Al." I leaned back, closing my eyes. "I believe a little nap is in order. I still have a softball game to coach. How about a movie and popcorn night in the quiet of our entertainment room?"

"Sounds like heaven to me," Lora agreed.

"I'm in," Al said, "but I want my own bowl of popcorn. You two scarf it down so fast, I hardly get a handful."

She drew laughs from Dannie and Amara who had been listening in, which helped rid Amara of her glassy eyed stare.

"We'll be having pizza after the game, you little glutton."

"I don't have to worry about my weight, Dad, but Mom on the other hand…"

And that's how the fight started.

* * *

The minions met us as per Denny's instruction, taking charge of our unhappy pirate. Having the kids on board, Lynn had to restrain herself with small facts of reality about what would soon be happening if her Huckleberry didn't tell us everything from the day he was born. Denny showed him a couple of movies showcasing Lynn's work in the past. Let's just say he was one terrified munchkin by the time Laredo landed. Jess met us with our limo so we could retrieve our vehicles from the Marina after Lucas gained Denny's word the Wolf would be completely checked over and shielded from any more EMP attacks. Denny didn't need much convincing. I could tell this attack out of nowhere shook him up. He went with the minions and prisoner to Pain Central for answers.

I arrived, accompanying Lora and Al with all the equipment I needed in our soccer mom van. A full crew of coaches arrived soon after, pleased to be participating in a simple girls' softball game, especially Lynn. I could tell she had rested during the brief few hours since getting home from the unexpected helicopter ride. Warmups entertained in humorous ways as I received the usual complaints about my pitching while Lynn coached the base running. Then the unexpected happened as the two opposing teams' fans and family arrived, taking their seats in the small sections of bleachers in a semicircle around the field. Yuri and Marko arrived to sit behind the opposing team's dugout. Everyone on our side recognized them, putting a grim aspect to what had been a lighthearted diversion. I grinned. Soon the bill for all this was coming due, and I planned on collecting interest.

Lynn bumped against me after delivering the player sheet to the umpire, escorted by the very happy Tonto who had mascot duty. "I see this day will be remaining interesting no matter where we are. I see that look in your eyes, DL. Dreaming about next Friday night, huh?"

"Oh yeah." It was then both Yuri and Marko waved at me. "I guess that answers the question whether they knew about our earlier adventure."

152

"Yep. It means they know a bunch more now about us," Lynn agreed, waving back at them for me. "You can have Marko the Assassin. I want Yuri. I can't stand the sight of that smirking prick. This is their cute ploy to let us know they're onto us. I bet they didn't like it we survived. I know Yuri didn't. After the training session this morning, I'm betting Marko will be sorry you survived when match night comes."

I kept my eyes locked on to the visitors. "Yeah, he will, Lynn. I know he has something he plans on springing as a surprise during the match. I don't know what the surprise is, but I plan on making it a two way deal. Yuri's all yours. Be patient until we smoke out his buddy, the Ghost. Then we will get real busy."

"Of course," Lynn said amiably. "Well, it looks like the ump and opposing team's coach are done stroking each other. You do know they're banging each other, right?"

Everything has a few bad kinks in it. "Yeah, I heard the rumors. It appears they're true. Manny's a good ump, and they don't get paid. He'll call a straight game."

Lynn chuckled. "You're so cute, you naïve little bugger. There won't be anything straight about this game. The fix is in. The only question is how far he'll go to keep tapping the minx."

"Hopefully not far enough to cause a riot. We have a few hotheads amongst our parenting core too. We've toned them down, but anything real obvious will set them off again. Maybe it will be a blowout one way or the other."

"If it is, it better be us on top, coach."

"Seriously, Lynn, let's keep the focus on the game for the girls' sake. I don't like Yuri and Marko deciding to take in the game. Here comes Clint."

Lynn put an arm around Clint as he moved next to her. "Casey's coaching third. I'm taking first base today. Tommy

153

volunteered to do the scorecard. Everyone else will be watching for trouble. This puts another new spin on things. Batter up, coach."

"Indeed. Lynn thinks the fix is in."

Clint nodded. "I saw how cozy Manny was with Elaine, and we're not the only ones. I heard some rumblings in our bleacher section."

"After this morning, I'd have to say it's a small thing, brother."

"Amen to that."

* * *

The game was a good one in spite of Manny's calling balls and strikes like his bedroom hopes were riding on them, much to Lynn's amusement. The parents settled on protesting each obvious strike Manny called a ball with a concerted groan. Luckily his paramour's team liked to swing at strikes, so I made sure our pitchers knew to not do anything fancy. They did well throwing strikes, and our fielding was as good as I'd hoped. We were leading six to four. Manny was showing signs of frustration from the parental groaning chorus, mixed in with timeouts called for private conferences by Elaine to protest something or other. Lynn comically substituted her own dialogue between the two in a whisper to me – very entertaining jewels like 'if you ever want sex with anything other than your hand, you better start calling the game like you mean it'.

So here we were in the last inning with the bases loaded, no outs, and the tying run on second base. Manny's strike and ball calling had returned to Coach Elaine's game plan, and our pitcher Julie was losing concentration. The parental groaning choir was heating up with the addition of Devon and Jesse, who had stopped by after their business driving stint, adding a couple more booming base voices for Manny to deal with.

"I'm switching Julie and Al," I said to Lynn. "Maybe Al can close this out."

"Okay, but let me handle it," Lynn replied, signaling for a timeout. "I want to make sure Julie knows she hasn't done anything wrong. Besides, I'd like to make sure Al's okay with it."

"Sounds good." Clint, Casey, and I were trying not to stand with our fingers laced through the cage links with our noses pressed against it. Girls' softball turned out to be more exciting than EMP attacks.

Lynn put an arm around Julie's shoulders, waving Al over from first base. Julie seemed happy with the decision, and jogged to first. Lynn put the ball in Al's glove, whispered some instructions, which Al obviously enjoyed, and returned to the dugout.

"What made her laugh, babe," Clint asked.

"I told her to slow pitch the next batter right down the heart of the plate, and see if she could put a kink in Manny's love life."

"Very cool," Casey remarked, while Al warmed up.

The next batter was Coach Elaine's best hitter, and she looked ready to eat her bat she was so ready. Elaine's team chanted the time tested 'pitcher has a rubber arm'. Al grinned, looked in with her death stare, and let fly a floater down the middle. The batter swung so hard I figured she might have caused a ten mile an hour wind. She topped it, fortunately, because if she had hit it solidly, the baserunners could have walked home. As it was, Al bounded off the mound, snatched the ball, tagged out the runner from third, and threw the ball to Julie on first for a double play.

The double play woke up our fans to a standing ovation, complete with hoots and howls. Lora was in the stands next to Lucas losing her mind, pumping fists, and swaying. Elaine stormed out of the opposing dugout to protest the pitch, the tag out, the throw out, the sun, the moon, too little gas, not enough oil, and probably the cosmic convergence. Manny listened intently, hearing disparaging remarks and boos coupled with Lynn staring straight at him from the dugout entrance, arms folded. Manny shook his head and yelled 'play ball', turning away from the raging Elaine to brush off the plate. Elaine had nothing left but to return to her dugout.

"Oh Manny, you poor devil," Lynn whispered to us three happy coaches. "You ain't gettin' any tonight."

Al struck out the next batter with three straight fastballs, two of which were swinging strikes, with the third strike a called one. The ballgame was over, and it was raining somewhere in Mudville. Al did a victory dance, and chopping hand forward step as when a football player gets a first down. We celebrated happily with the girls. We then lined up on the field for hand slaps of good game with the opposing Tigers, including the prancing Tonto, who lightened the mood when he also held up a paw for each Tiger player. We were the A's. Elaine's assistant coach led the Tigers, because the disappointed Elaine hit the showers before the good sportsmanship show. I noticed Yuri and Marko were gone.

Dannie and Amara, who sat with the girls in the dugout were the first to congratulate them after the hand slap ceremony. Amara in particular looked to have had a good time. We dressed them both in our A's green and yellow uniforms for the game so they would not attract attention. Lora joined us while we packed the gear, before traveling to our favorite pizza place. Lucas followed close behind with Dev, Jess, and Tommy with him. All were glancing at the parking lot.

"We have company, John," Lucas said. "I'm glad we had the last game for today, and all the kids have left for the pizza place."

I glanced around, seeing Lucas had it right before stepping around the dugout with our equipment bags. The grouping of

Middle Eastern suits halted at the parking lot edge, conferencing heatedly.

"It's the contingent that visited our house to accost Dannie, plus one," Clint said.

Amara noticed too. She ran over to clutch Lynn's arm with Tonto and Dannie at her side. "It is my Father. Can...can he take me?"

Lynn patted her hands while looking around at the smiling faces around her. "What do you think, boys? Can Daddy take Amara with him? Wait... don't answer that."

Lynn turned to grip Amara's shoulders. "We need to clear the air once more, kid. How sentimental are you about Daddy? If we're to keep you safe and help you relocate, Daddy might be one of the casualties we warned you of earlier. It's best you let us know how serious you are."

Tears streamed down Amara's face. "I...I want to live, Lynn. He's going to kill me."

Lynn straightened. "That's all I wanted to know. Stay behind us with Tonto, Dannie, Lora, and Al."

Lora put an arm around Amara, drawing her a few more steps in the rear. Dannie and Al stayed close with Tonto positioning himself in front of them, head cocked cutely to the side as Al petted him. We weren't in a big rush, so we stayed where we were.

"Not much doubt who tipped these butt nuggets as to where Amara was," I said. "Friday seems too far away right now."

"I'll flip you for Daddy, Lynn," Lucas said.

"You can have him, Lucas. Clint reminded me I'm seven months pregnant, and can't take a body shot. I'll warm him up for you though."

Lucas nodded happily. "Thank you."

Clint and Lynn took lead. The rest of us hung back slightly behind them, scanning the area for glints in the sun or unexpected reinforcements showing with a grenade launcher or machine guns. Casey held his gym bag with his hand on his MP5 I knew he carried in it. The rest of us, including Tommy, Dev, and Jess were packing. The meeting conference ended abruptly. A heavyset, gray streaked, black bearded man a few inches over six feet tall wearing a white kufi head cover, led the men toward us. He waved what looked to be a document at us while approaching.

Lynn held her hand in a stopping motion when the group were nearly ten feet away. "That's far enough, Porky. State your business from there. We don't want any misunderstandings that could end in multiple deaths."

That statement led to a finger pointing enraged rebuke. "Do not insult me! My name is Mohammed Nejem. I am here to take my daughter with me. I see her cringing ashamedly in that ridiculous costume! She will come with me now!"

"Amara?" Lynn called over her shoulder. "Would you like to go with your Daddy?"

"No!" Amara shouted out.

"Sorry, Porky," Lynn answered, not sorry at all, "Amara doesn't want to go with you. Since she's over eighteen, there isn't a damn thing you can do about it either. Save yourself some pain, and hit the road."

"I have a court order for you to turn her over to me!" Mohammed wasn't stupid enough to approach any closer. My Monster Squad looks anything but approachable. "Read it yourself!"

Lynn strolled closer, took the paper, and turned her back on Mohammed. She scanned the papers. She laughed after a moment, handing it over to Clint. "What's the sentence for falsifying court documents, Clint?"

"Five to ten years, and you're right, babe – this is a fraudulent document. Tonto?"

Tonto streaked around to Clint's side.

"Mark this for me Special Agent Tonto." Clint dropped the paper. Tonto immediately lifted his leg and pissed on the papers to much laughter from the Monster Squad, but cries of outrage from our party of goons. "Thank you, Agent Tonto. Return."

Tonto rejoined our group of ladies at the rear to fervent hugs and petting. As the goons became more agitated, especially Mohammed, with threats and shouts of anti this and that, Lucas took over negotiations. He walked straight into Mohammed airspace, staring up into his eyes with Marine drill sergeant precision. Mr. Nejem fell back a step, his eyes widening.

"So, you're the big bad daddy likes to beat his own teenage daughter with his fists and switches, huh? Want to try it on a man, you worthless piece of camel dung! Go ahead! Take the first shot at me, pussy. I'll bitch slap you until your two inch dick falls off!"

Mohammed had enough, and not in a good way. He did exactly what he should not have done. He took the bait. Mr. Nejem swung a nice looking right handed sucker punch at Lucas. Our own Mr. Blake batted it away with a left wrist strike, and bitch slapped Mohammed so hard, he catapulted sideways to the ground. He stayed on his back, rolling back and forth cradling his face. Lucas gave the rest a come on over gesture.

"Any other woman beaters want to try their luck with a man, or do you pussies only fight women when you're forced into unarmed combat?"

Silence with red, skulking faces.

159

"No takers." Lynn sighed. "I guess they figured to flash a phony paper, walk away with Amara, and beat her to death in private without any opposition, Lucas. We filed that one for you. We should have arrested all of you for using fraudulent court papers in the act of kidnapping a young girl. You boys would not do well in prison. For now, we want someone to tell us how you all knew to come here to kidnap Amara. If we don't get an answer to that question, then we get busy. By busy, I mean my friends and I will have to find out our answer the hard way. If you guys are not totally stupid, make it easy on yourselves, and give us a name."

I stepped forward. Lynn set them up nicely. Now, I get to see if I can deliver the goods. "As Agent Montoya/Dostiene told you, give us the name, or kneel on the ground with your hands clasped behind your heads. You have ten seconds to comply. If you don't, we take you into custody, and when I say take, I mean you perverted pieces of shit get to experience a little of what you dish out."

The game was up within those seconds as the Monster Squad moved on them in a semicircle with anticipation. The rage, anguish, Islamophobia card disappeared in an instant, leaving only open mouthed staring at us with fear. When the time was up, I moved instantly on the nearest one to me.

"Kornev! Yuri... Kornev!" His backtracking with hands up signaled the ending of this impromptu meeting of the minds.

"Okay... gather your Daddy figure off the ground, and get the hell out of our sight. I know this warning won't help you idiots, but if we see you again, no one else will... ever."

They didn't even mutter the usual clichés. They simply gather Daddy dearest by the arms, dragged him groaning to his feet, and whisked him toward the parking lot. "Damn, Lucas... that was one fine ass bitch slap. I think you may have fractured his cheek bone."

160

"Thank you, John," Lucas said formally, as the others echoed my compliment. "To say I enjoyed that shot immensely would be poorly descriptive. Watching him writhe around on the ground cradling his face was even more satisfying than I dreamed."

He broke character in an instant. "Damn it, Recon... grab the bags and let's go. I'm starving. Man... the thought of a nice pitcher of beer first has me drooling. You know of course you and Tommy are beer free tonight don't you, Dark Lord? You two are up in the event of accelerated action."

"Arrrrgghh..." I danced around in only partially acting pain. Yep. I didn't know about Tommy yet, but the night of confrontation would be tonight, not Sunday. It would be a dry night tonight for the Dark Lord. Tommy was laughing, because he didn't care, He knew everyone but Clint and Lynn would be slurping beer down with gasps and cries of pleasure on my behalf. "I'm fine, Lucas. It's a good thing we have The Lora. Otherwise, we'd be driving the van to the desert tonight chuck full of bodies."

"Gentlemen!" Lora strode into our midst. "Could we load the equipment bags, and get on the way to the pizza place without the references to carnage?

"Yes... Mistress of the excess pounds." I ran for it with equipment bags and everything. I still beat her to the soccer mom van, unlocked, loaded, and was in the driver's seat with the door locked before Lora slammed against the passenger side door. Ah... good times.

161

Chapter 7

New Game Plans

I broke the clown's neck left to watch the outside of Clint and Lynn's house. They decided to attack at two in the morning, and they were damned effective doing it. The house security system went dead before they entered the gate, along with the motion detector lights meant to turn on when anyone opened the front gate. Tommy and I moved in immediately in their footsteps. I knew with Tonto, the chances of anyone entering without warning of any kind was nonexistent, but he was visiting away from home tonight. We hurried along after them. I dropped the guard out of sight in the bushes after snapping a picture of his face, and uploaded it to Denny.

"Nothing seems to go right with you guys," Tommy whispered.

"Tell me about it. We'll shadow them in, but remember, Amara will already be in a safe room. She won't be in any danger no matter what happens out here. Put on the night vision goggles I gave you, and don't jump around drawing the dynamic duo's attention from the real bad guys."

"I won't," Tommy hissed. "Hell, I know better than to pretend I'm more than a backup guy waiting to bag and tag."

I grinned in the darkness under my own night vision goggles. "We're taking prisoners tonight, T. It was smart to have Jafar pick up Dannie and Tonto to stay overnight. It confirmed a fact Clint suspected. They have the house under surveillance, because after getting to know Tonto, there was no way in hell they would have attacked the house with him there. Our lookout had to die because I learned a long time ago never to leave a live enemy at your back, no matter how out of it or secured you think they are."

"What now?"

"We wait," I answered. "I've already texted Lucas and Casey. They'll find the getaway driver. I'm hoping the old man was one of the guys going in with the kidnapping crew. He looked old enough to be one of their fathers. C'mon, we have to be in position for close order backup if things go wrong. I doubt that will happen. With Clint, and Lynn waiting for them, the chances of escape or survival are very low. We'll go in, and help secure the prisoners if there are any."

"I thought you said you had to take prisoners," Tommy reminded me.

"I suggested you and I stake them out at the doorway on the inside, but Cruella vetoed my suggestion. She told me she has a neat plan she wants to try."

"I'm glad I'm not in on that experiment," Tommy replied.

"Amen."

That's when a loud twang sounded inside, followed by muffled thumps, and then silence until the screaming started.

* * *

"Laredo's head will be so swelled if this works we won't be able to speak to him without bowing first," Clint whispered. "It took him three hours to install after you gave him the idea. Some of these guys are not going to survive this."

Lynn patted his knee. "I'm sorry, did you think I cared? We retrieved Kornev's name from their cohort earlier. I know Denny wants a few more for his keychain, but he already gathered a shit load of intel from those first guys we gave him. It's time to have a little fun."

163

"It's a damn good thing he rigged a mechanical trigger," Clint said. "This EMP shit is beginning to piss me off. God knows how many things we'll have to replace. That was a surprise."

"Quiet... here they come. This will be so good." Lynn fingered the trigger connected to a release in the floor which would launch a two inch diameter solid steel bar to a ninety degree angle at waist level with bone breaking force. It worked much like a mousetrap, but didn't move past the ninety degree range.

Their front entrance opened. The men entered inside the narrow foyer silently, making sure to close the door with quiet deliberation. They stayed perfectly still while listening in the darkness for any reaction to their entrance. They moved in harmony, beginning to spread out. As they passed the spot where the entranceway widened, Lynn triggered the release. The bar shot into place with devastating effect. Bodies flew backwards into the foyer walls and entranceway door with such force, it took many moments for the victims to find their voice. When they did, they drowned out Lynn's applause and laughter.

* * *

Our entry into the house required some force as there were a few bodies writhing around behind it. Once inside, Tommy and I scanned the foyer with our mini flashlights. "Damn. This is a mess."

"Don't you ruin this for me, Cheese," Lynn warned, as she and Clint surveyed the damage. "That was lovely. Get to it boys. I'm seven months pregnant. I'm not doing search and seizures. They're all alive too. I want a team in here tomorrow morning undoing everything that damn EMP did."

I found the weapon they used, and handed it to Lynn. "I can tell this much even in the dark. That's a prototype."

Tommy, Clint, and I maneuvered the six thugs together, assessing the damage. The really noisy ones, we plastic tied, and gagged with duct tape. The groaners, we separated after restraints were in place. That done, I took pictures while Tommy aimed his light on each face. Denny could make sure we had the same group Clint sent pictures of before. I received a text during our show and tell. Clint and Lucas had the driver.

* * *

"There he is, Case." Lucas pointed at a Mercedes SUV parked along the roadside one block away from Clint and Lynn's home with the motor running. "Damn, a new GL. These suckers are livin' good."

"Don't even think about confiscating it, Lucas," Casey replied, driving by, and turning at the end of the street while Lucas ran the plate. "You have enough money to buy a fleet of them, you cheap prick. Buy yourself one."

"Why should I? His nice lookin' GL will just go to waste, or the minions will claim it." Lucas saw he wasn't getting any leeway on the confiscation from his partner. "Fine, another community property vehicle for the minions."

"Want to play rock, paper, scissors to see who gets to educate the driver?"

"I got it," Lucas said. "I'm going with an MP5 burst right through the windshield since I can't have the damn thing. When you box him in, it'll be over in a few seconds. I heard Cruella had Laredo rig some kind of trap for the ones entering the house. She's gettin' nasty in all directions lately."

"I heard because she put the minions on alert. I told Gus to call me when they get activated. You be careful with that fruitcake, Lucas. Want me to show you again how I got that cool nickname, Night-shot Casey?"

Lucas scowled in Casey's direction. "You bring up that lucky shot in the dark while backing the Cheeseburger's play on the bad guy one more time, and I'll put an MP5 round right through your head... Night-shot."

Casey enjoyed Lucas's upbraiding, turning off his lights as he approached the Mercedes GL. He angled in at such a way, the SUV could not go forward because of the vehicle ahead, and could not reverse because of Casey's block. Lucas leaped from the passenger seat just before their own GMC Acadia halted. The driver, with Lucas's MP5 pointed through the window at his head, instantly turned the situation into a calm takedown.

"Get the fuck out of the vehicle, and lay face down on the pavement! Do anything else, and I put a burst right through your head, Daddy."

Lucas sped Mohammed Nejem's journey to the pavement considerably when Nejem hesitated after exiting the vehicle with another overhand bitch-slap. The slap pitched Nejem into the GMC, and onto his knees. Lucas knelt on him with one knee in the middle of his back, forcing him flat with an anguished cry of pain.

"This is all I'd imagined, Case," Lucas said as he roughly searched Nejem for weapons and ID. "I hoped Mohammed would be one of the guys, but I never dreamed he'd be stupid enough to actually join in at the ground level."

"Yep," Casey agreed. "He's a genius. Throw him in the back once he's on his feet. We'll introduce him to the facts of life on the path he's chosen later. I hope Amara doesn't screw us over later after she understands Daddy there had to be sanitized."

Lucas pitched the bound and now gagged Nejem through the GMC rear hatch, and closed it. He rejoined Casey in the front with a big smile. A moment later they were speeding toward the Dostiene residence. "It sure was nice of Mohammed to join in the front line work. He gave me another golden opportunity. Smacking that perverted thing calling itself a father was just so nice. We read crap about these 'Honor Killing' assholes in the papers more and

166

more. I wonder what the hell goes on in any American's head considering allowing Sharia Law in to piss all over the United States Constitution. I can tell you one thing, brother: if it happens, I'm not sure what the hell I'll do."

"We're in the right place, with the right group, if it does," Casey replied. "There's no use beating it around in your head now, partner. Thanks to Denny, inadvertently through John, we have a sanctuary… at least for now. I guess we live in the present while we still have a Constitution to defend, and pray for better management."

"May as well pray for world peace," Lucas replied, his fists tightening. "I don't know about you, but I'm gonna' get me a piece before I allow the upper political echelon of stupidity to sell out the nation in a politically correct acid bath."

"I'm with you. Maybe we should start saving to buy an island. If all of us put into the pot, I bet we could. We'd make sure we had an airstrip on it, and a real good deep water pier approach. We could build a fortress on it, impregnable by EMP attacks or the zombie apocalypse for that matter. If things get too hot for us on the mainland, we could take the flag there for preservation."

"I'm in, Case!" Lucas sat up, his hands slamming the dashboard. "That is one exceptional idea! You've given me a goal. I'll let you keep the Night-shot tag."

"Can I keep referring to it without a bullet in the head?"

"Don't push your luck, brother."

Casey chuckled. "Understood."

* * *

I looked up from my triage operation as Casey and Lucas arrived with Amara's Daddy, figuring in my head how many of our Lynn 'mousetrap' victims would survive. I couldn't speak for possible internal organ damage, but it seemed we would have a full group of survivors to hand over to Denny. He loved it so much as to dispatch a full cleanup crew to the scene for extraction. Lucas and Casey seemed particularly buoyant as they dragged Amara's old man into the house of alternate lighting. Clint had his EMP protected satellite uplink with Denny on screen to observe. I did the medical triage, because I had a lot of experience, and I loved the entertainment value of Lynn mingling to terrorize my patients while Clint backed her up with Tommy overseeing.

"Papa did participate, huh?"

"He sure did, John. Lucas applied his second bitch-slap of the day for him," Casey replied. "I see the new intruder alert system worked well. I know you would have had the video if the bastards wouldn't have EMP bombed your peripherals, Crue."

Lynn sighed, making as if she were going to kneel on one intruder's ribcage as he hummed for mercy behind a duct taped mouth. "Damn right, Case! I was set to record anything except a prototype EMP attack."

"All will be well, Lynn," Denny said loudly from on screen. "Although as highly entertaining to watch as I'm sure your intruder alert invention was, we have them all alive to clarify this horrible invasion of castle Dostiene."

"I'm too tired to really show these boys a good time," Lynn admitted. "Send any uncooperative ones to the House of Pain if they are reluctant during questioning, Spawn. I'm going to bed."

"By your command 'Mistress of the Unimaginable'. Rest well," Denny said.

Lynn giggled as she moved toward the stairwell, giving Spawn the wave off.

"I'd like to work Daddy Nejem myself," Lucas said, grabbing the aforementioned father of ill repute's ear, shaking Nejem's head violently.

"I…I will answer anything… anything. Do not let this beast torture me," Mohammed begged.

Denny liked that. "I enjoyed his professing of compliance, Lucas. I don't appreciate his naming of you as a beast. Feel free to give him a sampling of your wares to gain also a modicum of respect when he speaks of you."

The rest of us backed away. It would be a valuable lesson for our survivors to see as well as Nejem. Lucas smilingly cut the bindings on Daddy Nejem, helping him to his feet from where we had seated him. Lucas patted his face. "Like Denny said, you've learned fear, but not respect. I'm going to teach you respect right now. I'll give you a couple of minutes to formulate whatever fight you want to oppose me with. Then… I'm going to beat you like a man. It won't be pretty to watch, but it'll damn well show your cohorts here we ain't the American pussies you all have been led to believe. You have thirty seconds to regroup, you woman beating sissy. For your sake, I'd recommend at least putting your hands up to defend yourself, girlie. Otherwise, I'll just boot kick you unopposed after I bitch-slap you to the floor again."

Nejem was done. He fell on the floor, begging forgiveness. Lucas backed away. It had never been his intention to force the point past complete capitulation and eagerness to surrender intel. "Like Crue said, Denny, if you get any resistance from these turds, send them to the House of Pain. We'll set things right. Speaking of Pain Central, have you had it cleaned out yet?"

"Already taken care of," Denny answered. "This action should quiet things while Yuri melts his communications network trying to find out where Amara's Papa and his helpers went. After a few weeks in Clint and Lynn's protective custody, I believe we'll be able to relocate Amara safely. How about sending her away to college somewhere?"

"Damn, that's actually a great idea, Den," I admitted.

"You act like I never have them," Denny complained. "Actually, it was Maria who suggested it."

"I'll find out if she'd like to do that and where," Clint said. "I'm thinking someplace North would be good, maybe Colorado State."

"She won't be drawing attention to herself, so any crowded college campus would be a good choice," Denny replied. "I like the North better than East. Amara would run into too many Islamists there, sympathetic to destroying the nation they're stealing blind already."

"That reminds me," Lucas said. "Case came up with a hell of an idea. We need to buy an island for when the political hacks import so many jihadists, they install Sharia Law, and we end up killing a whole bunch of people. We need an island sanctuary. We have the money. Hell, when we get this whacko 'Ghost' corralled, I bet he'll beg Crue to let him give us all his ill-gotten gains. I know Yuri will."

I could see Denny's face light up. I know the rest of us liked the idea.

"I'm on it! Damn, that's golden," Denny proclaimed. "It will be an outpost against the darkness. We'll need a deep water port if possible, and a landing strip for Laredo. We'll get it done no matter what happens here. We'll make it into our own personal resort until we need it, or a special place to take one or two rendition type terrorists. My team will be there shortly. I have to start checking out available islands that can work for Casey's idea. Spawn out."

"You sure lit a fire under Spawn, Case," I told him. "I like your idea more than I care to say. I love America, and this area in particular, but I see nothing but death and chaos if we keep doing what it is we're doing. Having an island sanctuary even as a short term safe place would be incredibly good. What made you think of it... the new baby?"

Casey shrugged. "Yep. That's the main reason, but a sanctuary where we don't have to worry about loved ones in a place where we could send the minions in as guards with their families too seems perfect to me. We have hard corps minions. Those guys can be counted on. They're part of our weirdo family now. I hate to say it, but we better save for island batteries to repulse the drones possibly sent our way too. With Denny's inside knowledge, we may be able to smuggle state of the art island protectors against drones into place too."

I absorbed the chorus of 'hell yeahs' with my mind racing at the prospects, but also with the downside where we're leaving people behind. I ain't saying this yet, but that won't happen for me on a personal basis. I'm a Marine. I die for the United States of America... period. The thought of allowing the turd world nations to simply overwhelm us without a fight pissed me off beyond the reality Casey voiced. Lucas slapped me in the side of the head.

"Don't read in facts not in evidence, Recon. We ain't abandoning America. We just need a sanctuary where loved ones and operations can be dealt with while we spearhead the resistance. Don't go deaf on me Probie."

I gripped Lucas's hands slowly after the first lightning fast grasp, making sure in an instant he knew he couldn't break free no matter what. "I know what we're battling, brother. The thought of making everyone we care about safe in a bad situation works for the greater good of turning us loose to do what we do best. I understand that."

Lucas relaxed as I let him go. "Then what's the problem?"

I shrugged because I wasn't sure. "I don't know, but you and Casey are right. We need a sanctuary like that. This latest bunch of revelations with allowing our enemies to filter freely into the country over our borders, while creating known terrorist training grounds protected under a suicidal interpretation of religion, is beginning to remind me of the boy plugging a hole in the damn with his finger. It's been a bad week, Lucas."

"Yeah, it has. Let's wrap this up for the cleaners, and get the hell out of here. I'm like Denny. I want to go home, get some sleep, and start looking at island real estate."

The rest of us enjoyed Lucas's pronouncement – our pack of break-in wolves, not so much. They stared, moaned, groaned, and generally shifted continually in pain. It was another twenty minutes before Denny's cleanup crew arrived. We didn't feel like celebrating, because other than another terrorist headache, all we had was a bad early morning shit-storm. We did what any other bunch of monsters would do, we started perusing island real estate on the satellite uplink. It even made me feel better.

* * *

Lora awaited my arrival at a bit after 4 am. She hugged me at the door with something flimsy on I liked very much. "Mama Mia, you feel good."

"I was worried about you. I had a premonition."

Uh oh. I never dismiss premonitions, especially one who has shared many close moments with me of the female persuasion. "We called in the big guns tonight just as I told you we would with Tommy and me taking point. If you could have seen the way Lynn's invention, put into place by Laredo worked, you wouldn't have worried at all. I only had one to handle at the door. Lucas and Casey grabbed the driver who turned out to be none other than Amara's Dad. They're all on the way to detention of Denny's choosing. We already know Kornev made it happen."

172

Lora clutched onto me hard with her face buried in my chest. "I...I don't know what I'd do without you. Forgive me if I channel my shrew sister Tess once in a while, making your life miserable. I'll do better."

I forced her out at arm's length. "Hey, you're not going soft on me, are you? We're partners. I'm in for the duration. I love you beyond life, and everything in it. God forbid you ever see what happened to the BBC reporter you thought I was sweet on, Natalie Radcliff, and that terrorist henchman that tied you and Al up here in our own home. Cruella and I helped those two into the afterlife in a way you'd probably dump me if you knew the manner in which we found out their involvement in the anthrax scare. It was probably something that would have made Jack the Ripper puke."

Lora blushed. "I made Lynn show it to me. She told me you make videos so it saves some time from having to do the interrogations the hard way. I talked her into showing me the video, but I only made it through about five minutes. Would... you know... rather be with someone like Lynn?"

Now that was funny. "There is no one like Lynn, babe... no one. Even my monster squad talks about Clint and Lynn being together in terms of the cosmic balance shifting. We have our own team – you, me, and Al. I don't expect you to be anyone other than the woman I can't keep my hands off of, and backs any play I make - whether it be UFC brawling, terrorist intervention, or deadly force. You're the whole package to me."

I began stroking all the areas within my reach through the nearly transparent black nightie she wore, while kissing her with due diligence. My soft passionate side descended into darkness without warning. I scooped her into my arms. Seconds later, we were in our bedroom with the door locked. We spent Sunday morning in the pre-dawn hours allowing me to prove I held no grudges concerning Lora's supposed off key day on Saturday. Al made our morning by having been really blitzed from all of her activities the day before, allowing both of us, especially me, to

173

sleep until ten, an awakening time unknown for many moons to the Dark Lord.

"Hey! Are you two still alive in there?"

Our precious Sunday late morning reprieve came to an end for the Dark Lord, called out by an unfriendly referee with a grudge concerning her breakfast not being on the table when she woke with smiley faced pancakes and bacon. I glanced over at Lora, lying in as bedraggled a sexy pose as I've ever seen... out cold. She never stirred at her mini-me's banshee shriek through the door.

"Be right out, Al, but only if you get your butt back in your room and hunt down your inside voice before meeting me again in the kitchen."

A giggle, and then a confirming, "yes, Dark Lord."

I threw on a jeans, tee-shirt, and slippers ensemble to amble out for kitchen duty. My buzz-cut hair looked the same as it always did when I glimpsed it in the bathroom mirror while washing up. The beard stubble would have to wait. In the kitchen, I made tea for both Lora, and her mini-me just the way they liked it. Al joined me with her ten going on thirty smirk. She sat down in her favorite spot where I had placed her tea.

"Well, Smirky, what would you like for breakfast?"

"I would like an omelet like you cook for Mom with tiny pieces of cutup onion, pepper, tomato and jalapeno mixed in it with Colby Jack cheese."

"I thought you hated all that stuff."

Al shrugged. "Mom gave me a bite, and I loved it. Who knew?"

"One omelet coming up. I may as well make one big enough for your Mom too. I'll serve her breakfast in bed this morning."

"Good idea, Dad," Al agreed. "You'll chalk up some brownie points for that play. What time did you get home?"

"After four this morning, but I have the day off from the banana suit today, so it's like a mini-vacation day." Al came over to watch me cut the ingredients into very fine pieces, and stir them into a bowl with five eggs. I added a few tablespoons of milk before putting the concoction on the burner with super low flame. Once I covered it, I made some rye toast. My timing was impeccable because I finished topping and folding over the omelet as the toast finished.

"I think I could do that the next time," Al declared. "Can I try it?"

"Sure, but only with me next to you, okay?"

"Yeah, that would be better. How the heck do you get those pieces of stuff so small with those huge fingers?"

"Practice... practice... practice." I readied Lora's heated tea, toast, and omelet on a tray. "Watch the Dark Lord walk your Mom's tray in to her."

I did the robot Dark Lord all the way into the bedroom with a very entertained Al, trying not to cough up tea and omelet. By then Lora was stirring around, squinting at the clock. "Oh God... is it really almost eleven?"

"Don't worry about it, babe. It's Sunday. Al liked your bite of omelet so much, she ordered one this morning. I made enough for you too with rye toast."

"Yum." Lora sipped her tea, and took a bite of omelet. "Delicious as usual. You have so many talents, Dark Lord. What's your secret?"

"Practice… practice… practice," I chanted once more as I slipped in nearer to Lora. Of course the phone rang. Such is life in monster land. When a monster gets too close to the light, a little darkness must fall. Al knocked on the door I had kicked shut.

"It's Uncle Tommy, Dad."

"That can't be good," Lora said.

"Jinx." I opened the door. Al handed me the portable while waving at her Mom. "Good morning, Mr. Sands. How may I be of assistance?"

"Sorry to break into your Sunday after our earlier mission, DL. Our man Eric Tamil called me. We have a bad guy to retrieve the bond on. It can't wait."

Eric's our paid snitch to let us know if he sees anything we might be interested on a bond retrieval basis. Like hell it can't wait. I'm glancing at Lora's innocent breakfast eating in her flimsy nightie, wondering how I can hint at Al going over to her friends' house somewhere for a couple of hours. I planned to make this morning only a preview. "We'll pick that weed Monday, T. Enjoy your day with the family. I'll be in the Bay tomorrow morning bright and early. I'll go with you to pluck the garden parasite out after training."

"It's Glock Sterner, John."

I straightened the hell up when I heard that name, my fist clenched around the phone in shatter mode, retaining a grip on reality with will power. "You could have led off with the name, Mr. Sands."

"Sorry, but even I need a warm up sentence before I spew that name, brother."

"Give me a second." I looked at the phone in my hand while holding reality images at bay. William 'Glock' Sterner gunned down my neighbors' two kids three houses down from me, and shot at the Sparks' twins, Kara and Jim, as the drive-by vehicle streaked away. Kara remembered seeing five guys in the car, laughing at them as they did it. My neighbor's teenage son wanted the easy life sellin' drugs, and rakin' in the money. He began sampling his wares, and the rest was history when Keith tapped into his sales money, thinking he could hide the skim. He was sixteen, and his sister Monique fourteen, when Glock fixed things for his employer, a piss-ant dealer name Roady.

I heard the shots, and ran out on the lawn, taking in the scene instantly. I grabbed the twins who were wailing away, wide-eyed and terrified, handing them off to their Mom as she ran out of her house. I called into 911 while running to my neighbors' house, sticking my .45 Colt under my shirt at the back. There they lay, pitched from the sidewalk onto their front lawn like broken toys. Their Mom was screaming at me to do something. I met her pounding fists with stoicism learned on the battlefield as I held her tight. There was no use in speaking.

I found them all but Glock. There were no survivors... only landfill. I didn't leave them for the police. I'm sure they were all abused by society, their moms, the system, the man, the whatever. I introduced them to responsibility for their actions with final penance. My bereaved neighbors fled from the unspeakable. I knew I couldn't change anything... except on my street. No one does drive-bys on my turf... ever. Now I had the shooter in sight. There would not be a bond ticket retrieval. There would only be death.

"I hope you don't think Glock will walk into the police station, T. If you do, then it would be best to send the info, and step off. If the info is good, I want Eric to get a grand. That's all I ask if it doesn't work out."

"I'm in to the end, John. I know those two kids' passing ate into your soul."

"Yeah… they did. It's not because of fate or anything else. We can't control shit. We protect our streets or we get used to being on our knees. I kneel to no one, not in defense or offense. Lay it on me, T."

"Eric spotted him outside the Lake Chalet Seafood Bar and Grill. You know the place, high end atmosphere, and the whole works. Eric says he's dealing, but he's dressed to the nine's. He looks like someone poured him out of a 'Gentleman's Quarterly' ad according to our man at the scene. Eric got the hell away and called me. He knows Glock would know him on sight. I don't know what kind of scam he has dealing in a spot like the Lake Chalet, but he damn well will be easy to spot. I know you, DL. I'm getting into my ride right now, and I'll be at your house in ten. I have my celebrity suit on like I'm going to a million dollar ad campaign meeting."

"I'll do the same. See you when I see you, brother." I got off the phone, and did a white trash cleanup with baby wipes. Lora watched me throw on my dark gray suit without comment. She knew something big had come up, and she didn't pretend to be a virgin newbie to what I was heading for. Lora spoke only when I finished, slinking next to me in only the way she could: impressive enough to wipe even 'Glock' out of my head for a moment.

"Hi, sailor… want to have a good time?"

Oh good Lord in heaven did I. "Don't do this you little minx… I'm warning you… don't do this."

Lora turned, fluffing her nightie up past her waist as she bent over looking back at me. "Forty seconds sailor, and you walk out with a smile, baby."

Damn it!

* * *

"You smell like a French whore house, DL, and not the perfumed scent. You went and tapped La Lora in the short time it took me to get over here, didn't you?"

I remained silent. I may have smiled.

Tommy smirked, turning to his driving. "Such is life. We live when we can. Any thoughts about what you want to do when we get there?"

"The good part is Glock hasn't seen either one of us. The bad part is you can be sure the deaths of all his compatriots have been known to him, including my name. Get this straight, T: Glock dies today. If you're not comfortable with that, drop me off when we find him. I'll call Clint to pick me up."

Tommy swerved off to the side of the road, pointing at me with attitude. "Don't even think about replacing me with that white-bread psycho. I called you, didn't I?"

I gulped air while making calming gestures at Tommy. "It's me, brother. I'm a little mangled in the brain. I detest this guy. You know what I did to his compatriots to get a lead on his whereabouts. He was slick, and getting off on it that he had protected his ass so well. Today, the bill comes due in a very bad way. It may be quick, or it may be lengthy, but my buddy Glock will wish he'd never come back to the Bay. He murdered two kids practically in front of my house, and fired a couple of shots at the Sparks twins, laughing as he drove off. Sterner has haunted my head ever since."

Tommy steered onto the road again. "We have a good approach plan, with brief cases, and looking to share a power lunch. I wonder what kind of gimmick he could have going where he can simply stand out there dealing like he's on the corner of

179

Foothill and International at midnight. I'm glad Eric left before he got spotted, but I wish he'd given us a hint about what the hell Glock was up to."

The rich get their upgrades from doctors usually, but with the changes in drug prescription rules, even prescriptions were hard to come by. "If he looks as good as Eric said, it's a perfect place where the clientele are comfortable, and the police presence is at a minimum. Unless the customers complain, he's golden."

"How do you want to play it?"

"We'll be walking toward the restaurant, smiling and talking. We spot him, walk over, and I act like I know him. It doesn't matter then what he does. He's coming with us."

"What are you packing in case he has reinforcements, your . 45?"

"Yep. What about you, T? Did you bring your Glock in honor of the occasion?"

"Of course. I should bring the riot gun, but it's too hard to conceal. He could have a pack of wolves in the background. You can bet he answers prearranged appointments there. If he's dealing the high end product, he won't be there by himself. We're going to spot them first, right?"

I thought that was a given. It goes to show I'm so into this I'm thinking like a teenager in the backseat with his date for the first time. "We have to. Otherwise we could have a few side-shooting idiots turning the place into a blood bath. They won't be real close to him, or it would be useless to deal out of a setting like the Chalet."

"We'll be careful, John. That's a wide street in front. We'll have plenty of room to do some scouting as if we're looking for a parking place. It's the main reason I drove my dark tinted Acura."

"Your tinting's darker than legal. I should report you, but the idea's good."

"Me!" Tommy stared at me for a moment at the stoplight in open mouthed shock. "You have your damn soccer mom van's glass so dark it looks like the Black Hole of Calcutta!"

"I can't let the softball gear get too hot in there," I answered defensively. It proves the old saying, those who live in glass houses shouldn't throw rocks. Damn soccer mom van anyway.

"Awww… isn't that sweet. Get your head back in the game, Dark Lord. Here we go."

The wide, one way Lakeside Drive fronting Lake Chalet Bar and Grill with two full parking lanes on either side, and two driving lanes, made for an easy scouting trip. The traffic on a Sunday afternoon amounted to a few cars going by in staggered form on the two lanes. I spotted Sterner in one pass. He leaned casually against a new black E-class Mercedes convertible working on the touchscreen of a tablet. If I were a cop, I wouldn't have given him a second look. Eric was right. Sterner looked good. Given the distance between the restaurant entrance and the walkway between road and restaurant approach, Sterner positioned himself in a perfect position to be seen from the Lake Merritt side or Lakeside Drive.

"The bastard has a nice setup here," Tommy commented.

"Let's find where his posse is, and then introduce ourselves." As we drove by, a couple walking around Lake Merritt approached Sterner all smiles and waves, admiring the Mercedes while conversing with Sterner. The guy shook hands with Sterner, and the deal was done. Waving happily, the couple walked off to pharmaceutical heaven. Tommy drove slowly while I watched with my mini-range finders. "Damn, that was just as slick as you please. Take it around again, T. I'm sure-"

"Check the fire-escape landing nearest the ground over here on the building by my side across from the Chalet."

I focused on the landing Tommy pointed out, and there they were, three out of place looking thugs with thigh high pants, hoodies, sunglasses, and ball-caps - the usual uniform of the day for 'bangers no matter what anyone says. The only problem is now they're a protected species. They can walk into any place of business, pull off an armed robbery, or shoplift at will, without being questioned or identified on security tapes. After all, their feelings might be hurt. I still remember that jackass councilman wearing a specially made suit with hoodie in solidarity with the poor misunderstood gangbangers. I did wonder if they had the final ladder rigged for a quick drop to the ground. See, no one in their right mind owning an apartment building in Oakland leaves the fire-escape ladder jacked all the way to the ground. The final ladder drops down from the landing nearest the ground. Shit, we'd have to either follow Sterner home, or coax his buddies down to get a piece. If we did that, we'd have to turn Glock into the cops.

Tommy rounded Lakeside to make another approach. He stopped well out of sight. "We're fucked, John. If you want him dead, we'll have to wait and follow. If we get the 'bangers down the ladder, we'll still have three more bodies. I know we could coax them down by hassling Sterner, but then what?"

"I have to hand it to them, T. That is one sweet spot with 'bangers occupying the high ground as lookouts and enforcers. I saw the one in the middle with expensive binoculars scanning the area as if he were bird watching on the Lake surface for rare species. One more time around. I didn't have a chance to see if the 'bangers actually had a way down from the fire-escape landing. It could be if they see anyone approaching who looks like trouble they text a warning to Sterner, and send one of the guys down through the building."

Tommy circled the block. He slowed way down so I could scope the particulars of the fire-escape as we approached. "No ladder to the ground, T, and only one of two apartments with access to the landing. Pull over here, and we'll watch for a while. I have an idea."

"Uh oh." Tommy parked in the parking lane on the right.

"Very funny. We'll wait until one of the 'bangers goes inside, showing us which window he goes through. It's the third floor, middle apartments. I'll go in, knock on the door, zap the one that answers, and go inside to wait for the other two. They'll investigate either whatever noise I make or their missing companion's whereabouts."

"Not bad," Tommy replied. "With those guys restrained, we can approach Sterner without worrying. I like it. What about the 'bangers?"

Oh well. "I don't like their chances." I was already fishing around in my equipment bag, retrieving my hotshot kit, and another couple pieces of clothing. I then took off my suitcoat.

"What's formulating in that Cheese head of yours? Hey... is that a hoodie?"

"Damn right. We're trying to have as little recognition factor as possible. I didn't invent the game." I slipped on my black hoodie, Oakland Raiders ball cap, and sunglasses. "How do I look?"

Tommy chuckled, shaking his head. "Like a big 'banger going into a 7/11 store to score without being recognized on video, except for the pants. Remember to keep your chin tucked. There goes one inside, John. It's the apartment on the left as you look at the building."

"I have my earpiece in, T. Let's make sure our communications work when I get to the door with a second check at the apartment door."

183

"I'll be listenin'. Be careful in there. Don't get your Dark Lord ass hung out to dry. If the entry is too risky, we'll find him later."

I slipped out of the Acura with a wave. The traffic was light, and I crossed while keeping eyes on the fire-escape landing. We were far enough down Lakeside Drive, I didn't get even a curious glance. At the apartment building, I picked a buzzer at random.

"Yeah?" The gruff female voice sounded hungover.

"PG&E (Pacific Gas & Electric). Building circuit check. Sorry to bother you."

"Oh... okay."

The buzzer went off, and I was in. "I'm on my way to the stairs. Can you hear me now?"

"I knew you'd pull that crappy ad saying out of your ass!"

Heh, heh... it was still funny to me anyway. I avoided the elevator, found the stairs, and bounded up them into a position outside the door of our suspected lookout post. "Outside the door, T."

"All three are on the fire-escape landing."

"Good. I'll let you know how it works out with the first one. Keep me informed on the other two."

"Will do."

I rang the apartment buzzer. There was the sound of a window opening and closing. Then I heard the clothing rustle of a hurried penguin walk to the door. I called out before he did the security eye in the door scan. "PG&E! Reported gas leak scan."

The door opened, and I zapped my brother hoodie, grabbed the clothes in a bunch at his neck while kicking the door shut gently. "Heading to the window."

"No movement."

I took out my hotshot kit, sent brother hoodie to the happy hunting ground, and put him off to the side. When you bake cookies, or even pot-roast, you can't rush the process. "Let me know when I get the next 'banger interested," I whispered.

"Of course. Speak of the devil. You have a bite, DL."

The window opened, and a loud 'eyyyyyy... echoed around the room. My deceased hoodie brother must have promised to bring something out on the landing for his brethren. I made no noise, waiting patiently for hoodie number two's decision. I wanted to do him as close as possible to the window, where the last hoodie would hear the application of electricity. He busted in trying to make an impressive pissed off entrance, but it's hard as hell to do it in penguin pants. He made it, and I gave him an Arc of the Covenant long dose, where he most definitely thought he saw the afterlife, by the way his eyeballs nearly launched out of his skull.

"The noise startled the last guy, John. He dropped his binoculars. He's listening by the window."

"Where you assholes at?" The last hoodie stuck his head in to peek, and I plucked him inside by the hood, letting him pitch onto his face with a yelp.

I lit him up, and then gave my last two contestants their final pharmaceutical adjustment. I helped them each into a chair nice and comfy, and stretched the first one on the room couch like he was sleeping. In a way he was. My work was done here. I shed my hoodie disguise when I reached the Acura. Tommy handed me my suitcoat.

"The partiers in the area will not like you wiping out their supply line, DL."

"We haven't snagged the pretty face of the operation yet. Besides, they'll have another crew on site by tomorrow afternoon." I straightened my tie and jacket neatly. I ran a hand through my buzz-cut hair while looking at Tommy questioningly. "How's my hair, T?"

"What hair. Quit preening, and let's collect Sterner. How do you want to do it?"

"We're going to arrest him. I have my FBI credentials with me. We flushed his backup crew, so we may as well do a straight on arrest. We'll collect his car too. Gus and the guys can work it over and add it to our fleet. It'll seem to their supplier that Glock took off with the car, product, and somehow aced his crew."

"Good one," Tommy approved. "Let me do it. I brought my credentials. I've never done it before."

I should have thought about giving Tommy a chance before. "Sure. I'll follow your lead. I'll cinch him into restraints while you read him his rights. We'll put him in his car, and I'll drive Glock baby right to Pain Central. We'll let Crue find out who his area supplier is, and then take him with us on our training voyage in The Lora."

"You're gettin' damn good at this shit," Tommy replied. "There's a parking spot three car lengths back from him. I'll pull in. We'll get out nice and loose, walk over to him, and box him in. He packs a knife, John, so if he reaches, Gronk him."

"My pleasure, Special Agent Sands."

Tommy parked. We didn't run over to Sterner, who remained engrossed in whatever game he was playing on his electronic gizmo. Hell, maybe he diligently worked an Excel spreadsheet for his drug sales for all I know. Tommy and I talked

186

amiably as we came abreast of Sterner. Then we boxed him. He shifted to see over his shoulder for the backup crew that would never come. He pulled the innocent outrage card with passion as Tommy held his FBI credentials where Sterner could see them. I watched his hands. I let him stick his electronic tablet in his coat pocket, but grabbed the wrist when the hand stayed down in the pocket. Tommy grabbed his other free hand.

"That's enough pocket pool Sterner," Tommy said, as Sterner's face began to register pain. "I'm Special Agent Sands. This is Special Agent Harding. You're under arrest for distributing and transporting narcotics."

Sterner listened without a word while Tommy Mirandized him, very smoothly I might add. Tommy must watch a lot of cop shows. When he reached the 'do you understand these rights' Sterner answered.

"Yeah. One word: lawyer."

"Of course, Sir," Tommy agreed.

I turned Sterner toward his car, plastic tied his hands behind his back, followed by his ankles. Tommy patted him down, confiscating his tablet, and a stiletto knife from the same pocket. I opened the passenger door on the beautiful black Mercedes, picked Sterner up and fitted him into the passenger seat. I could tell by the shocked look on his face as I buckled him in extra tightly, he had never been picked up and moved like that. Heh... heh. That's only the beginning Glock old buddy.

"Follow me over, T? I could use a ride home. I think Gus is on call tonight, but I don't want to call anyone else in for a ride."

"Of course. I planned to. It's still early. Do you have plans with Lora and Al?"

I moved the driver's seat all the way back and carefully slid into the Mercedes driver's seat. "I'm hoping only a movie and a beer."

Tommy handed me my equipment bag. "That sounds like heaven to me. I might have one with you before I head home."

I'd love to do the brothers Bud and Beam tonight, but I have an ocean jaunt tomorrow, so it's semi-sobriety for me. "You're on. Let's drop our pal off, and get to it. I'll text Gus right now. He lives only ten minutes away from Pain Central anyway."

By this time in the conversation Glock's face began to show a bit of worry. As I texted Gus and received his confirmation, Glock mumbled something about rights. I ignored him, and started the convertible, easing into the light traffic with Tommy on my tail. I would have to be satisfied with knowing we finally brought this asshole to justice... just not the justice murdering thugs think they'll get. I had no intention of touching him when we arrived at Pain Central. Anything I broke on Crue's toys, and my training day in the ocean tomorrow would be pole poking hell. She went to bed early. That did not bode well for Glock.

"Answer me, Harding! This isn't the way to any precinct. You're heading south out of the city. Where the hell are you taking me? I know you too – John Harding. I heard you were after me. I never did anything to you. What the hell's your problem?"

"You killed two kids in front of my house practically, and fired at two more. I caught everyone that was in the car with you that day. You made a big mistake coming back to Oakland, Glock baby."

"What the fuck is this?! You can't kidnap me off the street, and execute me! Listen... I have money. I can soothe the hurt feelings you think I caused. You can't prove shit! I'll pay the people. They'll be fine with it. Let me go and I'll make you and them rich."

I did enjoy Glock's offer to make me and everyone involved rich. He doesn't know it yet, but I will use all the money Crue makes this ass-wipe cough up in his accounts to do what he wants. It will be his anonymous after death apology for what he did. I'm sure Crue will find out all the names we need to make the fund transfers to the right people. Then I added a caution when dead man stopped talking.

"My advice is to shut up. I will make all the wishes come true except for the setting you free one. I know you've been bred from babyhood to believe nothing you ever do, say, or destroy is your fault. You believe the courts, public opinion, the very stars in the sky are here to help you do whatever sick shit flits through your mind at any time. I'm here to reeducate you on those beliefs, Glock. You will die tomorrow. If you help my assistant find out every single thing we ask you about what you've been involved with, maybe we'll give you a hotshot into hell without pain. If you resist for even a moment, my assistant, the infamous Cruella Deville, will make your passing so legendary that your victims will rise from the grave to applaud."

I glanced over at the well-dressed piece of crap next to me, noting with satisfaction he understood there would be no pleas, no lawyers, and no way out. There would only be death. I could tell after the initial acceptance he wasn't ever seeing a courtroom, goofy Glock became entertainingly adamant.

He smirked. "I will tell you nothing. Kill me now, asshole! I'm not telling you, or your assistant shit, homey!"

I had to pull over at that point. I admit I was laughing so hard I couldn't drive safely. "Thanks... thanks for that... Glock. God... it's good to laugh. For your own sanity, please think of all the helpful things you can tell us tomorrow. My assistant won't be pleased, but if you think of a myriad of facts making you interesting tomorrow, Cruella Deville will accede to my recommendation to simply give you the hotshot into hell. If you don't, buckle up pal, because nothing will save you from your overdue fate."

I stopped again a couple miles from our destination. I uploaded everything from Glock's mobile phone and tablet into my own before smashing them both to bits. Next, I took my Laredo made tracker device indicator. I went over Sterner's vehicle carefully, getting my only hit in the trunk. My scan of Sterner indicated he was clean. In the trunk I found the tracker near a pocket in his drug bag. These guys had it made, or they thought they did. His wares were all ready for transfer into a client's hand in exchange for money. I busted the tracker, did a quick secondary search, and we were on our way. Glock turned real moody when he saw what happened to his toys.

"Damn it, Harding! We can make a deal. These guys I deal for will make you beg for death. You haven't completely screwed them over. Set me free, and I can make this go away."

"I think not. You have your crew. I have mine. Mine makes yours seem like Disney on Ice, when all the cute young ladies and guys ice skate to music while Mickey and Pluto dance around them. What's the use in talking about it anyway? No one will ever see you again anyway. They certainly won't know what happened to you. I'm taking you on a boat trip tomorrow after Cruella Deville gets through convincing you to provide us with every fact we want to know about your misguided life, player. Don't bother bringing a fishing pole though."

That shut Glock up for the rest of our short trip. Gus opened our spacious garage area the moment I beeped. In I went to Gus's admiring inspection of the E-class convertible.

"Like my ride, Mr. Denova?"

"Oh John... this sucker is gorgeous. Tan leather interior... Mama Mia... do we get to keep her for loan outs?"

"Of course," I assured him as I noticed Glock staring at Gus with shock. He recognized our reformed kingpin of crime. "You guys will have to alter it a bit, but yeah, it's going into the vehicle pool."

"Gus Denova? What the fuck... I thought you were dead," Glock blurted out.

Gus let the amiable minion features wash away. In a split second he was the murderous cartel enforcer he carried with him inside. "Did I give you permission to speak, poser?"

Glock hung his head immediately, and Gus glanced at me with a smile. "Shall I entertain him or is he Crue's new toy?"

"He's awfully cute, but you know how Crue feels about anyone playing with her toys before she has a chance to unwrap them," I replied.

Gus nodded in solemn agreement. "Understood. What about movies, John. Can I show him a few Director Deville movie clips?

"If you do that, it'll be like someone yanked the remote out of her hands. You know Glock here will start spewing everything he knows, and everything he ate today. It's best you lock him down for the night. It'll give you time to do a computer mockup of what you'd like to do to help this fine Mercedes join our vehicle line incognito."

"Oh yeah. I'm calling Silvio. His wife and kid are visiting the in-laws down in LA. He said he wanted in on anything exciting."

"Leave the drugs he has in the trunk. I'll let Denny figure out what he wants to do with them. Tommy's outside. I leave Glock in your capable hands. His real name is William."

Gus pumped his fist. "Yes! Get the fuck out of my car, Willie, before I Glock you."

Chapter 8

The Assassin

Cruella arrived early with Clint after I left a text explaining Sterner. Gus brought him out from the holding cell with a neutral look of a jail cell administrator. I suspected Gus, Silvio, and Quays all worshiped Lynn. They knew instinctively if she cared about you, she would kill, maim, or torture anyone for you. Crue put an arm around Gus's shoulders, hugging him to her like a relative she hadn't seen since last Christmas.

"John told me he warned you to stay clear of my toys, Gus. I'm feeling the pinch of pregnancy, my friend. From now on, call me if you feel a warmup with results would work. I've already seen you look down and away. The 'Glock' did something that prompted you to show him a movie, didn't he?"

Gus shrugged. "Yeah… he pitched the slave card we were working for criminals without conscience. Silvio thought it was funny, and said we sure the hell are, and proud of it. When he failed in getting a rise out of us, he spit in Silvio's face. We didn't touch him, but I did show him the game show video of you conducting an interrogation cutting skin off for wrong answers. It's a classic."

Oh boy did Crue enjoy that for a few moments. "I see Glock boy has a surprised look of shock on his face since I arrived. How'd the demonstration go?"

"He threw up faster than Quays did when he saw it," Gus answered. "We made him clean all the cells, including his own, and then locked him down… Mistress of the Unimaginable."

"Well done, my treasured minion." Crue walked over to stroke the trembling face of Sterner. "I see in your eyes you're eager to help us sort this whole ill-conceived plan out so no innocents are harmed. If you impress me, you get a quick and not unpleasant death. Play hardball, and I'm cranky enough to take all seven months of my pregnancy out on you."

"Believe me, you don't want that," Clint added comically on cue, drawing suppressed amusement from everyone but Sterner and Crue. "Oh... sorry, Hon, did I say that out loud?"

After another moment of eyeball daggers, Lynn turned her attention to Sterner again. "My husband is right, in spite of the unfortunate way he said it. You've seen the film. When I get started, there are no take-backs. Please don't waste time bargaining for something you can't have. John already told me what you've done. This isn't the world court of bullshit. It doesn't always happen that assholes like you pay for gunning down kids in the street, but I'm betting those two in front of John's house weren't your first, nor were they your last. Shall Gus start recording, or do you want door number two: hell on earth?"

Glock looked up for the first time with resignation coloring his features. "Start the recording. I do not want to die screaming."

"Good choice," Lynn said. "Gus has a set of questions he'll ask. Pretend I'm asking them. If I have to interrupt the proceedings because my valued minion doesn't like your answer while he checks them on the satellite uplink in front of him, then I get involved in a very bad way. Do you understand? Don't say yes now, and maybe later, because you'll become my next video star. I have a really neat one involving a red hot poker, and your asshole. Oh boy, Willie, you don't want to become the star in that video."

"I...I understand!" The former 'Glock' and now Willie had the shakes already, so I knew he was concentrating.

"Before Gus gets started," Lynn said. "Tell us the bandit's name supplying the drugs for that very cool spot you had on Lake Merritt."

"Yuri Kornev supplies everything. The bastard brought me up from LA, saying no one would remember what I'd done... that I was history with the police."

Oh baby. Lynn and I exchanged avid glances of completion. "You were history with the police, but not to me. I'll sit in for this Lynn. Go rest. You'll need your strength for the ocean training session."

"Thanks, John. I may let Tommy handle the cruise on his own. Clint Jr. is making my life miserable right now. I'm still on board for a reeducation ceremony if my honeybun Willie forgets his place."

Clint put an arm around her shoulders. "I'll make you some tea, and whatever you think sounds good for breakfast, babe. C'mon, and challenge me."

Lynn leaned into her monster mate with affection. "An omelet I think would soothe the Clint Jr. roller coaster ride on my stomach."

"Right this way, my dear. We'll be in the kitchen, brother. Sing out if you need the poker heated."

"Will do," I replied, getting in front of Willie with my chair. "Go ahead, Gus. I'm a great truth detector. To be truthful, Willie, I'm praying you make me doubt you. You didn't see the videos of Director Deville's red hot poker movies. I'd love to see you get the treatment, because I know we're only calling due a small number of your transgressions. Don't worry though. We don't break our word about a quick exit if you answer truthfully. Go on, Gus."

Over the next hour Gus took Willie through every instance in his pathetic life where he caused pain, heartbreak, and death. By the end, I wanted to take him on a tour of the unimaginable myself, but I don't break my word to anyone... ever. When he ran out of things to say, I gave Willie his promised hotshot to hell, but I hung on to his hair at the end as he faded away into eternity with regret. Gus noticed and placed a hand on my wrist.

"Let it go, John. This one won't ever terrorize anyone."

"Yeah… I know. He did something I never expected. He made me hot for getting into the ocean and busting the shit out of some poles. I don't think Crue is into the training this morning though. Tommy will have to do."

"I can fill in for the Mistress of the Unimaginable, John."

I looked him over, and saw he wasn't kidding. Uh oh. Well, the fight's won in the trenches so the path is important. "Are you sure, Gus?"

"Oh yeah."

He was indeed, and we fed Willie to the fishes beyond the Bay. It was a good day. For the first time since it happened, the picture of those two neighbor kids' bloody bodies, didn't pop into my head when I passed their house.

* * *

'Rique met me at the car with Earl following closely behind. They were in plain clothes of course, maintaining the pretense they were doing a security job. "John? How the hell are you feelin', brother?"

Okay, this was new. I looked over at Tommy, but he shrugged, looking like he had no clue what this unexpected meeting was about with our Oakland police brothers. "I'm fine. What the hell has your panties in a bunch, 'Rique? This isn't like you and Earl doing a faceoff before a fight. What's the problem?"

We were parked a long way from the warehouse, so I knew we must have a great crowd on hand. Tommy and I liked the outskirts arrival as in the old days. We were only a block and a half away, but it set me on edge that our security detail would meet us at the car. I could tell Tommy felt the same way.

"Nothin'," 'Rique replied. "We were wondering why so much money is on The Assassin, considering he's never fought a UFC fight. Right now, the odds are even, which seems strange to us. I admit Earl and I threw down some serious money when the odds evened up. We were wondering if there's something we don't know about."

Damn. Even odds on an unknown like Marko, even with his backstreet record, did not compute. I could tell Tommy felt the same way. "I don't know of anything. I don't plan on losing, but anything can happen. Did you two hear I was throwing the fight from someone?"

"No, John," Earl answered. "We thought maybe you were sick, injured, or something."

"This is weird," Tommy agreed. "I figured John to be at least a three to one favorite. We'll ask Alexi when we get in there. Maybe he knows. John's ready though, so I like your chances to make some money, guys."

"Thanks, Tommy," 'Rique said with obvious relief. "C'mon with us. Your crew's already inside. They didn't know what the story with the odds was either. We'll walk you two in."

"Protecting your investment, huh?"

"That's right, brother," Earl said, leading the way with 'Rique on our six.

The line wound out the building, and around the corner. The old warehouse only received a facelift inside. The outer graffiti covered ramshackle appearance kept its flavor of desperation. A loud murmur built as we passed our soon to be audience with the usual catcalls, some supportive, some not. It used to be no one would even recognize me on fight nights. I waved amiably at the big mouths. With the newly remodeled inside, complete with UFC type cage and seating, we didn't have to pay as close attention to the detractors as in the old days when they'd be standing around our blood stained matting. It was still a slight shock to see the remodeled inside. The admissions crew waved us inside while blocking off the line for a moment. A guy dressed in a suit with a beautiful young blonde on his arm, wearing one of those short peek-a-boo dresses, added some humor to our entry.

"They ought to make you buy a ticket, Harding!" His pronouncement drew laughs, even from me.

I stopped to look over at him. I didn't recognize either the suit or his date. "Did I cost you some money or something?"

"Yeah, but tonight, I'm getting it back, loser."

I grinned and nodded before continuing inside. "Damn, Tommy, I'm not getting any respect tonight. Hey Jess, did you hear the news about me losing the fight?"

Jesse Brown patted my shoulder in commiseration as Earl and 'Rique veered off with a wave. "Yeah, brother... even odds. We thought maybe you were in a car wreck on the way over. Another few minutes and you'll be the underdog in the fight."

Alexi Fiialkov waited by the cage with our referee, Jack Korlos. We all shook hands.

"You have heard about the odds, John?"

"We sure did, Alexi. How'd that happen?"

"I have no idea at the moment." Fiialkov had his game face on, so I figured he was in the dark about it too. "I will probably not find out why until after the fight ends, hopefully in our favor."

"That's my plan." Korlos led us into the cage, where Dev and Jafar waited in our part of the Octagon. Tommy checked our

198

equipment bag while I shed my sweat-suit, handing it to Jafar. My hands were taped already, so Dev helped me with my gloves while Jess worked over my face with salve.

"I wish this was a five rounder instead of under the old rules," Tommy said. "We can't do shit for you."

I shrugged. We were getting spoiled anyway with the UFC rules. Tonight we go until one of us can't go on. "I guess I better take care of business then."

The guys left the cage, and I turned to face The Assassin. Marko looked confident, but he didn't look amped or anything. He's a big, bad looking dude, but so am I. In the audience behind him I spotted Denny and my crew sitting apart halfway up the seats. Their main purpose was to be on the lookout for 'The Ghost'. We had no idea what he looked like, but they were busy checking the audience for anyone interesting, sending pictures to Laredo stationed at our central computer station at Pain Central. I erased their part from mine, allowing the monster I chain inside to emerge, the thing I keep hidden from Al and Lora. They had only seen glimpses of him.

I slowly stretched, working my arms and grinning. I remembered the first time I unleashed it. Hiding because I knew my old man would be arriving soon, I could only wait to find out if he was drunk enough to pass out, or ready for another of his son reeducation beat downs. Dad found me, and the beast within. It's possible I beat him to death. I don't know, because I didn't care. I left him where he lay. Once unlocked, the beast never left me fully again. I stared across at Marko. He grinned back at me. We shared the monster inside for a second while Jack went to each of us for final checks, Marko and I remained silent through Jack's inspection with warnings of what would happen if we didn't follow his order to stop. We understand, but sometimes the monster doesn't.

Jack stepped away, shouting his last remark to be heard over the rising crowd noise. "Nod if you're ready!"

We nodded, never taking our eyes off of each other. Marko flew at me with a flurry of jabs and combinations. He had been measured when I took his blow at Tommy, and found wanting, so I didn't give his power much respect. I shot a right hook under his rib cage when I timed his left jabs correctly. Oh baby, did that one make him see the light. I followed the right hook with my deadly behind the knee slap kick that buckled him, but then I found out suddenly why Marko the Assassin charged in to shoot a bunch of jabs at me. My eyes felt like someone had thrown acid into my face. I side kicked the bastard onto his back, and ran over to where my crew were grabbing the cage links in surprise at my movement.

I have no idea what they thought. Their outline beyond the cage was blurring to slurred amber pieces of light as the fire fury in my eyes heated to my pain threshold. When you have a monster inside, it reacts to pain, bad times, threats, and imminent death or dismemberment in ways not imaginable for common folk. The monster screams, tearing the inside of its cage apart, insane with a vengeance beyond hurt. Only a last reasoning plot, and the burning pit of fire behind my eyeballs corralled the beast for a momentary hope of relief until I could kill the son-of-a-bitch.

"My eyes! Throw water in my face hard!"

Tommy never hesitated. He threw his own water in my face. Jafar followed suit, throwing his bottled water into my eyes. By then, Dev and Jesse had confiscated water bottles from a few of the patrons, yanking them out of their hands, and returning to dose me in the face through the cage links. The pain eased slightly, but I knew I didn't have much time.

"Duck, John!" Tommy's order was followed instantly with compliance.

A right hand smash sailed over my head to hit into the chain links. I hit the mat, rolled to the right and onto my feet, blinking water, and whatever the hell shit it was on Marko's gloves with passion. I resisted the urge to blot at them with my own hands,

200

knowing in spite of the pain, any agitation of the chemical bath pounded into the area around my eyes would be multiplied. I let out the monster with a roar, turning to hit what was close, another right under the ribcage that shut off further attack for a moment.

I heard Marko suck wind. I pounded the blur in front of my blinking eyes until Marko wisely got on his bicycle. Yeah, my corner was giving Jack hell about Marko's gloves, but there wasn't anything he could do about it. Provable fouls screw the betting into the tank, but the match has to end first with me letting Jack know I couldn't go on. That ain't happenin' ever. The crowd screamed their approval. They didn't know what was happening, but they knew I had the short end of the stick. The background noise made it impossible to depend on my ears.

The Bulgarian Assassin came in for more jabs to give my eyes another dose. I ducked into his midsection, took an elbow to the top of my head I could tell split the scalp. Hell, I couldn't see anyway, so the blood wouldn't be a problem. I used my momentum, picked him up, and slammed him into the cage. We hit so hard because of my misjudgment we both bounced off, separating slightly as we hit down. I recovered first, shifting into a full mount position on the mat over Marko, raining hell down on him with hammer fists until the damn stuff burning my eyes forced me to stagger where the guys were prepared. They screamed at me so I could follow the sound.

"Open your eyes, John," Tommy ordered, as I clunked into the cage with my forehead.

Pure will power helped me get them open as I received streams directly in the eyes from squirt bottles they rounded up for me. We only had seconds. It turned out, Marko could recover fast too.

"Drop John!"

201

I instantly did as Jess warned. Marko's foot hit into the cage where my head would have been. I rolled left, but Marko kept balance after the kick, and dropped with an elbow smash to my face. Only slightly off target, it tore skin in front of my ear, and gave me a terrific star vista with exploding suns. He didn't pull the arm back quickly enough though. I nearly ended the fight with an arm-lock, but missed it by a split second. Marko leaped away, scuttling to his feet before I could try a mount again. Rage is such a weak word to describe my pain filled mind. I decided to trade some agony with a different tactic.

Marko approached with care, watching my blinking eyes, as I bobbed and weaved more than I'd ever done in a fight. I lanced out with my own jabs. When I missed my target, I heard him grunt approvingly. He wouldn't be so happy if my tactic worked. Marko peppered my face with jabs and crosses, which I absorbed in order to entice a full power hook from him. When his right hand reached into my face to measure me while spreading its poison cheer, I knew the left hook was on its way. The moment it began to mash into my head, I spun as if blindly knife-handing the pole while in the water. The spinning slash I launched caught Marko completely off balance as he finished the hook. My knife-hand strike missed the knee I intended for my target, but it hit Marko's thigh so hard he screamed in pain while falling to the mat, gripping his thigh. Before the poison forced me to close my eyes on the blur, I saw him using rolling and kicking to get against the cage for support. By then my eyeballs were burning through the back of my pounding head while the crowd roar rattled the old warehouse sheet metal.

My guys directed me with sound again, as I moved drunkenly toward them. Forehead kissed cage with squirting relief bombarding my face while I willed my eyes open to a narrow squint. The water could only dilute the pain, but it would help me finish that asshole Marko off. If I didn't have a mouthpiece in, I would have already ground the tops of my teeth into dust.

"It may be over, Hard Case," Dev shouted approvingly. "Jack's asking Marko if he can go on."

"Fuck that! I'll kill that cocksucker!" I blinked, squinting again at my opponent's position. He regained his feet, using the cage. His hands worked his injured thigh with hard strokes, kneading at the strike area worriedly.

"We need to get your eyes fixed, dummy!" Tommy wasted his time talking at the monster. "We don't know what the hell he put on his gloves! Let him quit, and you can get him later!"

I kept my monster mouth shut, gritting my teeth while ordering my eyes open further with small success for another dousing. I couldn't do shit if Marko quit. I wouldn't be able to avoid the sapping I'd get from Jack. If Marko recovered enough to try me again, then game on. I'd have to take a real bad eye attack this time to end The Assassin for all time. The monster seethed inside, rattling my brain with blood rage.

"Damn it!" Tommy tipped me off Marko decided to keep hoping he could blind me to the point I would be ripe for plucking.

"He's coming, John," Jess said, as the amped crowd heralded the decision with wall to wall noise.

"But slowly," Dev added, giving Jafar time to keep double bottle squirting my face. "Your eyes are so swollen, can you even see to go on?"

"Watch me." The monster turned to plod toward Marko, all semblance of anything but a killing strike gone from the equation.

As Dev had warned, the reduced opening I was capable of limited anything but an amber blur with black gloves approaching with a limp. I had no peripheral vision. While I could see the blur, I launched a sidekick on target enough even partially blocked to jettison Marko to his back. I couldn't chance following it, because I very likely would miss my target completely. The crowd loved it though by the noise. Marko… not so much. I hoped he was saying his prayers.

He regained his feet easier than before, having blocked my side-kick partially. Marko wisely circled me, jutting quick left and right smacks into my head. I kept my eyes tightly shut, trying to keep open the option to see something when I needed to. Confidence caused a speeding crescendo of blows. I felt the blood dancing off me like rain. I weaved in nonstop side to side motion, faking leg strikes to keep Marko wary. My timing would have to be spot on. I opened my eyes to the tiny slits permitted by the swollen sockets as he began grinding his left fist into my face. Measuring done, he threw the right. I darted right while leaping. I came down with all the power I could muster in a knife-hand strike to his neck. I heard the crack like a lightning strike on a dead tree branch.

In moments, there was dead silence. I landed on my feet, bobbing and weaving as if expecting another attack. I knew The Assassin would not be attacking anyone unless the zombie apocalypse started in the next few seconds, and Marko did it with his head rolling around loosely on his shoulders.

"Can you see, kid?"

"Not a thing, Jack," I answered truthfully, as cursing screams echoed at me from Marko's people.

"Fights over," Jack said, raising my hand to a deafening cascade of sound.

"We're here next to you, Hard Case," Dev informed me. "Don't swing. Anything you feel will be friendly. Jess is standing between you and Marko's crew."

I nodded, feeling the blessed ice pack pressed against my eyes. Someone peeled off my gloves while the ice pack was held in place, and a peroxide towel by the smell of it cleaned my wounds gently. A stool pressed into the backs of my legs.

"Sit down, dummy, and tilt your head into Dev's hands. Keep bathing the cuts, Jafar." Tommy was not pleased. I did as told. Dev removed the ice pack while Tommy I think pried open each eye, and a solution of something hell-a-soothing poured into my eyes. I could hear the peroxide making my bloody wounds bubble and the familiar warming sensation the wet application causes.

"You murdering bastard!" I recognized Kornev's voice. "You forfeited the fight with that illegal strike, you son-of-a-bitch! Let me go... you-"

I heard Dev laugh before Jack's angry voice. "It's okay, Jess. Let the asshole go. I'll sap him if he comes any closer."

Gagging sounds in Kornev's voice range sounded as he gasped for breath from what I assumed was Jess's choke hold.

"Listen closely, Mr. Kornev," Jack ordered. "Do you see my security guys with gloves on guarding the scene for the detectives to arrive? They will be paying strict attention to no one touching your fighter's gloves. They're with the Oakland Police Department. Hristov's gloves will go to their lab to confirm whatever the hell it was you put on them. The coroner has been called I'm sure. My other security team confiscated all of your corner equipment. John couldn't even see with the shit you poisoned him with. You fucked with the wrong guy, asshole! Now get the hell away, and wait outside the cage, or I'll ask Jess here to escort you. Believe me, you don't want that."

I smirked a little because although Jack Korlos is scary, and proficient as hell with his fists or a sap, Jesse Brown when motivated will turn your head into mush if he connects with his right or left hand bombs. Kornev stormed out of the cage with his tail between his legs I'd bet, because even with the eye solution and ice, I had a feeling this night would be spent in the emergency room. I kept away from the thought of blindness. If it was true, I did for the bastard that did it to me. My crew would take care of

Kornev. We would have anyway, but Cruella Deville kind of likes me. If he blinded me, I knew when the guys collected him, he would learn what happens when you fuck with us from Crue. If I'm blind, I'll find a way to check out. I know Clint, Casey, or Lucas would help. Lora and Al would be well taken care of. I lay back against the chair with the ice pack on, thinking maybe bloody me up with some cuts, give me a razor sharp bayonet, and let me swim in the Bay. The more I thought about it, the more comfortable I got. I'd go out with my boots on. Hell... we could party before it got done.

"What the fuck you smilin' at, cracker?" Tommy broke my mild reverie with attitude. "I know what the hell you're thinkin'. If the shithead blinded you, ain't no one in your crew goin' to help you to the other side. Lora would declare war."

"Shut the fuck up, Tommy." Dev knew. "The man can pick his pleasure. I already know he's thinkin' his mates from CIA. They won't pussy out like you."

"That's right, Tommy," Jess's voice joined in. "The decision ain't yours to make, partner. Quit mind readin', and let's get John the hell out of here to the hospital. It's not like Earl and 'Rique won't vouch for it."

"Take me to Earl and 'Rique," I told them, listening also to the crowd undercurrent playing in the background. "Let me talk to them. Hey, Dev... did all the politicos scurry away like rats on fire from a burning ship?"

I could tell Dev and the guys were scanning the crowd. Jafar beat Dev to the answer.

"It is just so, John. I see no one in Oakland political circles. All their front row seats are vacant."

"Yeah, kid, they probably streaked for the door two seconds after that honey of a strike I launched on poor old Marko, God rest

206

his soul in hell, the dirty, no good, rotten prick. Steer me next to him so I can kick his corpse."

That statement received the enjoyment I'd hoped for. I held onto the ice pack, and stood. The eye solution and ice pack eased the pain considerably.

"C'mon, dummy," Tommy said, grabbing my arm. "Make your case so we can get some medical attention. Earl?"

"Yeah, Tommy?"

I could tell Earl was near me on the right. "Can I go get my eyes looked at? I'd like a head-start on anything that would prevent me from ending up blind."

"No problem," Earl stated with emphasis. "Are you headin' to Highland?"

"That's where I'm going, brother. All our cell-phones are on. If anyone gives you shit, give them my whereabouts and number. I'll handle every call personally."

"Don't worry about it, brother," Earl said, gripping my shoulder. "I hope there isn't any permanent damage. That was sick."

"I'm fuckin' glad you killed that bastard, John," 'Rique stated. "We'll put this whole damn thing in the light it should be put in."

"Thanks guys," I said, as I was led away. "Hey... do you see my monster squad?"

"They're spread out, none of them near the cage," Tommy replied.

"That's a good sign." I sighed with satisfaction. "Did Laredo text you, kid?"

"I will look as you exit. Go to the hospital, John. I will follow every aspect of this case. I will update info for Tommy every few minutes after we reach the hospital until Denny or someone arrives.

With a hand on Tommy's shoulder, I cleared the cage entrance. There were regular media there foaming at the mouth to ask questions there were no answers for. Even they could see my eye dilemma, especially if they had observed the fight. No one knows about what they actually see. They report whatever the hell they think gives them street cred with the down trodden, including thugs, murderers, rapists, and psychopaths. The truth died a hard death decades ago with the fifth estate. The only thing left of those times when they reported what actually happened without bias are some hula hoops and Barbie dolls. By the questions being shouted at me, I couldn't tell if these people had even seen the fight. I stopped for a moment to have some fun, because one idiot asked if the fight was rigged. My eyes had stopped trying to explode out of my skull, and I couldn't resist.

I dropped the ice pack to my side for a moment, drinking in the gasps of shock. I knew the area around the eyes extending to my hairline, and down to my mouth had to be swollen hideously. The swelling reached my mouth because words had to be thought about while speaking. "Did someone ask if we'd rigged the fight so my opponent died, and I was blinded? Write his name down, Tommy. I want to know it in case I can see again. We'll make him the next rigged death."

There were some chuckles before he followed it with another gem. "Why didn't you quit, Harding? You could have protested the fight later. Were you just looking for an excuse to get your third killing?"

Then it hit me. I knew his voice. This was the same reporter from the 'Rattler' fight asking if I'd broken the Rattler's jaw after the fight ended on purpose, and tying it to the two deaths in my matches before.

208

"Are you there, Jess?"

"I'm here, John. I'm readin' minds too tonight. You want to know if this is the same jackass media asshole from the Rattler fights, right? It sure is."

Shit! This incident would be hard enough to play down without me shooting my mouth off. "I'm very sorry The Assassin died tonight. He wouldn't have if he hadn't blinded me. Frankly, he died in the cage resulting from his own actions. I don't quit in the cage for anyone. He could have killed me just as easily. I ain't allowing you assholes to portray The Assassin as a victim. I used the knife-hand strike to cripple his left upper arm pressure point, but by then my eyes were swollen shut, and struck high off target."

That lie sounded sincere to my ears anyway. I detected the flashes going off, and I knew the video clips were getting an excellent illustration of how bad my face looked along with the still pictures. I had to do this, or Denny would have a hell of a time in spite of testimony from Earl and 'Rique in my favor to keep me from being charged. The silence meant I'd made my point, so I put the ice pack against my eyes again.

"I think you wanted him dead, Harding," the same reporter shouted out as we began to move again. "There is no such thing as an accident with you in the cage. You're a monster. You should be banned from any fighting, especially the UFC!"

It annoyed me how close to the truth he was; but I'd put on the only show I could, and by the way Tommy kept tugging on me, I figured he thought the same way. Hell, I am a monster. "I can't fix this reality for you any way you would like it, shithead. Marko Hristov had an agenda coming into the cage – to cripple me with some kind of poison on his gloves, which was damned effective. Unfortunately for him, his plan backfired. Goodnight. I have to go try and save my sight."

209

"You should be charged with murder, Harding!" The reporter called out as we continued. By the less than pleased grumbling undercurrent amongst the people there, the sight of my face at close quarters must have made an impression. Tommy threw my windbreaker over my shoulders.

"If you don't kill that ass-wipe, I'm going to do him myself," Jess said as I could tell we'd cleared the building by the cool air hitting me, blowing away the smell of desperation.

"It wouldn't be so bad if he wasn't right," I admitted, taking in deep breaths of the night air skimming in off the Bay."

"He's stalking you," Dev added. "There's not much doubt about that. We should have had his name on the list after the first Rattler fight."

"Time for that later. I know Tommy's still here. I can smell that aftershave shit he bathes in, Eau De Toilette or something. Where's Jafar?"

The guys were enjoying my line about Tommy's aftershave too much for Tommy to reply for a moment. "I sent Achmed the Terrorist ahead for the car. Denny texted me. He said they'd meet us at the hospital. They had a few likely suspects to tail away from the warehouse, and they all left when the Oakland politicos scrammed. Crue texted me personally to say you get a day off from training for the neck strike. Alexi is busily running down items of interest from your win, and to have his own crew checking any indication of the 'Ghost' guy."

Gee thanks, Crue, but my training days are over for a while. People were streaming by us, oddly quiet in their passing. That happens when you're with Dev, Tommy, and Jess. I let the ice pack drop for a moment, and squinted open my eyes a bit through my troglodyte swelled folds of skin. I scanned around with a smile. "Hey… I can see you guys."

Jess laughed, peering into my face. "I don't know how. I can't even see your eyes."

"Dev, you still have that stuff you rinsed my eyes out with?"

"Yeah, John. The doc gave me a whole bottle of it, because he had to go pretend he could wake the dead. Here."

Dev pressed a bottle into my hand as Jafar drove alongside. "Thanks. I'll ride in the back, Tommy, and douse my eyes again on the way. It must be promising I can see a little though."

"You're right, dummy, but you still should have cut out the moment we knew what they did to you. You know we'll have to hunt for next of kin, right?"

"I know. We were so focused on Kornev's life, we discounted Marko." I slipped into the back, lying across the seat. "I'm going to be okay. You and Jess head for home, Dev. I'll call you later."

"Okay, brother. I want to hear from you tonight though," Dev said.

"What he said, John," Jess added. "If the A's or Giants play a spring training game tomorrow, let's watch it at your house with refreshments... that is if you can see the TV. Tommy? You know all those old TV shows. Who was that white cracker detective who worked cases blind?"

Tommy chuckled. "Ah... Longstreet. It was Longstreet."

"If things don't work out, Longstreet, you could work cases blind," Jess was revving up. "Oh hell yeah! I can see it now. You could get a parrot to sit on your shoulder. It could be trained to talk, and say 'Cracker' every couple seconds."

They were still enjoying that one a few minutes later when I had to smack Achmed the Terrorist in the back of the head to get him driving toward Highland Hospital. I leaned back to bathe my eyes. I couldn't tell what the stuff was, but man it sure made my eyes feel better. The downer no matter what would be Lora and Al appearing at the hospital before I could get through the emergency room red tape. I figured hours before I actually made it to an examining room on a Friday night in Oak-Town. I smiled during the trip thinking about the blind detective moniker and Jess's parrot.

Lucas met us at the Highland Hospital Emergency Room entrance. I had my eyes covered with icepack in hand. Tommy, Jess, and Dev bracketed me while Achmed the Terrorist parked the car. I knew this because I heard Lucas's one word greeting, along with everyone within a block of the building.

"Recon!"

I could picture him pumping his fist. At least he didn't call me a pussy for not somehow knowing in advance what Marko would do. "Hey, Lucas... how's things going in Denny-land?"

"Still in limbo, John. The troops are in the field, including Denny. He knew you wouldn't want to get blinded for nothing. We have it narrowed to two possibilities. Denny and Casey are on one, and Clint and Crue are on the other. I have the duty here in case Marko's surviving family or Kornev's gang decides to pay their respects. You should have seen Crue in the stands. She was funnier than hell. When someone told her to shut up and sit down, Clint nearly had to carry her out in spite of the assignment. After you gave Marko last rites, Crue celebrated, very weirdly for a pregnant woman heading for month number eight I might add. The prick who told her to shut up tried to throw something at her, but Clint had been watching him, and chucked a quarter at him. It hit dead center in his forehead. The guy collapsed like he was shot. Needless to say, we had a good time, but had to play catchup on the guys we suspected of being the 'Ghost'. It turned out Crue had the inside track on her bet of a woman being 'The Ghost'. She's one of the two suspects we're tracking."

"Damn, Lucas, that's all good stuff."

"C'mon, Longstreet," Tommy ordered. "We need to get the hell inside. Jafar's here now. We have to start waiting in line for some service. You know how many damn emergencies happen at Highland on a Friday night."

"Longstreet?" I could hear the question in Lucas's voice. "Never mind... I'll get that story later. I filled out all the cards on John. They have all the info needed for the emergency room gateway to service. The staff know what to expect. I turned over a sample of what they doused Marko's gloves with. The lab will already be working on it, because I had a private chat with the lab attendant who was less than enthused about anything he'd actually have to work on. After I shoved my Homeland Security ID in his face, the slacker got to work. He said he may have some preliminary findings in another hour."

"Thanks, Lucas. I can see a little bit, thanks to the solution Alexi's Doc gave Devon before we left. How do I look?" I dropped the icepack down again. I expected some laughs from my mentor, Lucas. I got silence instead. I could see his craggy facial features scrunching in head shaking disapproval.

"Damn... I'm glad I didn't eat anything lately, Recon. Otherwise, I'd barf it up on your shoes. You look like a fruitcake repackaged for too many years on the Christmas gift circuit."

I waited patiently for the he-haws to die down. "Please tell me Lora and Al haven't arrived yet, brother."

"Nope, but Lora's been burning the text line into Denny's phone trying to get details, because we've been keeping mum about the fight. Denny didn't figure you would appreciate us detailing the match with that low down piece of shit Marko for Lora's appraisal."

I sighed in relief, as Tommy yanked me inside. "Thanks, brother. I'm hoping they can do something about the swelling before Denny caves in on the details."

"Not to worry," Lucas said, grabbing my other arm as a guide. "He shut his phone off. He sent his better half over to your place with the facts, and a plea to stay where she is until we get you looked at. Maria can smooth things over while we see if the doctors can counteract that hideous face Marko pounded into place."

Yep, we chuckled over that pronouncement. "Denny played it just right. I owe him. Maria's a great choice for go between."

We all sat together in the emergency room. I'm sure I received a lot of attention from my fellow would be patients in Highland's Tower of Babel emergency room area. On any given Friday night, Highland accounted for a plethora of illegal aliens, gangbangers, and domestic violence recipients. It made for a rather long wait to be seen by anyone with a white coat for people who actually paid taxes, and were citizens of the United States. I'm a great waiter though. In the Marine Corps, I learned nothing good comes to those who do not wait well. Sitting with a quiet Lucas next to me, while Tommy and Jafar flitted around or complained in mumbling tones illustrated my point. I remember the line from the movie 'A League of Their Own' Lora's sister Tess made me watch against my will. An actor in it, Tom Hanks, declared when one of his female hardball players had an emotional moment, 'there's no crying in baseball'. In the Corps, there's no crying, complaining, or take-backs, especially in Recon. We live by the feud, and keep our shit internal for disbursement later. I already tagged the main participant, so I waited with stoic acceptance. I had quiet plans for everyone else involved. We had a mission if I could see.

A short hour later Tommy led me into a curtained off cubical to be seen by someone. A nurse's aide took my vitals in between. I had kept the fresh icepack on my eyes Lucas had coerced from an attendant in the emergency room, so I figured the

214

swelling would at least be kept at bay. The female doctor took away my pack, and examined me while introducing herself.

"We have the preliminary results from the lab on what you were exposed to, Mr. Harding. It is thankfully non-lethal, or permanently debilitating. I believe you were allergic to some ingredient in what appears to be a pepper spray type formula used in actual defensive sprays, although diluted. I will give you a shot that should negate the effects without having to do a more involved testing phase."

"Thanks, Doctor Kaye, I really appreciate that. I can see now out of the swollen ugly slits. How fast do you think the shot will work against the swelling?"

"Nearly immediately. Please call me Jan," she said while administering the shot. "I've seen your UFC fights, Mr. Harding. I confess to being a fan of that brutal sport. Why in the world would you fight backstreet warehouse brawls with the possibility of maiming or even death?"

I grasped her hand. "Probably stupidity in your reality, Doc. I promise to keep out of your emergency room as much as my reality allows me."

She laughed. I took that to be a good sign. Doctor Kay was a short, plump, and very likable person on initial contact, from my admittedly small scope of vision. "Yes… please take better care of yourself, Mr. Harding."

"Can't do that, Doc, but your compassion is much appreciated. Is it okay to leave?"

"I think so, but if you're experiencing pain, I could write you a prescription for painkillers. I'd imagine they would be a good thing."

"No thanks. Pain is my friend. Thanks for seeing me so quickly."

"No problem. I won a lot of money on tonight's fight, palooka."

Now that was funny. "Good to know, Doc. See ya' later, much later, I hope."

"Ditto," Doctor Kaye answered.

Tommy handed me my sweats while Doc Kaye left. I hurriedly put them on, thinking I had mere moments before my female entourage would bust in ripping me a new one. None of that happened, and I left the curtained partition dressed for a quick exit. As we walked where people were milling around and waiting, I covered my features once more with the ice pack while Tommy guided me.

"Don't want to hear people barfing, and kids screaming, huh dummy?"

"That's just hurtful, Tommy."

"Heh... heh."

Chapter 9

Little Things

I caught hell the night before when I came home. No, it didn't matter I couldn't see a cell-phone let alone call from one. You know how it goes. Yes Dear, I knew I could have clued in one of my companions to call. No Dear, I didn't want to worry you until I found out all the details. Yes Dear, I realize I look hideous… thank you for noticing. No Dear, I wouldn't think of touching you in the mood you're in. Yes Dear, I thought of Al's feelings, which was exactly the reason I didn't want to face either of you until I came home with the facts. Lora greeted me, out for blood, even while wincing at my Elephant Man Face, which was a lot better looking than thirty minutes before. Maria had done an excellent job of containing Lora, but couldn't completely defuse my wife's left out feeling. I tried to explain I wasn't on my death bed, so no blood, no foul, right? Fail!

Here I was, making a bunch of finger foods for my afternoon spring training baseball game between the A's and the Giants, marveling at modern medicine while steering clear of my fuming wife. Al forgave me in seconds, having slept through it anyway, especially when she found me sleeping on the couch. Hey… it happens to the best of us. Al put dip into bowls, and fixed the treats onto separate serving plates for me. It would be a full house for the game including the minions.

"I think your face looks better than when I saw it this morning, Dad." This was the first time Al broached the subject of my looks or the fight. She had sampled the mood her Mom was in, and decided time needed to pass before any discussion. Lora left for a friend's house without a goodbye, so the two of us decided retreat had indeed been the best part of valor in this case.

"Thanks, Al. I can see a lot better."

"I saw the news." She glanced at me, while biting her lip to keep from saying more.

"I can't hide it, kid. It is what it is as Lynn would say. They're ruling it accidental because of the on scene testimony from Earl and 'Rique. I'm glad they were working security. Marko was the first guy Jack Korlos ever lost in the cage as a referee. I feel bad about that. He's a good man. I know his testimony helped the ruling too."

"I'm glad the softball game got cancelled because of the rain. Otherwise, you would have scared the team into a forfeit."

I grinned out the kitchen window at the wonderful spring rain. Although whatever the injection Doc Kaye gave me worked wonders overnight, I still had the red eye express going along with some swelling. Otherwise, I felt damn good. "Yep. The girls would have been shunning me today, if their parents allow them to play with me as a coach. I may need Lynn to take over, while I work with you away from practice like we've been doing anyway."

"If they make you quit, I'm quitting too. So will Lynn."

Uh oh. I hadn't figured on a protest. "C'mon Al. You're the team's star. We don't quit. We may get canned, but we don't quit. They can't ban me from watching your games or coaching you. Bottom line... we don't quit... ever."

"Okay. I see your point, but I don't like it. Without you there, Lynn's going to kill someone though."

"Nope. Clint will be there," I refuted her logical assumption. "Lynn would be more careful of her temper. Do you think we have enough snacks?"

Al shook her head. "Not if Uncle Jess is coming."

218

"I'm ordering two extra large pizzas too."

"Better make it three, Dad."

"Right you are," I admitted.

"Mom's really pissed," Al stated, mentioning the elephant in the room for the first time. "She put you on the couch right from the hospital. That's cold."

I chuckled at that apt assessment. "Can we keep the Lora retribution between us? Otherwise, Lynn will lead the guys in barbequing me this afternoon."

Al grinned, glancing sideways with that annoying pixie look she gets from her Mom. "What's in it for me?"

"Why you little... okay fine... no Beeper jokes for two weeks." I had been rocking the house with Justin Bieber jokes lately, getting quickly onto Al's last nerve. My imitation of his screeching voice tones entertained the troops to no end, but sent Al into fits of angst.

"Make it three."

"Deal."

* * *

Al and I settled in our guests with trays set all around my large home theater room. A common thread we monsters shared in the entertainment arena is baseball, including Lynn, and her acolyte Dannie. Her enthusiasm for the game turned into invective quite easily when one of her least favorite players blew an at bat with runners on, or committed an error on the field. My ability to see, and the prior night's deadly ending drew only mild comments. It was simply another phase of the mission we were on that ended with complications. I left them to answer the door. I only had one man not here: Denny. Having no prisoners in custody allowed

Lynn's minions to all attend. This was to be a business meeting too with both Laredo and Jafar keeping their satellite laptops at hand. We knew now who the 'Ghost' was.

Surprisingly, Maria came with Denny. She was showing in her seventh month even more than Lynn on her way to becoming a Mom. Denny led her in with solemn demeanor I took to mean trouble with our latest step forward. Maria hugged me.

"I'm sorry, John. I tried smoothing over your incommunicado hospital trip with Lora. I brought Samira with me, hoping a double team effort would suffice. She listened, but was unimpressed. I enticed her to have a couple glasses of wine with me. It didn't help. I could see the polite veneer ready to peel away when you came home."

"It's not your fault. It'll be fine. She's visiting a friend today, and Al's entertaining in the viewing room if you'd like to go ahead. I see in Denny's face we need to talk. Please don't share any Lora acrimony with the crowd or we'll be playing pin the tail on the donkey all afternoon with me as the donkey."

Maria laughed. "Of course, John. I will say nothing. Hopefully, Samira did not rat you out to Lynn already. They did talk this morning, because Lynn called her while she was talking to me."

Damn it! "I did not know that. Thank you. He-haw... he-haw."

My donkey acceptance was even a hit with Denny. Maria scooted onward to our entertainment room. I guided Denny toward the kitchen where I served him a double Beam and had one myself. I toasted him. "Semper Fi."

"Semper Fi, brother," Denny clicked his glass with mine. "Lynn saw a note get passed to Kornev near the end of that bloody dangerous fight you were in last night. She kept eyes on who the courier returned to. Laredo ran the picture through every database at our disposal. He then hacked into Russia's Federal Security Service files. Laredo created a worm to open anything, disguised as coming from a Chinese source. The picture had the Phoebe Christova name attached to it. She started in the Bulgarian Secret Police. With her name, Laredo got the hell out, and began searching for clues. She kept her real name, because she never thought the Russians had it, or a file. Christova has homes in Paris, London, Amsterdam, and a villa on the French Riviera. No other name we checked last night had so many arrows pointing to it. I believe without doubt Christova is the 'Ghost'."

I sipped the Beam brother, wondering why Denny was suddenly staring off into eternity in silence. "You left me hanging. Any chance of my hearing what your reservations about her are?"

"Sorry." Denny snapped out of his reverie. "I was ordered not to tell you this, so I'm telling you. Interpol got close to her on a deal in the Nigerian port of Lagos. She employed Ricin gas on the crew and the converging Interpol team. Half of the crew, and three quarters of the Interpol agents died from effects of the gas. Christova had been tipped off. She has spies everywhere. Because it took place in Nigeria, the chemical weapons attack was squashed."

"So what's stopping us from taking her out from long distance?"

Denny paused, finishing off his double Beam. "They want her alive. Otherwise, with the intel I've given them from last night, she'd already be dead. It's amazing how priorities change when the dipshits in control decide maybe they could get a few sentences more after the edit."

I'm used to it. It's why my monster squad will always be a 'Rogue' element. We exist because nothing else is working, yet if our backers fear reprisal, they throw us under the bus in a split second with an endearing wave of goodbye. "If she can pay off enough people to do in an Interpol team with Ricin and get away with it, we'll need to move fast on her, Den. If she finds out about us, and you can bet she suspects someone's playing around in her sandbox, she won't hesitate like our handlers are doing. We've taken out a bunch of key players. Kornev, I'm sure realizes he's missing men who have disappeared under very suspicious circumstances."

"I'm with you. Christova accomplished a cover-up using chemical weapons in an international port of call, and buried it, along with the Interpol agents sent in. She has a place in the Stinson Beach area. We found it under a holding company she's carefully kept three levels back from. The 'Ghost' reminds me a lot of Maria's brother, Terrance."

"I agree. We had to get him before he got us, and he came close. I understand the big boys want to know all her planning details, but sometimes you need to smash-"

My i-thingy gave that stupid ping noise. I looked at it. "It's Lora. Maybe she's not mad anymore. Hey, Hon, I made all the-"

"Something's wrong, John," Lora cut me off with a FaceTime wave off. "I went to see my friend Tracy today instead of pretending I didn't mind being left out of your hospital decisions. You remember where she lives in Piedmont, right?"

"Yep. Nice house, and husband Pete. What's wrong?" My trouble meter pegged with a ping much like the i-thingy.

"Ever since that bitch from the BBC and her henchman took Al and me prisoner in our own damn house, I've checked every suspicious car or truck anywhere within three blocks of us. I thought this silver SUV followed me this morning from 35th Avenue, but I didn't see it again until I reached Tracy's house. Now it's parked a couple houses down from us with two guys in front who are not going anywhere."

I was running into the entertainment room with phone in hand as I listened, fear, rage, and desperation jetting into my head.

"Stay where you are, babe! Get your friends somewhere in the house you can barricade now! I'm on my way, line open and listening."

My burst into the entertainment room with hints of tragic happenings had my monster crew on their feet, all humor or levity gone in an instant. "Silver SUV with two guys not moving near where Lora's friend's house is in Piedmont. Get in the safe-room right now, Al and Dannie! Dev, Jess, Casey, Jafar, Lynn's minions, and Lucas go home, lock and load immediately with all family safe in sight. If you don't have anyone, Maria, go with the girls into the safe-room. Clint, Lynn, and Denny will be with me. Don't argue! Get the fuck out of here and where you need to be."

There were no questions where family would very possibly be in danger. My three active forces without loved ones in danger hovered with me while the others left. There was no use in whining or protecting in an afterthought. It would be hell on earth if we didn't act in time. It was nobody's fault but mine. I assumed days to find the responsible parties. Hopefully, Laredo's workings would save us. If not, then I kill until the situation is resolved or I'm dead. The one thing about being part of a monster squad that I'm sure would humor someone when hearing the name is the definition of monster. Look it up, multiply it by ten, and you have my squad in perspective... everything but imaginary. We have done things that would make a monster from imagination puke.

Lynn grabbed my arm. "I didn't drink. Let's do this. I'm driving. God in heaven have mercy on these assholes. I won't. We survive because we have a Bay area lair against the darkness. If we don't protect it, who the hell will? That was one sweet swipe you took Marko's life with, John. C'mon pussy... step the hell up and get 'er done."

"That's right, John!"

I held up the i-thingy for Lynn to see with Lora doing her snarly face. "Now see what you've done, Lynn."

223

Lynn waved, smiling with pleasant carefree visage, before turning to the darkness. "Get off my line, you jingoistic turd! If I want feedback from you, I'll beat it out of you!"

Oh God... I laughed after hearing Lora's bleating yelps as I kept her on line while running for tools in my safe-room. Clint and Lynn packed their own everywhere they went, so they had only to wait for me. Denny accompanied me, trying in his usual middle of the road-kill fashion not to take sides as Lora was burning the digital connection into dust particles. Denny picked out and donned his favorites from my stash of armament, weapons, and party favors.

I cut Lora off from hearing our side of the conversation. "I know we need to take this bunch in for questioning. That said, I'm not taking casualties on our side to get it done. If I don't like things, I am going to shoot everyone in the head, and figure what the damage done is later when we bring Christova's empire down around her ears."

"Agreed. What the hell is that?"

I was stripping out of my clothes and into a police uniform, complete with all the paraphernalia to go along with it, including regulation utility belt and holster. Yeah... I dressed like Lora's life depended on it. "We get into position, and I stroll to the window and throw a banger into the back, if it's closed. If it isn't, I do that trick Lynn pulled on the last batch of ambushers we caught, knock on the window, only instead of a hooker I'm an officer of the law. The driver opens the window, and I throw in the banger. Boom... and we have prisoners."

"Or the driver shoots you in the head," Denny replied.

I grabbed my bag, and we hustled out. Lynn and Clint waited beside Denny's Ford Excursion. Lynn caught the keys thrown her, and we piled into the Ford. I directed Lynn. When we neared Mountain Avenue where Lora's friend lived, I tapped Lynn on the shoulder and she drove to the curb.

"They live on the corner of Sharon and Mountain Avenues. Lora said they're parked on Sharon Avenue two houses down. I figure Lynn drives next to them. I get out, pop a banger in there with Denny and Clint covering me. After we restrain the survivors, I'll drive them in their vehicle to Pain Central while you three follow Lora home. I didn't have much to drink. Once Lora's safe, we'll have an info gathering session."

"I have a feeling we missed our chance on the 'Ghost'," Denny said. "I smell setup. We know who she is, and what she looks like now. I'm betting taking Lora was her plan to leverage an escape from the Bay Area. She's on to us. Let's do this, and reassess our next move."

Clint pointed as Lynn steered onto Sharon Avenue from behind our targets. He had his range finders, trying to determine if he could see movement in the SUV. I asked Lora to take a peek. She told me the two she saw earlier were still in the front seat, but she couldn't see anything else. No sense putting this off.

"The driver's window's open, John."

"Ready when you are, Lynn." I pulled the pin on the flash-bang grenade, holding it in my left hand, keeping my right free for something unexpected. Clint carried an MP5 Heckler and Koch machine pistol. Denny chose a .45 caliber Colt. If my plan hit a snag, I'd duck. There was no question in my mind who would win a gun battle. My uniform would only give me a couple seconds surprise factor.

Lynn drove alongside the GMC Yukon. In seconds I was standing next to the driver's side window. The uniform shocked the two in the front for a moment as hoped. My hand shot in past the driver's body before he could get a word out. I released the bang, ripped free of the driver's clutching hands, and ducked. The resulting blast made Lynn's already proven attack mode on parked vehicles my favorite. I opened the driver's side door, and tossed the driver to the street where Denny restrained him quickly. Clint went into the back with Lynn on his six, while I ran around to handle the passenger.

The occupants were in miserable shape. There were two other men in the back. One had been too close when the grenade went off. He was dead with part of his jaw missing. The others were secured quickly before the neighbors decided to call the real police. I patrolled near the Yukon where everyone peeking out their windows could see a police presence. Denny and Clint put our prisoners in the rear cargo area, including the dead one. From start to finish with me behind the Yukon's steering wheel, only ten minutes had passed. I left, leaving Lora to my partners, while I drove to Pain Central. Gus was free to open the place for me, having dropped his family off with his fellow minions. The door was open when I arrived, so I could simply park inside. I helped Gus put the dead guy in a body bag, and transport him to our freezer for keeping until we went out on the boat. I did triage on our unhappy guests, patching superficial wounds, and washing off the blood.

Gus searched the Yukon while we waited for our interrogation expert to arrive. We would have shown them a movie of Lynn in action, but they were still too disoriented from the blast for it to work. "I didn't find anything, John. They don't even have license or registration for the Yukon in there. I texted Jafar and Laredo the plate, and vehicle identification number. Did they have anything on them?"

"Not a thing. I'm betting they're Bulgarian, but we'll have to wait until their brains stop rattling around in their heads." Denny had already taken pictures. Gus used our electronic fingerprint scanner to send on the prints for Laredo and Jafar to work.

Denny, Clint, and Lynn arrived a few moments later. My patients began groaning in painful recovery of their senses. I'm

226

certain their hearing would be a problem for the time being. The survivor from the back had two busted eardrums I'm certain. His friends from the front were in much better shape. Lynn looked them over with professional curiosity. She turned to Denny after only a moment's inspection.

"We may as well put them away for the night, Den. I doubt we'll be able to get anything useful from them right now. I think we'll have to use the more gentle approach if Gus can stay tonight. He can show them the movies when they recover a bit. Can you stay, Gus?"

"Yes, of course, Mistress of the Unimaginable. I wish to look over our new addition to the fleet. At this rate, we will be able to simply provide a one way escape vehicle to be ditched somewhere on the other end."

Lynn pinched Gus's cheek. "You are so cute. Good thinking. We may have to add another building if these jerks keep invading our territory with new vehicles. Lora said you owe her, John, and she's going to collect in the coin of the realm whatever the hell that means."

"Nothing good, I'll wager. I guess it doesn't count when I launched an immediate hit squad action to save her, huh?"

Lynn laughed. "Apparently not."

"Everyone has checked in without any problems," Clint added. "She could have sent multiple teams. She must have smelled how close we were."

"No one is leaving the area without us knowing it unless they do it by car," Denny added. Even then they're in trouble, because anywhere with a bridge crossing is on alert for any license Laredo found belonging to her. Trains, boats, and planes are being watched since the first moment Lora called."

227

Hell, that is good news. It means Denny has a bit extra he hasn't shared. "You have feelers into every suspected leak's communications waiting for him or her to warn Phoebe, don't you?"

"Very good, John. You're damn right I do. Laredo and I have a code. When I hit code red, he launches everything within our power to track all assets in our investigation. He has a list of people above suspicion, and a list we keep in the loop from sheer necessity. That one is a very short list. If Christova receives a warning, I'll know who sent it. They won't ever send another, because we will erase them from this dimension. As Clint pointed out she could have sent multiple teams or tried to blow up John's house with all of us inside. It's a new day in the neighborhood for now. We close security holes with extreme prejudice. Our notoriety for dispensing blood and fear is what keeps us safe. I'm afraid we need to have another example."

"We have Maria, Lora, Dannie, and Al in lockdown. If you know where Kornev is, I'm going to settle accounts with him first tonight. We can let Alexi work the port security for the time being while we find Christova." Denny had it right. We may as well buy the island in the middle of nowhere right now, if we keep allowing shots at our home base.

"Gus, walk our disoriented trio to holding, please," Lynn said. "Use a cattle prod if you have to, but get them out of here."

Gus smiled, took out his stun gun, and fired off an arc. "On your feet ladies. I will then unclip your feet. Do anything other than walk where I tell you, and I'll give you a hummer like you never had before."

They couldn't hear real well yet, but our guests were coherent enough to follow orders. I reached down, and yanked them to their feet, where Gus clipped the ankle plastic ties. "Shoot them in the head if they try anything, Gus."

"Will do. I will be back in a few minutes. If not, we're going to need more body bags."

Gus herded them on their way while Lynn turned to us. She clutched Clint's hand. "I'm done boys. I will not endanger you by acting like I'm running on a full tank. This seven months pregnant business only allows me one adventure a day. Drop me off at John's house. I'll collect Dannie and Maria, and head for home."

I could tell Clint was surprised and worried. "Go with Lynn, Clint. Denny and I can handle Kornev. We'll call in Casey and Lucas. They will have secured their homes by now, and are probably ready to eat nails waiting for a target."

Lynn began to protest, but Clint grabbed her in a shoulder embrace, shaking his head. "Are you sure, John?"

"Very sure. You don't look well, Lynn. We've been pushing the hell out of you with softball practices, terrorists, and last minute crap like today's scrap. Have a glass of wine with Maria while Clint and Tonto watch the house."

Lynn nodded, and Clint led her away without further comment.

"I'm not used to seeing Crue like that," Denny said. "Usually, she'd cut me for trying to keep her out of an op. Maria's been tired as hell lately too. C'mon. I'll text Casey and Lucas on the way. I know where he's at, but we'll need a few more toys to take him out tonight."

"Let's get loaded. We'll take Gus with us to drive. Those clowns in lockdown won't be going anywhere."

Gus was jogging toward us by that time. He heard part of what I said. His face lit up like he won the lottery. "I'm in! I don't give a shit what we're doing."

"Come with us," I motioned for him to follow us to our armory. "We'll need you to get armor on. I know you've shot an MP5 before. That's what we're taking tonight. I'm glad I cleaned my M107 after the boat attack. Do we have a location where I can get a few shots off to clean around his building, Denny?"

"We do indeed, and it will need some cleaning around the outside before we hit it. I hate to say this, but we'll have to hit hard after his guards are down. Are you sure you're feeling well enough?"

"Very funny." I take the first hit as usual on the way in. "That'll be a scramble to reach the entrance after taking potshots at the guards. Gus? Can you shoot?"

"I shoot well, but I have never shot an M107 before. I'm sure I could cover you four against attack though."

"That's all we need. I have a Barrett QDL silencer on it, but it's always best to space the shots if you can. I'll have to use it in quick succession, so when I hand it over to you, wait as long as you can before firing. Otherwise, take the thing off and fire away. I'm hoping that won't be necessary. Where's his hideout at, Denny."

Denny grinned while loading what he would need. "The Hayward hills, in a nice spot where all the vegetation is only now turning green between the house and the road. No one frequents the road unless they live on it. It's about a hundred yards to the estate. Before you ask, yes it has a balcony, and there is a guard there."

"So, you went recon on Yuri's ass without telling the rest of us, huh?"

Denny shrugged. "I watched what happened after the fight is all, but I did get an eyeful, and pictures I haven't had time to share. Our Christova didn't show at the after fight wake, but a bunch of other notables did. A few were politicians with wives too stupid to filter their donor list. Laredo and I filed a handful of credible participants in shady dealings at the port Christova has now lost access to, except by permission from Alexi."

"Let's go rain on their parade." I led the way out to the EMT vehicle we had in our fleet. We were going to stay big on this one. An emergency medical tech vehicle draws two seconds of attention, as people believe it's there for an emergency call. We'd be there for an emergency call... just not the one of popular conception."

* * *

Lynn drove home with Dannie and Maria in the backseat. The way Clint kept glancing at her while pretending he was paying attention to the road was beginning to ping Lynn's radar. "Hey... man from nowhere, why the hell do you keep glancing at me as if I'm the last chicken McNugget on your dinner plate. I'm getting worried about you, Clint dog."

Dannie giggled at first when Clint didn't speak, but added her own perception to the mix. "I'm worried about you too, Lynn. You've been tired all the time lately, and you look even more pale than usual."

Lynn stared at Dannie by way of the rearview mirror that had Dannie, cringing to her side of the backseat, clasping hands together, and staring straight into the back of Clint's head. Lynn smiled. "Thank you for your input, 'Eve of Destruction'. Is there anything else you'd like to add?"

"No... Mistress of the Unimaginable," Dannie replied, using her minion's card, because although she knew Lynn cared about her, she was also aware of what Lynn was capable of in an all too personal way. Like Maria, who had kept silent, she had been on the receiving end of Lynn's interrogation techniques.

"Dannie's right," Maria broke the girlfriend code, and endangered her personal friend credentials built up over the months. "You look like hell, Lynn. I'm pregnant nearly as long as

231

you, but I'm not beginning to resemble the 'walking dead'. Have you been to the obstetrician lately?"

"We went to her appointment at the beginning of the last week," Clint answered for her. "She said Lynn was doing fine, and liked the exercise she routinely does in addition to coaching softball.

"Maria and Dannie are right. I do look like hell. I've been popping the thousand prenatal vitamins they gave me, but I still don't feel right. We'll make another appointment. Maybe another ultrasound test would be a good idea."

"I think it's a great idea," Clint replied. "I figured if I mentioned it, you'd gut me like a trout."

Clint's remark lightened the mood. He checked his tablet while they approached the house. "Uh oh. We have company. All our motion sensor lights are on. Denny's crew only finished repairing the EMP damage yesterday. They better not have another one of those damn prototypes or I'm going to be pissed. I hope they didn't try to go in. We have security bars everywhere in addition to alarms, and door deadbolts that would stop any common burglar."

"You're worried about Tonto!" Dannie became suddenly energized, her hands gripping Clint's seat. "I hope he's okay. This is bad."

Lynn and Clint started laughing at the same time.

"The only thing Clint's worried about is guys as helpless as the ones we picked up stalking Lora actually breaking into our house," Lynn said. "We'll need to hire one of those crime scene cleaning teams."

"You've seen Tonto in action with people around in an outside environment, Dannie," Clint said. "If four guys like the mooks John adjusted today broke inside, we'll have to clean Tonto, and head for a hotel. When he's alone, he won't bark, growl, or

232

even pant. Tonto will leap, rip a throat out, and hide, waiting for the next opportunity. I texted Amara to get in the safe room. She texted back she's inside, and Tonto is on alert by the door."

"Jesus…" Maria mumbled. "He…he's so cute though."

"I have audible, and the alarms aren't going off so maybe we'll get there before we need to stay elsewhere at a hotel that takes bloody mouthed dogs," Clint said, still checking his iPad. "Park a block away, babe, and I'll go see what we need to do."

"I can't back you reliably, hon. We have Jafar in reserve. Maybe we should give him a call." Lynn smiled at her mate with sweet helpfulness. Clint growled.

"Have I done something tonight to deserve being insulted? This is good. I turned off the security lights." Clint exited the vehicle in a second with MP5 with silencer in hand.

"He doesn't know how many men there are, Lynn," Maria whispered as if trying to keep Clint from hearing.

"It wouldn't matter, girlfriend. When Clint rigged an escape out of Mexico for me with Denny's help, bringing John, Lucas, and Casey in on it, he had to do a side job for the DEA. Clint went inland, and wiped out an entire Cartel drug convoy by himself in the dark, carried one of the wounded guys a few miles, tortured his account numbers out of him, killed him, and made us and Laredo rich. I think he can handle a few burglars."

"You two are like the demonic convergence," Maria said, squeezing her friend's shoulder. "I'm taking you to a specialist tomorrow."

Lynn reached over and covered her friend's hand. "No complaint from me there. I feel like shit. I admit it. I'm worried. Maybe something is wrong with the pregnancy. I'm not taking chances. I didn't know how I'd feel about having a Clint Jr. Now, I can't think of anything else. I'll be ready tomorrow when…"

Someone banged on the driver's window. Lynn turned slowly, as both Dannie and Maria let out startled yelps. She whispered an urgent toned order. "When I open this door girls, hit the floor."

Lynn rolled down the driver's window, smiling at the hooded and masked figure pointing what looked to be an Uzi at her head. "Hello, officer. Was I speeding?"

Lynn's complete disregard for his threat startled the gun wielder, but only for a second. "Get the fuck out of the car, bitch!"

"Okay, Dexter, but give a girl some room. I'm seven months pregnant. I have to-"

"I will help, bitch!" The man did exactly what he should not have done. He let the strapped Uzi fall to his side on its strap, while opening the driver's side door, grabbing Lynn by the hair, and yanking.

Lynn came with the gunman's yank in a rush, eviscerating him from his groin to the top of his ribcage with her razor sharp butterfly knife, ripping upward while smiling into his mask, the knife parting flesh, clothing and belt. She stripped the Uzi away as he fell screaming to the road, clutching at his spilling entrails. The other hooded figure behind him had only enough time to try and point his weapon before the short burst from Lynn's confiscated Uzi stitched across his head. Lynn turned with a deep breath as if sniffing lilacs in a garden, and fired a single round through the screamer's head.

"I wonder who sent these cherries after me. It's all fine, girls. Are you both okay? I didn't mean to-" Lynn collapsed, the grainy blackness washing over her. "Shit..."

* * *

234

"Finally!" The hooded figure outside Clint and Lynn's house entrance mumbled as the security lights went out. "T2, do you copy?"

"We copy. We have a suspect vehicle parking down the way. It may be just neighbors."

"Don't take chances. Jog down and have a look. Then return to position."

"Understood." The man receiving the orders shrugged at his companion. "We will be careful and check the car. I doubt they are anything but neighbors, but let us do it, and get back where the action will begin. I want these people who think Allah is a joke. We will teach them all, brother."

The two jogged toward a onetime meeting with Lynn Montoya Dostiene, while their two cohorts stayed near the house entrance. The one who had ordered his two men to their death spoke in a hoarse whisper. "I do not hear the dog. Perhaps they took it with them."

When his companion didn't answer, he moved in a crouch to where the other man should have been. He was there, his throat slit from ear to ear. Sweat ran into his eyes under the mask. He whirled around, the Uzi he carried pointed in panicked manner in all directions. When he turned a second time, his labored breathing beginning to come in gasps, he felt his head pulled back. A blade pressed against his throat. Blood flowed warmly under his shirt. The man held his breath, hands releasing his grip on the Uzi to allow the weight to fall on the strap over his shoulder.

"Hello," Clint said. "You didn't call first. That's bad manners."

A man's screams started then, followed by two short bursts of an Uzi. Clint, who had been in the process of taking a prisoner, instead slit the second throat of the night. He took the Uzi with him at a dead run to where he had left Lynn. He went past a man with little of his face left to another masked eviscerated man in a growing pool of blood. Maria and Dannie were kneeling next to an Uzi armed Lynn, groggily acknowledging her friends concerned pleas. She spotted Clint, resting her head against their Toyota Rav.

"Hey, Cowboy... look what I found. They sent a couple of... Snow Whites after me and the girls."

Clint dived down to her side looking for gaping wounds, but there was only a little blood staining her pants. "Are you wounded, babe?"

"We have to get her to Alta Bates Summit on Hawthorne. It's only a mile away, Clint," Maria said. "I called ahead to have a pediatrician specialist there I have on call. She knows damn well she better get her ass over there to meet us. I'll drive. You get her in the back."

Clint wasted no time picking Lynn off the roadway. He slipped into the driver's side rear compartment after Dannie held the door open, and closed it when he was inside with Lynn in his arms. She ran around to leap into the passenger side front. Maria turned around over the bodies of the men Lynn had killed, only then seeing a few lights coming on in the neighbors widely spaced properties. Clint called Denny while hugging Lynn to him. She relaxed against him, a weary lethargy stealing over her. When she heard Denny's voice, she grabbed the iPhone from Clint.

"Spawn! I'm seven months pregnant, and I just killed two men. What did you do? Cleanup on aisle seven... and make it quick, or we'll be the talk of the neighborhood." Lynn didn't listen for a reply. She gave the phone back. "Time for a nap."

"Clint?"

"What she said, Denny. Two dead by my front door. Two more dead by her hand in the road. We're on our way to the hospital. Lynn may be having a miscarriage. Can't talk right now. Don't let anyone enter my house. Tonto is on guard."

236

"Got it, Clint. Call when you can, brother. Worry about nothing else."

Clint put the phone away, watching Lynn fading. "Talk to me, babe. Chatter away, so I know you're okay. You can nap in the hospital while doctors and nurses have you hooked to everything they have in the place."

Lynn's eyes opened wide suddenly. "Would...would you leave me if I lost Clint Jr?"

Clint swallowed the first sob he could remember since he was four years old as her question lanced through his mind, and right through his heart. "I love you more than life itself. I'm never leaving you... ever! Get that through your Cruella Deville head!"

"Okay then... maybe I'll stick around." Lynn began to drift again, but again became animated, clutching Clint's hand. "Don't you kill him to save me! You hear me? I...I'll know, and we will be through. Give me your... word!"

Clint couldn't speak. He tightened his jawline to the breaking point while not looking away from the only female he had ever loved. He stayed silent, with sobbing noises from Maria and Dannie plaguing the conversation. Lynn gave up all pretense of threat, tears streaming down her face.

"Please, Clint... please?"

"Okay, baby... you have my word," Clint lied to her for the first time.

* * *

Clint, Maria, and Dannie huddled together. Lynn had been taken in for emergency Cesarean section surgery. From the moment they entered the hospital with Clint carrying Lynn in his arms, the doctors joined to Maria body and soul took over all aspects of her wellbeing immediately. It was the first time he could remember where threats or physical action could not help or change a situation, leaving Clint watching her taken away with his fists clenched at his sides. He signed what he was presented with for the surgery, Maria glaring at him as he refused to choose his unborn son's life over Lynn's. She knew better than to comment. Denny had made it plain to her Clint was easily one of the most dangerous men alive. At the time of the telling, Denny warned her to never take sides against him for any reason, and whatever she heard said or done concerning Clint to keep silent for eternity.

Clint sat with his fists clenched while leaning back in the waiting room chair staring into eternity. He pretended no comfort for his companions. In his world, he had friends he would die for, but in love he had only two: Lynn and Tonto. He believed in God, but he knew better than to ask for the life of a nearly psychopathic killer with only one more undeserving of life, he himself. Lynn's constant shrugging declaration of 'it is what it is' singed his soul. In spite of it all, he began reciting prayers he knew from a Catholic childhood orphanage/foster care time. They helped rein in the beast prowling within his mind.

One of Maria's obstetricians pranced toward them, all smiles. Clint shot out of his chair as if on a catapult, his approach startling the doctor to a halt. The searing look on Clint's face made the woman who was delivering good news wish she had sent a nurse out in her stead. She took an involuntary step back, realizing on an elemental level the man rushing to confront her would snuff her life out without a second thought. She held up her hands in placating and urgently sincere fashion.

"Your...your wife and baby are fine. We have to keep the baby under constant care for now, but I believe he will survive. Thank God you got your wife here when you did."

Clint covered his face with both hands, turning away. He stood there whispering words of thanks to a force beyond reasoning, or in his and Lynn's case, beyond retribution. Maria and

Dannie swarmed him happily, a group hug Clint was sure Lynn would have barfed at seeing.

Chapter 10

Changes

I watched Denny's face as we three listened to Clint's call, and Denny responded. We were in a sniper's nest facing Yuri's property from the dense brush and trees across the way, awaiting Lucas and Casey. The three of us worked our way from nearly half a mile down the road, along the hillside dip, through the brush across from Kornev's house. It had taken only moments to set my M107 into position. Until Clint called, we were busily using our range finders on the exposed targets guarding Yuri's supposedly impregnable estate. There were only three lackadaisical simpletons pacing around while pretending to be observant. Inside the house, our infrared display off Denny's tablet indicated four more people. After Clint's call, Denny reached out to his own contacts. He stated what he needed, and then listened with growing displeasure.

"Listen! Do not speak anymore, Langstrom. You are a go between to filter unwanteds. If you want to become an unwanted, say anything other than yes sir, your will be done."

Denny speaks the lingo well, because he now has a position to make nearly anyone through the chain of command up to the President take notice. In our circles, where we operate, Denny's word means compliance or death, because the notoriety needed to stave off attacks on our home area have met with retaliation that could not be ignored. In our circles as well as our enemies', my West Coast Avengers are feared and respected, depending on the intelligence level of people we have to interact with. The ones on our side never take anything for granted, especially our patience with dolts who screw with us. Denny disconnected after hearing what he wanted to hear.

"Frankly… I can't afford to lose Crue. I'm willing to write you off in place of her, John."

That drew muffled levity in a horrific situation we could do nothing about.

"I don't speak grief well or empathy for that matter," Denny went on. "Whatever they need will be done on my word no matter what the consequences. We may need that island of escape sooner than I had planned. We're going to make a statement here after I find out where Christova probably went. There will be no needles or deals other than death. I've been ordered to take Kornev alive. That ain't happenin'. He sent the team that put Lynn in the hospital. We don't have three days in the desert on an anthill with his nuts covered in honey, so we'll make do with what we have tonight. I don't think we should wait for Lucas and Casey. The dead men over at Clint's place might have managed to get a warning out. Do you have a problem with going in with us, Gus?"

Gus reached out to grasp Denny's wrist. "I love Crue. She is the reason I am here with a family I may see share my good times, and the kids grow into adults with children. Any entity causing pain to my mentor will die by my hand or a hand I am supporting. Do not doubt me!"

"Well said," Denny acknowledged. "Let's get this shit done, and go see how our Crue is doing. I know John can ace these three cardboard cutups fronting Kornev's house without a second breath. What would you like to do then, John?"

I had been thinking about speeding this intervention up, and the violent outlet of emotion ever since hearing Lynn tell us she'd killed two men while seven months pregnant, and asking what we'd done. "I think you're right about not waiting. If you want to do this now, you and Gus should do a broad angle approach within about twenty yards of the entrance. Do it slow, while I monitor your success, or end any threat from the three gazebos watching the house. If you make it to your positions without my interference I

241

will then take out the three guards, and charge the entrance from here. I will take that door down. Then it's party time. If we can take Kornev for questioning, we'll do it on the spot, and deliver his dead body to complete your orders, Den. I'm with you. No more leaks, and no more possibilities of leaks. No one walks away from here as players to be named later. For all we know, the Nigerian government is supplying info to Christova. Be aware of booby traps getting into position. Any bare areas of ground sprinkled with debris are suspect."

"Absolutely. I like it," Denny said. "Any questions, Gus?"

"I am ready. It is nice of them to light up the house front, is it not, John?"

I grinned because I was thinking the same thing. I didn't even need my night-vision scope. It's not that I faulted their logic. Anyone seeing armed guards in front of a house tend to go on down the road, looking for easier targets. The cops or neighbors might make some complaints about an armed compound to ATF or the FBI; but if the men are simply walking the perimeter without assault rifles, there wasn't much the authorities could do about it besides harassment. "Yeah Gus, that is very nice of them. Go take over guarding my ramming assault path. I will be along shortly. Remember to fall in behind me. Even cement heads need backup."

"We'll double click when we're in position," Denny said, before mumbling, "John... you pussy."

I assumed firing position with a slight chuckle. "Get moving. I have you covered."

I didn't bother watching them. I watched my targets. If they reacted they died now. If they didn't react, they died in another minute or so. The .50 caliber payloads I had in the clip were capable of going through them and the house wall, but mine were machined to hit and pulp whatever I aimed at. If I missed my target, there would be a warning to the men inside as my missed shot smacked into the wall. I breathed evenly, index finger along the trigger guard while waiting. When I received two sets of clicks, I had not seen a single indication the three guards had heard anything. With no night-vision goggles, and the porch lights on, we could be assured they couldn't see shit out in the darkness. I waited until one walked to the furthest end of the porch, looking around the corner of the house. I blew his head clean off.

To his cohorts I'm sure it appeared he tripped and fell over the railing. The second man nearest him actually laughed. He walked over to get a close-up laugh at his guard brother. He tripped over the railing too without his head. The third guy was no dummy. He went for the door, but never made it. His brains did though, along with pieces of his skull. As his body pitched against the entrance way, I was up and running. I had mapped out my approach, knowing exactly where to leap, and where to pump arms and legs.

It was a damn fast barricade smashing pace. When I hit that very impressive door, it held, but its frame died a gallant death, fragmenting into wood chips around it. Once through the door, I rolled to my left, drawing and providing cover fire for Denny and Gus to get inside with my .45 caliber Colt. To my surprise, Denny, Gus, Lucas, and Casey streaked through the door, fanning out. No one inside gave up. They had automatic weapons, so they died before they could use them. There were only three, a different count from the infrared reading. We searched the inside of the house in professional haste with our two additional assault team members. Then I heard a groan by the front.

"Hey guys, I think I know where our fourth culprit is," I called out, moving to the entranceway framework, crashed onto the floor. I wasn't stupid enough to lift the damn thing, and get a few rounds through every one of my appendages exposed. When my guys retreated around me, I pointed at the entranceway that was continuing to groan. "I think we have the rat we've been hearing squeaking."

They all knelt where they could fire in the event the person under the entryway door planned on shooting in all directions. I heaved it off our mystery person, holding the entranceway in the air like a lean-to in the middle of the woods. My shooters first saw to my safety, and then dragged the prick out from under.

"Let it go, John," Lucas said.

I dropped it. I saw with a big smile it was Kornev I'd drawn to the entryway. "Well hello, Yuri. You cannot believe how happy I am to see you. That poor arm of yours looks broken, booby. Let's make sure, shall we?"

Yuri screamed like a girl scout with a vampire bat attached to her neck, and I hadn't even touched him yet. I made shushing sounds while my entourage watched with grim anticipation. One of ours was hurt, and all were under threat of attack. When that happens, things get wild. You get to meet the monster squad few ever see, and none ever tell the tale of. When Kornev ran out of vocal power, turning his output into sobs, I knelt next to him with his clearly broken arm in my grasp. I didn't go with fancy. I broke it, twisted it, and ripped it free of his body at the elbow joint. Yuri passed out, silence remained. The monster squad wasn't here to listen to our own voices. Lucas handed me the propane torch he had in his bag. I threw Kornev's detached hand and forearm off to the side. I fired the torch, and cauterized the stump, but kept the flame on. Casey threw water in Yuri's face. He gagged, gasped, realized his predicament, and screamed again, his anguish heightened as he waved his stump, held in horror by his other hand.

I smashed him with a hammer fist in the face. "Hey! We're not here to mourn your deformities, Yuri. We have questions, and we don't have time for elaborate interrogation tactics or that pussy shit like water boarding. You get the torch. Want another demo after I rip your other arm off at the elbow?"

"I'll talk! I'll talk! What... anything... what is it you want?" He sobbed convincingly through his guarantee to tell us

244

everything. Then Gus, Lucas, and Casey held him in place while I gave him a ten second refresher course with the propane torch on his stump.

"Sorry, Yuri, I thought I saw a little more blood seeping out," I apologized as Kornev hit a high noted scream I don't think has ever been heard before. "Okay... I think I got it. Now I want to know where that Phoebe Christova bitch is. If I don't find out in the next thirty seconds, I'm going to roast your balls in five second intervals until I do."

We listened then, because nothing could shut Yuri up short of a bullet in the brain. If everything with Lynn was okay, I bet I'd get a laugh from this session when I related my off the cuff method. After about forty-five minutes with Denny recording directly to our IT wing of the monster squad, and them lighting our vast internet starship of information on fire, he gave me the cut sign. I then broke Yuri's neck with a violent but heartfelt twist, making him look like he was auditioning for the part in an 'Exorcist' remake where the kid turns her head a hundred and eighty degrees around. I did it with feeling, having wanted to since the first moment I laid eyes on the creepy son-of-a-bitch.

"Well, damn. Took this a bit on the personal level, did we?" Yeah, Casey noticed.

I ignored him and the general amusement from my other companions. "Do we need to secure the property, or move on this now, Denny?"

"If Christova slipped by the force I have in play right now, nothing we do will help. Yuri didn't know how she would leave, or her route to Lagos. That she would go there answers a few questions I admit didn't come into play before. I think we can agree she owns some high end power in Nigeria. She'll also be calculating ways to take us out of her picture here on the West Coast since we moved fast enough to screw her. Our Phoebe will be thinking she's safe in the Lagos home port. She doesn't know we now have her on our radar. I know we have assets in Nigeria. We'll monitor her until we can get the Sea Wolf EMP shielded and ready to go."

Denny didn't like the subsequent silence at his declaration. "What?"

"That's a lot of ifs, ands, and buts unspoken in there, Denny," Casey was the first to say. "You have the part where she'll be spending the equivalent of a small country's gross national product to have us killed, right... probably nuked from orbit? If we wait around until the stars align in the sky for this, we may as well shoot ourselves in the head."

"We still have the leak in our own hierarchy to deal with," Lucas added.

I put in my bit then, because I agreed, but I knew instinctively Denny couldn't do a damn thing instantly. "If Laredo or Jafar find out who we need to seal in the leak department, it will make any movement on Christova overseas safer. We'll need the Sea Wolf. Any other plan will be broadcasting intent unless we did it through military channels, which is also a bad idea. We can get Alexi to ship the Sea Wolf to a neutral port in another country like nearby Ghana. I know they have a deep water port in Takoradi. Then we can sail an intercept course with the yacht Yuri says is her mother-ship in Nigeria. I hope he's right about the location she lays low in."

"Good one," Denny said. "That would indeed keep us off everyone's radar if Alexi would agree to move the Sea Wolf for us. Yuri's claim she has a love/hate relationship with the Nigerians would make it easier for any assets I can move into place to track whether she's on her yacht or not. As John pointed out, we have to get the one she's contacting in our own circles before we risk a mission on the open seas. I'm sorry, but we have to bide our time until we get the targets. Let's get the hell out of here, and go see how Crue and Clint are doing."

"I pray to God they have people real good working on her," Lucas said. "If something happens to her, Clint will be an unknown factor."

"Agreed," Denny said. "Let's hope we get there in time either way it goes. We can't afford to lose either one of them, and losing both would damn near close us down for the time being. That mix can't be duplicated. Let's spread out, grab anything looking even remotely interesting. The train pulls out of the station in ten minutes."

* * *

Clint stared at the tiny thing in the incubator with fear. His heart pounded like nothing he had ever experienced. He had done things without raising his pulse that would have caused cardiac arrest in most normal people. The sight of this microscopic human being with a wisp of hair threatened to tear his heart out. Clint accepted with a smile the label monster squad for both he and Lynn. With any predatory force on earth, he knew the challenge of winning with Lynn at his side would be negligible. They reveled in being two of the most dangerous human beings on earth. They would kill, torture, maim, or dangle in a purgatory of hell anyone getting in the way of their mission. Here was a mission he could do nothing to achieve other than wait and watch. His fists tightened involuntarily as mayhem seeped into his mind. He turned away, needing Lynn as his stanchion against the darkness.

* * *

Lynn perceived her surroundings in blurred form. Her first thought was she had been captured, and her captors stupidly left her unrestrained. Reality flowed over her in a slow wave of anticipated killing to helpless confusion. She recognized the parameters of what she had done on a step by step meeting with the unknown. Lynn gripped the rails of her bed with white knuckled intensity, every nightmarish outcome flashing into her consciousness. Recognizing she had an IV inserted, and numerous

247

diagnostic patches attached from surrounding machines gave her pause for only a few seconds. As she reached for the first thing to pluck off of her, Clint streaked into her room with fear highlighting his features for the first time she had ever seen. It shocked her into immobility. He clutched her hand while kneeling next to the bed, kissing it with reverence, and something beyond Lynn's grasp for a moment. Then light shone on a darkened landscape. He needed her.

"I'm here, baby." Lynn said. "How are we doin', Cowboy?"

Clint buried his face in her hand, obviously fighting off never before felt emotions threatening to unmask him as a normal human being. Lynn watched him take hold of reality in a slow reckoning, a recognition she adored about him. Her mate didn't cry out in helpless anguish or fall into a fetal withdrawal on the floor. It was not in his nature or hers. Clint planted a final kiss on her hand, looking into her eyes without wavering.

"He's okay right now. They have him in an incubator for warmth. He carries monster genes, so I don't want you to worry. I didn't think you'd wake this soon. I should have known better. I love you so much it makes me feel like one of those clowns doing romance movies on the Lifetime Channel."

Lynn giggled with a rasp, the tube inserts in her nose making their drying presence known. "Can you take me to see him?"

Clint stood with a mission in hand. "Thy will be done, babe, even if I have to decimate the population of the hospital to see it done."

Lynn's brows furrowed. "Don't you dare touch anyone inappropriately, Clint Dostiene! I'm certain a simple request, and a few hoops I might have to go through will be the extent of what we need to do."

Clint's eyes welled up. He grasped her hand in both his while kissing her on the forehead. "You have my word on it." Clint was at peace with the second lie he gave during the visit. He grinned while enfolding Lynn in his arms. Anyone trying to prevent his mission completion had better have kissed all their loved ones before leaving home.

* * *

All members of the monster squad waited in the designated area, drawing looks probably never seen by regular visitors. They jutted to their feet as one when spotting Clint walking toward them. The monster squad knew better than to speak or slice into Clint's approach with stupid questions, and whining for knowledge. We stood stolidly, hoping and praying for the best. Outward rending of clothes and shrill screaming in anguish would not be demonstrated by us. We didn't need to convince anyone of our caring for the public to see.

"Lynn is fine, and will be able to see little Clint in a couple hours. He's in an incubator for preemies right now, but Maria's obstetricians like his improvements. It's good to see you all."

We greeted his news in true monster squad form, by swarming him with relief. We killed and tortured without mercy, but we're kind of needy when it comes to loved ones. Crue was one of us, and there are only a handful.

"I've had the area around your house sterilized, and Amara is with Maria and Dannie at our place, Clint. Dannie brought Tonto with her, because I didn't know how long you'd be tied up here." Denny paused for a moment as if uncertain how to go on. "Anyway, Maria let me know we're building an obstetrics wing into your house, complete with everything they have here, and a few extras her obstetricians noted down. They will be in rotating attendance, and on call, so you and Lynn can bring the baby home right away when all is safely stabilized. I have people working on it right now, gathering what's needed."

249

Clint grabbed Denny by the shoulders. "Damn… I don't know what to say. I-"

Denny waved him off. "It's a small thing, brother. We have the money, and when Laredo finishes confiscating Yuri's holdings, we'll have even more. Maria thought it all out. I'm putting her plan into effect. Thank God you have all the security in place, and didn't walk into a trap. We're on this, Clint. Laredo's looking for an island retreat too."

"Damn right, brother," Laredo confirmed. "I have a few possibilities. When we seal that bitch Christova's fate, we'll have the assets to do anything we want."

"C'mon then," Clint urged, releasing Denny. "I'll take you in to see Lynn. She's barely out of recovery, and already steaming to get into a wheelchair for a Clint Jr. visit. I'll let her know the good news on the hospital wing edition to our house later. She'll flip. They can't allow her in the wheelchair yet, but it will be soon. A visit from the gang may take her mind off ripping the IV's off, and running down the corridor."

"Are you sure it's safe for us to see her?" Jesse was getting anxious, and funny. "She gutted a guy, and popped the other in the head on her way down. There's no tellin' what she'll do with all of us in the same room with her. They took her butterfly knife off her, right Clint?"

Needless to say, Clint enjoyed Jesse Brown's take on the visit as he guided us down the hall as did we all. Lynn was sitting up in the bed. She had a private room, if not for money, then for the sake of safety for the rest of the hospital. I smiled when meeting her eyes. I knew they'd put her under for the operation, but it looked to me as if she had completely obliterated the anesthetic, the operation, and all other aspects of everything in the hours since taking the lives of two men. Yep, she was a monster to be held in awe. Her minions ran to her side, heads lowered comically by plan

I'm sure, with hands palms up. It was hilarious, and Lynn absorbed it with grinning acknowledgement.

"Awwww... so sweet," she cooed. "My minions all here with me in this special moment. Okay... I see uneasiness in Jess's face, weirdness in everyone else's... except for Samira. What's wrong, my young disciple?"

The minions had gotten off their knees, clasping Lynn's hand with big smiles as they moved away. Samira hesitantly walked forward, very pregnant with Jafar's baby, and obviously concerned for Lynn's welfare, but also fearing in a mother's way for her own child's eventual delivery.

"I am so sorry about your complications, Lynn. Did you have any indication something was wrong?"

Lynn shook her head. "Nope. I lost it after I put the Uzi burst through the second guy's head. I faded. Buck up, kid. You're young. Everything will be fine with your baby. I'm older. Everything that can go wrong usually does with us non-teenagers. I'm glad for the visit. It softens my baser tendencies to allow Clint to wreck mayhem on the hospital until I am in the same room with my son. Believe me, it has not been easy to keep my husband from a rampage. He only thinks I don't know what he's thinking."

"In my defense," Clint said amidst more hilarity, "I wished also to see my wife with her son. Those brainwaves may have set off a stranger protection gene in my wife, where she pretends to care one way or another about the human sheep around us. My bad."

"Get the fear of death off your features, Sam," Lynn said finally. "We still don't know what will happen, and yet here we are, all laughing like hell. It's a moment to moment world, kid. Enjoy the good ones, and we'll stick together through the bad ones. I hate to break this up, but I have to take a short nap before my designated meeting time with my younger Clint. He's mildly in

251

trouble, but his Dad and Mom are at the scene. Now go on home and get some rest. I'm sure it will be needed if we are to kill every bastard involved in this assault on a poor innocent pregnant woman."

Samira hugged her, stifling the tears and fears in the presence of her mentor. "You are an inspiration… an evil, killing one, but still an inspiration."

"And don't you forget it. Now, out of my room. Leave the man from nowhere with me for comfort's sake. If I need an intervention for my beloved if he starts going off the deep end during this trying time, I will text you."

We exited the room with waves at our monster squad torturing department. Once outside Lynn's room, we monsters met for a brief period to divvy responsibilities. I had already called Lora to let her know my plan, so she and Al would be staying in the safe-room for the night. "I'll take first watch tonight. I'll go until 8 am."

"I'll take the dayshift," Lucas said. "It would be just like these bastards to dress as doctors, and make visits with no one the wiser. They ain't got a prayer of foolin' us. That was stand up stuff building a mini-intensive care unit right in their house, Denny. Maria must be having a positive effect on your no account, lyin', thievin' ass."

Denny smiled. "Yep. There's no use denying it, but thanks for putting it in such a wonderful manner, Lucas."

Lucas grabbed Denny around the shoulders. "That's what I'm here for, Spawn. I hope you have contingency plans for your own. Do we need to have a presence at your residence?"

"Nope. We're at DEFCON one at my house. Every one of us needs to make sure all security measures are in place. This attack may definitely be related to the visit from Amara's Dad's bunch. Shitheads doing honor killings would be open for anything

252

from their homeland area. If we had the next target, we'd be hitting it. I know Laredo's working on it with Jafar's insights. That's good enough for me. When we launch on a lead, the rules of engagement are kill or be killed. We have contingency plans in the works for Christova. We will be careful so that bitch dies no matter what the consequences."

"How are your eyes, John?"

"Fine, Case. I had no trouble with sniper duty. I'll keep you all updated in texts. I'll get acquainted with one of the nurses on staff tonight, and make sure no one gets to this level the staff doesn't know on sight. I have all my ID's with me. It's possible Christova knew she needed more than one decoy to get free of the area. We already know Amara's Dad had connections with the rat pack working in the same circles as Kornev's people, and the Nigerians. Samira, I'll need a fill in coach for Lynn next week. Do you want the job?"

"Yes! I will substitute for Lynn. I cannot do as well, but I can learn from you what my duties must be."

"We'll see you tomorrow, John," Denny said. "We still have prisoners to question."

"I have the duty tonight at Pain Central," Gus said. "I'll prep them come morning."

"Goodnight, my friends," I told them. I had a gut feeling this night would be a long one as I watched my crew leave in hushed fashion. I went into Lynn's room to talk with Clint. He sat next to the sleeping Lynn. He had one hand covering hers, and the other inside his jacket, probably on the butt of his Colt.

"I'll be with little Clint," I whispered. Clint grinned and nodded.

I found a middle thirties nurse with blonde hair and a scowl in charge of the floor. She didn't look happy to see me. I showed her my FBI credentials, explained the situation, and the danger involved. She warmed to me the moment she saw my name.

"John Harding. I saw both 'Rattler' fights. God, those were bloody affairs." She held out her hand. "I'm Connie Fortino."

I shook her hand. "So, you're a UFC fan, huh?" It might be easier to get guard duty in the preemie ward than I thought.

"My husband and I are hooked. Do you think they'll give you a title shot?"

"I don't know whether you heard, but I agreed to an off the books fight that didn't end well. It's the third death in the ring. I'll probably be lucky to get another UFC shot at any fight."

"I heard something about that on the news. That guy... the Assassin, tried to blind you. What made you take a fight off the circuit? You're really popular after those 'Rattler' fights. My husband said you'd get a title shot maybe this year. Wait until I tell him you're an FBI agent. How the heck did you get into the FBI?"

"It's a long story, Connie. About tonight. Could I give you my mobile number, and you text me if you see anyone suspicious on the floor, especially a doctor you don't recognize?"

"Sure, but where will you be?"

"With the Dostiene preemie. We believe the baby may be a target. I don't want to stick out like a sore thumb around there. I do have to make sure no one gets near the baby, but the people who are supposed to be there."

"I'll get you a lab coat. You really don't have to worry though. There are eyes on the preemies every second of the day. The nurses working there know everyone, including the doctors. We don't allow anyone inside either the nursery or intensive care, John. I'm fine with you staying. I'll get you access, and introduce you to our team, so they'll know you."

254

"Thanks for doing this, Connie. I know you could give me a lot of grief instead of helping me."

Connie smiled. "I'm thinking tickets to the next UFC match if you get one, ringside."

"You bet I'll get them for you. It doesn't even have to be me. I'll get you tickets for the next big match, and all the trimmings getting there, and staying."

"Come with me, Mr. Harding."

* * *

The doctor approached the desk all smiles, a tall black man with the manner of a confident physician, complete with nametag, clipboard, and attitude. Connie texted John anyway before smiling at the approaching man.

"Hi, can I help you, doctor?"

"Yes, I am here to check on the Dositiene baby," the man said with an accent. "I am a specialist called in by the family, Doctor James Turay. It was impossible for me to arrive any sooner. Can you please take me to the child?

"Certainly," Connie said, stalling for time. "May I see your credentials please? The parents are here of course. I can call the father to go in with you if you'd like, Dr. Turay."

"That won't be necessary." Dr. Turay reached inside his lab coat, seeing Connie's eyes widen a split second before a hand clasped his reaching wrist, in an until now unimaginable grip. He screamed out in pain involuntarily as the hand on his appendage continued squeezing until pain filled his world along with the sound of his wrist bone fracturing.

* * *

I slipped off my shoes the moment Connie texted me as I dozed near the baby intensive care ward. It was one in the morning on my iPhone. Angling against the hallway corridor, I slipped into position away from the white coated phony at Connie's desk. I didn't want her killed because I wasn't prepared to end the threat the moment it began. She had a job to do, and I had no doubt she would die to fulfil her responsibility – not happenin' on my watch. My timing was a bit on the close side as I approached him from the rear. He went for what I'm sure was a silenced automatic of some kind to pop Connie, and hurry on to execute the staff in the baby ICU along with Clint Jr. I don't think so. Jutting forward at the final clearing stage for his piece, I latched onto the offending wrist with extreme prejudice. After all, what the hell did we care if his wrist hung by skin shreds or not. The pussy started screaming, so I had to Gronk him with my now well practiced knife-hand strike to the base of his skull. When I landed, gauging the way he dropped, I thought I may have miscalculated the force. Oh well... it's an inexact science. Doc Ock or whatever his name is crumpled to the floor.

"Damn, John... that was an illegal strike. Bad John... bad." Connie was peering over the desk at the downed fake Doc while I frisked him. When she saw me take the silenced H&K 9mm auto out of his custom holster, I heard her gasp. "He...he was going to kill me. Shit! I hope the prick's dead. Thanks, John."

"We needed him alive, Connie. I think he'll be okay. I'm sorry for the timing. I didn't mean for there to be any danger if one of these assholes arrived unannounced. I owe you two sets of UFC ringside seats of your choice after this close one."

"Hell... I'd have killed him myself for that deal."

Oh man, Connie was good. We were enjoying the hell out of her statement as Clint arrived in full combat mode, and game face on. It's not a pretty sight if you're on the opposite side of the Clintster. It means you have split seconds before you take your last breath or scream and pray for it if you're still alive after he takes you. I patted Doc Ock with false compassion. He was indeed still living. Sucks to be you, Doc.

"I'll put this as Lynn would like, John," Clint said. "Did you break my toy?"

I straightened with all the paraphernalia I had confiscated from Doc Ock in hand, while backing away. "I only played for a moment, Clint. He's still alive."

Clint still didn't crack a smile. He knelt next to Doc Ock, and hit the call button for someone, waiting until he heard a voice. "Quays... get over to the hospital right now, my friend. I have a pickup for holding, and it can't wait."

Clint smiled then after acknowledging whatever Quays said, holding Doc Ock's pulverized right wrist in the air while staring at me. "You are a very bad man, Mr. Harding."

I waved his criticism off. "I had my friend Connie's wellbeing to take care of, brother. That the Doc still lives is a badge of honor for my restraint, 'man from nowhere'."

"Should I call the cops," Connie asked, having stared from me to Clint repeatedly during our small verbal exchange.

After securing Doc Ock for me with plastic ties at the elbows and ankles, Clint straightened then with his own FBI credentials in hand for Connie's perusal. "This was an assassination attempt to cower my wife and I from pursuing an investigation into a terrorist cell here in the Bay Area. I'm hoping you will keep this in confidence, Connie. We're on the track of monsters who would launch WMD's on us. I'm sorry you were caught up in this."

Connie gripped his extended hand with both hers. "Say no more. No way I share anything from this with anyone, including the cops. Your son is my first priority! No one touches him unless they go through me first!"

Clint patted her hands with feeling. "Thank you. It is a difficult time for us in this terrorist cell era. I wish the government would take their commitments to our wellbeing as seriously as you do. John and I are in your debt. You may call the debt in at any time. One of us will answer it depending on your part in the problem."

Clint pressed his card into her hands then. "Keep this near. It is a projection onto everyone you love. Count on us if you have a real problem. I will trust you to know the difference. If you ever see anything weird here at your work, we would welcome the information you give us concerning the incident."

"Thank you. I won't let either of you down," Connie answered. "What happens to this guy?"

"We have another agent taking him into custody," Clint answered. "He will be interrogated and charged for his crimes. If you'd like, I'll keep you informed about the investigation as much as possible."

Connie looked into Clint's lying eyes, buying the whole package. "Not necessary. I don't care what the hell you do with him."

Clint nodded. "If you change your mind after we leave, just call. I'll update you."

"Fair enough," Connie said. She reached over the counter to grip my arm. "Thank you for my life. When you get clearance, can I tell my husband about this? I mean... will you let me know when it's okay to explain tonight to him?"

"I sure will, and I'll tell him personally of your part in it," I told her. "After all, you'll need some kind of explanation for your UFC sojourns."

"Yeah, I will. Chad's a great guy, and he never gets jealous. He always claims he can stand up to comparison... and he can,"

258

Connie replied with conviction. "I always tell him the truth, because he says he can't bury what he doesn't know."

Clint and I enjoyed that statement, liking Chad without ever knowing him. "Good enough, Connie. Thank you. We will be taking little Clint to his home far quicker than expected. I wish that-"

I heard the elevator open around the corridor. The sound of running feet meant it disgorged people near enough they thought a running assault would send us into brain freeze. Yeah, okay boys, let's do this right now. I leaped over the counter, pulling Connie down, while popping back up to fire a volley in backup to Clint's. Bullets sprayed in our direction wildly, I guess hoping they would find a target. The smell is unexplainable. It is a mixture from hell, involving fear, gunpowder, cordite, and the sweat of delivering it, except if you're Clint and me.

We delivered death in single shot hell, because every round we fired struck target. We're head shooters. They don't wear armor there. In seconds, the four man backup team for Doc Ock lie strewn across the corridor very near our greeting counter, the only indication of their presence a splattering of bullet holes in the greeting area, and the last twisting death rattles of four men in need of a priest rather than a hospital. Screams echoed out from the rooms too of shock and fear. I waved Clint away.

"Go Clint. Lynn will be ripping her tubes out to get here."

"Don't take chances, brother. I'll text Denny," Clint yelled over his shoulder on the way to harness an awakening Cruella Deville.

I popped in my spare clip, before patting Connie's hand, with my eye on the dead and dying.

"You did excellent, Connie. Your hearing will be back to normal in a little while, although your area around the counter will smell like the gunfight at the OK corral for the time being." I pulled her up into a position where she could see there was no danger left. "They pulled out all the stops on this one. Thank you for your courageous help. It means a lot to us. We'll have your back for all time. There were a few extras we weren't counting on. Are you okay?"

"I...I think so. What did you guys do to deserve getting a case like this?"

"We're in the middle of keeping a bad presence out of our port system. I wish I could tell you more, but I can't. Stay here behind the desk. Once Clint makes sure his wife is settled, he'll calm the others down. I have to secure the scene before help arrives."

"Will help arrive?"

"Oh yeah," I told her while moving around the desk again to check on the four men with partial heads. Clint already had one of our people on the way. He'll request a team now. There's no keeping this quiet. We mistakenly assumed there would only be possibly one shooter if at all. To attack an obstetrics newborn ICU like this will gain us more publicity than we care to have, but we don't get a choice in this one."

"I'll go do something I can do, check my staff in the NICU, and help your friend calm the patients."

"That'll work, Connie. Thanks."

"Ever get worried you've picked the wrong careers?"

"Not yet, but the day is young."

* * *

Clint jogged into Lynn's room to find her lying unmoving, and breathing regularly. He grinned. "I ain't going near you until I see both your hands, babe."

260

Lynn chuckled, and put away her butterfly knife in the serving tray drawer. She positioned her adjustable bed more comfortably upright, being careful not to raise the angle too far for her surgical sutures. "Spill it. How many dead?"

"Four, and one survivor John Gronked the first after he pulverized the guy's wrist. We, my dear one, appear to have become a main target for this Christova woman while she flees the area. It seems from Denny's perspective, she may have made it. Kornev told Denny and John under duress Christova has quite a luxury liner near the port of Lagos, Nigeria."

"What the hell put a bug up her ass about us?" Lynn began sipping from her ice water.

"I'm thinking our Amara connection, and the prior 'honor killing' asshole posse had something to do with it. We must have mangled one of her treasured minions during our adjustments. Remember, Denny traded players to the Nigerians, along with Amara's Daddy, and his crew. According to Kornev, she has a lot of friends in the upper echelons of power in Nigeria. I'd wager Amara's Dad, or the gang of enforcers Denny placed may have had more of a connection with Christova through Kornev than we knew about. We pissed her off but good. That's for sure. Attacking the obstetrics floor of a major hospital means two things – they figured to get away with it, and if they didn't accomplish it quietly, they didn't care how loudly they did it. This very high profile attack won't do them or us much good in the media."

"It is what it is. Can I go see my boy now, or do I have to get really upset?"

"I'll go get a nurse to help with all the meters they have you hooked to. I saw some patients walking around with their rolling tree of meters and IV bags, so maybe you can walk there while we skirt all the police I'm sure will be here soon. I should know better than to ask this, but wouldn't tomorrow morning be-"

261

"You do know better than to ask! The boy's probably starving by now."

"Sorry. On my way." Clint hurried out to do Lynn's bidding, and nearly ran into Connie. "Oh… hi Connie. My wife would like to see our baby, and do a feeding if that's possible. I think when you take a look at her, you'll help me get her in a position to try a few steps. She and I can stay in the NICU until the police thing wears down a bit."

"We sure can." Connie strode into the room, looked over Lynn's readings, and did a blood pressure check. "I think you're good to go. I'm Connie by the way."

Lynn shook her hand, before Connie began moving the rolling tree to the side, and positioning it so Lynn could try sitting all the way vertically before swinging her legs over the bedside. "Don't try and stand for a moment. We need to see if you can stay upright without dizziness or nausea, okay?"

Lynn swung her feet over to the floor, where Clint quickly put slippers on her feet. "Glad to meet you, Connie."

"Connie alerted John to the fake Doc getting ready to kill her and our baby."

Lynn stood without help, balancing herself without gripping the mobile meter tree. She then hugged Connie. "Thank you. I'm sure Clint gave you our card. It's good as gold if you ever get into trouble. Now, c'mon Clint, I have to make a pit-stop before I see Clint Jr."

Clint assisted her in the bathroom, and then fell in behind Lynn with one hand on the diagnostic meter and IV tree, and one hand on Lynn's waist so he could catch her if this first trip out of bed didn't go well. Connie guided the way, but glanced continually back at her followers, uneasy about allowing Lynn to visit her son so soon after the delivery. Outside the room, she helped both Clint and Lynn into sterile masks before entering the room. While Clint watched with anxious anticipation, Connie showed Lynn how to use a breast pump. With Lynn comfortably seated, Connie explained how to hold a baby like little Clint, who was only a bit over two and a half pounds, and sixteen inches long.

At Connie's direction, Clint sat near Lynn, where she supported his son's head, enjoying the look of total concentration on his wife's face. Lynn had no trouble getting the baby to feed from the bottle. "He seems hungry."

"He's doing well in every way we watch for," Connie replied. "His breathing is good, which is a very healthy sign in preemies. The lungs are the last organs to fully form. On a scale of one to ten how's your pain level, Lynn?"

Lynn chuckled, and then realized Connie was being serious. "Oh yeah, you mean from the operation. It's not much worse than a five second stun-gunning... maybe a five. It's cool though. I'm fine."

Clint stifled amusement of Lynn's pain comparison to her day to day reality, but noticed Connie's odd expression. "It's okay, Connie. Lynn doesn't really have an internal pain meter. The only time I've ever seen a pained expression on her face is when I asked her to vacuum the living room."

The three went into a whisper soft, muffled set of snorts in the hushed atmosphere of the NICU. Little Clint seemed to like the vibrations.

* * *

Gus and Denny arrived before the police. A CIA crime scene forensics and cleaning team Denny scrambled entered the floor seconds later in well-marked uniforms with Homeland Security in large letters. I had Doc Ock on his feet by then with his ankles released. To say he was a sullen, angry captive would be putting it politely. The good part was he didn't bother demanding treatment he was never going to get. I had already taken pictures of everyone, along with DNA samples. We always like to be thorough when erasing enemies off our list.

"This is the only live one, Gus. His right wrist is broken, but take no chances with him. He's a professional baby killer. Christova sent him to murder little Clint. Can you make the baby killer feel at home back in Pain Central until morning?"

Gus smiled at Doc Ock. "You are very lucky our Pain Central leader, Cruella Deville won't be coming in tomorrow, but I will take good care of you, amigo. Should I take him now, John?"

"Yes. Take him. We'll work out the details tomorrow. I'm sure Denny scrubbed the police presence. What government agency are we taking over the scene under this time?"

"Homeland Security. I let all our backers know, and delved into favors all the way to the White House. We control everything on the West Coast as of right now until we fix this situation. Laredo's at Central now watching every line for confirmation with Jafar next to him. I see we won't have to worry about much other than cleaning. I'll talk to you later. I want to go with Gus if you can take over here. I have a number for you to call for anyone giving you shit. The guy on the other end of the line will shut them the hell up quick. C'mon Gus, let's take this tough guy here in for the night. My guys know you're in charge, John. They'll take care of everything without much direction. I'll see you tomorrow morning. Keep us up to date on Crue and the baby."

"Will do." I took the card Denny gave me. He had a few last words for his crime scene team before he and Gus took Doc Ock. I figured I lucked out. Lucas would be here to relieve me at eight, so I could get home in time for the Dark Lord's Lora and Al show, highlighting I'm sure the horrible time they had, relegated to the safe-room for the night. I decided to retreat to my chair outside NICU, check on my favorite monster couple, and sit for a snooze until morning.

Chapter 11

Leak Fix Discoveries

I actually managed some quality sleep time, the only disturbance a Clint Jr meeting with Mom and Dad in attendance. Lynn looked remarkably better than when I saw her last. I have no clue how she could be traipsing around after the day and night she had. Lucas relieved me, kicking himself for not staying with me.

"I might have known you'd get all the fun, Banana."

"Hey… what happened to Recon?"

"What did you do for me lately besides ace me out of the killin'?" Lucas was smiling again. "I smell disinfectant. How did Denny's team work out?"

"Excellent. He's billeted them out on the West Coast permanently because he can trust them. He texted me, they handled Clint's neighbors, and scoured the scene there too. Their cover story is violent home invasion stopped by the FBI special task force. Mom and Dad are with baby Clint now. It's feeding time again like every couple hours or less. They wanted me to bring you in the moment you arrived."

"Hell yeah, I want to see the baby." A dark shadow passed over Lucas's face. "You're stopping at Pain Central to make sure that phony you stopped last night was treated well, aren't you?"

Indeed I am. "Did I give you some reason to insult me this morning, Lucas?"

"Just checkin'. Man, I wish Crue was feeling well enough to educate him. We'd have a video we would only need to show a few seconds of to a perp, and they'd be screaming to tell us their tale. Let's see the baby."

The staff around the NICU knew me well by then. We could see Lynn and Clint together feeding the tiny bundle. They waved as we put our masks on and outer tie on surgical gowns and hair covers. Inside, Lucas melted. The monster who trained three of us monsters knelt like a five year old on Christmas morning in front of Lynn.

"Nice to see you, Godfather," Lynn delivered the line with deference, her head nodding.

"Godfather," Clint acknowledged, also with the head nod.

"Huh?"

"You'll be Clint Jr's Godfather when we get him babtized," Lynn said.

"I will?" They had Lucas then. He stared at Clint Jr like he was delivered on the wings of an angel. "Oh my God... are you serious?"

"Hell yeah," Lynn said. "Who'd you think we'd get to do it? You trained Clint, and I'm only alive because of things you've taught me while I was breaking into the monster squad."

"He's so tiny," Lucas muttered.

"Maria's obstetricians told us he'll grow fast," Clint said. "Even the nurse was optimistic because of his lung development."

Lucas covered Lynn's hand where she held the Clint Jr bundle. "You look hell-a-better, Crue. I'm glad Recon was here with the 'man from nowhere' to protect my Godson. I trained them. They damn well better know how to protect him. Are you feeling better, kid?"

267

"I sure am, Pappy. My boy's so tiny I have to be in top notch form. You wait. He's going to be a monster."

Lucas laughed, patting her hand. "It wouldn't be bad if he became a doctor."

"Well sure… he could do that." Lynn grinned at Lucas. "Disappointing, but manageable."

We monsters enjoyed that Cruella Deville declaration. We had so many unknowns going in this monster excursion there really wasn't anything left but jokes. "Congratulations, Lucas. The boy will have an ancient in his life to guide him… I'm not sure to what… but he'll have the ancient."

Lucas pointed a finger of retribution in my face, complete with snarly drill sergeant face. "You wait, Mellow Yellow. Your time's comin', and it will be bad. I don't know what you're still doin' here anyway. Don't you have a home? All you're good for is killin' and malingerin' like an old egg suckin' farm hound."

Mind you, Lucas delivered this entire line in a hushed whisper with us three knuckleheads and Clint Jr listening with rapt attention. I waved. "I'm going. I'm just glad it's daytime, and the threat's over. Otherwise I'd stay for a double shift."

Mellow Yellow made good his escape with rapid but silent footsteps out of the NICU before the ancient got his feet under him in pursuit.

* * *

When I reached home what did my wandering eyes see but my fight corner brothers, Dev and Jess. They began apologizing almost before I got out of the car. I waved them to silence. "It's been a long night, brothers. Give me the short version. First… is it an emergency, because I have to say hi to Lora and Al before I go over to Pain Central.

"You know Jess's Mom," Dev said. "Jess has a problem in that Florence won't accept any favors from anyone. She lives in that old house of hers on Coolidge Avenue by herself."

"She won't move in with me," Jess cut in. "Since I bought the new house in Walnut Creek, she thinks I'm sellin' drugs or somethin'. Every time I say come live with me, Mama, she starts rantin' about not getting involved with violence. She shows up at my door this morning, and surprises the hell out of me. My Mama thinks the idiots messing with her house are there because of my imaginary criminal lifestyle. She thinks I'm a damn kingpin of crime or something, John."

I unfortunately start laughing my ass off, and Devon joins in against his will. Now I'm getting a snarly face from Jess. He waves me off. "Don't you never call me brother again, John Harding. Disrespecting me and my Mama when I come to you for advice. That's just wrong!"

I grab Jess's shoulders while trying to keep my disrespectful ass in check. "Jess! I haven't even cleaned my gun from popping a couple guys at the hospital last night. I'll change clips right now. I'll go to Mama's house, and shoot every gangbanger for a mile in the vicinity of her house right through the head. Let's go!"

Jess snorted, trying not to bust out laughing himself while framing words to explain, but Dev beat him to it.

"Not to downplay this crap happening to Jess's Mom, it's the new paradigm when gangs get run out of familiar territory. They establish a presence in Section Eight housing supposedly going toward the needy and downtrodden – yeah right. They're hitting Jess's Mom's block right now. She's been vocal about not letting them in, meaning Section Eight housing bottoms out the real estate values while introducing a violent factor. The bastards have already thrown crap through her windows, and painted graffiti on her house last night."

My monster side welled up in spite of all the proverbial irons in the fire already. "First off... when did you start using words like paradigm, Dev? Secondly why is this the first I've heard of your Mom's problems, Jess?"

"Until Mom banged on my door last night, I had no idea it had shot past her protests, and into a war. I know we're up to our eyeballs with plots and crap. Dev had to talk me into coming over here after what you, Clint, and Lynn had to go through. I'm the youngest of six. My brothers and sisters have all moved out of the area. You, Dev, and Mama are the only ones I know still livin' in the city. I see Earl and 'Rique over at The Warehouse when I take Mama out to eat, but they can't do shit about this. It's like that damn 'Knockout Game' they tried to launch around here. We can't let this shit happen on our turf."

"First off," Dev says, pointing at me, "fuck you, John. I may not know as many languages as you, but I certainly know this one better than you... prick. I knew we'd have to move on this quick or the assholes doing this will already be taking over around Florence's house."

"I agree. Sorry... I couldn't pass up the paradigm dig. After all the action at 1 am in the hospital, I did get some decent snoozing time. Come in and have coffee with me, while I say hi to Lora and Al. We'll kick around a few options about what to do. Your Mom's in a nice section of Coolidge. Why the hell would those idiots put Section Eight housing in that area? It's been a dismal failure everywhere they've done it. The gangsters send in dupes to qualify, and then take the houses over for everything from crack dealin' to meth labs, and prostitution. C'mon inside, and let's hash this out."

Lora and Al swarmed me when I cleared the door. I have monitors in the safe-room, so once I texted them I was on my way home, they were watching for me. "I smell breakfast."

"We heard you guys talking, and started scrambling every egg in the house," Lora said, holding on to me. "There's plenty of coffee. Al and I will finish the eggs and bacon for you guys."

"God bless you, Mrs." Jess rubbed his eyes with shoulders heaving in joy, as if he were Bob Cratchit, receiving word of a raise in salary from Ebenezer Scrooge.

Once we were seated in the kitchen with coffee, Al went to work on me. I could tell her heart wasn't in it, and she was acting on behest of her Mom. "You should have called, Dad. You knew we'd get one of those streaming headline things about a terrorist hospital attack on the TV."

"I couldn't send anything out, because I had to keep the line completely open, including blocking you and your Mom for a while. I had Denny let you know we were okay. That was the best I could do until this morning."

Lora delivered a heaping platter of scrambled eggs, with Al adding toast and the bacon on separate plates. It reminded me I hadn't had anything to eat for quite a while. "I'm getting you a burner phone for your equipment bag, so you can at least send a text that you're okay, and still keep the main line clear. We heard what you were saying, Jess, on the monitor. Does your Mom really think you're a crime boss?"

"It's being the youngest. When I joined the army with Dev, she nearly had a stroke. Then I got into doing the back alley fights after my discharge, and she had my whole family ragging me. Losin' Dad so sudden a few years back messed with her mind. She's so convincing, I had brothers and sisters crossing me off their reunion lists, thinking I might get assassinated at their houses. When Mama banged on my door, and began shouting about my chickens coming to roost, my Karen nearly laughed herself into a coma. She tried explaining I stopped criminals not helped them. I showed her my FBI credentials a hundred times since she started hinting I was a crook, but she says they're fakes. It's been funny

271

until now when I'm getting blamed for gangsters messing with her home."

"Florence thought I was a good influence on Jess until he joined the army with me," Dev explained. "Now she won't listen to anything I say. She thinks I'm in on it too. Jess is lucky he was able to convince her to stay at his house. If this wasn't so serious, I'd get John to dress like Vito Corleone, and we'd pretend he was guaranteeing to look into it since she thinks you're part of the gang anyway."

Even Al liked that idea, but I thought it would get us in a deeper hole. "What I should do is take her over to the San Francisco FBI office, where Sam and Janie are stationed now. She couldn't deny you were an agent then, Jess."

Jess shook his head. "Those two hate our guts. When Denny pulled strings to get us in officially, Sam nearly blew a gasket. Remember him storming into our office to protest, John?"

"Yeah, the ungrateful bastard. I'll get Janie to be our greeter, and Sam better keep his mouth shut. He's a good guy. He just doesn't understand when you need certain talents in certain places, you can't wait for all the red tape to finish unraveling. I'll set the wheels in motion. I have both their private lines. Those are official FBI credentials. She must think you're a hell of an artist to make a set like that. Now, let's hear your ideas on the plague being visited on Flo's home in the meantime."

"Like you're aware of, John, these punks shoot first, and ask questions later. Jess and I were thinking of getting a line on this bunch through Laredo and Jafar. Then we hit their crib. I've seen you in action. You could fill in for Crue in a second. We're hoping the ones behind this action are other gang hierarchy thugs, or possibly some local guys thinking to make a name for themselves. If it's a Cartel establishing a presence, we're well aware that would be bad news."

I sat back in my chair after Dev stopped speaking, considering seriously we had too many coincidences. We had an attempted takeover of the ports, a 'Bulgarian Ghost', and soldiers from the Nigerian Boko Haram contingent, all making their presence known with other local thugs thrown into the mix. "I think we're lucky in a way, Jess. There are damn well too many coincidences around here since we heard about Phoebe Christova. It may be a small sprout on a larger tree, but we may as well take care of this business, if only to find out what their first move after entails. Wait one."

I called into Central Command, located of course with our holding cells, and Pain Central. "It's your nickel," Laredo responded. "I'm a little busy here, John."

"I think we've inadvertently ran into another thread from Christova with gangs using the old 'Section Eight' poor and downtrodden card to take over distribution points in Oakland. Can you delve into that and get back to me. If the lead looks promising, would you let Denny know? He's there with Gus. Maybe they can get something tangible from our many new guests."

"Jafar got here only a few minutes ago. We'll work it right away. Damn, I hope you're wrong. God only knows what the hell is going on with what I've already traced in terms of payments, and our main leak. It's not good, brother."

"We had far too short a vacation. I'll be glad when we purchase that damn island."

"Amen to that. Gotta' go, John. Talk to you in a few."

"Yep." I disconnected, to face my audience. "By the sound of things I don't think I'm far off on the connections part of this. Laredo's praying it's not true, but from the tone of his voice, and what he's found out, we may be in for a world of hurt."

"Great!" Dev looked like I felt. "I was hoping for Jess and Mommy issues, easily rectified with a couple of beat-downs to the right people."

Jess nearly coughed up the egg he'd swallowed whole in a piece of toast. "Me and Mommy issues... oh... it is so on, Dev. Payback's a bitch, buddy."

I enjoyed the interaction completely. These two had been together since grade school, fought the same fights in school, and on a battlefield far from home. They had each other's back without question, which is why I didn't discount anything they came to me with. "If you two are done grab-assin', I think I know a way to bring this into the open for extra inspection."

"You do?" Jess didn't look convinced at all; and Dev merely smiled, knowing he'd hear the plan in real time, so who cares about the threads connecting it.

"It depends on Laredo and Jafar getting us more info, such as the trademark name of the group causing the damage. We need a rival cartel card for bait."

"You've been playin' with sharks in the Bay too long, amigo," Jess said, staring at me, while hoping I hadn't lost my mind. "Give it to us plain and simple, John."

"I like Dev's idea of a gangland Godfather presence. I'm thinking we have three experts in Cartel business who could put a sting in place we could really bust this wide open with quickly."

"The minions! Damn... that is pure genius. Those guys would kill each other in hopes of getting the Godfather role." Dev paused for a second. "It has to be Gus. He can out quick his two buddies with adlibs easily, and this role may require some big adlibs. Jess and I will be part of his gang, of course. We need a long range player, and two more short range specialists. I'm thinking Lucas and Casey would cut us all up if we aced them out of a role like this."

"You're thinkin' Chicago bad news bears fronting for a Cartel," Jess stated. "We strut around in thousand dollar suits with hats and the whole enchilada! I like it. We can do this! God knows what lowlife pukes we can get to bite on the lure."

"You guys are nuts," Lora said, sitting down with us and Al, who was hanging on every word as if it were a raft in the middle of the Pacific Ocean. "Keep Flo with you until the police handle this neighborhood invasion."

Dev and Jess laughed like hell at that declaration before they noticed Lora wasn't smiling. Jess stared right at me. "You never told her, did you?"

I knew right away what he was talking about, but I had never saw fit to pass that particular info onto my wife. "It never came up in conversation until now, Jess. Gee... thank you for that gem."

"What?" Jess went into his all innocent persona, shaking his head in forlorn fashion, while lowering his head, and placing his hands palm down on the table. Of course he had to lay his fork down too, which I'm sure didn't appeal to him. He soldiered on. "You can't blame me because you kept relevant facts about your neighborhood from your lovely wife."

"Yeah... I can." It was too late for any of that, as I noticed the down at the mouth look I was getting from my wife. Damn, it seemed like only days ago she was okay about everything from my past and present. This is what happens when too much leeway is given - too much more gets assumed by force of will: her will.

"Please explain it to me, Jess," Lora said, with invisible claws out, and verbal fangs ready to maim and dismember. "I don't think I have heard about those adventures."

Dev was shaking his head virulently at our less astute brother in arms. Jess looked like a wolf caught in a bear trap.

"Go on, Jess. It's a small thing. You're right. It is my fault for not reciting the odd history of my surrounding neighborhood. Please fill Lora in on all the details."

"Yeah, Uncle Jess!" Al pipes in on the conversation she shouldn't have been around to hear about anyway.

"Uh... well... you know... John's street had a bad element in it. You remember when your sister was working with that law firm here, there were a lot of break-ins, and the gangs drifted around these neighborhoods like they owned them. Then John moves into his house, and suddenly the sun came out, the birds sang, and the sky was blue. Good Karma, I guess."

Okay, that was funny. Even Al was laughing. Not Lora, but who knows why she latches onto anything these days. My beloved wife has always spouted the right words about understanding my lifestyle, but I believe there's always been a disconnect waiting to surface. Apparently, the warning gong went off, and I didn't pay attention to it. Al saw her Mom's face and stopped enjoying Jess's very entertaining explanation.

"I hear what you're saying now, Jess," Lora stated with precise wording. "In other words, the landfills around the area became thug burial grounds. My sister mentioned something about a pimp she represented who gutted her cat, while making advances on her. She told me the pimp was found a couple weeks later, after she hired John through Tommy to protect her, in a dump on 12th Street. It's amazing how this Karma thing works."

Dev was starting to get a little grim about Lora's sarcastic angle. "Yeah... I heard about that. Your sister's still alive, and pregnant with the first child to be calling you Aunt Lora, huh? I guess that Karma thing ought to be left alone to do its work in peace, Boss."

Oh my, that was good. Lora's face went from sarcastically evil to a 'good Lord in heaven, what the hell am I doing in a split

276

second. She stood, went around, and hugged Dev. "Thanks, Dev. Some thing in my brain has snapped. All my prior protestations about understanding John's endeavors have become ranting crap, criticizing him. I'm going to go do something useful like laundry."

Lora came to me next. "Jesus, I don't know what the hell's wrong with me lately, John. I'm sorry."

Knowing instinctively Lora thought when she goes off into a weird tangent I might bolt on her, I stood, enveloping her in my arms. "I'm never leaving you, unless you kick me out, Hon. Maybe I should have told you about-"

"No... you shouldn't have told me about any of this." Lora sealed my mouth off with her hand. "Most I've guessed from talking to Della next door. I'm not this naïve. I know mentioning the police being able to end the threat in Flo's neighborhood was stupid. Hell, they want to lynch cops when they take a stand anywhere in this dumbass city. I can only imagine the fallout for the Blue if they try and rescue a neighborhood from unknown sources. C'mon, Al. Want to help me with the laundry?"

Seeing an opening in her Mom's unusual behavior lately, Al stepped up. "Sure, Mom. I want to help. Don't be mad. Dad knows what he's doing. I'll help if he's a little slack on chores, and I don't care if he has to get someone to fill in as my coach. He's stopping terrorists! We're playing softball... big deal! Like Lynn always says, 'it is what it is'. I know we can't be part of everything like the fights, and altering what he has to do, but if you ever go psycho on me, I'm staying with Dad. I know he's my real Dad no matter what the DNA claims. My real Dad hasn't even called me in months!"

Uh oh. I've been so busy with my crap, I hadn't given Al's plight a thought. Her Dad's an okay guy. He lives elsewhere with a family. Blaming him for anything is a crock, but Al writing him off like she did is one step too far in the blame game. "Have you called him, Al?"

Al knew in an instant she'd screwed up. It took a few moments before she shrugged. "No, Dark Lord, I didn't. I'll call him tonight. I shouldn't have said that. I guess we should go do something useful, Mom."

"Thanks for breakfast. It was great," Jess said, with Dev and I echoing his compliment.

"No problem," Lora answered on the way out with Al in tow.

"Back to business. We need to find out who the hell is moving into Flo's neighborhood, and what they're selling. Then we may have to lean on someone to find out where they hang out unless Laredo and Jafar can get a read on them. I'm certain they know you, Jess, so when we drive you into the neighborhood with the Godfather minions, we'll let you do the talking. I'll ask the guys we're questioning this morning if they know of anything being started in the neighborhoods on a grassroots level. That Nigerian hit-man they sent in to kill the baby will probably know something about local area operations. The Bulgarians we have will be able to substantiate whatever the fake Doc says. I'm glad we have roots around the ports here. Apparently, they're in high demand to ship some very dangerous cargo from the East to the West, including terrorist soldiers."

Dev and Jess exchanged agreeing looks.

"What do you want us to do, Dark Lord?"

"I think it would be good if you two went over to Flo's house in the thousand dollar outfits we mentioned before, check damage and entry on the house. Drive something impressive, and not that old beater of yours, Dev."

"My old beater makes that piece of shit Chevy you hold onto look like a scrap yard reject. We'll go in Jess's Chrysler though in spite of your insults."

"Good choice," I replied. "Remember we want 'Wall Street' chic gangsters."

"You hear this jeans and a t-shirt manikin talkin' to us, Dev?"

"It explains his disrespect for his brothers in arms, Jess. He's like when that woman Gertrude Stein described Oakland as 'there is no there there'. The same goes for brother John's expertise in dressing," Dev added, while the two comedians stood away from the table in a huff, joining on their way to my door. "His mama dressed him funny, and now he's taking it out on everyone around him."

"No, Dev," Jess corrected, "John don't even know who his mama was. Maybe his Daddy wanted a girl, and got John instead."

Damn it! That was a solid gold serve. "I'm watchin' you, Jess. You must have a ghost writer writing your lines for you - no way you create that one yourself. Admit it, you're using Dev's writer. That he even knows who Gertrude Stein is makes me uncomfortable."

They laughed their asses off all the way out the door with Dev making call me gestures with his hand as a phone to his ear. I grinned at their departure, trying to figure out a way to separate Lora from Al for a quickie. Yeah, even we monsters have needs. I wracked my brain, but thought of nothing other than maybe an Al visit to a friend's house. With Al, you have to be careful, because she's onto everything her Mom and I formulate as a plan without her. She loves to serve it at an incredibly opportune time without remorse. I gave up, and simply joined them in our laundry room. The looks Lora gave me as I helped with the clothes promised bonanzas in later dark hours.

* * *

"Dark Lord," Denny enunciated in true Spawn form. "Did mommy finally let you out of the house?"

"She did indeed allow me out to play. Have we any new toys to play with?" I sat down with our monster minions at the Pain Central conference table. Lucas and Casey attended too, so something must have broken free in the info department. They all looked relatively happy, so I figured them to be the bearers of good news.

"First order of business is the remarkable interrogation of Yuri. We showed it to our three Bulgarians, and Doc Ock as you call him. When I told them you were coming in to interrogate them later in the morning, they talked until I thought I'd have to stun-gun them into silence. I believe you broke new ground with that technique. Secondly, we have the name of our leak, thanks to Jafar. He traced an IP address in Christova's e-mails to one of our supposed benefactors, Senator Kaline Nikolov. He and Laredo followed it along its slimy trail. She is the one. Ever consider assassinating a sitting Senator, John?"

"I am now, but I bet you have a plot in mind far better than simply killing her. Spill it, Den. Don't make me have to beg."

Denny slapped the table. "We're going to double her up. I already have so much on her since we've found her name, she's my bitch to eternity, or she will be bound as a traitor. She will do our will or I will put her in the general population of a prison for the rest of her life. I swear to God, John, if she barters her way free, I will slit the bitch's throat with my own hand."

Well, I see Denny is in for the duration of this. "Good start. I can see all the positives in supplying false info to Christova through this Nikolov connection. It buys us time as well as eyes on target. On a local level, did you make anything out of these neighborhood threads I texted you about?"

"We are yours, John," Quays proclaimed. "Silvio and I will support Gus as the new Godfather of crime in Jess's neighborhood. We've reached into the network with our contacts. We can manage a slight rip-off of the Los Zeta's Cartel. We have a rather goofy plan we'd like to spring on you though."

I liked Quays Tannous. He'd been through a lot, and he was unwaveringly on our side. Plus, he was a bloody monster like his two Lynn minions. "Make me believe, Quays."

Quays chuckled. "We know where this swarm of cockroaches are. We will go there today and barter, but we need your okay to do it."

Fine, I'm intrigued. "What the hell do you guys have in mind?"

"Quays formulated the basic concept," Silvio said. "We have money much like the Cartels do. Why the hell shouldn't we fight these suckers with money? These gangbanging idiots fight for nothing but to last another day as slaves to their drug bosses, and addicts as bad as any of their customers. Why not offer them a real choice… after we show them strength."

I was beginning to get a chilly liking for this plan. "I have a feeling I'm going to get personally involved in this, my friend. I see it in the humor covering your features. Tell me how."

"We've all seen these movies where one side proclaims to spare all the bloodshed between two opposing factions with champions. With your permission, we're going to create the Oaktown Cartel. We'll need a champion to sell this novel idea. Any ideas, John?"

"I'm your man, Quays." This had a flavor to it I liked. "When do we start?"

"Tonight, after we finalize the details today. We already have it in the works. They have a big bad from Columbia, nearly seven feet tall I understand, and kills with his bare hands rather than disgrace himself with a weapon. When we put out the rumors the neighborhood was off limits, and under our protection, they offered this fight deal. We read trap all the way, but we figured to let you decide what to do with it. We texted Dev and Jess to be subtle in their recon of Jess's Mom's house. You could of course be killed in a trap, which is what we think this is, but we'd have our own guys in place who have your back to the death."

Who needs time off and vacations. I could watch 'The 300' every night. I believe the same as those fabled Spartans from long ago. Who knows the truth of legend? I wouldn't mind carving my own. "Where would something like this take place? We would need to recon the area before I arrive like some rube on his first trip into trouble."

"We won't proceed unless we find out the spot they have in mind," Silvio replied. "The moment we find out, I'll let Lucas or Casey know. I would imagine you'd want them for the long range backup."

"Yep, I want Lucas and Casey long range. Tommy and Clint will be at my side if Clint can get away from his duties at the hospital for a few hours. I want the rest of you dressed to the nines like Hollywood gangsters, packing body armor, and MP5's in case I lose. We don't lose, by the way. I may lose. Then it's open season on your idea, and our potential Oaktown Cartel."

"Earl and 'Rique are in on this too, John," Quays said. "We called them, because they're our touchstone to keep our brother Blue's out of this. They heard rumors about this new strong-arming tactic to push through Section Eight housing, and contacted Denny, who in turn asked what we thought about it."

"So, they won't relay the meeting place until later, huh?"

"That is how they specified it. They'll know the place. We get the details a half hour before the meeting, but we're going to push for more when we go over there today," Gus answered. "If they won't give us the meeting place, I'll text you for a decision. A half hour is a damn short window to operate in."

282

Lucas moved beside me, gripping my arm. "You do know this is a horseshit trap, right?"

"It moves our timetable way ahead if Christova is connected in any way, Lucas. It's good to get this local crap put in our laps like this. It widens our database of info as to what's going on in our home base area."

"If you lose and live, I will of course turn the rest of your life into a living hell. You know that right, Recon?"

"I would expect nothing less." I gripped his shoulders. "Don't let me get cut short from my duty. I don't want some cherry picking me off from far away before I get to face Goliath."

"You have my word on it… Marine."

That's all I needed for this. "I'll get rested, if there's nothing else to discuss. Come get me when it's time, guys. Hell of an idea, Quays. I hope we can use the money in a long range reclamation deal with the gangs. We'll need to confiscate more from people no longer able to use it. I have to go home, and make this right with Lora. She'll probably toast my marshmallows, but this fight with the big guy is too good to pass up. I hope Clint can make it."

"I'll talk to Clint," Denny promised. "I won't pressure him. If he can't make it, I'll stand in for him. Are you sure you're up to this? We can do it another way."

"It's what I do. These gangsters have been watching too many movies. They believe the outcome will be me dead on my back. I'm thinking we're through playing around, and things will be getting rough until we lock down Christova. With Quays idea of an Oaktown Cartel, we could get fed info from multiple sources while squashing the gangs that don't conform. It's a hell of a trial run, but I like it. Do we have enough money with all we've confiscated to pull off something like he has in mind?"

"We sure do," Denny replied. "If we land Christova, it will be jackpot time for confiscation. I will go to work on our Senator leak right now. Go home, and get some sleep, John. We'll handle the details the rest of the way."

"Will do."

"Hey John," Casey called out as I walked away. "You do know there won't be any rules in this hack fight, don't you?"

I grinned back at Casey. "I'm counting on it, Case. We can't win any chips if we don't gamble some. Don't forget to pack your MP5 too, Night-shot."

"You got it, John. No one will interrupt from outside, and if Clint's with you inside, there won't be any interference there either."

"Maybe you should stay and rest up here, Recon. Otherwise, we won't be sure if Lora will allow you to show for the match," Lucas zapped me.

I walked out with much laughter behind me.

* * *

Oh baby, this is what it's all about. I walked into the large grubby shed with a smile of recognition. It even smelled of fear and desperation. A single large fluorescent light array hung from the rafters in the middle. Under the light, the debris had been scraped away so a weighted mat could be laid into place. Nothing but shadows existed beyond the mat area. My retinue of Godfather minions, along with Dev, Jess, Tommy, and Clint were at my side, and at my back. They dressed as we had decided, all in thousand dollar suits, and matching hats, with light overcoats we built holders for the MP5's into. Luckily, this wasn't summer on the Bay, and the temperature inside the shed felt to be no more than the high 50's. Tommy met my gaze, grinning from ear to ear. Yep, he and I were home again.

284

"Was Lynn okay with you going, Clint?" I was a little worried about Crue's take on this.

Clint nodded. "She said come back with your shield or on it."

"Cool."

"I don't know how all this is going to play out, but I'm glad you let me come," Tommy said in a low keyed voice.

"Drop if there's gunplay. Man, you look good. What did Rachel say about your duds?"

Tommy chuckled. "She wanted to keep me at home to role play as the black Bonnie and Clyde."

Now that was entertainment. The mooks on the other side thought we were laughing at them, including their giant. Good Lord, he was big. Bad part for him was, he'd been having it so easy killin' people, he'd let his gut grow. The giant was out of shape.

"What you laughin' at," the lead mook called out. All of them had a hand inside their coat with a threatening gesture against our imagined disrespect. I wasn't worried. I had Clint. The chances of any mook across the mat clearing their coat before Clint shot them all in the head were slim and none.

"Anything we want to laugh at, Tony Soprano," Gus fired back. We were here to make our presence known, not take shit from a bunch of cheap thugs. "Are we going to do this or do you need to change your pants?"

The lead mook pointed at our very dapper Gus, gracing him with what I'm sure was his scowling killer look he practiced in the mirror. "After Kong gets done with that pussy you brought, I'll have him rip your head off too. Get on the mat, girlie. Here's the rules... there ain't no rules. Whoever's left breathin' wins."

285

I guess I'm girlie, so I stepped on the mat with my hands in position. Kong and I both had mixed martial arts gloves on. He had been smiling ever since we walked to the mat. I like a happy guy. He had a mouthpiece in so I guess he figured he might get hit. We didn't shake hands. Kong swung a round house left hook I think would have decapitated me if it had landed. I ducked, and smacked the inside of his left knee with my own hello kick. That got his attention. Kong stopped smiling, and gimped a step backwards, so I smacked the inside of his right knee with a real pile driver smash. Kong dropped to his knees. I wasn't here to prolong this thing, so I put a flying knee right between his eyes. It blasted him off the mat where he skidded into his fellow Sopranos.

I stayed where I was, not wanting to follow him into thug central where I'd only be in the way if Clint had to kill them all on the spot. The mooks scrambled getting Kong back on his feet. I could tell the birdies were playing amongst the starbursts inside his thick skull. He could take it. That's for sure. My knee to his forehead should have killed him. Kong wasn't too steady on his feet, but he was mad as hell. He smashed his gloves together, and roared. I never saw that coming. I glanced at Tommy, but he was too busy laughing his ass off at Kong's roar to give me a clue what he thought about it.

One thing I did know. Kong could roar, but no way would he be rushing me after those kicks. He didn't. Kong plodded toward me, serious as a heart attack, hands in position, crouching to protect his legs. He threw some nice left right combinations without the leg action he needed to really get power into them. I stepped inside, and fired my own combo into his ribs. He belched out a grunt of pain that smelled like he'd been eating road kill for a week raw. His hands dropped, and I hit him with a left upper cut mostly to get his breath turned in a different direction. It dropped him on his ass, so I stepped away, and smashed a right roundhouse kick to his left temple. Goodnight sweet prince. Kong dropped sideways to the mat, snoring before he hit. I shrugged at the lead mook.

"Want me to kill him? I know you said the fight's only over when one of us ain't breathin'. Do I have to end old Kong, or is comatose okay for the win?"

I could hear my guys laughing, but the Sopranos stared open mouthed at Kong. Then lead mook tried a quick draw. Clint put a .45 slug through his head spattering his companions with brain matter as it exited.

"Unless you want to die, keep your hands at your sides," Clint warned. "I won't tell you twice. You want to take it from here, Gus?"

"Thanks, Clint. We're taking you guys with us for a question, answer, and recruitment session. We'll give you an option then to join us and expand, or get the hell out of the country. We'll have to put blindfolds on you gangsters, and restraints. I think once our profitable enterprise is explained thoroughly, most of you will take our offer to go legit."

"Fuck you! Fuck this! I-"

Soprano number two got a new eyehole in his forehead. Clint made clucking noises. "I'm sorry. Did you assholes think we're voting on this?"

"Now… whoever wants to go with us to hear the details of our offer get on your knees with hands behind your back," Gus stated. "Anyone else who doesn't want to go with us, bend over and kiss your ass goodbye."

The remaining five dropped to their knees with hands behind their backs. I checked on Kong while the other guys restrained our new guests going to Pain Central. Kong was not doing well. I walked over to one of our detainees. He tried to pretend I wasn't staring right at him, so I knelt, and took his chin into a nearly bone crushing grip.

"I want to know about Kong. Are the rumors true he's a killer of men, women, and children?" I was only asking, because it would mean one fewer passenger. We'd be doing DNA, fingerprint, and picture checks on the other five. If any of them were guilty of the same thing, they would not be getting a deal. They would be getting the Bay cruise.

"Si... Kong is a very bad man."

"Thanks." I returned to Kong, and snapped his neck with a slow deliberate positioning, followed by the final twist of death. I turned to the detainees. "Anyone else guilty of such behavior, say so now, because we will be checking. If we can, we'll give you over to the authorities. If we have to find out the hard way, the ending will be very bad."

No one else indicated they were like Kong. I'd bet the guys who Clint shot were the two in the group much like Kong. "Okay, no takers, so let's get the blindfolds on, and go get this party started."

"Wait!" The guy I'd asked about Kong wanted to discuss a bit more, and he was sweating bullets in the coolness doing it. "There are four men in position, and probably moving on the building now."

"Did you guys hear that," Clint asked our own protection outside. He was in direct communication with Lucas and Casey.

"We heard," Casey drawled. "We didn't want to interrupt business for simple statistics. It's messy outside the shed, so watch where you're walkin', brother."

"Will do," Clint acknowledged. He made a throat slitting gesture at me. "Case said watch the path we follow to where we parked our vehicles, or we're apt to gather DNA on the bottom of our shoes."

I patted my informant's face. "Good one. That piece of information earned you a step ahead of your companions in the survival game, except it isn't a game. We kill when we're surprised. Actually, that's not exactly true. We get surprised, and then we kill the surprise party people. The ones who knew about a surprise party get to exit life through the seventh level of hell. Believe me... you don't want that. Is there anything else we should know before we go outside?"

Silence. Boy, are they going to like the scene outside, where Lucas and Casey probably did double taps through the head of these guys' backup soldiers. Such is life if you tread into monster land. I'm immediately thinking by the monster minions' happy looks, they think these guys with us now are in control of a local bunch of shitheads throughout the city. Quay's idea of forcing local gangs into our Oaktown Cartel might be the biggest positive play we've made so far. It was time to go.

The Kong match had my blood boiling. I expected more, and got less. For this operation, that was a good thing. It never ends well for amateur, sadistic bad-asses. They're really scary for blue collar folks, including men, women, and children to face. They usually look like Kong, so big, one deadly look from them freezes the blood of hard working people trying to raise families while working for a living. That's where we come in. I lead monsters more deadly than Kong ever imagined. We didn't come here to this shed to lose or negotiate. We arrived to kill or be killed. Sure, we had some nice plusses added on with a personal touch, like brother Jess's Mom's house taken off the hit list of gang's that shouldn't exist.

"I think we're done here," Gus said. "Let's take our new friends incognito to their surroundings, and head for Pain Central."

Gus went over and embraced a surprised Clint. "Thank you. We needed you here, Clint. I'm sorry we took you away from 'The Mistress of the Unimaginable' at this time. Please tell her that her minions pray for her wellbeing, and Clint Jr's, every second."

I could tell Clint was startled. He patted Gus. "I will tell her, Gus. I'll tell you a secret because we're here and it seems appropriate. She loves you guys. Lynn already threatened Denny with extermination if he tried to take you guys out, and I back any play she makes known. You guys are golden with us."

Gus backed away, swiping at his eyes. "Thank you for telling us that, Clint. Let's herd these new recruits to their destination. I feel we will make a big splash with this idea Quays invented. He should be Godfather of the Oaktown Cartel."

"No way!" Quays strode next to Gus, his hands waving off Gus's declaration with emphasis. "You're a natural, Gus. Silvio and I are agreed. You'll be the Godfather we keep in front of the Oaktown Cartel, and it's not because we need an easy target. Anyone targeting you better have all their last wishes in print."

Everyone thought this in itself was entertaining, I glanced at Clint with a grim Cheeseburger look. He nodded and smiled.

"Let's go. We'll sort out this killer ambiance later. I like your idea though, Gus. I'm going now to join Crue at the hospital. Watch your phones. There will be pictures."

"Don't forget about post natal depression, Clint," Jess inserted into the discussion. "It's a serious deal, and we need to watch out for any signs of it in Crue."

"Don't worry about that, Jess. If she shows any sign of that post natal depression, I'll just beat her with my belt. She'll be fine."

Oh my, did we enjoy that word picture for a few moments.

Chapter 12

Riding the Wave

Denny attended our Oaktown Cartel recruitment conference with high expectations. I could tell from his body language, and the excitement he couldn't keep from his features. I didn't like any of this, but I knew the results could be incredible. If they came to fruition, Quays idea would spread around our home base area in a positive tidal wave against the worst of society's element. I'm not on a crusade, but this Cartel sham might allow us time and misdirection we vitally needed. Earl and 'Rique showed too. I had filled them in on every part of our plan. They signed on to our CIA, Homeland, and FBI plot to report any suspicious activity. Denny had provided money, and credentials for their help. He never asked for their participation in anything, other than warning them of an impending operation.

"I'd love to see this work," 'Rique said, "but there will be many of these gangbangers who will say one thing and do another. If it worked, we could make real progress in taking the neighborhoods back that are being terrorized now."

"My partner's right, guys," Earl agreed. "This scheme will be your toughest one so far to pull off. Using the gangs you recruit to enforce this Oaktown Cartel front will be really tricky. I know you have three experts on gang hierarchy and control. I hope to God they're successful, and this doesn't turn into a blood bath. That attempted killing at the hospital by a hit squad has everyone from the Mayor down running for cover."

"Those pussies run for cover no matter what happens," Lucas replied. "I think if the way these gangster wannabes reacted to seeing their four guys with heads blown off on the fight shed's outer entrance was any indication, we'll get cooperation. They're enjoying a video of John's interrogation of Yuri Kornev as we speak. If that doesn't convince them we will do anything necessary to install our own Cartel presence, nothing will. I like our chances."

I agreed. "Think of an underground source for information like this. We can be spread out across the city and area. Sure, there will be drug addicts clamoring for their fixes. Well, boo hoo, that won't be happening except in the bad sections of our littered metropolis without neighborhoods. I was leery of this project myself at the start, but I'm warming to the notion every second. Hey, if it doesn't work, we'll shoot them all through the head."

The monsters enjoyed my final solution for failure. Good thing, because that was exactly how I figured to do it. I'm sick of gangbanging scum calling the shots in Oakland. They terrorize the neighborhoods where decent people live, while letting professional whiners protest every single action by the police, thanks to the bought and paid for asshole media. We needed to change perspectives. If we failed, we needed to kill more bad guys. Works for me.

"We'll back your play within reason, John," Earl said. "We know you guys are dedicated to the survival of America, and our politicians are not. Hell, like Lucas said, they throw us under the bus in a split second. 'Rique and I have to walk the tightrope, but we'll call Denny if we hear of something unexpected coming your way."

"We will fix things slowly, Earl," I told him. "I know if we move too fast, we'll screw our chances of making progress. Once we repair a problem we have with an internal affair, we should have more time and resources to smooth things on our new project. In the meantime, we did successfully end the takeover on Coolidge Avenue, which could have been a wild-west distribution point in the middle of a blue collar neighborhood. That win should get us some slack with the city. Gus has something we'd like you to put into the city fathers' hands which should distract them a bit. Go ahead, Gus, make your presentation."

Gus passed out folders Laredo and Jafar had put together from our new recruits. "Our informants have names, money transfers, and video linking some very influential people in Oakland politics with a Section Eight housing scam to put drug operations into place in strategic neighborhood areas. We know who started buying their way into this, and we know she's not interested in running drugs. She's trying to create a shipping network utilizing our own neighborhoods instead of warehouses for acting as intermediate safe houses for weapons of a sophisticated nature: electromagnet pulse weapons which could put our entire nation in jeopardy. Her name is Phoebe Christova. We're working with Alexi Fiialkov to stop her cold."

Earl and 'Rique were staring at each other in open mouthed shock, having perused the folders Gus provided, and the names in them. We needed Earl and 'Rique with us on this. "Any Oakland political figure trying to mess with you two will find out how extensive our researching capabilities really are. It won't be necessary after you hand over these folders in person to do any preaching or threatening. Our ploy will be more impressive when carried out by two rank and file police officers."

"Jesus, Mary, and Joseph," 'Rique mumbled. "It's no damn wonder this city is always under siege."

"It explains why we're not getting any backing no matter what we do," Earl added. "If your guys can get this info, then it means the names in these folders are already in the hands of the wrong people. What happens when these jerks in office can't control anything, and the gangsters owning them start squeezing, John?"

"Any one of a few things," I answered. "They can resign, go into rehab with cries of 'I'm so sorry', or they can do what the hell they're supposed to be doing in office. We're not backing away. We'll expose them, one after another. They'll have to make their own decisions on their next moves. Denny agreed with me on

293

this. The police officers risking their lives every day needed to know what they're up against, so they can take precautions."

"So we're not supposed to keep this secret then?"

I grinned, because I loved this part. "We don't care what you guys do with the info, 'Rique. We're as sick of listening to your bosses talk about crime prevention, taking back the neighborhoods, and how they're behind law enforcement a hundred percent as you guys are. Then the first outcry from gangbanger love puppies, and they throw Blue under the bus. I think it's time to try something new. As you say, we have three experts on the interior workings in the thug world."

Earl held up his stack of folders. "We'll get on this right away. Where's Denny at?"

"He's in Washington by now, gathering a band of our backers together to end our own internal affairs problem. Don't worry, Laredo flew him there, and is monitoring everything going on here. If we hit a snag, both Laredo and Denny will fix it. In the meantime, we will be coaching girls' softball, and checking on Lynn, and the newest addition to our monster squad."

"One other ah... situation, John," Earl said. "There have been a lot of bodies, the latest in an old warehouse shed, we figured was connected to the price of doing business getting gangbangers in line. We've also received complaints about a number of missing men, phoned in by the people working for that Christova you mentioned. Are they all dead?"

I hesitated for a moment, because we hadn't read in Earl and 'Rique on our prior collections. What the hell, I'm not keeping two guys I trust implicitly in the dark. "They're not dead. The Bulgarians we were holding, Denny traded to Russia, because they were linked with two bombings there. In return, Russia will provide logistical help on another deal we're finalizing to get Christova. We only have one man in holding: an assassin I call Doc

Ock, because he's the one who led the attack on the hospital, seeking to kill Clint and Lynn's baby. We're not trading him, and you won't ever see his face except on the side of a milk carton, so it would be best to forget any rumors moving in police circles about a fifth guy at the hospital."

"Understood, John," 'Rique acknowledged. "When are you all coming over to The Warehouse? The guys ask about you bunch all the time."

I glanced around at my monsters. "I think when we get Lynn, Clint, and Clint Jr out of the NICU, we'll sponsor a night for the Blue with all of us in attendance. The Clint Jr. baby wing has been completed at their house, so we're hoping for Lynn and Clint Jr's release in the next couple of days. Clint Jr's already gained a couple of pounds, so he may be really close to release.

"Damn! That's outstanding news," 'Rique said. "Lynn makes my blood run cold, but she believes in everything I do, and she's not hampered by guidelines. She's like watching my evil side make everything happen the way I want it to."

"Tell 'em, John," Casey said. "They'll get a charge out of it, and they couldn't do anything about it anyway."

I did as Casey directed, including Lynn's line she told Denny after she gutted and shot the two men thinking to attack their residence. By the time I finished the story, everyone was enjoying my Cruella Deville dangerous moments before birth tale.

"Holy mother of God," Earl said, covering his face with his hands. "I'm glad she's on our side. Please tell her hello for me, and I'm praying every day for her recovery, and the wellbeing of Clint Jr."

"Ditto!" 'Rique said with feeling. "We do not wish Diabla to take anything we say or do the wrong way. I have less fear of the Cartels."

295

It was entertaining to hear verbal mumbling in the same vein from the rest of my crew. I understood Crue as Clint I'm sure did, and as the rest of my companions did on an elemental basis. When you piss her off, you'd better have a safe-house somewhere, much like a 1950's bomb shelter, where your breathing, food, and waste production cannot be detected. Otherwise, Crue would hunt your ass down, adding on hours of unspeakable torture according to the time it took her to locate you. And yes, we minions of the 'Mistress of the Unimaginable' would be helping. It's best to stay in touch with the darkest side of any enterprise. To do otherwise provokes consequences unimaginable to normal folk.

"I think we all see eye to eye on the main item on our agenda. Let's go work our angles in preparation for the coming of the Oaktown Cartel. We want everything in place when we put the now extinct 'Coolidge Avenue Section Eight Fraud's' con-artists back on the street under new management. We'll see over the next few weeks what kind of rats they draw into the light. It will be the Oaktown Cartel's enforcement arm to smooth the rough spots."

"For their sakes, they better leave town before the Oaktown Cartel gets its gun moll back from the hospital," Gus said.

"Amen to that," Earl added, with reverent agreements from the rest of our conference members.

* * *

Cloudy and humid, our first week of May felt in the comfortable mid-seventies at noontime first pitch. Al's team made the playoffs. We were getting our butts kicked. The girls played hard, and nearly error free ball, but the Cardinals had a team mostly on the upper age limit for our league. Their pitcher threw high heat, and their batters blasted our pitching into the furthest reaches of the park. They batted to the six run limit two innings in a row. Here we were, leading off the third behind twelve to two. Our girls stared off into space as Samira and I tried to ease the agony of defeat, but they weren't having any.

"It's okay, Dad." Al became the spokesperson for the team somewhere in midseason. "We'll play as well as they are when we're in our twenties too. I think their pitcher has two kids, and drove a Buick to the park today."

That comment loosened them a bit. It was a free-for-all afterward for best one liner describing the ages of our opponents. Casey and Jafar enjoyed the insult-a-thon far too inappropriately for coaches, but sometimes these kids' sporting events can only be enjoyed in a humorous vein, and Al had found it.

"You're up first, Kelly," Samira called out, as the umpire was giving us the evil eye.

Twelve year old Kelly with an auburn hair ponytail sticking out the back of her cap paused near Samira. "I think you should get the ump to check the pitcher. She has a beard stubble, and her Mom in the stands called her Tommy."

"Kelly!" Samira gasped, turning away with clipboard and free hand over her face, as Kelly's teammates and coaches inappropriately enjoyed the moment once again. I gestured the unrepentant Casey and Jafar to their coaching positions.

I put a hand on Kelly's shoulders. "Go get something started, Kel."

"I would, but the Cardinals are so big, I can't see an open spot to hit the ball."

"Good idea. Bunt the sucker."

Kelly giggled and nodded. What the hell? We worked on our bunting every practice. Nothing else seemed to be working. Kelly's fast, so this could be interesting. I signaled Casey on third base what we were doing. He acknowledged, and it was game on. Kelly didn't show bunt until the last second. She dribbled it perfectly up the first base line. The pitcher beat the catcher to the ball, scooped it, and threw it into the right field corner. By the time the right fielder relayed the throw in, Kelly was ambling across home plate with a bunt homerun. While we celebrated a bright spot in the day, the Cardinal's coach went ballistic. She went right into the face of her pitcher, arms waving. Such is life in girls' softball land. I'd go to killing bad guys full time before I ever pulled a stunt like that. Luckily, the pitcher's Mom rushed out onto the field with fists clenched, and fire in her eyes. That ended the coaching diatribe, but almost in a fist fight. We kept our mouths shut on our side. The umpire finally stopped hiding, and came out in front of the plate to yell 'play ball'. I turned to the girls.

"Bunting practice, anyone?" Oh boy, did the girls ever get into that one. The inning ended on us being held to the six run rule. Our pitcher, Wendy, who had been pitching a terrific game, firing it right over the strike zone, pulled me aside.

"I...I don't want to screw us again, John. Maybe you should substitute for me."

I shook my head, as Samira put an arm around Wendy's shoulders. "You pitched great. They're hitting your fastball. Remember when we worked on throwing a change-up? It's the same arm motion until you let go of the pitch. Mix them up at your discretion. It doesn't matter if we have another bat around by the Cardinals. We're competing, kid. That's what it's all about. Another thing I need you to keep in mind. They may go the bunt route against you. Keep your calm. Turn, check the runner's progress, and throw a strike to first base. I already went through that with our catcher Karen. Call off Karen, if you think you have it. Otherwise, let Karen handle the play."

"Got it. Thanks, John." She ran to the pitcher's mound without hesitation.

"You are very good at this, John," Samira complimented me. "I love this. It takes my mind off of my soon to arrive daughter."

"I won't hint at knowing that feeling, but your being here to sub for Lynn has been terrific. I'm hoping the girls can learn to compete without malice. That last inning was hell-of-fun. I'm glad the pitcher's Mom made the Cardinal's coach scurry away. The Mom showed restraint in handling it, with a message to that airhead, reading her players out like they're getting paid for being here."

"I have video clipped many moments to Lynn. She is enjoying every moment, but she's a little demanding. Lynn has made remarks such as 'grow a pair you imbecile', and many more like that in regard to your coaching. She is engaged at every level of this game." Samira hesitated with her head lowered. "I am in fear of her, John."

"Relax, kid. You grew up in an Afghan cave. What the hell are you afraid of?"

"Lynn is an elemental force," Samira conceded. "She commands fear as if it were the natural state of things. I will remember what you have said though."

"Remember this then. Lynn loves you like her own little sister. I doubt there's anything you could do to piss her off."

Startled, Samira is staring at her tablet fearfully, "And yet she sends me this."

Samira held her iPad for my viewing of Lynn, staring close-up with her face in a Cruella Deville interrogation moment face. The text was 'are you ignoring me, baby Sis? That will not go well for you'.

"What do I do, John? She owns me."

"Tell her to… oh hell… give me your pad." I texted 'screw you, harpy. I won't send you shit from now on… bitch!', and sent it. In seconds we had a reply - 'heh… heh… I know you're texting for Sam, Cheeseburger… you pussy! There will be blood'! I

299

handed the pad to Samira once again. "Sorry, I should have seen that coming. You would think Clint Jr would be filling every Cruella Deville moment."

"She probably has him doing the dishes and laundry already," Samira replied.

We enjoyed that ace a few seconds too long, because instantly, on the iPad came this text: 'you two are not doing one liners about me behind my back, are you? Send me more clips... damn it'!

Sighing, I gave Sam a break, and did a clip for Crue of the inning starting. It seems although my coaching sucked, my precognitive powers were right on the money. The first Cardinal batter bunted down the first base line. Wendy streaked off the mound, picked it clean barehanded, and fired a strike by the head of the runner to Al on first base. Oh yeah! I sent the clip, and got an instant clip back with Crue dancing with the tiny Clint Jr. He gained weight steadily. Lynn and Clint spent every second doing the skin on skin preemie thing, nursing him along. We outsiders were not allowed in yet because of possible contamination. Maria's pediatrician specialists told Lynn if Clint Jr kept making the same startling improvements over the next couple weeks, they could have visitors.

"Lynn looks nearly like her old self," Sam said as she watched Lynn's clip over my shoulder. "She told me she's working out every day with Clint. I'm not sure I would like to guess at what she's getting into shape for."

"Probably not the details." I began another clip. Wendy threw a beautiful changeup the Cardinal batter was so out in front of she could have swung twice. She threw a fast pitch next the girl looked at for strike two. A foul tip popup to Al made the second out of the inning. I kept the clip going for Lynn's amusement as the Cardinal's coach emerged to argue about Wendy's delivery. The umpire pointed out it was the same delivery Wendy had in the first two innings, ending the discussion with a loud 'play ball'. In reply, I received a call to arms.

Lynn texted an all business note about Lucas calling Clint to report some friends of his had a lead on how Christova managed to get out of the Bay Area undetected. She added Clint would meet us at the pizza place to supply details. She ended with an order to keep the clips coming. I did as ordered. We lost by two runs, but we were in it to the end.

Samira showed them a clip Lynn did with Clint Jr in her arms during our team meeting at the end after we congratulated the Cardinals.

"I'm proud as hell of the way every one of you girls competed right down to the end," Lynn said. "I hope I can get another chance to coach you all again sometime in the future. God bless you all! That was one fine ass game!"

Lynn's fist pumping finish had the girls standing and pumping fists with her. When the clip ended, I simply shrugged with a smile. "What Lynn said goes double for me. Let's go get some pizza."

* * *

At the pizza place, all of my crew attended to congratulate the girls. In addition, Denny showed with Lucas and Clint, with Crue's minions, Gus, Quays, and Silvio. Even Laredo walked in, smiling and shaking hands. The gang was all here and they had their game faces on. Their approach quieted our celebration somewhat, but the girls' parents were morose anyway. It didn't register with them their kids came back from a 12 to 2 disaster to compete to the last out, and have fun while they overcame all kinds of crap. Al was happy, and exuberant in retelling the tale of how they nearly won the game. She didn't take credit for initiating the light hearted comment that started it all. Although that works to cement her in as a great teammate, I'll remember what really sparked the A's to their comeback. For now, we sipped, ate, and listened to very entertaining renditions of what went on through the game. After a while, even the morose parents perked up.

We waited until most of the parents and kids hit the road, leaving a couple of Al's closest friends, her fellow team smartasses: Kelly, and Wendy. Al approached us with a request I could see was eating her up from the inside out. "Kelly's parents want me and Wendy to spend the night. Can I... please?"

Lora looked to me. She wasn't one to ignore reality. "You have your iPhone. We want a FaceTime with you once every hour, even if it means I might hear strains of the great Beeper in the background (Beeper being my pet name for Justin Bieber whom Al loves, and whom I'd rather open a vein than listen to). We will be on call at all hours. Any problems, let us know, and I'll be there. Keep your iPhone with you at every moment, kid."

Al bowed slightly, with her 'Yes Dark Lord' usual comment. She gripped my hand in both hers. "You were great today, Dad. Thanks for a great season."

I covered her hands with my other free one. "I loved every moment of it. Even if I have to give up coaching by popular demand, I promise to be at every practice and game."

"I know you will," Al said with conviction, easing her hands away, and hugging her Mom. "I'll see you both tomorrow. It's Saturday without practices or a game. Whatever will we do, Dark Lord?"

I grinned while glancing around at my fellow monster squad faces. "I'll think of something."

"You better not! We have tickets to the A's game at one," Al warned.

I leaned into my chair, arms folded. "We'll see, depending on how well you do tonight checking in, my little lamb."

"That's blackmail! There will be blood!" Having lanced me with the usual Cruella Deville line, Al left in a huff with Lora following.

"I'll get her cleaned up, and with a bag of necessities for the overnighter, DL," Lora said. "You'll be coming home tonight, right?"

I glanced at Denny. He nodded. "I will indeed, and God help you. The Dark Lord cometh on a night uninhibited by children."

Lora turned to plant both hands on the table, eyeballing me with a smile. "Ooooohhhhh... I'm so scared, Dark Lord. Bring it!"

With that said, Lora twisted away to join a giggling Al.

"Wow, you really put them on notice, DL," Clint said.

"Don't go there, 'man from nowhere'. We all know where your mind is ranging. Apparently, some new information has placed us a hell of a lot closer to moving on Cristova. I've been waiting patiently for the payoff. It's been a long time since we put the minion overlords in charge of the dreaded Oaktown Cartel. So far we have a little under half of Oakland raising fists when they hear the name mentioned. It's been a surprisingly easy takeover."

"With Gus's ploy of champions fighting for control over disputed territory, I'd say it's been easy for everyone but you," Denny said. "What are you now... five and oh?"

"At least we've been keeping the number of dead at a minimum." Yeah, we're taking over control like in that Brad Pitt movie, Troy, where they send him out to fight the other army's champion instead of fighting a costly war. Of course I have to hear how far I fall short of Mr. Pitt in the looks department... constantly. Besides, my adversaries are amateurs.

"Clint can tell you," Gus said. "Crue hounds us without mercy for clips of our Oaktown Cartel business. I think she's planning on a coup to takeover operations in a month or so with the baby strapped to her chest."

"She has me watching the whole damn Sopranos series night after night," Clint admitted. "Last night at dinner, she stuffed gauze rolls or something in her cheeks, and turned on me from the sink, talking like Marlon Brando in the Godfather. Gus is right, guys. Lynn's out of control."

Oh boy, it was many moments before any of us could speak after that word picture.

"You punks think this is funny," Clint said with a straight face. "If I hear one more threat when I don't jump to do her bidding fast enough of 'how would you like to sleep with the fishes', I'm going to eat a bullet right in front of my son."

"Okay, 'man from nowhere'," Lucas cut into the comedy act. "I have two Marine buddies who have flown from LA to join us. They own a security firm in Anaheim, called Red Dragon Security. It's a little like Blackwater. They provide protection for executives and workers abroad. That anti-American jackass, Michael Moronas, tried to hire them because he would be in Lagos, Nigeria for a time, aboard a yacht with the name Orion. We all know who owns the Orion. What we didn't know until my friends called me was that Moronas flew his long haul private jet out of San Francisco with passengers, because the asshole wanted Red Dragon to provide a security force to fly out of SF with him. This happened at the exact time we had an all-points bulletin on Christova, trying to nail her before she could leave the area."

That explains how we missed her. "The bastard flew Christova away right under our noses."

"Lucas's Marine buddies told Moronas they wouldn't piss on him if he was on fire after the multitudes of times he's insulted the troops, and refused the job," Denny said. "Our Christova alert reached them too late, but they've followed Moronas's trail since then, checking when he'd be returning to the states after his vacation stay aboard Christova's yacht. He'll be in LA, and the best part is he has a warrant out for his arrest for assault from one of his slave laborers helping him with his films. He thought he was above the law, and didn't show for the court date. The bonding company ate the big one, and they want him brought in."

"I see that smirk," Clint said. "You have a plan behind those beady eyes. Spit it out. You've prepped us enough. He's been stringing me along ever since Lucas clued him in."

"We're heading to the Gulf of Guinea in a matter of days. Moronas will be arriving in LA in exactly two weeks from now. I want you and Crue to apprehend that traitorous asshole, using our Hollywood Bounty Hunters in a TV episode. Use Clint again as the federal agent taking him into custody. This will be high profile, and hard as hell to pull off. The problem is he's the most famous traitorous asshole on the planet. He can't just disappear... unfortunately. Moronas knows a hell of a lot more about the Orion yacht. I want you to take Dev and Jesse with you, along with Crue's treasured minions. They know the area intimately down there. If this won't work for you, Clint, say so now. We know what you've been through despite the disrespectful jokes about your lovely wife."

"I wish I could go with the other pirates, but this is a plan I can sell with me in it to Lynn. The bad part is you have to lose your love child expectations about Moronas. We need freedom to educate him, and turn his ass from the dark side. Anything less will bring crappy results."

"That's why we're here, Clint. Laredo is zeroing in on an island we may be able to hide from our detractors. Naturally, we will have our own extradition code, meaning none. I confess there might be a time when we're all on the island with the way our government handles threats to homeland security."

Lucas pounded the table. "Hell yeah! If it takes us having to go into exile while fighting for the United States of America, then bring it on! They'll have to nuke us from orbit."

"That won't happen, Lucas," Denny said, leaning into the table. "There will be no casualties on our side without retribution unknown in the states. Laredo has the targets. We won't go easy, my friends. I will take the first hit! I vow if I see it coming, I will front it with everything I have. I confess that even with Lucas's contact with Red Dragon Security, this op may go off the rails into unknown territory. I trust his take on this security firm with my life. They're the real deal – God fearing Americans and Marines. Anyone uncomfortable about the future, speak now."

Silence. Deadly and forbidding. It had to be asked, but no one at the table made a sound. We were in for the long haul. We admittedly couldn't dance worth a shit, sing, or pretend we cared for the refuse of society. We staked our lives on the real Americans, working their asses off, only to be taxed for the downtrodden gray zone of need.

Two men entered, dressed in black and slate gray business suits, short cropped gray hair, white walled on the sides, with lined faces showing the wear of years, both lean and a little under six feet tall. The one in black spotted Lucas waving, smiled, and gestured to his companion. They approached with eyes taking in every detail of their surroundings. Lucas hugged each one while the rest of us stood.

Lucas turned toward the table, introducing each of us, before gesturing at his friends. "This guy in black is Charles Bucholz, and his partner, Jan Sallaz. We chewed some of the same ground together in country, long ago in a hell hole we should have made into a parking lot. They own Red Dragon Security."

"Just Chuck," Bucholz said in a gravelly voice while shaking hands.

"Call me Sal," his partner greeted us in a pleasant bass tone as he in turn shook with each of us. "We're mighty dry, Lucas."

Lucas grinned. He grabbed a couple chairs while we made room for them with the rest of us behemoths. Lucas poured them a beer. "I brought the guys up to date."

"Sorry about not getting the memo on that rat bastard, Moronas," Sal said. "Chuck and I would have taken the job, flown here, and thrown Moronas and that Christova bitch onto the runway after we disposed of the security on board."

"We're here to set things right," Chuck added. "Hell, if we had known about the bond issued, when the scum sucking dog missed his court date, we would have snatched Moronas into custody ourselves. If we hadn't said some unfortunate things to Fathead when he tried to hire us, we may have been able to approach him about the security gig when he returns to the states in a couple weeks."

"Lucas told us you guys mentor that TV crew, Hollywood Bounty Hunters. Chuck and I like the idea of busting the prick for a TV audience. We really don't do bond work anyway. If we can help with logistics, setup, or security, count us in. It must be fun helping those TV people. We saw the episode where they handed over Gus Denova to the FBI. Great stuff."

Sal couldn't understand what we were all laughing about suddenly. Gus gave him a little wave. "I'm Gus Denova. Clint and John were the FBI Agents who took me into custody. I've been rehabilitated."

"It's a bit confusing, but we'll have to explain things in small doses, Sal," Lucas said. "We'd appreciate the help down in your area. We're hoping our interrogation and director supreme will be able to lead the operation."

"That's the woman you call Cruella Deville, right," Chuck asked. He looked around our table. "Good Lord... Lucas sent us the vid of the game show she did on those BBC terrorist supporters. She's incredible. I hope she gets to spend some quality time with Michael Moronas. How's Lynn doing, Clint? We heard she's your wife, and just gave birth to a son under very bad conditions. Lucas said she gutted a terrorist, and shot another one through the head with the first terrorist's gun. Damn! You lucky bastard."

After the enjoyment of Chuck's Cruella Deville appreciation, Clint dived right in. "She's fine, and if she gets aced out of any more operations, she'll gut me… her words. Yeah, Lynn is my soulmate… unfortunately for the rest of the world. It will be great having backup in LA while we bust this Moronas jerk. I heard what he said about snipers, and the people fighting for his right to mouth off as a fat windbag, who is frankly worthless. If ever the universal Jihad works, Moronas will be the first one beheaded with a dull butterknife. In answer to your appeal, Mikey will definitely get some reeducation via my lovely wife."

"Good enough," Sal said. "We watched the two Rattler fights, Harding. Is it true you're doing back alley street fights for control of different parts of your city?"

I glanced at Lucas because I had no idea how much he'd told them. The fact he sent the game show vid to them means they know a hell of a lot already. "We have an off the books operation to regain control of Oakland's neighborhoods. It was Quay's idea to interest these gangbangers in a winner take all type match with side betting. I have one on for tomorrow night. It's weird, but it's working."

"We'd like to see it, if you don't mind us being around, John."

"Sure, Chuck," I replied. Hell, why not? "It's no big deal. These matchups provide me with ways to stay in the fight game, and keep my skills honed. Our former Russian gangster friend, who tips us off on anything bad happening at our ports, allows us to use the warehouse converted into a fight arena he owns. We have some fun with the side bets, so my partner Tommy practices his skills while the match goes on. We've been warned though through back channels it would be bad if there's another death in these matches."

"How do the gangs take to being aced out?"

"They either abide by our one on one matches when they accept the venue, or we destroy them, Sal," I explained. "So far, that's only happened once. The Oaktown Cartel is a definite presence on the streets now. We're helping the cops, and they're tacitly agreeing to the extracurricular fights, meaning they look the other way."

"I like this," Chuck said. "You guys do things the rest of us only dream about. Whatever's working for you, we're right there with you, and no questions asked. You're risking a lot with a UFC career doing these street fights on the side. I hope the neighborhood gains remain worth the risk."

"So far, so good."

* * *

Oh crap. The packed warehouse might see an upset in the making. Miguel Romero's Father clued us into the Asian Crips moving into his neighborhood because of it being partially zoned for commercial shops, which had a large Asian ownership. The Asian Crips terrorized the shop keepers, collecting protection money, and selling drugs out of the shops. Gus worked his magic setting this winner take all match in place, with Alexi supplying our venue, and Jack Korlos as referee. The Crips loved the idea, because when Gus met with them, he brought a contingent of Oaktown Cartel converts with him – former gangbangers and enforcers, now on our payroll. Seeing they were outnumbered three to one, the Crips agreed to terms. Gus told me they liked the idea a bit too much for his liking. Now, I understand why.

Right out of the gate, I took a roundhouse kick to the head I never even saw. It stir fried my brain. I pawed around on my back, blocking kicks from three guys - at least that was the number my triple vision relayed to my brain, accompanied by the familiar little birdies chirping between my ears. Only my continued Bay pole poking, shark tag regimen kept me conscious. This mixed race Asian kid, calling himself Dragon Hands, was faster than the damn Rattler, and he enjoyed his work. Maybe an inch smaller than me, nearly the same weight, with arms and legs like corded steel, he showed martial arts skills practiced from childhood. I glimpsed another roundhouse kick on the launch pad as I tried to scramble to my feet, whipping over at the last split second to smash a closed fist into the kid's right knee joint.

Dragon Hands screamed out in pain as I caught him coming in. The strike spun him into the cage and down. I twisted over without getting on my feet, and side-kicked him in the chest. I missed his head, which was what I aimed at, but the strike blasted him into the cage, and face down on the mat for a moment. The kid could take it though. He crab crawled away from me to the other side of the cage, while assessing damage. I did the same. His first killer roundhouse still had me trying to join images in my head, but I lurched again to my feet. I didn't attack him, because I wasn't sure whether or not I'd take a few steps, and fall flat on my face. It was a standoff for long moments with the crowd rattling the old warehouse walls with sound. Hands furiously worked his knee while rasping air into his lungs against the cage.

I was afraid to look at my corner for fear vertigo would put me on my ass. I could imagine Tommy calling me every name in the book, thinking I had been overconfident. In the stands, I'm sure Lucas was disavowing my Recon nickname for his friends' amusement. Hands approached warily, testing his leg for support. I knew one thing for sure: he wouldn't be landing kicks with either foot. He would need his right leg's support to strike with his left, and by the way his knee joint was already swelling, I figured another right leg strike wasn't happening either. My vision cleared a bit, but I hesitated to initiate an offense. Hands went for the takedown. I bopped him a glancing blow with an elbow strike. It drew blood.

On the mat where he put me easily, Hands began snaking arms and legs around my head and arms faster than I could think, going for triangle chokes, arm bars, and everything in the book. I rolled, twisted, threw elbows, and became entangled in a nearly closed triangle choke. He had my left arm and head locked with his left leg. Grainy darkness began to descend with Jack Korlos on his knees watching to make sure I didn't die on him. The ocean tide of doom roared in my head. I rolled to my knees, lifting Dragon Hands with my last few seconds of consciousness, and him squeezing with all he had. Unfortunately for him, I made it to my feet. I ran the big spider monkey head first into the cage.

Jarred from his mounting, Hands hit the cage, and down on his back. I dropped with an elbow shot to his head while seeing stars, light flashes, and for some reason, Smokey the Bear. Smokey didn't help my aim. I missed his head in a stumbling downward strike where I nailed his hard as a rock stomach instead. It was enough to blast the air out of him, allowing me to lurch away from Hands before those steel leg cables and arms wrapped around my damn head again. I did remember to shoot in a satisfying heel kick to his head I was sure would give Hands his own opportunity to see Smokey.

I crawled the hell away fast, grabbed some cage, and pulled myself upright. The crowd noise seeped into my battered brain again. They were near to lifting the roof off. Man, was it loud in there. Either that or the band played on in my own head only. When I thought I could face Hands again without falling on my face, he was still on his back, rocking weakly back and forth, trying to stay conscious. I grinned. Time for the old running football kick. I charged across with murderous intent, only to be intercepted by Jack Korlos. He shouldered me off course.

"Fight's over, kid. He tapped out already."

"One more for the road, Jack." The monster broke the chains in my head. He demanded an accounting. I eased Jack bodily along with me. I planned to stomp Smokey the Bear right out of his head. Every joint in my body ached.

"No more killings in my cage, John!"

I stopped, partly in respect for Jack, and partly because Hands was already cringing against the cage, unable to get away, but conscious enough to know he was near death. I let my arms drop. "I'm good, Jack."

I pointed at Dragon Hands. "Good fight, Dragon. Damn… you're in the wrong business."

Jack let me go, but stayed in between me and Hands. I turned without any more comments, heading for my corner. There wasn't any announcements or cameras, only the absolute bedlam going on in the crowd. The Crips were unhappy, but they were surrounded by not only Godfather Gus's Oaktown Cartel guys, but my own crew of deadly killers, smiling at the scene with anticipation. The Oakland politicos fled the scene. Jafar threw a wet towel over my head. Tommy grabbed me by the ears, his face two inches from mine.

"Tell me you didn't half ass this fight nearly into your own death match!"

"He clocked me with the roundhouse, T. I didn't even see it."

Tommy nodded. "Okay then… sorry. Maybe an hour each day, treading water on the Bay with your hands straight in the air will keep you safe in the first few seconds of a fight."

"He won the damn fight, T," Dev said, working the arm pinned by Dragon Hands against my head, while Jess worked the shoulder. "That guy is hell-a-good. He shot that kick so fast to John's temple, it looked like a shoulder rocket."

312

"Brother, I don't know how the hell you came back from that strike," Jess added, helping me strip off my gloves. "Hell, you should have died during the triangle he had on you."

"I saw Smokey the Bear. He strangled me so long, I saw old Smokey."

I watched with grinning appreciation as my admission elicited raucous enjoyment from even Tommy. "Only you can prevent forest fires."

That one had Jafar almost on his knees. Another day, another lesson in life. "How's our gang negotiations going?"

"Could be better," Dev said, gesturing at the outside the cage altercations. "It seems they weren't expecting to lose. It's being handled."

"I hope to hell Gus can recruit those guys into the Cartel," Jess added. "I think we could substitute Dragon Hands into the matches in place of you, Smokey."

"Gee, thanks." Not a bad idea. "After that match, I'm beginning to see your point."

"You were going to kill him, John." Naturally, Jafar comments on that segment of my match. "He knew it too. I think he was trying to crawl through the cage links as you were dragging Jack along with you."

"In my defense, it was the blood finally rushing to my head. I guess this was a bad one for Lucas to bring his friends to. Let's get the hell out of here. I need refreshment."

Jafar held his iPad for me to see with an impatient Cruella Deville, holding the tiny Clint Jr. She pointed at me with a big smile. "Hell of a fight, Sissy. You nearly let that high school kid kill you. Nice pickup and run his head into the cage though. Lucas is going to ream your ass."

"Nice to see you too, Lynn," I replied while my cage brothers mocked me. "Clint Jr. looks wonderful. I'm sure you've heard we're arranging a new directorial gig for you with full entourage."

Lynn went feral instantly. Her countenance went from pleasant teasing to torturous mistress of the unimaginable in a split second. "When I get my hands on that traitorous asshole, there won't be enough of him left for the Hollywood bunch to transfer to the Feds. I know you guys will be overseas with the Wolf by the time we get Moronas in for his reeducation seminar. If the weasel knows anything that will help, I'll make him beg to tell it."

"Anything you can do is great with me. I'm betting he has the exact coordinates of where Christova's yacht is parked. Have fun. Every time he opens his mouth, I want to stuff a grenade down his throat. You can only imagine how pumped I am about having him in your hands. Don't mess with your Hollywood collaboration. You're first rate as a director. The minions are the best support you could ever hope for in scene staging. Between Clint at your side, and Lucas's friends' Red Dragon Security on tap, the episode could win a Grammy or whatever the hell award they give out."

"Thanks, John." Lynn calmed down noticeably, hugging Clint Jr to her. "I need this gig down in LA. I'm going nuts. I'll have one of Maria's doctors with me, and Laredo has our private jet converted into a baby clinic. I'm in shape like never before. I can do this."

"I know you'll do great things with our Hollywood Bounty Hunters. We need you, so ease into our crap at your own pace. I've already heard from Gus and Clint you're opting for a takeover of the Oaktown Cartel."

She chuckled with a wave off gesture. "The Godfather stuff was just to yank Clint's chain, although I wouldn't mind being the shadowy syndicate boss behind the scenes."

"I think it's a perfect role for you."

"Go easy on the celebration, Hard Case."

"I will, Lynn."

Jafar turned off his tablet. "She threatened me with extinction if I didn't give her a ringside delivery of the fight. I was so worried for a while, I almost cut her off by accident. I would have been so dead."

I put my arm around his shoulders. "Let's get out of here, little brother. I'm sure Samira wants you with her as she orders your whipped ass around the house in the late stages of her pregnancy."

"That's just mean, John."

No one else thought so. Jack Korlos joined us after making sure Hands was okay, and able to leave the cage with help from his buddies.

"I thought he had you, kid," Jack said. "I won't even pretend to know what kept you conscious while ramming Dragon Hands into the cage. I keep getting the uneasy feeling I really will need to sap you one of these days."

I held out my hand, and Jack shook it. "It won't be anything personal. Hands flipped my switch temporarily. Thanks for stopping me. I know you were looking to make sure I didn't get killed either."

"It was close, John. I'll say that. See ya' in the funny papers." Jack walked to Hands' cage entrance to avoid the crowd gathering outside our cage exit.

Alexi met us outside the cage with Miguel Romero's Father, flanked by his fight game assistants Jim Bonasera and Ray Alexander. Ray was sullen, which meant he had bet against me

315

once again. Alexi was excited to say the least. "Frank wanted to say thanks, although you nearly lost his neighborhood to the Asian Crips."

"Tell me about it. Good to see you, Frank. How's Miguel doing?" Frank's son Miguel had to go through an unfortunate reeducation process with Lynn before we had him repaired at the local hospital. He turned on the gang with Lynn's help that was trying to kill the Gomez family – Celia, Joe, and their son, Ricky. Miguel's in the Marine Corps now, like Frank before him.

All smiles, Frank held his phone to my face cycling through pictures of a lean, mean Miguel in dress uniform, and in khaki's with other Marines in a dry sandy looking place I figured wasn't anywhere around here. "He's in Afghanistan. I did one of those Skype conversations with him last night to tell him what you were doing. I just sent him the video of the fight. He texted me a moment ago, he thought you lost."

"Yeah, that's the popular opinion, Frank. I'm sorry I came so close to leaving the Crips in charge of your neighborhood. If there are any loose ends, you know who to call. Godfather Gus will take care of it."

Frank shook my hand. "It was never in doubt. I heard Lucas scream 'Recon' when you slammed the Crip's head into the cage. I have to go home and tell my wife the good news. She was ready to force me to move when I just got the house paid off. I thought I'd end my days in a prison cell after going Crip hunting."

"We can't have that, my friend. Let us handle your light work."

Frank chuckled as he walked away with a wave. "Will do."

"How much you lose on the fight, Ray," Tommy asked as if he cared. He hated Ray Alexander. "I tried to get a piece of that action, but I heard you're on limited funds."

"None of your fuckin' business, Sands!"

"Wait for us elsewhere, Ray," Alexi ordered.

One look at his boss, and Ray walked off with his fists clenched.

"He dropped five large," his former partner, Jim Bonasera admitted. "Alexi nearly had to take a bunch off Ray's debt, because odds were at three to one against Dragon Hands. We've already had a hundred thousand hits on the YouTube fight. It's titled Asian Crips' Dragon Hands nearly decapitates John Harding in the cage."

"Wonderful. Thanks for sharing."

"All is set for celebration at The Warehouse," Alexi said. "Your FBI friends, Sam Reeves and Janie Labrie, contacted me, wondering if you'd be there after the fight. They have a special request after you briefed them on your hoped for arrest of Michael Moronas."

"I owe them a meeting. I didn't think they'd give a crap one way or another about Moronas, but with a fugitive arriving from overseas, I wanted them to be apprised of what we were doing. I hope they haven't been spreading the word, or the Moronas gig will fall through. Even Sam was gracious when Dev, Jess and I brought his Mom to the San Francisco office."

"They convinced her I wasn't lying to her," Jess added. "Between getting her neighborhood back, and finding out I'm not a criminal, my Mom's happy as hell. She's told all the neighbors I'm with the FBI and the security firm. I'm golden with her and the family now."

"I wonder what Sam and Janie want," Dev said. "They sure helped Flo to see the light. It's nice not to have her think I'm the instigator that turned Jess into a criminal."

317

"I'll get a shower, and we'll go solve the FBI mystery with the Bud and Beam brothers."

"Dragon Hands squeezed your damn neck so hard, you'll probably have to use a straw," Tommy said.

Chapter 13

Duty Distribution

The Warehouse called to me. We worked our new Oaktown Cartel endeavor every spare minute. The minions handled every facet with extraordinary skill. Watching them in action entertained us without peer anywhere in our crime busting lives. Dev, Jess, and Tommy alternated driving the limo for the minions and enforcer crew. We never allowed them to only go with gangbanger recruits. Clint, Casey, Lucas, and I alternated in pairs to make sure nothing happened to our Oaktown Cartel Godfathers. Lynn lived vicariously through live feeds of every action. She and Dannie looked after Clint Jr like a couple of mamma lions. Clint told us Lynn was in the best shape ever, just as she claimed. The moment the baby didn't need to be isolated, Lynn promised to be all over everyone's business.

Denny now controlled our leak obstacle in the Christova operation. He turned Senator Kaline Nikolov from New York with a Laredo and Jafar onslaught of offshore transactions, communiques, and even sexual dalliances. He owned her, and we had eyes and ears on everything she did. She fed Christova whatever the hell Denny wanted her to concerning our movements, and that we were stumped by her disappearance. We kept waiting, since we ended her imported EMP threat in the planned port takeover, but she left her yacht, the Orion, at different intervals we had yet to track down. We hoped to use Moronas to make sure she was on board when we came for her in the Sea Wolf. Once we finished our business with Christova, Senator Nikolov would have three choices, die, resign, or become our pawn in a much more complicated game.

We entered The Warehouse to cheers from our Oakland PD friends. They knew we were the Oaktown Cartel. They also knew how we were achieving our limiting the gangs to certain areas of the city where they could be more easily monitored. Unfortunately, we knew there was no way to shut off drugs in our city. That would take an act of God. We could only limit it to areas where neighborhoods of real people weren't affected. Our PD friends understood the difference. They lived it from one day to the next without backup for what they had to do. Earl and 'Rique were the first to greet us, having come over directly from their security gig at the warehouse cage fight.

"Damn, John, that was a close one," Earl said.

"We thought you ate the big one when Dragon put the leg triangle on you," 'Rique added. "I thought you guys who fought UFC were tougher than that."

I endured the roasting in good humor as Marla delivered my brothers Bud and Beam. I downed brother Beam after toasting my PD friends, and then quaffed half of my Bud brother. We adjourned to the reserved part of the bar for our meeting after I complimented Marla on her superb timing. She served my companions as efficiently as always at our spot. It was then I spotted Sam Reeves and Janie Labrie. They approached us with some reluctance. I motioned them over.

"Monsters," Sam said, nodding his head in comical form.

Janie hugged me. "We thought the young gangster ended your reign as street champ tonight, John. That kid was awesome."

"Thanks for the great meeting with Jess's Mom. She's finally convinced Jess is on the straight and narrow. I heard from Alexi, who should be here shortly, that you two have something to discuss in reference to our planned Moronas arrest. How can we help?"

"Janie and I know it was you and Clint that accepted Gus's handover from the Hollywood Bounty Hunters," Sam Reeves stated. "We know you bunch don't do anything half-ass, so we know you have the goods on this bastard. If you think we at the FBI don't hear his absolute bullshit, think again. We can't stand his fat ass. I'd like to burn his ball cap off with a torch."

"We'd like to be the FBI agents your Hollywood people hand Moronas over to," Janie said. "We could use a few comments of course about Sam and I being the consulting agents on the case. What do you think, John?"

"I think it's a great idea. Clint will be busy helping Lynn, and I'll be out of the country." I looked up as Lucas, Casey, and our Red Dragon Security guys arrived. "There's Lucas with his Southern California security contacts. I'll introduce you all, and get this Moronas handover set in stone. One thing we need to get straight though. We're questioning Moronas before you touch him. He will probably claim all sorts of bad things having to do with our treatment of him. Can we possibly downplay his crap?"

"After what he said in the news about our youngsters on the front lines being cowards, I'd settle for him being able to breathe," Sam said.

"Ditto," Janie reiterated. "Talk about the scum of the earth... that fuck is it!"

Lucas led his friends to our bar position, grinning and shaking a finger at me. "You know only your last ditch stumbling mayhem into the cage with Dragon Hands saved you from a dressing down of biblical proportions, right Recon?"

I lowered my head in pretend anguish. "I am so ashamed, Grandpa."

Lucas gave me a V8 smack on the forehead I had lowered in comical deference to his statement. "I'm watching you, boy. Don't make me have to get into your training first hand again."

"Sam and Janie would like to do the handover of Moronas into FBI hands in the TV segment. They know we have to question him first. I told them Red Dragon Security is collaborating on the capture." I then introduced everyone.

After the introductions, Jess hugged Sam and Janie. He figured never to be looked on as anything but a criminal mastermind by his Mom. The FBI agents took his effusive thanks with good humor, knowing Jess was probably more capable and trustworthy than half the agents on their own staff.

"Anytime, Jess," Sam said. "I thought for a moment Flo was going to have a stroke."

"She was pretty emotional," Jess admitted. "She told me she figured a couple guys would jump out and clamp handcuffs on me, and the joke would be over. It turns out Sal and Chuck were doing a security gig at the same time Dev and I were in the sandpit, protecting some contractors flown in for a construction consult."

"We appreciate the extra cloak of accountability on taking Moronas in," Chuck said. "We will handle all scene security, and make sure this happens for Director Montoya/Dostiene just as she wants."

"I have to admit," Sam said with a shake of his head, "that episode was incredibly good. It bothers me a serial killing psycho can be so good at so many things, but Lynn has talent. I bet you guys don't know we contracted her husband to catch her when she was killing rapist/murderers. He even went down with the rest of this bunch to get her from the Cartel she ran afoul of down in Mexico. Now, she's upset the balance of nature, and given birth to a baby fathered by one of the most dangerous men on earth. Clint Dostiene and Harding killed four assassins in the hospital she delivered the baby in. God knows what's next for that poor child."

"One of these days, Sam," Janie admonished her partner. "Clint will take offense at one of your cute little zingers and rip your throat out."

322

I gestured at the entrance, where the rest of our crew were arriving. "There's Clint now, with Casey and Jafar. Maybe you'd like to entertain Clint with a reenactment of your take on his child, Sam."

Dev put a hand on Sam's shoulder as he was about to speak. "I know how caustic you can be, brother. Do us a favor, and don't say anything that could get you killed right here in the bar."

"You're on our plus list after being a standup guy at the FBI office," Jess added. "Don't piss on the good Karma."

Sam grinned. He'd been through the verbal wars with Clint before. He also knew what Clint was capable of. "Understood."

Clint walked right into my airspace. "Hell of a fight, John. I wish I'd seen it in person, but it was awful good on our big screen in surround sound from Jafar's hook-up. He told me he explained about almost committing suicide by cutting our feed accidentally. I don't know if I could have saved him from Cruella Deville's retribution. Clint Jr. started crying when the Dragon Hands put you in the triangle leg choke. Lynn's been doing the skin on skin therapy with the baby, and he can detect even the slightest mood change in Lynn. It's funny as hell. Lynn has to throttle herself down when she's in direct contact."

Clint gestured at Sam and Janie. "Who ordered the federal hand puppets? Are they finally making a Disney movie or something?"

Okay, sure... the Monster Squad may have enjoyed that a bit too much. Chuck and Sal definitely liked the interchange after hearing Sam's initial remarks. I did a rehash quickly so we could get down to business.

"I'm glad you guys will be with us on this," Clint told Chuck and Sal. "My wife is the most dangerous woman on the planet, guys. Sometimes we've run into situations during filming best handled in advance rather than during filming. She tends to

323

allow her real life persona blend into the make believe scenes. I've known Sam and Janie for a while now. They'll do what they can in their roles as FBI agents. Frankly, I think I should stand in for Sam. God only knows if he can handle even a two word transfer scene."

Janie nearly came unglued during Clint's roasting of Sam. To his credit, Sam put an arm around Clint. "I deserve that. Congrats on your new son, psycho."

Clint shook Sam's extended hand. "Thanks. Lynn and I will be on our best behavior down in Southern California. We'll have our son along to keep us in line."

Janie hugged Clint with real emotion. "I'm so happy for you two. It will be a real pleasure seeing Lynn with your son. Sam and I will make sure everything in this goofy 'episode of the tragic and pretend' proceeds perfectly. Do you think it will be safe enough to bring your son along, Clint?"

"Safe for whom, Janie?"

Janie laughed, patting Clint's cheek. "Yeah, that was a stupid statement. Thanks for approving our tapping into this bust. We need a little boost. We're living in a 'what have you done for me lately world' at the Bureau."

"No problem," Clint replied. "We need you and Sam. These times are getting more desperate by the moment. Think about the consequences if our crew had not been in on this EMP infiltration and production crap. Good Lord, they sent some bozos in with a prototype and took out my very expensive security setup. If someone upstairs doesn't get a handle on this immigration and infiltration cluster-fuck, we may as well start buying our damn prayer rugs now. That Moronas mutt is a prime illustration of liberal idiots with money, willing to back anyone who professes an anti-American agenda. I wish to God we would elect a God fearing American who declared actual war until we beat these bastards!"

Oh my God, that was good. I grabbed Clint around his shoulders with the rest of my crew, including Red Dragon Security, pumping fists into the air. Yeah, we're a little sick of the status quo. "I can tell Lynn has unmasked the monster, my brother. I bet you have to hear all about it on a daily basis."

Clint stared right into my eyes. "Whatever you imagine, multiply it by ten, and you will have the Cruella Deville input down pat."

"I heard that!" Crue's voice nearly burst Clint's eardrum. He grimaced, and tore his earwig out to hold it away from him as if it were a piece of used toilet paper between his index finger and thumb.

That was funny! Clint was tapped into Crue's world even now. She wired him. "Oh my God, brother, Crue has you on an audio video leash."

Clint shrugged. "Did you think I'd be allowed out of the house without the ball and chain along in some manner? Not to mention, the baby cries if he doesn't hear my voice every few minutes."

"What!? Did you just call me the ball and chain!?" The squawking earwig was too much. We had a break in all discussion for temporary humorous mayhem. Alexi joined the celebration with smiling recognition he had stumbled into something unrelated to terrorism.

"I…I have a spare room if you need one, Clint."

"Not necessary, John. I have to be back home in an hour, or Crue punishes me by making dinner for a week. It's more than any human being can endure."

"You're toast, man from nowhere! You'll be eating out of Tonto's dish until the devil serves snow-cones in hell!"

Clint kept smiling as Crue roasted him in tiny squawks until finally, he shoved the device into his pocket, and unclipped his button camera, stuffing it into the same pocket as the ear piece. "I hope we have something for my woman to do in the near future, or I'll be needing an island refuge soon."

Our phones began going off moments later. We checked, and turned them off one at a time as Crue called one after another. The bar phone went off shortly after the last of ours was turned off. Marla, who had been enjoying the hell out of the Clint roast, looked at Clint for help. She signaled her other bartender to let it ring.

"What the hell do I do now?" Marla picked up the phone, confirmed who it was on the readout, and handed it to Clint. "She's all yours, Clint. I know better than to blow off Cruella Deville."

Clint took the phone. "Hello, Dear... I..." He started laughing midway through his stammering hello. He had to hold the receiver six inches away from his ear before getting near enough to the mouthpiece to say something. "Calm down. I was having a little fun." He grinned. "Yes, I know. When the baby goes down for a nap, it will be unarmed combat time. Just a warning – if you try to Tase me on my way through the door, it won't go well for you. I'll have Jess come over and slap you around a little."

"Not happenin', Crue," Jess called out with conviction.

"I will. Okay... goodbye." Clint passed the phone to Marla again. He looked around at all of us with a big smile. "I have to keep her juices flowing. She says she's ready to go to the mattresses."

"I can't wait to meet her," Chuck said. "Sal and I have heard so many stories about her, we would have taken on the job just to see her in action."

"She'll be questioning Moronas for sure then, right?" Sal wanted confirmation.

"I guarantee it," Clint said. "Now, before we discuss logistics, Justin Bieber called. He wants the next shot at the Cheeseburger."

* * *

Lynn moved only when needing to with Dannie and Amara at her side. Clint Jr clung to her happily, bound to her chest. She watched the Hollywood Bounty Hunters arrive in the same place where they had filmed the last FBI handover. Clint, along with the minions surrounded her inner circle. Everyone was in position at the Casa Ado restaurant for the dress rehearsal. With hands patting the baby, Lynn scoped the scene in every detail, from the interaction between participants to the camera guys she knew very well. They had already rehearsed the takedown of Moronas at the private airfield he was flying into soon. Lynn used the cover of making an episode of the TV series without mentioning who they were after landing there. Lynn felt it would be a piece of cake once they confirmed arrival time with Red Dragon Security people monitoring the airport.

The Casa Ado restaurant acted again as the backdrop to Lynn's hoped for scene after Moronas went through a short reeducation lesson in the very near future. Clint, Lynn's minions, and Tonto, acted as her bodyguards, and troubleshooters. Tommy, Jess, and Devon interacted with the Hollywood Bounty Hunters, making sure equipment was at hand when needed, or anything on the set needed shifting at a moment's notice. At 10 pm, Sigfried Kadelus, their head cameraman indicated to Lynn the lighting settings matched his previous work at the spot filmed on the earlier episode.

"Good, Sig. Let's run a full on clip from when Kensy and Kevin walk Moronas to the FBI agents, including lines. Do you remember the sentence you're supposed to say when Kensy hands over Moronas, Tommy?"

"Yeah, Crue, I have the line down pat. We should have Sam and Janie here to practice. You know they'll flub this scene. A hundred bucks says that cardboard cutout Sam will forget his seven word line – 'we'll take him from here, Ms. Talon'."

"If I want any input from you Sands, I'll cut it out of you," Lynn stated, waving the Holly wood Bounty Hunters into action while listening to the snorted laughter around the set.

"Incoming." Clint pointed at a convertible screeching to a halt at the end of the alleyway, they were filming in. Six guys who jumped into the street, with penguin pants allowing a rather weird dismount from the vehicle, shuffled toward them. "This doesn't look good either. What the hell? Do these guys patrol their gangster areas?"

"Take the baby, Dannie," Lynn disengaged from her harness with Clint's help. Dannie took the baby, and faded to the rear with Amara, behind the minions who did not bother hiding the fact they had hands on weapons. "Let's not start a war here. We haven't filmed our scene yet. We don't collect Bozo Moronas until later. Tommy, Jess, and Dev... stay where you are in front of the Hollywood's. Les and Kev... c'mon out with them as a precaution."

Ex-Hell's Angel, Les Tavor, along with his Hollywood Bounty Hunters' enforcement wing partner, Kevin Halliday, moved alongside Tommy's group. Lynn grinned at Clint, as the march of the penguins took a few moments from their car to the scene. One of them in front recognized Lynn from their last disastrous confrontation, and stopped dead with his guys running into him.

"What the hell you stoppin' for, Jet?"

"I know this woman's crew, Speed. We don't want to do this. They just filming some goofy reality show... that Hollywood Bounty Hunters gig, only the real bad asses work the scene. C'mon... they ain't stayin' long."

"Man... I did not take over the reins of this party to back down from some mo-fo out-of-towners." The one named Speed gestured at Lynn. "You on our turf, bitch! You want to operate here, you have to pay the toll."

Lynn sighed. She was so into the director's duties, she didn't care about the extortion racket, figuring maybe a quick payment would keep their later filming of the real scene without incident. "Okay, Betty, what'll it cost me?"

"Oh no... you did not-"

Speed moved in threatening gestures toward Lynn. The prior acquaintance called Jet, dashed out in front of Speed, signaling the rest of their crew in placating form. "Don't reach! The man backing her play is a shooter." Jet tried to dissuade Speed's approach as the man pushed against him. "If you do this, Speed, you'll have her knife carving you some new initials, and her shooter will clip pieces off the rest of us if we're lucky! Step off this time, brother!"

"Get away from me, pussy!" Speed shoved Jet away, while pulling his own knife. "Bitch likes to brawl with the blade, huh? Let's do this! Think you bad, huh? I'll carve you a new pussy in your face."

"You're so cute," Lynn said, her own butterfly knife not only appearing, but doing tricks from one hand to the other, while occasionally flipping it over her shoulder, and catching it in perfect position for an attack. "I was going to let you Bambi's go on your way. Now, that's not an option. Tommy? Work your magic, and get us a little payment for this damn interruption."

Tommy walked into the middle without a flinch either way, smiling and gesturing. "Your man Jet here knows how this works. We don't show skills without a price, gentlemen. I'm giving three to one odds my director carves this tootsie roll pop until he begs for mercy."

Tommy took out a wad of cash. "Let's see the money young gentlemen, unless your balls have shrunk into your chest."

His target audience checked each other with an uneasiness borne of foul beginnings. That did not mean shit to Tommy. "Oh… I'm sorry tough guys. You're not doing transactions with poor saps kneeling with their hands clasped in prayer. It's a new day in the neighborhood, you gangster wannabes! Put up, or shut up!"

They wanted no part of the match, but they bet, all but the one who knew Lynn and Clint. Jet wanted no part of wagering. He refused to put any money down. He glanced away from his companions to see Lynn and Clint smiling at him. Tommy coerced, and ragged the other men with expertise until he had maxed the bets to the most he thought possible. Tommy met Lynn's gaze with a nod.

"These campfire girls are all in, Crue. They're beat before the cuttin' even starts."

One reached inside his hoodie at Tommy's words. No one saw Clint draw. His bullet took a notch from the young man's shoulder. "Next lesson is a deadly one, gentlemen. I have my young baby son here on scene. Anyone else even sneezes with their hand moving, and I will put a bullet into each one of your heads before you take another breath. For full disclosure, I want the rest of you to take your hands and grab onto your clothing. Anyone I don't see grabbing, gets a third eye."

They grabbed clothing, including the wounded one.

"Well now, we have the preliminaries on the board. C'mon, Betty. Don't be shy. You think you're hell on wheels with a knife. Come get some, pussy."

Speed had been watching the preliminaries with surprise. It was plain he had never faced down professional killers before. He watched Lynn do knife tricks even while he was looking at his own knife with suspicion. Rage flared as Lynn's countering features revealed plainly she had no fear, and no mercy waiting for him.

Speed jutted a thrust toward Lynn unexpectedly. Lynn batted it away while carving a six inch line of blood up his attacking forearm.

"Oh yeah, baby, bring it. By the time we're done dancin' no one in your crew will even recognize you," Lynn told him while Speed watched the blood drip to the pavement from his forearm. "Have you ever heard that song, 'Bad Bad Leroy Brown', Betty? He messed with the wrong cat. When they pulled old Leroy from the floor in the lyrics to the song, he looked like a jigsaw puzzle with a couple of pieces gone. That'll be you, Betty. Now c'mon. Lace up those pink panties, and let's finish this bet."

Sweating in the cool air, with his gang shouting for him to cut the bitch up, Speed crouched into a careful ready crouch, no longer angling for anything other than survival. He had not even seen the swipe Lynn cut his arm with. Lynn made kissing noises at him, finally dropping her arms to her sides.

"Well shit! Is this a knife fight or a ballet lesson? Damn… so all you other sissies follow this big girl around doing anything she wants you to do, huh?"

Speed heard the mumblings from his men. He shot straight at her, his knife hand flicking out from what he thought was an unexpected angle. Lynn dropped to one side, leg whipping Speed face first to the pavement. Before he could move, she ran over him, slicing him from the small of his back to the top of his neck. Speed's shirt and leather jacket parted into halves. The blood welled from the thin red incision. Lynn twirled the knife around from hand to hand, stooping to clean the blade in between revolutions on Speed's clothing.

"You want anymore, Betty?" Lynn was crouching next to Speed's head, continuing her knife tricks around his ears.

"No!" Speed held his hand up as he rolled slightly to his side. "I'm done."

"Pay up, kiddies," Tommy said, moving amongst the others with Dev and Jesse at his side. "That's how it's done. Lesson learned, right? Don't be shy. Show me the green, children."

The gang paid without comment. Speed scrambled to his feet, letting his clothing drop away as he ran toward the convertible with his disgruntled gang members close behind. Tommy, Dev, and Jesse watched their retreat with Clint on the opposite side of the alleyway.

Lynn put an arm around Jet before he could follow. "I can use a smart guy like you, Jet. Our Hollywoods need some color in the ranks. Although Les and Kev are good protectors, I need a streetwise ex-gangbanger to help keep my little Kensy safe. How would you like a job, kid?"

"You mean be on TV?" Jet looked around at the others in confusion. Kensy walked over to take his hand.

"Lynn's our boss and mentor. If she wants you with us, you're in, Jet. I think she means for you to be our guy who can spot any gang trouble before it happens. Is that right, Lynn?"

"Exactly," Lynn replied. "Your job is to make sure nothing happens to our make believe bounty hunters. We want good safe scenes. Sometimes the kids have to get into harm's way for a moment or two. Les, Kevin, and you will make sure nothing bad happens. I'm certain you can spot a bad situation, right?"

Jet warmed to the idea immediately. "Sure I can. I can't go back even to grab my stuff though. They'll kill me."

"You let us worry about that. We'll have to make a statement so your home-boys don't cause problems after the filming ends. Les? Do you have room at your place for Jet until we find him his own crib?"

"Yeah, Lynn," Les answered without hesitation. "He can bunk in with me for as long as he needs. This is a great idea. We can use him. I have plenty of room at my new place."

"This will be a good training project for him to be with us on," Kevin added. "Chad... I mean, Mr. Dubrinsky, our lawyer can help you with any law problems you have hanging over your head."

"Good! Breaks over. Let's get this last run through done," Lynn ordered. "I have another feeding in half an hour."

"Now that scene disruption was what entertainment is all about," Clint said, patting Jet on the back. "Welcome aboard, matey."

* * *

The limousine drove alongside the parked private jet as Michael Moronas hurried down the plane's stairwell with briefcase in hand. He wore his signature glasses, ball cap, and hair sticking out all around the brim. The rest of his clothing could be described loosely as casual. The scarf he wore accentuated his triple chins. Tommy met him at the stairwell base to take the bags from the plane personnel following him. The limousine trunk popped open as Moronas stopped to glower at Tommy.

"Where the hell's by regular driver?"

"He is ill, Sir. My asssociates and I were sent to make sure you were picked up on time," Tommy answered with professional courtesy while storing the bags in the limo. He then hurried over to open Moronas's door for him. Moronas hesitated for a moment, but then leaned in. When he saw Lynn and Clint waving at him, he started to back out. Clint grabbed his coat and shirt at the neck. Moronas tried to cry out as Clint jerked him inside to the floor, but the grip choked off any sound. Tommy followed him in, slamming the limo door once he cleared the frame. Jess sped away an instant later. Clint jammed his shoe down on Moronas's neck, pinning him to the limo floor.

"Stay quiet, and I won't have to break something on you, Michael," Clint said.

Lynn duct taped his mouth with Tommy yanking Moronas's head back for access. Tommy added a plastic tie to restrain their new interrogation subject. "I've been looking forward to sealing that big fat mouth of yours until I could question you personally, Mikey. Oh what fun we're going to have."

They exited the airport without incident. Clint eased his foot off on Moronas's neck. Tommy and Clint helped the bleating Moronas onto the seat between them. Lynn watched the red faced Moronas with professional interest. His bloated body heaved, trying to breathe through his nose, snorting air as if he had ran a marathon race.

"I can tell this is going to be easier than we thought. He's already close to pissing his pants, and I haven't even zapped his nuts yet." Lynn chuckled as Moronas's eyes widened, and the bleating increased in volume. "I think I hurt his feelings. Did you think I'd ask a few questions, and not make damn certain of the truth, Mikey? My associate is going to show you a few movies of me in action with other uncooperative types. By then, we'll be at our interrogation warehouse we've appropriated just for your visit. Show him the criminal proof our first class research department found concerning photo, video, and documents, proving Mikey has been consorting with known terrorists in action against the United States of America. That should warm him for us."

Tommy lifted the iPad he already had cued to the desired collage of still pictures, videos, and documents of money transfers to his accounts in illegal offshore banks. After the indoctrination ended, everyone in the limo but Moronas was having fun at his expense. Lynn was the first to notice the furrowed brows, accompanied by the pouty expression she had seen in many of his media photos.

"Uh oh, Mikey thinks this is a joke, and he's getting punked. I don't like that expression." In a split second's time, Lynn zapped Moronas's groin for a five second journey into living hell. If not for the restraining gloved hands of Tommy and Clint, Moronas would have launched like a guided missile through the limo roof. He passed out.

"Was that as good for you as it was for me, babe? I can't stand the sight of this guy," Clint said, while slapping Moronas into consciousness.

Tommy raised his hand. "That was so good."

"We loved it here in the front, Ms. Daisy," Dev responded to much amusement.

Lynn grabbed Moronas's chin while giving Devon the glare of retribution. "Wake up, pussy. I'm not done with you yet."

Moronas vibrated into consciousness slowly, small high pitched squeaks of abject terror puffing out the duct tape. He closed his eyes, and started to sob when the only sight he saw was Lynn's merciless stare.

"When I get done interrogating you, princess, those crocodile tears you're shedding now will feel like spring rain. Before we hand you over to the FBI, I'm going to teach you respect for this country that you've been shitting on since you were born. On the way along our love America first trail, you're going to tell me everything you know about Phoebe Christova; and honey, I have fact checkers you never in your wildest dreams believed existed. I bet you're getting hot just thinking about cooperating right now, aren't you, Mikey?"

Moronas knew two things with absolute certainty: these people would torture him to death, and they would love doing it.

He bleated miserably behind his duct tape covering while nodding in assent violently.

Lynn pinched his cheek, sighing with regret. "Yep, that's what I figured. You're damn lucky I have a crew of friends in harm's way hunting for Phoebe. If I didn't, I'd make you scream for me to kill you, princess. There ain't no take backs for what you've said about our troops. My advice after I get through with you - embrace God, the flag, and most of all every man or woman in uniform. If I ever hear another slimy assed, traitorous spew from your lips again, me and the 'man from nowhere' here will appear magically by your bedside no matter where the fuck you think you can go undetected. We will execute you then in a way the devil himself would puke seeing. I hope you take this little talk to heart, princess, because oh my God are you not going to like the consequences if you ignore it. Do you feel me, princess?"

Another violent head nod in the affirmative answered Lynn, complete with nearly hysterical bleating.

Lynn knew she destroyed him with one application of her attitude adjustment policy, but she craved more after having to research the smarmy, traitorous crap, the bastard spewed on a daily basis to the media. That he would garner media attention to his worthless anti-American documentaries by also denigrating the troops fighting for his right to speak in a free country hit a chord in Lynn, not meant for business like acceptance. She ripped off the duct tape.

"Honey?" Clint noticed the death grip his wife had on Moronas's cheek. "Be careful, babe. We don't have the info we need for our guys."

Lynn glanced at her husband as if coming out of a trance. She smiled and nodded, but then grabbed Moronas's chin again in a hurtful grip. "Please screw us over, princess. I will make your passing from this earth legendary. You have no clue what I am capable of if you don't do exactly what I say; but honey, I will

336

teach it to you. You, Mikey, are going to become a great American... or you will be dead! As God is my witness, I will make you sing the praises of this great country, or I will have you screaming under my knife!"

Michael Moronas met Lynn's gaze with nothing short of terrified respect. "From this day forward, I... I will never put a bad light on the United States of America."

When Moronas saw Lynn's less than satisfied look, he amended his statement immediately. "America is the only reason I have been allowed to say what I have said. My statements have been unforgiveable."

Lynn released him with disappointment written over her features. "Sam and Janie are in town. Let's get Mikey to contact Christova, and then get our film in the can."

Moronas began to speak, only to get a light slap in the face from Lynn. "Don't say another word until I tell you to. Got it?"

Moronas nodded.

* * *

Denny met them at the safe-house he procured from local assets. He grinned at Moronas's head down furtive glances at their choice of venue, noticing Lynn no longer thought he needed restraints. Moronas followed her with hands at his sides. Tommy, Devon, and Jesse took seats in the living room. Dannie and Amara were making the baby smile, making faces, and snorting noises. Lynn's minions busily engaged in turning part of the living room into a communications network capable of reaching The Sea Wolf while networked with Laredo at their Command Central.

"You handle the rest Clint. I'll feed the baby. I've missed the little bugger already." Lynn pointed at Moronas. "If Clint has to call me into the kitchen because you're being uncooperative, you do understand what I'll do to you, right Mikey?"

337

A quick head bob of acknowledgement with eyes on his feet answered Lynn's question.

"Good. You may speak when you get in the kitchen." Lynn gathered the baby into her arms, adjourning to the bedroom down the hallway from the living room.

Clint accompanied Denny into the kitchen with Moronas. "I take it the warmup was all that was required, huh?"

"Yep," Clint answered. "Mikey is ready to begin his penance. He wants to help us in the worst way. How are things going in the Gulf of Guinea?"

"Bad start. The first contact they ran into after leaving port in Takorada was a Nigerian patrol boat, looking to make a score off easy pickings as the Wolf entered Nigerian waters. You can imagine how that went, but Jafar sent the footage of the entire event as ordered by the Mistress of the Unimaginable. The minions will have the live feed as per her orders in place shortly."

"I'll check the battle after we finish," Clint replied. He pointed at a chair. "Sit, Mikey. My boss will conduct this interchange. Treat him as if he were Lynn sitting opposite you, and I won't have to actually have Lynn sitting opposite you."

"Yes, Mr. Dostiene."

Denny sat down with his satellite laptop, and a digital recorder. "As you know by now, we're not the police. Everything you say will be used against you unless we cut you some slack. We're ending threats to our homeland, which you won't be from now on. What kind of deal did you strike with Christova, and is it ongoing?"

"She needed to leave the San Francisco area. We had met at parties a couple times, but I knew nothing about her, other than we shared... I mean used to share the same beliefs. Phoebe paid me a hundred thousand dollars, and guaranteed to finance my next two documentaries. I got her on board my private jet, and we went to Lagos in a roundabout route. She talked me into listening to a deal while we cruised on her yacht, The Orion. If I would smuggle in small shipments of items from overseas on my jet, I could write my own ticket for a blockbuster film, or be paid for every shipment."

"Did you agree to the deal?"

"Yes, Sir." Moronas knew better than to philosophize about why with the two men he now shared a room with. "My stuff hasn't been selling. I had hoped my remarks about the troops would stir the notoriety factor for money backers, but the opposite happened. My productions are in limbo now. The deal with Phoebe would have put me back on track."

"On track?" Clint grabbed the table to keep from choking Moronas. "If you ever managed to pull off this crash of the American system, you do understand useless traitors without any skills other than their lying mouths would be put to death first, right?"

Seeing the rage building across Clint's features, Moronas held his hands in defensive form. "Please, Mr. Dostiene… I will do whatever you and your wife tell me to do. I believe you can reach me anywhere. Even if you don't believe I'll ever change, believe I would never do anything in the future to piss off either of you."

Clint relaxed with a slow headshake of acceptance. "It is what it is. Sorry, Denny. Go on with what you're doing."

"You only said what I was thinking, Clint. Okay… did you put anything in the works for the near future involving meeting with her again, or transporting something for her?"

"Yes. I was to return with items I received after contacting a Nigerian national, Isaac Kalu. I have his phone number."

"Did you get any of this news, Clint?"

339

"We were busy prepping a prisoner for interrogation, Den. There is a certain order to things, even in our racket. Mikey had to learn what would be in store for him during the rest of his life if he decided he was a tough guy."

"Hell of a job you two did. I believe this news is just what we've been wanting to give us an edge. How soon were you to contact Kalu, Mikey?"

"Right away, Sir. I was to fly the items into Lagos two days from now. I would be happy to follow through with that plan under your guidance if you wish."

Denny laughed. "Ah... no, you won't be going anywhere, Mikey. I believe I'll ask my companion Clint if he and his wife would like to go confiscate whatever Mr. Kalu has in his possession Christova wants."

"We'd love to do that, Denny."

Denny leaned forward with his hands clasped. "Here's what I need you to do, Mikey. I want you to contact Christova, and tell her you will meet her in three days out on her yacht with the items she requested. In the meantime, you'll help my associate Lynn Dostiene film your turnover to the FBI. We'll keep you of course, but the episode won't air for a while anyway."

One glance at Clint, and Moronas stared down at the table. "Anything you want done... I will do."

"That's what I wanted to hear."

* * *

Isaac Kalu thought he heard something. He sat up in bed next to his mistress, trying to figure out what had awoken him. He stared into the darkness, his dream of sexual pleasures rushing away from his mind like a fast moving stream. Then he heard a woman's chuckle. Kalu looked toward his female companion, praying it was her. His paramour did not stir at all, even when he nudged her.

The bedroom light flashed on, blinding his night vision. Kalu reached for the Glock 9mm he had in his bedside stand drawer. A hand slapped his sharply.

"Keep your hands at your sides," Isaac heard the order from a masked apparition near him with gloved hands.

"Oh baby, you have it all, don't you, Isaac," a female voice asked him as he blinked with hand shading his eyes from the light. "You keep your mistress here, while telling your wife and four kids you're on a business trip. Nice. Unfortunately for you, you're dealing with terrorists in our country, and on our radar. We don't allow that. We have some friends in danger I'd cut you into sugar cubes to keep safe. We're here for info to keep them safe."

"Who are you people?" Kalu continued to shade his eyes as they adjusted to the light. "I don't think you know who I am."

"Did you hear that, Cowboy? The big timer thinks we don't understand who he is. Actually, we're enjoying our moment waking you from your girlfriend's side. Now that you're awake Isaac, we can get down to business. I want you to explain every detail of the transactions going on between you and Phoebe Christova."

Kalu folded his arms over his chest, looking away. "Arrest me. I will tell you nothing. I will have your badges when this is over."

"Badges?" Lynn repeated, complete with accent. "We don't need no stinking badges!"

Clint manhandled Kalu onto his stomach, plastic tying his wrists behind him, and then his ankles. After rolling the Nigerian onto his side, Clint straddled him, jamming his head still against the bedding.

"Wait! What are you doing?" Kalu tried to move his eyes to see, but could not move a fraction of an inch.

"I will explain to you why you're going to tell us everything we want to know before your girlfriend wakes from our extra dose of dreamy sleep potion." Lynn held a small bottle where Kalu could see it. "This my reluctant informer is a slightly diluted mixture of sulfuric acid and water. I am going to get a tiny bit into this eyedropper. That drop into your inner ear will make you think your brain is about to explode."

"No! I...I'll talk. I'll tell you everything!"

"Ahhhh... so helpful," Lynn said. "Wait until I put this drop in your ear. You will beg me to let you be helpful. Just a little taste to get you on board the helpful train."

Lynn slowly uncapped the bottle, handed the cap to Clint, and received the eyedropper. With Kalu pleading, and actually spewing out details, Lynn released a small droplet down into Kalu's ear. The pain left the man breathless. His body bucked under Clint in silent horrific vibrations. When he found his voice, it was a gasping, gagging breathless scream.

"I think he gets it now, babe."

"I should give him one more to grow on," Lynn stated. "He's too noisy. One more drop will quiet him down."

Kalu heard through the pain, turning his screams of agony into a prayerful begging to be able to tell them anything. Lynn squirted a neutralizing baking soda solution into his ear.

"You and Jess can come in now for pickup," Clint said.

"I don't know why we have to transport Gizmo to the safe-house. We could have recorded everything here."

"Denny wants to make sure. The excitement in his voice when he called us at the hotel meant Laredo must have found something extra out about Mr. Kalu. We'll drop him off with Denny and go back to the hotel. We have a big TV filming day tomorrow. Besides, we already had fun helping Jet retrieve his belongings. I talked with John's lawyer friend who runs the show. He loved your recruiting of Jet. Chad told me Jet will be the missing ingredient as far as insights into places where they need to shoot scenes when our crew isn't with them."

Jess peeked into the room, earning a hands on hips look of displeasure from Lynn. "Get in here, Snow White. We have places to go."

"I have to be careful, Crue. If I barf, I have to clean all the DNA before we leave."

Lynn and Clint enjoyed that pronouncement as Devon and Jesse lifted Kalu bodily from the bed, carting him out to their rented SUV.

"I hope Denny can make this extra crap with Kalu worth all the trouble," Lynn said.

"One thing I know about Denny," Clint replied, while gathering Kalu's clothing and belongings into a bag, "he doesn't order anything extra. Kalu knows something Denny wants."

"Works for me. I need to hone my skills down a bit more. What did you think of my reusing my old sulfuric acid drop method?"

"I love that one, babe. If we could figure a way for it not to leave a mark, I like it the best."

"I'll check Kalu's ear when we get back. It all depends on the amount of time between the drop being administered, and when we add the neutralizing solution. Practice is a key."

"Yeah, it is," Clint agreed. "All set. Let's go make memories."

Chapter 14

On the High Seas

"Incoming!"

"We just got here, Case," I called to our lookout. We entered the Gulf of Guinea in Nigerian territorial waters only an hour before.

"We can outrun them," Lucas said from his position at the helm of The Sea Wolf. "What kind of boat, Night-shot?"

"Nigerian patrol boat, complete with flag. Have Achmed the Terrorist call out to them on the radio."

Jafar came up from below decks with the prototype EMP handheld weapon our benefactors provided us. They knew an at sea firing would not be ruined by collateral damage. In place of a nuclear basis, the HERF gun Jafar held used high energy radio frequency microwave pulses. We didn't want trouble, but we needed to know how far the Nigerian government was in bed with Christova.

"I think Achmed is rewriting our script guys." I saw the worried look on Jafar's face. "Easy kid. What's the problem?"

"How close do we allow these guys to approach, John?"

"What's the effective range on the weapon?"

"A 150 meters for a moving target. I do not wish to be fish food before we get started on our objective."

"Why you little pussy!" Lucas always takes exception to doubt.

Jafar smiled. "I knew that would get him."

The kid had already been out with the rest of us pirates on a couple of missions. Since becoming Achmed the Terrorist by acclamation, Jafar reveled in his new nickname status. "Don't worry, Lucas. Achmed will protect you."

"You better hope that patrol boat has a dinghy, Achmed!" Lucas took the verbal shot from Jafar with revenge in mind. "You'll need alternate transportation when this encounter is over, you little mole on the asshole of a camel!"

Jafar was soon bent over at the waist while enjoying Lucas's threat. "I do not take threats seriously when mouthed from antique relics who barely have skills to steer a boat. I'll bet we could have recruited Justin Bieber to play your part in real life."

Silence for a moment before loud, guffawing laughter floated to us from the bridge. "Good one, Achmed."

"They're hailing us," Lucas said a moment later. "We are to stand down, and show ourselves with hands in the air."

"Yeah... that'll happen," Achmed mumbled while sighting our EMP weapon. "Whenever you're ready, Cheese."

"We're testing weapons here, Achmed. Start firing, and I'll do the range finding chores."

"On it." Jafar began aiming at the patrol boat approaching at flank speed. Nothing happened until it reached nearly a hundred yards away.

"It's drifting," I told him, watching through the range finders as the patrol boat slowed to dead in the water. "Now what? You can bet they have conventional weapons."

"I see only one alternative to killing them," Jafar said. "We can leave the boat without going any closer, and claim they are

346

mistaken if they've reported us. It would not bode well for us to do so. We can also interact with them, which I don't see as a viable alternative."

"Ditto," both Casey and Lucas said.

"I'm of the same mind, but we have no idea that will work toward our safety with meeting the other boat. In fact, we have to assume these guys reported us already before making their approach. I thought Denny had the Russians interceding on our behalf, along with the Nigerian government people he gave over our Boko's to."

"They're not liking this new development." Casey kept the patrol boat under observation from his perch. "I see some guys roaming around on the deck with conventional weapons, and then there's the-"

Machine gun fire stitched the water ten yards behind our fantail. Lucas sped away at flank speed.

"Machine gun," Casey finished his report. "Damn! This is a little early on this excursion for rogue government elements. We can't risk damage to the Wolf at this stage."

"Or any stage," Lucas added in my ear, having put on his com gear. "Achmed needs seasoning. Let him fire an XM307 25mm airburst on their asses while we contemplate our predicament with Denny."

"Agreed." I popped out both the XM307 grenade airburst and .50 caliber machine gun nests. "I'll get on my M107 for single targets, little brother. When Lucas swerves into position, I'll call out the range, and you let loose over them as we practiced."

"Will do." Jafar climbed into the nest, while I readied my M107 sniper rifle in the other nest. "I am ready when you are, John."

Casey climbed behind the .50 caliber machine gun for support. I steadied the M107. "Okay, Lucas. We're ready for a strafing run."

Lucas circled the patrol boat's position. I called out range as Lucas slowed to dead stop, flanking the boat. Jafar fired a burst. The carnage through my scope after the blast looked complete. The patrol boat did not sink, which made the next decision all the more important. If Jafar's burst sank the boat, we would drift amongst the wreckage for useful debris. If it stayed afloat, we'd decide whether to board it or not. We had time now, because the Wolf was safe from stray fire. Lucas called in to Denny, who was in Command Central at the House of Pain with Laredo. The Wolf had extensive radar equipment, but Laredo could provide satellite imaging while watching our backs for unseen visitors. We timed our high seas adventure in conjunction with a carrier group in the region.

"Very nice, Achmed." I scanned the patrol boat's devastated deck and bridge. If there was anything alive, the survivors would be below deck. "Let's adjourn for a pirate meeting with Captain Blood."

Lucas turned the shielded satellite laptop so we could give Captain Blood a few amusing pirate talk lines. Achmed in particular performed our pirate ritual with enthusiasm. Captain Blood, and Laredo enjoyed the show while checking on other possible rogues on the water.

"Okay... enough you pirates," Denny (Captain Blood) said. "I ordered an AWACS (Airborne Warning and Control System) aircraft launched to watch the Guinea Gulf for intruders until we can get you into range of Christova's yacht. Clint and Lynn have Moronas. We're working on an added player in the game now, a Nigerian named Isaac Kalu. I'll keep you informed as to what we find. I will leave boarding the patrol boat in your hands. If you don't like the looks of a boarding, make the boat into dust. We're working on a live feed from Crue so she can harass you guys."

"Arrrhhhhh… we'll make you walk the plank for that one, Blood," Lucas said.

"That's better than getting tuned up by Crue," Denny replied. "I'll be in touch. We'll leave this line open from now on unless we lose your signal."

He signed off, but Laredo came on a moment later. "I'm here, so shout if you need something."

"Will do." I turned to my pirates. "Input?"

"It would be good to check the boat," Jafar said. "What if they have another EMP device? That would be helpful to know. Think about a Nigerian patrol boat being rogue, and disabling anyone they feel like out here."

"Achmed's right," Casey agreed. "It wouldn't hurt to swing by, and check the boat. You and I could snap some pictures of what's left for faces amongst the crew, John. Laredo can cross reference any faces, and let us know if we have a hot one. We can find out if our own EMP gun worked below decks too. It sure turned their bridge control off."

"Let's do this," Lucas said. "We need to get clear of this area. You guys keep watch for anything moving on the boat while I do some closer passes."

"Aye… Ahab, you tool," Achmed acknowledged. Lucas is quick. Jafar barely cleared the bridge in time. Lucas returned to his control seat, pointing at me and Casey.

"I blame you for this continued disrespect, Cheese."

"Of course you do, Ahab. C'mon, Case, I think Ahab's getting ready to blow, and he doesn't have a white whale to blame it on."

"On your six, Cheese," Casey said, waving at Ahab.

Lucas did maneuvers near the patrol boat, hoping for a reaction. Not succeeding in that endeavor, he flanked the patrol boat broadside, while the rest of us scanned the deck. Nothing but dead bodies polluted the boat, at least on the topside. When I say we scanned the deck, I mean we each had our own personal area to graph, looking for any sign of danger or something interesting. Failing that, we decided to board. Lucas eased us in close, and I jumped aboard with Casey and Jafar backing my play with MP5's. We didn't use car tires to prevent damage along our railing. Casey inflated our buffer zone, and I tied us together. Casey leaped over then, leaving Achmed to guard our backs, with Lucas ready to speed us away. I detached the Wolf, allowing her to float away. We could not have our ship tied to this hunk of junk.

Casey and I took pictures and DNA samples of the six man crew dead above decks, guarding each other against interference from below decks. I had brought aboard a couple of flash bangs for the below decks area. I planned to be polite, while gathering prisoners for interrogation. There should have been no need to get confrontational. Wrong.

"I'm dropping a grenade down there if I don't hear a voice! Speak now, or else!"

I was answered with automatic weapons' fire from below. I shook my head at Casey. "I get no respect, Case."

"I see that." Casey caught the flash-bang, tossing it below deck in the same motion. We both turned away with hands covering ears.

The resulting explosion blew not only the patrol boat's lower deck apart. It also threw Casey and I out into the ocean like ragdolls in a tidal wave. I stayed conscious only by gripping my MP5 in both hands, concentrating on not letting go while I sailed into the air. When I began descending toward the ocean with foggy blackness turning my vision from high-def to the pit of darkness, I turned in flight. Holding my MP5 out in front of me, I cut through the debris without injury entering the water. I immediately surfaced with MP5 slung now to my back. I spotted Casey face-down in the water only twenty yards from me. I stroked through the debris at an Olympics breaststroke charge.

I flipped him onto his back, not seeing any wounds. I gripped his back with one hand, and worked his chest with the other, putting rib breaking pressure on his chest in measured compressions. I didn't quit even when Lucas brought the Wolf next to me using our electric trolling motors. A split second before I drifted to the fantail for retrieval, Casey spewed seawater, choking into consciousness. Lucas and Jafar jolted him onto the Wolf's deck, coughing and hacking while holding in a knees and hands on deck position. I scrambled aboard after searching and finding his MP5, which had caught on the side of a patrol boat hull piece. I slung it around my neck, and crawled on board. Jafar pushed an oxygen mask into place over Casey's nose and mouth, with Lucas helping to prop his partner in a sitting position.

I stayed on hands and knees near my three shipmates, taking deep breaths as I watched Casey's eyes taking stock of his surroundings. He grinned at me. We'd been in combat before, in situations where death walked along with us, arm in arm. Casey reached with his hand to grip my shoulder. Lucas put a hand over his. Jafar added his. Sometimes, no matter how bad-ass and prepared soldiers facing deadly situations are, we end a fight in God's hands.

"Oh well, kids," Lucas said. "I think maybe we better revise our battle plan. You boot-camps are going to get yourselves killed before we ever see that Christova bitch. If you girls will excuse me, I'll start moving the Wolf onto our objective."

Jafar waited until Lucas gave Casey a quick smack to the back of the head, and then walked toward the bridge. "Is this a good time to ask what happened?"

Casey took off the oxygen mask. "Combat, kid - sometimes dumb and unexpected. God bless us everyone."

I flipped over to my back as the Wolf accelerated away from the patrol boat debris. "Amen to that, brother."

* * *

Lynn grabbed Moronas by the ear, her face inches away from his. She and Clint had been on their way with the Hollywood Bounty Hunters for the final scene, transferring Moronas to FBI agents Sam Reeves and Janie Labrie, when Denny called them after final confirmation of what Isaac Kalu planned to transfer through Moronas to Christova: Sarin in weapons grade containers with engineered dispersal systems attached for any attack through any venue.

"We just heard what you would be transporting into Europe through Christova from a source here in our land, you fucking weasel! It was Sarin. Christova planned to use it first in the United Kingdom with traceable leads back to us as the originators, killing thousands. If I find out you knew about any detail of this, I will find a way to get your ass into our custody again, even if I have to raid the prison where you're held. We will make a video record of your death over the ensuing month which will be used as the ultimate measure within human capacity to administer pain without death. Only one thing will keep you from that fate: information. You spent days in contact with Christova aboard her yacht, The Orion. Tell me something useful right now, or I play all of this out, and when I discover the truth later, God himself will come down on earth to escort me into hell for what I do to you. Do you understand me, princess?"

Moronas shook visibly with fear. He had left one detail out, hoping to play his knowledge of it for later consideration after any implementation of the weaponized gas by Christova. "Christova has Sarin on board The Orion. Any attack on her yacht will release the gas, built into a trigger mechanism she controls. There is an escape pod built into the yacht's starboard side master suite where she stays."

Lynn turned to her grim faced husband. "Did you get that, Clint?"

"I got confirmation from Denny, and John. They were listening," Clint answered. "What do you want to do, babe?"

"I would like to skin this bastard right now." Lynn released Moronas's ear, pushing him away in the limousine. "Good Lord in heaven would I make him scream. We'll do him later if something goes wrong."

Lynn smiled at Moronas as he cringed into the corner. "I hope you learned your part for a one take filming, princess. Every retake we have to do, even if it's the fault of our other people on set, and you get a nineteen million volt dick jolt from the new 'Terminator' stun gun I'm experimenting with, on that two inch joint of yours. Oh baby… what times we'll have if the film crew is having an off day."

* * *

The four of us sat on the bridge, glancing at each other more out of commiseration than anything else.

"That bitch, Christova, is a monster," Lucas said, providing the rest of us monsters with some comic relief.

"If Interpol would have catalogued her usage of Ricin more specifically in her last getaway, we might have been able to anticipate this," Jafar said with a need to state something more palatable than the information we received from the states.

"It's a small thing, little brother." Something struck me solidly in my approach addled brain – too many days as shark bait alongside The Lora. "I have an idea."

353

The loud collective groan from my compatriots brought a smile to my lips.

"The Dark Lord has a plan," Lucas said, holding out his hand to Casey. "Can I borrow your Colt, brother? I'd rather shoot myself in the head now."

"No way!" Casey backed away from Lucas. "That would leave Achmed the Terrorist to finish me off because it's against my religion to commit suicide. You do me first, and then the Colt is all yours, brother."

"What about me?" Achmed realized he was left out to merely observe. He turned to Lucas with his hands and features in pleading form. "Case is right, benevolent one. You will have to shoot both him and me before escaping this trail of tears."

Lucas waved Achmed off with passion. "Not since you disrespected me, Achmed."

"Okay, that's enough comedy for now. Are you three comedians going to listen or not?" I put on my surly Cheeseburger face for them.

"Spit it out, Dark Lord," Lucas ordered only after more moments of hilarity.

"Denny has The Orion on satellite now in constant surveillance. We know the damn blueprints like our own mothers-"

"Except for you, Recon. You don't know your momma," Lucas corrected me in midsentence.

Another gap in my recitation ensued with Casey expanding it with his own gem, claiming to be my father in a very credible Darth Vader voice.

I held up my hands. "Can I go on now, or do we allow Christova to steam off into Never/Never land? With Denny and

Laredo accessing satellite coverage of Christova's yacht, I can make an approach, and get on board undetected. Denny told me he has the Seal team we normally have as our backup aboard the carrier force with our old friend, Lieutenant Commander Tom in charge. He'll be thrilled I want to avoid our usual carnage."

"How in hell do you plan a boarding without them noticing, you... never mind," Lucas said. "How?"

"We have to watch them from satellite. When they allow scuba diving or launches from their fantail, I'll swim to them like I belonged. Hell, they won't notice another diver coming on board. Once I'm on, I need to get the passengers off into the water with the carrier group approaching. We already know Christova has upper echelon guests, including this time a couple of royal figures from the Netherlands and Sweden. It's how she's covered herself since the Interpol attack. Once on board, I will get to Christova immediately while Jafar drives the Wolf for Lucas and Casey to board The Orion. Then, of course, all hell breaks loose. We will all have our gas masks on; but if I don't reach Christova before she hits the Sarin gas switch, they may be looking for new royalty in a few places. In any case, I want Lieutenant Commander Tom and his Seal team to land a few minutes after Lucas and Casey, with all the rafts and personnel needed to evacuate the yacht. It will be up to us to make sure no bad people survive in the rescue."

"I have to hand it to you, Recon," Lucas said. "That plan sucks. Let's do it."

"If it was easy, anyone could do it, right Achmed?" Casey clapped Jafar on the shoulder.

Achmed was not pleased. "I want allowances and guarantees if somehow during my piloting of the Wolf any damage occurs, I will be unaccountable. Otherwise, I shoot myself through the head right now."

* * *

"That's a long swim, Recon," Lucas said as I slipped into the water. We had decided on a mile for safety's sake. "It's a good thing I put you through your paces out in the Bay."

"All I have now is this damn thin black wetsuit, pappy. I'm cold."

Lucas pushed me at the forehead away from the Wolf's fantail. "Step up, pussy."

My mile swim with the GPS gear I had was a walk in the park, in addition to the fact the waters in the Gulf of Guinea were many degrees warmer than the Bay. I wore the same black wetsuit skins as the other divers we had seen through satellite imagery doing dives aboard The Orion. I carried only a waterproof bag with an MP5, a .45 caliber Colt with silencer, some clothing, and a gas mask capable of filtering Sarin gas for a short amount of time. How short was an experiment I didn't want to test out with me as the test subject. Hell, if I didn't get to Christova fast, there would be a lot of Sarin gas experiments. I left in plenty of time for the dive parties, scuba diving off The Orion, to do their dives by what we'd been observing, and arrive in time to board with them. I wore a single tank with regulator, and a weight belt to keep me down. I snorkeled the entire mile, on a mission, rather than sightseeing. Luckily, any scuba diving close to Lagos was a waste of time because of totally murky waters, and pollution. The Orion held position far away from shore, near a reef outcropping.

I had a full tank of air when I arrived at the dive spot The Orion's guests were frequenting. They were in two dive teams of five: the escorting master diver, and two scuba teams of two. I decided to stay near the hull of The Orion, waiting for the haphazard exodus from the water normal for divers off of a boat. As I hoped, my exit from the water went unnoticed as the other divers joked around, shedding equipment, and telling tales. I stayed in a partial crouch near the railing with one of the dive teams blocking my appearance. Once shed of my wetsuit, I slipped on the jeans, t-shirt, com unit, and slip on shoes in my bag while the others grab-assed around. With my weapon bag strapped over my shoulder, and one hand on the silenced Colt, I proceeded to the area of the ship we believed Christova was in. I tested the com unit, getting a double click in my ear.

The first ship's crewman who looked at me funny, I Gronked, and dragged to an unoccupied space. Bringing him to consciousness was rather daunting, but doable after five minutes. "Where is Christova?"

The man's eyes fluttered as he regained consciousness. "I... I think she's dining."

"Take me there or I put a bullet through your head." The silenced muzzle of my .45 Colt awakened him to full compliance. "If she's not there, I'm going to kill you, and find another helper."

"She...she's there. I just left the dining room."

"Let's go." I jerked him to his feet with such ease it shocked him for a moment until he noticed my size. We didn't pass anyone official in the corridor, so I didn't have to kill anyone. When we reached the dining area, I spotted Christova in seconds. "Stand here on the floor and live. Cry out for help, and die. Undertand?"

He nodded. I walked over to Christova's table. A few eggs would have to be broken to make this omelet. I shot the two men in back of her in suits through the head, threw the table over, grabbed Christova off her chair by the neck, and turned. I shot two more running at us amidst the screams while backing to a corner where either my guys arrived or Christova and I died.

"I have Christova," I broke radio silence for the first time on my com unit. "We're in a very loud, screaming portion of the dining area. I have cover, but life expectancy will be limited to how fast you guys come aboard. There will be no gas."

"We boarded ten seconds ago," Lucas said in my ear. "We were watching, and we're headed to you as we speak. The Seal team lands in ten minutes, so Case and I will join you momentarily. Pop that bitch if things get nasty."

"I sure will." I grinned at Christova, who stared at me in horror with my razor sharp blade against her neck drawing ever so lightly a thin trace of blood. With my right hand, I held the Colt, ready to execute upon approach. Four commando type guys burst professionally into the room, looking for I'm sure, their employer, Christova. "Bye, bye, doll-face."

As I came within a heartbeat of slitting Christova's throat, my monsters arrived. Short bursts from MP5 automatics, and there were four dead mercenaries on the floor. I don't have mercenaries on my crew. I have USA trained monsters, who never hesitate, and who ride for the brand: The United States of America.

"Over here, guys." I helped lady Christova to her feet where she sobbed piteously while holding her throat.

Lucas laughed. "Oh lady… if you think that little paper cut is bad, wait until you meet Crue. You had your minions try and kill her baby boy: my godson. She's going to teach you the meaning of pain, baby."

Amen to that. I smiled, thinking about another vacation time ahead, possibly longer than that short stint we had after the 'Rattler' fight. Al said something about wanting to try soccer. Maybe they needed a coach. Then I thought of Lora wearing that last black, sheer slip of a thing she tortured me with. Oh yeah… life was good.

* * *

Phoebe Christova awoke in darkness. In moments, she realized every movable part of her body was restrained on a table with her legs wide apart, and her knees up. Phoebe also knew she was naked. When she started whimpering, and calling out, demanding to know where she was, a single light bulb turned on over the table. A minute later the sound of footsteps approaching from the darkness chilled her to the bone. The sixth sense of danger and death jolted her system into full awakening. A blonde woman with a green soccer jersey leaned over her with a smile so frightening, Christova squealed slightly in anguish.

"Hello there, girlfriend. I'm Lynn Montoya Dostiene. You decided to send killers to execute my baby boy, Clint Jr. I know who you are. My friend, John Harding, gave you to me with a list of questions. You will answer those questions, and then give me access to every account you have money in. Unfortunately for you, I'm not interested in answers or money. I will get them for my friend, but you and I have a more personal debt to settle. I'll be right back."

Christova began weeping, knowing nothing could dissuade the woman walking away. She had been in the Dostiene woman's position many times, loving every second of fear oozing from her victim. When she heard footsteps again, and saw a reddish pointed glow in the darkness, Phoebe strained to see what it was. When she realized what was in the approaching woman's hand was a red hot poker, Phoebe screamed, jerking at her bindings with every terrified ounce of strength in her body.

"Ahhhh… isn't that sweet," Lynn said. "Nice practice, baby, but let me show you what a real scream sounds like."

The real screams started a moment later.

The End

Thank you for purchasing and reading *Hard Case Book V: Blood and Fear*. If you enjoyed the novel, please take a moment and leave a review. Your consideration would be much appreciated. Please visit my Amazon Author's Page if you would like to preview any of my other novels. Thanks again for your support.

Bernard Lee DeLeo

Author's Face Book Page -

https://www.facebook.com/groups/BernardLeeDeLeo/

BERNARD LEE DELEO - AUTHOR'S PAGE -

http://www.amazon.com/Bernard-Lee-DeLeo/e/B005UNXZ04/ref=ntt_athr_dp_pel_pop_1

AMAZON AUTHOR'S PAGE (UK) -

http://www.amazon.co.uk/-/e/B005UNXZ04

39490486R00206

Made in the USA
Lexington, KY
26 February 2015